A CITY OF SACRIFICE NOVEL

ALSO BY MICHAEL R. FLETCHER

GHOSTS OF TOMORROW
BEYOND REDEMPTION
THE MIRROR'S TRUTH
SWARM AND STEEL
A COLLECTION OF OBSESSIONS
SMOKE AND STONE (CITY OF SACRIFICE #1)

UPCOMING RELEASES

THE MILLENNIAL MANIFESTO
ASH AND BONE (CITY OF SACRIFICE #2)
BLACK STONE HEART (THE OBSIDIAN PATH #1)

SMOKE AND STONE

by Michael R. Fletcher

Cover Art: Felix Ortiz (https://www.artstation.com/felixortiz)
Editor: Sarah Chorn

For All the Hungry Gods

TABLE OF CONTENTS

BASTION - A REALLY BAD MAP

Population: ~250,000
Diameter: ~250 miles
Each ring is divided by a wall
The outer wall (Sandwall) has no gate

Grower's Ring
Tenements, farm lands, menageries

Crafters' Ring

Senators' Ring

Bankers' Ring

Priests' Ring

The
Gods

The Sandwall: Separates Bastion from the Bloody desert.
The Grey Wall: Separates the Growers from the Crafters.
The Wall of Lords: Separates the Crafters from the Senators.
The Wall of Commerce: Separates the Senators from the Bankers.
The Wall of Faith: Separates the Banks from the Priests.
The Wall of Gods: Separates the gods at Bastion's core from the Priests.

AKACHI – UNBREAKABLE INTENT

The entire city of Bastion is comprised of a single stone, two hundred and fifty miles in diameter, some seven hundred and eighty-five miles in circumference. In all Bastion, from colossal Sand Wall to the Wall of Gods at the centre, from the simplest Grower's tenement, to the columns of the Senate, to the mighty vaults of the Banks, to the towering spires of the central churches, there is no seam to be found.

Bastion is a manifestation of perfection.

—The Book of Bastion

You can't put this off any longer.

Standing outside Bishop Zalika's chambers, Akachi lifted a hand to knock and hesitated.

Why had she summoned him? He'd done a passable job of leading yesterday's sermon and there was no way she knew about last night's attempt to sneak into the wing housing Precious Feather's acolytes with Nafari. In spite of his friend's claim to know a secret route, they'd been wholly unsuccessful. After spending three hours wandering, lost in one of the Northern Cathedral's sub-basements, they eventually found their way back to their own room. They hadn't actually managed to get into trouble.

Much as they'd wanted to.

More likely Zalika had invented some imagined trespass and was now going to punish Akachi for whatever it was she'd dreamed up. Luckily these things were rarely as bad as the real trouble he and Nafari found.

Bishop Zalika hated him. Well, she hated his father, the High Priest of Cloud Serpent. Her loathing of Akachi was incidental. He was an innocent victim of whatever past she and his father shared.

Mostly innocent.

He hadn't known about their enmity until arriving in the Growers' Ring.

For those born in the Priests' Ring there were two paths: work as support staff to the people who shepherded the souls of all Bastion, or join one of the priesthoods and really become someone of consequence. All Akachi's life, his father talked about how he'd someday follow in his footsteps. He'd make the journey to the outer ring, become an acolyte of Cloud Serpent in the Northern Cathedral, and earn his way back to the heart of the city.

Why didn't he warn me about Zalika?

There was no point in stalling. He'd have to face her eventually and receive punishment for his crimes, real or imagined. Reaching up, he rapped on the oak door.

"Enter." She sounded angry.

Breathing deep, he pushed the heavy door open and strode into the room. As Bishop of the Northern Cathedral, her quarters were palatial. The finest furniture and art crowded the space. Oak and leather sofas. Silk pillows. Thick rugs. Lustrous oil paintings depicting scenes from Bastion's past hung on the walls. One showed a beautiful woman with skin dark as the space between the stars and the body of a terrible spider being thrown from the wall by a giant skeleton with a necklace of eyeballs. A colossal tapestry, twice the height of a man and as wide as six lying head to toe, showed the Last Pilgrimage, the shattered remnants of humanity fleeing their dying world, escaping to Bastion. He hadn't seen anything like it since leaving his home in the Priest's Ring. So much rich colour.

The big woman stood waiting, arms crossed. A cloak of owl feathers hung from her shoulders and swept the floor, sighing with resigned disappointment each time she moved.

She looked him over with a show of distaste. "You're late."

He wasn't. "Sorry, Bishop."

"What do you know of the Wheat District?"

"I heard it's pretty rough, Bishop."

"So, nothing." She sighed in annoyance. "What do you know of the Loa?"

"Heretics. Worshippers of Mother Death." He glanced at the tapestry. "They seek to end her banishment, return her to Bastion and overthrow Father Death."

She stared at him, waiting.

"They…uh…use crystal magic, channel sorcery through stone. But their powers are limited with Mother Death's influence unable to breach the Sand Wall—"

"I didn't ask for a lecture."

He rather thought she had.

"There's a Cloud Serpent church in the Wheat District. It has been empty for years. Centuries."

Was she going to send him out there to clean it? Would she punish him by having him mop abandoned churches? There were a lot of empty parishes in the Growers' Ring. He could spend the rest of his life out there. No one would ever hear from him again.

Head bowed, he said nothing, waiting.

"The parish is yours."

Mine? His own parish at nineteen? That was even younger than his father! "Thank you, Bish—"

"At least until I can find a *real* pastor."

Ah. There it is. He should have known. "I'm honoured, Bishop," he answered, keeping the hurt from his face.

"Don't be. The nahual originally assigned this posting was assassinated on his way out from the Priests' Ring."

"I—"

"As was his replacement."

"Oh."

"As was her replacement."

"Ah."

She examined him with pebble eyes, wet and angry. "As was his replacement."

"I see."

"Doubtful," Bishop Zalika said, fat earlobes swinging like greasy pendulums. "Try not to die before your replacement arrives." She held out a sacrificial dagger.

"I shall," he said, accepting the knife. "Try not to."

He examined the obsidian blade. *The smoke is the souls.* That's what the *Book of Bastion* said. He felt its death creep up his arm, a bone-shattering cold, and seep into his heart. It poisoned him.

Swallowing sour bile, he said, "Bishop, judging from the colour, this dagger has killed thousands." He wanted to retch, to hurl this vile thing away. *Can't show weakness.* "Should it not make the trip to the Gods' Ring to be cleansed?" The gods would drain the souls from the blade so they might be reborn.

She sniffed at him and shook her head in disappointment. "It's the only one available."

Liar. He wanted to refuse, but a pastor without a sacrificial dagger was unheard of. The stench of death wafting from the knife twisted his stomach. As a pastor, it would fall to Akachi to punish those who broke the laws laid out in the *Book of Bastion*. Minor offences were punishable by whipping and could be carried out by the local Hummingbird Guard. Serious offences, however, were punishable by sacrifice on the altar. The act was, his teachers told him, a beautiful thing to send a man to the gods. Critical to the survival of Bastion, no duty was more sacred. Damaged souls, those who strayed from the Book, needed to be cleansed so they might be reborn.

Could he do it? Could he open a man and bleed him for the gods? He knew how, had attended countless lectures on anatomy. He'd even sat in on several sacrifices.

I can if I have to, he decided. *I won't let my father down.*

But this foul and soul-polluted dagger... Zalika did this on purpose, no doubt.

"When do I leave?" he asked.

"A squad of Hummingbird Guard await you in the courtyard. Due to your tardiness, they've been in the sun for hours."

He opened his mouth to protest and she waved him to silence.

"That reprobate, Nafari, will join you as will Jumoke. He's an acolyte. Totally useless."

"Thank you," said Akachi with real gratitude. Nafari was his only friend. They grew up together in the Priests' Ring. Jumoke, he didn't know. Just another faceless acolyte.

"This is a punishment detail for both the acolyte and the Hummingbirds."

And not for me? He wanted to ask what they'd done, but her expression suggested that might be a bad idea. *Her expression suggests everything is a bad idea.*

"Have you not kept them waiting long enough?" she asked, returning to her desk and shuffling papers as though he'd already left.

Exiting her Chambers, Akachi found Nafari, tall and handsome in a way that most women seemed to like, waiting in the hall.

"She called you a reprobate," Akachi told him.

"I am. You ready?"

"No. You?"

"Nope. Let's do this."

They found Jumoke awaiting them in the Northern Cathedral's great hall. Seeing Akachi, the skinny boy dipped a quick bow, coal-black hair falling in his face, and followed along a few steps behind. The acolyte carried a large pack, likely loaded with whatever supplies a new pastor would need. He dripped with sweat and blinked often, looking pale and gritting his teeth as if in pain.

Had he been recently lashed?

"You all right?" Akachi asked.

"We're leaving the North Cathedral, right?"

"Yes."

"Then I am fantastic."

"Need help carrying that?"

Jumoke flashed a pained grin. "Nah. I earned this."

A colossus of stone, not a seam or a crack anywhere to mar its perfection, this church was the religious centre of northern quarter of the Growers' Ring. Sweeping arches, towering spires, impossible bridges suspended upon nothing but the will of the gods, all part of the single stone that formed Bastion. So different than the utilitarian solidity of the rest of the Growers' tenements, the cathedral reminded Akachi of a giant spider's web. And home. All the Priests' Ring was as beautiful as this grand church.

The work of the gods humbled him to the core of his soul. *They made this for us.* Humanity brought itself to the brink of utter destruction and the gods built this bastion, took in the few survivors, and sheltered them from the world they'd killed.

He spent so much time dreaming of escaping the cathedral, but now that he was doing just that, it felt unreal.

A pastor. Well, kind of.

A grand adventure like the stories Mom used to read to him at bedtime. Tales of dark alleys, evil street sorcerers, and gangs of thieves defeated by heroic nahual and sorcerous nahualli. Life as an acolyte, and then later as a newly anointed priest, had been nothing like that.

Though when I dreamed of escape, I did think I'd be beginning my journey inward, back to the Priests' Ring.

Priests of every denomination bustled about the cathedral's great courtyard, intent on the daily business of maintaining and running Bastion. Here, in the Growers' Ring, where grey seemed to define the world, the priests were an explosion of colour. Nahual of Snake Woman, vestments blood red, ceremonial shields worn over their backs, strode past, spears of ebony used as walking sticks. Father Death's priests sweated under their multi-coloured cloaks of owl feathers. The nahual of Skirt of Vipers, robes mimicking the colouration of one deadly snake or another, went about the business of running the crèches and raising Grower children. Akachi even spotted the occasional banded red, white, and black of his fellow nahual of Cloud Serpent.

Seven Hummingbird Guard—three women, and four men—all wearing crimson armour of hardened leather in spite of the heat, awaited Akachi, Nafari, and Jumoke at the main entrance. The squad watched his approach through narrowed eyes.

The woman in charge nodded greeting. "I'm Captain Yejide. We've been assigned to you." She exuded coiled strength, unbreakable intent.

The Hummingbird squad stank of leather and sweat, and for the first time Akachi found it a comforting scent. They'd keep him safe from the gangs of the Wheat District. A priest of Cloud Serpent, he wasn't trained in violence or the arts of war. At least not in physical violence. As a nahualli he had sorcerous means of finding and defeating foes.

He wanted to ask what they'd done to earn this posting as punishment, but instead said, "How long are you staying?"

"Until assigned elsewhere, Pastor."

"He's not really a pastor," said Nafari, winking at Akachi.

Akachi ignored his friend, who'd clearly been listening at the Bishop's door. "Have you ever been in the Wheat District?" he asked Captain Yejide.

"Yes."

When she didn't elaborate, he said, "I've spent all of my time here in the Northern Cathedral. This is my first time out among the Growers. Is it really that bad?"

"Last week, two Guards were found bound to the district whipping post. Throats cut."

"But Growers are forbidden weapons and tools! What could they use to cut a throat?"

She looked at him like he was an idiot and he decided she might be right.

"The whipping post is in the central square," she said. "Yet somehow no one saw anything." She wiped beaded sweat from her forehead. "Most of the time they just kill each other. Every street corner has a gang of Dirts claiming it as turf."

"Dirts?"

"Growers. Most Dirts are too stupid to be dangerous, but there are so many of them..." She shook her head, mystified. "It's a hotspot for the Loa as well. The heretics have their own secret churches hidden in the basements of Grower tenements."

Dirts. The derogatory term left Akachi uncomfortable. As long as he was an acting pastor, his purpose was to educate them, to teach them the Book, and to protect them from their own ignorance. They were what they were. Hating them for being stupid was like hating a cow for being dull. He would do better. He would accept them for the flawed people they were and do what he could to improve their lives. He would bring them the Book and the Word as was his calling.

How long was he supposed to remain in the Wheat District? If his replacement left the Priests' Ring now, they could be in the Growers' Ring in eight or nine days. Less, if they rushed. No matter what Zalika said, even a temporary posting as acting pastor was a rise in rank and status. Would this be enough to begin his journey to the heart of Bastion?

A little over a week and I might be headed home!

Father would *have* to be impressed.

Taking a deep breath, he calmed himself. Priests were to serve in each ring as they earned their way inward, back to the gods. This posting, temporary and trivial as it might be, was the first step on the journey home. Even so, it would be years before he returned to the Priests' Ring and saw his parents again.

"How long will it take to get to the Wheat District?" he asked.

Captain Yejide glanced at the sun, squinting. "If we set a hard pace, we might make it before night."

"Let's move, then."

The Captain nodded, whistled a sharp blast, and the Hummingbirds formed a loose guard around Akachi, Nafari, and Jumoke.

Leaving the Northern Cathedral felt like leaving his home in the Priests' Ring all over again. Everything he knew lay behind him.

'It's time to leave your childhood behind.' Akachi's father said that as Akachi left their home in the Priests' Ring.

They were his last words before sending Akachi away.

Not 'I love you.'

Not 'I'm proud.'

But rather an admonishment not to disappoint.

Akachi had been twelve. Now, at nineteen, after seven years in the Growers' Ring training as an acolyte, he was an anointed nahualli of Cloud Serpent, Lord of the Hunt, and following in his father's footsteps.

It's time to leave your childhood behind.

I think I have, Father. He considered last night's attempt to sneak into the wing housing the acolytes of Precious Feather and winced. *At least I've started*, he amended.

Akachi slowed as they stepped into the street. Standing shadowed in the doorway of a tenement, a young woman caught his eye. She was beautiful, skin flawless, the whites of her eyes impossibly bright, almost as though she was lit from within. The woman stared at him, unflinching appraisal, face devoid of expression. Where the other Growers were filthy, bent with years of labour, she stood tall and proud, back straight.

Too clean. She looked like she'd be more comfortable in a priest's robes, yet there she was, wearing a grey thobe like all the other Growers. He imagined her in the revealing robes of a nahual of Precious Feather.

Turning a corner, Akachi and his Hummingbird retinue left her behind.

The group walked south, following the Grey Wall separating the Growers and the Crafters. So huge was Bastion, the wall's gentle curve was undetectable. It went on forever, disappearing in the wavering haze of heat, like it split the world in half.

It kind of does.

The Growers were roughly half of Bastion's population. The other half, the Crafters, the Senate, the Bankers, and the Priests, all lived on the other side of that wall.

"The Grey Wall," said Nafari, "separates everything interesting from everything not."

"*We're* on this side," said Jumoke.

The sun crawled higher, murdering the last hints of shade.

Some time later, when Akachi's stomach grumbled in complaint, he realized the priests and acolytes back in the Northern Cathedral would now be sitting down to lunch. The Hummingbird Guard showed no sign of slowing or stopping to eat.

Though all the districts along the Grey Wall were in theory identical, all lined with repeating patterns of streets, tenements, central squares, and churches, each was, in some way, distinct. Every district came with its own scents and sights. The Growers also changed. The men and women of the Bovine District stank of manure. In the Potato District, Growers wore the dirt they spent the day toiling in. Some districts smelled like horses or pigs, and some reeked of fish or rotting vegetables. Everywhere he looked he saw the products of the Growers' labours carted out behind teams of oxen, overseen by squads of Hummingbird Guard. Everything grown in this ring was taken to the Crafters' Ring where it would be turned into the food, tools, and materials, that kept Bastion alive.

Akachi's hunger became a background distraction, replaced by a more demanding thirst. And still the Guard showed no sign of stopping. His feet hurt, unaccustomed to such abuse.

They walked, following the wall.

Slitted eyes tracked the group's progress. Sometimes clumps of ragged Growers would follow a dozen strides behind them for a few blocks before breaking off. Captain Yejide noted them but did nothing.

Am I going to be assassinated before I make it to the church?

That would certainly please Bishop Zalika.

"Are we there yet?" asked Jumoke, grinning when the nearest Hummingbird shot him an annoyed glance.

Glares of hate followed Akachi and his retinue everywhere. Whether it was due to the presence of the Guard, or his own robes of Cloud Serpent, he couldn't tell.

Or do they hate all priests?

None of the lectures in the Northern Cathedral prepared Akachi for the seething anger, the obsidian edge of discontent surrounding him.

After hours of walking, Captain Yejide said, "We're in the Wheat District now."

They passed a church of Sin Eater. The nahual, dressed in countless layers of painfully bright white, face hidden beneath a voluminous cowl, stood in the centre of the street. The priest's head swung back and forth as if seeking sin by smell alone. Sin Eater's nahual wielded their power to cure or spread disease with a righteous fury. Even Akachi would be expected to attend service in that church at least once a month for confession.

Can't imagine I'll get up to much sinning out here.

Nafari, on the other hand, would no doubt find a way. He was already chatting up one of the Hummingbird women.

Captain Yejide led them through winding streets, eyes sharp. Turning a corner, she slowed, and held up a hand. The Hummingbirds, always alert, took up positions as if expecting attack.

"What is it, Captain?" asked Akachi. He scanned the alley. Piled garbage littered the street. Red sand dusted everything.

Nostrils flared, Yejide tested the air. "Going around will add an hour."

Around what? Akachi only saw more of the same. "An hour?" His feet hurt from walking and he felt like he'd sweat out his last drop of water two hours ago. *I'm going to sweat dust.* He saw nothing amiss. "It looks quiet."

"Your decision," she said, waiting.

Akachi shot Nafari a questioning look and his friend shrugged, abdicating responsibility.

"On the one hand," said Jumoke, "the alley does look more like an adventure than the main road."

Akachi ignored the acolyte. Though the Hummingbirds had their backs to him, studying the streets and alleys, he felt their expectation, their impatience for a decision. He'd never been in charge of anything before. He hesitated, unsure. *What if I choose wrong?* But it was just another filthy alley. Could this be some Hummingbird hazing ritual, or were they testing to see if he took the longer, more cowardly route?

He glanced at the Captain. Her utter lack of expression told him nothing.

"We cut through," he said. "If this district is to be my home, I need to see it. And the Growers need to see me." He wanted to add something about how showing fear would reduce the respect of the locals, but in truth he was just tired and wanted to get to his new home so he could lie down.

Captain Yejide led the way.

The first clod of ox shit hit Akachi in the chest, staggering him. The second, still moist and heavier for it, connected with the side of his head. Sparks arced across his vision.

Blinking, he found himself on his knees.

NURU – THIS PATCHWORK PANTHEON

Beyond the narcotics, there are two materials lending themselves to use in sorcery: wood, and stone. Church-trained nahualli carve strictly in wood as stone, crystals in particular, are conduits for Mother Death.

—Loa Book of The Invisibles

Sorcerous narcotics swam Nuru's blood like river snakes. She stood at her table in the basement of the tenement Chisulo's gang shared.

Twelve lashes for possession of a crafted construct.

A makeshift contraption made entirely of scraps of wood held together by hemp rope and more scraps of wood, it wobbled whenever she touched it. Omari stole it for her the year the five of them left the crèche where they grew up. She couldn't imagine where he found it.

Focus on what you're doing.

When she moved, the hundreds of pale bones tied into her knee-length charcoal hair clacked and whispered, soft and hollow. Though mostly collected from rats and mice, some of the bones were those of snakes and cats. The sound relaxed her.

The table held Nuru's most valued possessions. An assortment of narcotics—*sacrifice on the altar,* her mind helpfully supplied—sat in stolen glass jars and wood bowls. *Fourteen lashes for the glass, eight for the bowls.* A selection of crude wood-working tools she made herself from shards of rock lay beside a half-dozen unfinished carvings. *Six lashes for simple self-made tools.* Wood shavings littered the floor. She had three sheets of crisp clean paper left of the twenty Omari stole for her last year. Her quill, a sharpened seagull feather, rested beside a glass jar of ink she'd made from blackberries, eggs, and water. Beside the quill sat the flake of flint used for sharpening it. The quill and jar, glass cloudy, worn thin by a thousand generations of Growers passing it from one street sorcerer to the next, were treasures beyond value. *Three lashes for the quill, twenty for the ink.* Chunks of wood sat arrayed across the top edge of the table. Each had been selected because she'd seen something within, the potential for a carving. Four stones lay along the right side, there to be used as weights to hold the corners of her precious paper.

She blinked. How many lashes was the paper? She couldn't remember.

Even without the narcotics, her pathetic belongings were enough to see her sacrificed on the altar.

Risk everything for some small shred of control. If she chased the dream, she risked a lot more. She risked her soul.

A single wavering tallow candle, stinking of rendered beef fat and smoke, lit the basement. *Thirty lashes for the false light.* That pinpoint of yellow light, too bright to look at in her heightened state, danced sinuous shadows in her peripheral vision. Sometimes she saw snakes. With Isabis, her viper, lurking in the dark, she might not even be hallucinating.

Today was different.

Today she saw a spider.

A spider with a woman's body, she corrected.

She knew why: The dream.

So vivid as to be realer than real, the dream demanded attention. It demanded recognition. It demanded action.

The near-completed carving of a crow caught her attention. After working on it, slicing and carving with clumsy tools for over a year, it was almost finished. It wasn't great. The beak didn't look quite right, and the feathers lacked detail, but it was the best she could manage. Once finished—assuming she cured the aldatu mushrooms she grew down here exactly right—her nagual talent would allow her to take its shape. She would *become* the bird, fly through the air, look down upon Bastion. She wanted that, wanted it so bad. The taste of freedom, even if just for a brief while.

Rather, she *had* wanted it. Now she wanted something more.

I'm going to carve the spider.

There were two possibilities. Either she'd had a particularly vivid dream and it meant nothing, or *something* had reached out to her.

She knew better than to ignore her dreams.

She also knew better than to trust things that had the power to reach into a sorcerer's dream and plant a need.

Ally, banished spirit, or demon, she didn't know. Perhaps some ancient sorcerer had been thrown from the Sand Wall and her soul had lived on, gathering power.

It wants to use me for something. Maybe it craved vengeance, or to complete some unfinished task. Perhaps, after millennia as a formless spirit, it hungered for a taste of reality.

Well I want something from you too.

Power.

Control.

Having studied the darker arts and tested her power against other street sorcerers, she felt confident she could control the spirit. She'd give it some of whatever it desired, and in return it would aid her.

Nuru had planned on finishing the crow today, but it no longer mattered.

Setting aside the incomplete bird she selected one of the jars and rattled the single dose, three dried seeds in a dusting of green powder, crumbling in the bottom. A mix of foku and gorgoratzen, such narcotics were the purview of the nahualli. If discovered, she'd be loaded onto a penance wagon, hauled out to the Sand Wall, and cast into the Bloody Desert. The mix would sharpen her senses, improve recall, and aid in retention. *They don't want us thinking clearly*. It was hard to come by. She couldn't imagine what Omari, the gang Finger, traded to get it.

Nuru ate the blend of gorgoratzen and foku seeds. Then, just in case it contained even the slightest trace of narcotics, she licked the dust out of the bottom of the jar. Her tongue felt like sun-dried leather, swollen and heavy. She'd remember every last detail of her dream in incredible detail. If she missed a single element because she was distracted, the carving would differ too much from the reality of the dream and be useless as a channel.

Isabis moved in the dark, dry scales on sandy stone. Chisulo sat upstairs drinking. She heard him shift, the box he used as a chair, groaning. "Time for a war," he said, over and over, trying to convince himself.

You're a good man. Too good to lead a street gang in the Wheat District. But he was all they had. A fierce protectiveness filled her. Perhaps, once this carving was finished, they wouldn't have to struggle just to survive. Maybe they wouldn't have to fight to protect their meagre turf from the likes of Fadil. *I'll keep them safe*, she vowed. *Whatever it takes*.

All their lives they lived what amounted to an unnoticed rebellion. Growing up in the crèche, they'd shirked their responsibilities, defied the nahual at every chance. The day they left they swore to stay together forever. Forming their own little street gang, they claimed a street corner in the Wheat District as their own. For the most part, the nahual ignored them as harmless.

That's about to change.

Everything was changing.

"Time for a war," Chisulo repeated.

Not if I can help it. Her heart ached with concern for her friends. *I'll protect you all.*

Outside, somewhere in the distance, a woman cried, a broken, wailing sound.

Nuru swayed, the gentle clatter of bone on bone lulling her, separating her from the world above.

She forgot the stone under her bare feet and the constant hunger in her belly. She forgot Chisulo.

She forgot herself.

The narcotics in her blood thinned the veil between worlds, the wall between realities. Beyond that nebulous barrier lay spirits and demons, allies and dark forces, dead and banished gods.

She laid her crude carving tools, flint chisels, fire-hardened wood, and wedges of hard stone, out on the table. Leaning in, she examined her collection of wood chunks. She saw a rat in one, and a small dog in another. In none of them could she see the spider.

Use stone, not wood.

Could that work? The old woman who taught her sorcery always used wood. The nahualli always used wood. Stone would be so much harder to work, her tools insufficient for the intricate detail needed.

Wood is weak.

Where did that thought come from?

Spotting a chunk of catlinite, rust-red clay hardened into a shard of stone, in her collection, Nuru saw the potential for a spider locked within.

Yes. Stone.

A human head, eyes red as the brightest rose, skin the rainbow black of crow feathers. A sable curtain of silky hair fell the length of the human torso, draped the spider's bulbous abdomen, and swung between viciously barbed legs. From the waist up, she was a gorgeous young woman. From the curve of her hips on down she had the jagged and angular body of a hunting spider. A black carapace, wet and glistening, armoured her lower body. Legs long and bent, her knees rose up above the woman's beautiful face.

So much black.

So much flawless black.

The gods are at war. The spider spoke in silk and ash. *Lines are drawn, sides chosen. Southern Hummingbird and Cloud Serpent hunger for war. Smoking Mirror breeds chaos as is his way; Father of Discord, he can do no less. Sin Eater wants to burn it all. Father Death hasn't left the underworld in ten thousand years. My mad children require a firm hand. This patchwork pantheon is in turmoil. I have chosen you, my beautiful Heart.*

Nuru blinked.

Stone shavings and shards littered the table top. In the centre sat the spider, still trapped in catlinite. It possessed none of the life she saw in her hallucination.

My mad children require a firm hand. What did that mean?

Nuru examined the incomplete carving. When finished, the six legs would be needle thin at the tips, so fragile.

She glanced at her sad collection of tools. "I can't do it. Not with this garbage."

I need proper tools, a Crafter's stone-working kit. Real paints and brushes.

Somehow, she would get what she needed. Nuru knew this beyond any doubt. Though she couldn't imagine how, it would happen. The nahual claimed the gods provided to the deserving, to those in need. Seeing as those same nahual said street sorcerers were 'damned souls,' and would toss her from the wall, she knew it wouldn't be *their* gods doing the providing.

I have chosen you, my beautiful Heart. Somehow it sounded like a title.

Whatever this thing was, it had clearly long gone mad. Thousands of years trapped beyond the light and life of Bastion would do that, she supposed. Madness, however, was not a problem. If anything, it would make the spirit easier to trick and control.

She remembered the lithe body atop the terrible spider. Shivers of fear and revulsion ran through her. But there was more. She wanted to see the spider again. She *needed* to see that girl. So beautiful. So terrible.

For some reason the spider reminded her of Efra. The girl lived on the edge of Chisulo's gang, never quite inside, but not outside either. Sometimes she stayed with them, attended meetings, rarely talking, mostly staring at Chisulo. Sometimes she disappeared for weeks, only to return looking like she'd been mauled by one of the big cats in the menageries. The vicious scar bisecting her face from right eyebrow to the left side of her chin, reinforced the impression.

The spider—the female part—looked nothing like Efra. Too many curves, too flawless. And yet there was something there. This carving was important, the most important thing Nuru ever made. Efra was important too.

Could Efra be the key to getting the tools and paints I need?

That felt right. Nuru trusted her instincts, listened when the world whispered hints. Somehow, Efra was part of this.

AKACHI – THE GUARD DO NOT GO LIGHTLY

The war of the gods ended with the near extinction of humanity. With so few mortals left to worship them, the surviving gods starved. In a desperate attempt to save mankind the last gods created Bastion, a city formed of a single piece of stone pulled from deep beneath the Bloody Desert.

Bastion is the last city of man; beyond its walls is endless death.

—The Book of Bastion

Growers, filthy thobes stained in shit and blood, erupted from every doorway. Faces wrapped in grey cloth, only their eyes, slitted with rage, were visible. They attacked the priests with sharpened sticks and rocks clutched in fists.

The Hummingbird Guard retreated for a moment, creating a wall of flesh and leather around Akachi, Nafari, and Jumoke. Shuffling sandal-clad feet and muscled legs created a cage through which Akachi viewed the world. Yejide grunted as a Grower hurled himself at her and was neatly shouldered aside to be kicked in the groin by the Hummingbird at her side. A hollow *crack* echoed off stone and a woman lay an arm's length from Akachi, blood leaking from her ear. She blinked once and didn't blink again.

Get up. Fight.

Except he didn't know how. Priests of Cloud Serpent learned no martial skills. His power lay in his sorcery. With no narcotics in his blood, he was powerless. Knowing the fierce reputation of the Wheat District, should he have dosed up before leaving the Northern Cathedral? But that was hours ago! Whatever he took would have left his system by now.

Half rising, he was again knocked down as one of the Hummingbirds backed into him, driven by the weight of the attackers. They clawed at the Guard's armour, stabbed at him with fire-hardened spears. A Hummingbird took the spear from one Grower, shattered the nose of another with its blunt end, and then spun it with nimble fingers to stick it in the throat of the man he took it from.

Where the Growers screamed insults and curses, the Hummingbirds fought in silence. Where the Growers' eyes were lit with murderous hate, the Hummingbirds wore calm masks of deadly intent.

The young Hummingbird Nafari had been chatting with broke a man's arm, twisting it, using her cudgel as the pivot, until the bone popped. She moved like magic, weaving a spell of destruction. Hard fingers stabbed eyes. Knees found soft bellies. Vicious elbows shattered jaws, crushed noses. That cudgel was everywhere, sometimes a fulcrum, sometimes a stabbing weapon, sometimes a club. But never crude. She moved like she was three steps ahead of her opponents.

That's their sorcery.

Yejide made her look clumsy.

A spear, tip carved sharp and coated in dripping shit, stabbed at Akachi from between two Hummingbirds. Yejide caught it in a fist and shattered the man's cheekbone with her cudgel. He opened his mouth to scream and fell silently, choking as the Hummingbird beside Yejide caved his throat in.

Too many. There are too many!

The weight and stink of Grower flesh threatened to drown Akachi. Scores. Hundreds. Thousands. An entire district of hate throwing itself against seven Hummingbirds. The Guard staggered, retreated another step, crushing him.

And then, space. Three Growers grabbed Captain Yejide and dragged her from the formation, exposing her. She fought, kicking and spinning, lashing out with deadly precision. Someone hit her from behind, pitching her to her knees.

Already the remaining Hummingbirds were closing ranks, filling the gap left by her absence.

They aren't going to save her?

A man kicked Yejide and she caught his foot, but another grabbed her from behind, wrapping a scrawny arm around her throat. Releasing the foot, she struggled to pull loose the choking grip, but the man who kicked her grabbed her wrists, held them.

They'll kill her.

Why weren't the Hummingbirds trying to get to her?

He understood. *They're protecting me.*

Choked from behind, arms held by another man, Yejide's eyes unfocussed and her body slumped, limp.

Gathering his feet under him, Akachi lunged through the closing gap, shouldering aside one of the Hummingbirds. Grabbing the man choking Yejide, he dragged him off the woman, shoving him so he fell sprawling into several other Growers. Someone Akachi didn't see hit him in the face and his eyes watered. He fought near blind, terror giving him strength, kicking out at the man who held Yejide's arms.

And then the Hummingbirds surrounded them, the entire formation having moved in unison. Akachi huddled over Yejide, sheltering her with his body. She blinked up at him, eyes regaining focus as her wits returned.

"Don't you ever do that again," she said, voice raw.

Someone screamed in visceral agony and the Growers ran, scrambling in all direction, abandoning their dead and wounded. The Hummingbird Guard straightened and surveyed the scene.

"Anyone hurt?" asked Yejide, climbing to her feet.

"I dislocated a finger," said one of the men, a giant stuffed into red leather.

"Aw, poor muffin." Yejide grabbed the oddly bent finger and yanked it straight until it popped back into place. He looked bored.

"Akachi?" she asked without looking.

"Fine," he said, rising. He clawed ox shit from his face, grimaced at his right hand, the knuckles scraped and swelling.

"I'm fine too," said Jumoke. "Thanks for asking."

Yejide ignored him.

The acolyte seemed remarkably unfazed. He grinned at Akachi. "Adventure turns out to have been overrated."

"I can't believe they attacked us in broad daylight," said Nafari, brushing himself off. "What did they hope to achieve?"

Captain Yejide eyed the fallen Growers littering the ground. Many lay still, but some, curled around their wounds, moaning in pain. A few were trying to crawl away, dragging themselves toward the nearest tenement entrance.

"The Loa pay them in narcotics and food for dead nahual," she said. "They have to bring proof. Flesh with the right tattoos. Anyone bringing in a live priest is promised food and water for the rest of their lives, freedom from working the fields." She turned to Akachi. "What is your judgement?"

"Judgement?" He shook, tremors of adrenalin aftershock running through him. "I... I don't know." What was he supposed to do? A conflicting surge of emotions—the realization he'd survived, anger at being attacked, the dregs of fear—scattered his thoughts like fleeing Growers.

"The punishment for attacking nahual is death," said Yejide.

Sacrifice.

It is a nahual's holy duty to shepherd the souls of Bastion. How many times had he been told that? His teacher's words ran through his thoughts. *To send a damaged soul to the gods to be cleansed and reborn is the most beautiful experience. Nothing will bring you closer to the gods.*

A beautiful experience. This was his holy duty.

Father would never hesitate.

Akachi felt the vile sickness of the sacrificial dagger emanating from his pack where he'd stuffed it.

"Bringing the wounded back the church for proper sacrifice will slow us," added Captain Yejide. "They'll likely stage another attack in an attempt to rescue their friends."

He wanted to go home, wherever that was now. He didn't want to face another attack.

"We should move fast," he said.

She took that as some kind of decision and nodded to the other Hummingbirds. "Break them."

Akachi watched in horror as the squad spread out and systematically smashed the wrists and ankles of all who still lived, conscious or not. They broke bone to dust. As with the brawl, they worked in silence. Those receiving their sentences were less quiet. When the squad moved on, Akachi, Nafari, and Jumoke once again at the centre, they left behind a discordant choir of misery and pain.

"Why?" he asked the Captain.

"A message: The Guard do not go lightly."

NURU – BRITTLE AND SHARP

*The fifth age ended in catastrophe and the death of a world. We live now in
the sixth age, the age beyond life, the age of apocalypse. We live a nightmare. We are
damned souls, doomed to a slow and rotting demise.*

—Loa Book of the Invisibles

Searching the dark corners of their tenement basement, Nuru
found Isabis, her black viper, coiled and dozing.

"How's my pretty girl doing?" she cooed, caressing the snake's
scales, feeling the dry strength of her. "Want to come upstairs and scare
Chisulo?"

Isabis raised her head to examine Nuru.

"That's what I thought."

Retrieving the snake, she looped it around her neck where it
promptly fell asleep.

Collecting five crude wooden mugs, she filled them with fomented
apple cider she aged in stolen barrels previously used for carting toma-
toes from the Growers' ring to the Crafters'. Cradling them in her arms,
she carried them up the stone steps to the ground floor.

Chisulo sat on an over-turned wood box in the tenement's communal eating room. Having recently shaved his head again with one of

Omari's flint knives, his skull was a mess of nicks and scabs. He glanced up when she entered. Seeing Isabis sleeping around her neck, he paled and shuffled his box a little further away. "I wish you wouldn't do that."

"She's a viper, not a constrictor."

He rubbed at his broken nose, squished to one side. "Still. Gives me the spine shivers."

"Where are the others?" she asked, placing one the mugs on the table before Chisulo and setting out the rest where her friends would sit.

Chisulo shrugged. "They'll be back soon. Everyone knows we have a gang meeting today."

Calling them a gang always seemed funny to Nuru. Five friends who'd known each other since they were in the crèche, scraping a living by selling narcotics from their one street corner of turf. Six, if you counted Efra. The girl never could decide if she was in or out.

She ran a hand over his scalp, enjoying the prickle of stubble.

I can't lose you. I can't lose any of them, but especially you. She loved his stone sense of right and wrong, but worried. *You're too quick to put yourself in danger to protect your friends.*

Ignoring the contact, he eyed the stained wood mug filled with cloudy cider sitting before him. "What's that?"

She let her hand drop. "Cider. Mostly."

"This stuff undoes the knots life ties in me."

"Poetic."

"And leaves me feeling awful the next day, like an entire family of rats shat in my skull."

"Less poetic."

"Mostly cider?"

"I added a little something to help with the fight." She should stop this, convince him the war could wait until she finished the spider. He'd listen. He'd do as she suggested. Fadil, however, wouldn't wait. The rival gang would take their hesitation as weakness and strike. They could lose everything they'd fought for.

Chisulo drank, swallowing quickly. "The things I'll suffer for a buzz."

The tenement—two bedrooms, a communal front room, a waste closet where they shat and pissed into a hole, and a basement—was identical to every home in the Wheat District. Only the furnishings, what little there was, and a handprint smear of stolen grey paint over the door, faded to almost nothing, marked it as theirs. Bomani did it in one of his many moments of drunken recklessness. Nuru had been sure the nahual would command them to wash it away and dish out lashings to all involved, but so far, the priests ignored their pathetic rebellion.

Home.

Chisulo rubbed again at his flattened nose. Happy broke it during a fight back when they all still lived at the crèche. Since then it had been crushed two more times, though not by Happy. Chisulo long ago gave up on straightening it.

Happy arrived first, ducking to enter and brushing the shell curtain aside with a hand that looked capable of crushing skulls. His grey thobe stretched tight across his broad shoulders and chest. The big man intentionally chose clothes too small when the priests handed out new garments each month. Red sand dusted tight curled hair the colour of oak bark. Many mistook Happy for a man much older than nineteen. This morning he looked like someone asked him to eat dried goat dung.

"Happy," said Chisulo in greeting.

Happy nodded to his two friends and collapsed onto a box. Meaty hands, fingers like over-stuffed sausages, made fists, knuckles popping. He glared at Chisulo from under bushy eyebrows. "I was with Kayla."

"I know."

"She has the most fantastic—"

"We know," said Nuru. "You talk about them continually."

"Worth talking about," grunted the big man.

"We'll start the meeting as soon as soon as the others get here," said Chisulo.

That, too, was funny. Chisulo's meetings usually revolved around talking about how they were going to grow the gang and sell more erlaxatu, and each week nothing changed.

The spider will change that. It was going to change everything. If, that is, she found the tools to finish it.

Omari entered the room slapping the beads aside. He stood blinking at his friends, eyes red, chest heaving to catch his breath.

"What—"

"Bomani," said Omari, interrupting Chisulo. He blinked and tears ran free. "Fucking Fadil."

"No," said Chisulo, a quiet denial.

Happy's knuckles popped like cracked whips. "What happened?" he asked, voice rumbling threat.

"Fadil. His gang. They killed Bomani. Just now." Omari saw the mugs on the table, grabbed one, and downed it in a single swallow. "Fucking…"

Nuru couldn't speak. Words were gone from her, stolen. *It can't be.*

"I sent him to see what Fadil was up to," said Chisulo. "This is my fault."

Except it wasn't, not really. He only sent Bomani because Nuru told him to. *It's my fault.*

She couldn't move. "Are you sure?"

Omari swallowed, baring teeth in a silent snarl. "Amza saw it all."

Amza was no friend to Chisulo's gang but would never lie about something like this.

Bomani dead. Nuru couldn't fit her mind around the idea. There had to be some mistake. It must have been someone else. *Bomani is too damned mean to die.* "There must be—"

"No," said Omari. "Amza was sure. He said…" Omari grabbed another mug and raised it to his lips, pausing when he realized who it must have been set out for. Closing his eyes and whispering something Nuru missed, he drained the mug. "Amza said they smashed him until he was unrecognisable. The priests won't even be able to tell who he is. Was. Fuckers."

She wasn't sure who the fuckers were, the priests, or Fadil's gang. *Doesn't matter.*

Happy stared into his full mug, unblinking. He slid the cup to Omari without a word and Omari nodded and drained it.

If they killed Bomani, were they coming here next? Should they run? Hide? Should they try to strike back? A maelstrom of confused emotions flooded Nuru. Rage, fear, loss, and pain. She didn't know what to feel and so she felt all of them. She wanted to lash out and hurt someone. She wanted to huddle her remaining friends close and protect them. She wanted blood, and she wanted to run and hide.

"Fadil grabbed Efra." said Omari. "She was following Bomani for some reason. Amza saw that too."

His words cut through her confusion. The spider. Efra. She was important, somehow. "We have to go get her," said Nuru.

I need her. She felt a stab of guilt at her selfishness. Efra was hard to like at the best of times and certainly didn't go out of her way to make friends. Nuru wasn't sure how she felt about the girl. Sometimes she caught Efra staring at Chisulo like she was either thinking of stabbing or fucking him and Nuru could never tell which. Efra was intense about everything, rarely smiling. When she did speak, half the time Nuru wondered if she was smarter than the rest of them. The other half she knew she even crazier than Bomani. She was cute. She was scarred. She was small, hard like the stone of Bastion, and yet brittle and sharp like obsidian.

She scared the shit out of Nuru.

Oh, Bomani. I'm sorry, my friend. Can you forgive me?

Did the dead ever forgive? The nahual of The Lord preached of a dark underworld filled with souls awaiting Father Death's judgement and the chance to be reborn. They made it sound like it was beneath Bastion, as if you could get there by descending enough stairs.

Nuru imagined Bomani there, alone, knowing he was dead because she told Chisulo to send him.

I got him killed.

Chisulo stood. "We're going to get Efra."

A twisted knot of rage and loss, Nuru and her friends headed for Fadil's tenement.

She grabbed Chisulo's hand, held it tight.

"Tell me you have a surprise, something to tip the odds." he said, his dread of her sorcery writ plain on blunt features.

She nodded and brought out a viper carved in wood from within her thobe. Painted ink-black, it fit in the palm of her hand.

"Oh gods," he said, "a snake." He shuddered.

Bomani. Nuru remembered all the times her friend's short temper got him in trouble. Bomani could never turn his back on even the mildest, most accidental, slight.

What happened?

Had he died cursing her?

Was it a bad death?

Such a stupid question. Was there any way being beaten could be a good death?

The other Growers saw Chisulo's little group and stayed well clear. By now, everyone knew what happened to Bomani. No one wanted to get caught in a gang fight, no matter how small.

Glancing at Chisulo, she saw fear in the rigid set of his shoulders, his clenched jaw. Even Happy looked scared. The big man walked like he had to push himself forward. Only Omari showed no sign of fear. He looked angry. Angrier than Nuru ever saw him before.

Chisulo noticed her attention and said, "Of all the scary people I know, Fadil and Sefu, Bomani and Omari, you are easily the scariest." He took a steadying breath. "Thank the gods you're on my side."

Was that supposed to be a compliment? She'd never understand men.

"We have to rescue Efra," he said, watching her reaction from the corner of his eye.

He doesn't want to do this, doesn't want to fight. And yet he kept moving forward because he knew it was the right thing to do and could do no less.

"We have to hurry," said Nuru.

They ran.

Rounding a corner into Fadil's territory, she spotted the gang's tenement. Five strides from the entrance, a huge pool of blood browned in the sun, staining the street. In the centre lay Bomani, crumpled and broken. She recognized the shape of him. Not far from Bomani lay Sadiki, one of Fadil's men, his skull misshapen, dead eyes swarming with flies. At least Bomani took one with him. The stench of rotting life clung to everything.

Striding to the home, Chisulo entered without stopping.

And his friends followed with him.

AKACHI – SINS OF TOLERANCE

Whoever utters the truest name of a god must be put to death. The whole com-
munity must stone him, whether alien or native. If he utters the name, he must be put
to death.

—The Book of Bastion

By the time they reached the church of Cloud Serpent, Akachi, Nafari, and Jumoke, shuffled with exhaustion, their robes soaked through
with sweat. Blood and bruises aside, the Captain and her squad looked as
if they'd gone for a leisurely morning stroll. No one talked about the attack.

From outside, the church looked like every other church in the
Growers' Ring. Ancient stone, rounded from relentless millennia of wind
and sand. No cracks or seams. It was big enough to hold a few hundred
standing Growers at worship, with chambers for a dozen or more staff in
the back. Dead trees and a tangle of desiccated weeds littered the courtyard. Akachi ran his hand along the trunk of one tree on his way to the
main entrance. The ancient wood, wormed through with holes from generations of insects, crumbled beneath his touch.

A week. Maybe two. Then he and Nafari could put this place behind
them. Zalika made no secret of the fact she wanted to replace Akachi

with a real pastor. Where they'd be sent after that, he had no idea. *Anywhere has to be better than this.*

"How long has this parish been empty?" Nafari asked.

"Bishop Zalika said the church had been abandoned for hundreds of years," answered Jumoke.

Akachi studied the rubbish-strewn grounds. "I wonder what happened to the last pastor."

"Murdered," said the acolyte. "They dragged her from the church and sacrificed her in the public square. They flayed the tattoos from her living flesh, and then opened her ribs to expose her heart to the gods. It's an ancient Loa practice. I read about it—"

"We've read it too," said Akachi, not wanting to hear more. *Let's hope Zalika calls us back before that happens to me.*

Or had the last pastor done something to deserve such a gruesome death? No. The Loa heretics must have incited the Growers to such violence.

Captain Yejide and one of the other Hummingbirds, a man with a beard too big for his face, drew their cudgels and took the lead.

"Wait here," the Captain said, leading the Human Beard into the church.

The rest of the squad took up positions around the priests and watched the street.

First, in a trickle, and then in increasing numbers, Growers shuffled past.

"They're returning from the wheat fields," said Nafari.

They looked tired, soaked in sweat, and filthy.

Akachi felt the weight of eyes. With the sun sinking toward the horizon and the day's heat finally relinquishing its grip on Bastion, the Wheat District seemed peaceful.

He remembered the crush of struggling bodies, the grunts of effort, the wet sound of wood on flesh. Angry glares. Bared teeth. A dirty Grower choking Captain Yejide with a scrawny arm, her eyes rolling back as she lost consciousness. They tried to stab him with a sharpened stick covered in shit!

It's a lie. Peace is a lie.

At least it didn't smell as bad as many of the districts they passed through.

"It's empty," said Captain Yejide, exiting the church.

Akachi nodded his thanks and entered. He stopped at the threshold. Total destruction. Broken wood littered the floor. The pulpit, a raised section of stone for the residing pastor to place his prepared sermon on, had been sloppily painted in what might have once been red but was now a faded pink. Quotes from the forbidden Loa *Book of the Invisibles*, painted in the same pale pink, adorned the walls.

'The Black One is the oldest god.'

'Mother Death built Bastion and we betrayed her.'

'Open yourself to the stone and Nephthys shall fill you.'

'On the day of fire and smoke, when the fields burn, and the wells fill with ash, Kālarātri, the Destroyer, shall return.'

Like all young priests, Akachi had read the book. Being forbidden just made it all the more tantalizing. Why else would the library of the Northern Cathedral have so many copies?

'Know your enemy,' said his history teacher.

He remembered passages speaking of the Last War, when the rings of Bastion battled for control of the city. They mentioned Mother Death, the original Lord of the Underworld. She'd been cast out by her husband for plotting to betray the pantheon. Though the *Book of the Invisibles* claimed it was she who had been betrayed.

This doesn't make sense. Growers can't read or write. Had the Loa defaced the church? *But if the Loa heretics are literate, they must come from the inner rings.*

Even the Crafters could only read enough to follow craft-related instructions and do simple maths. Could there be renegade priests? Had the Loa infiltrated the church, or had they always been there?

"Home sweet home," said Jumoke, passing Akachi on his way into the church. "I call first pick of rooms!"

"Absolutely, young acolyte," agreed Nafari. "As long as you want the dirtiest, most cramped quarters."

The boy whooped in mock joy and went in search of his room.

Standing at the entrance, Akachi examined the hall. In the Crafters' Ring there would have been pews of stone, all part of the rock of Bastion. In the Priests' and Bankers' Rings, oak pews were adorned with soft cushions of rich materials. Here the main hall was a large and largely empty stone room. Growers stood.

Before the raised pulpit sat the sacrificial altar. Troughs and runnels lined its surface and the floor around it. It held him entranced. He'd been to the lectures, read the passages in the *Book of Bastion* detailing the rites of sacrifice and bloodletting. He knew how, but couldn't imagine doing it.

"The most beautiful ritual," he whispered, remembering his teacher's words. "Never closer to the gods."

Will I have to sacrifice someone?

Having recently been attacked by the very people he was supposed to preach to, he knew the answer. It was, he knew, his holy task to guide the souls of his district. They were his wards, his responsibility. If they lived in contradiction to the Book, that was his failure.

Was that why Zalika sent him here?

One week. Maybe two, he repeated.

He'd get the church cleaned up, do a few sermons to the locals, and have everything ready for his replacement. When they saw how good he'd done, they'd send on word of his success, and Zalika would hate him all the more.

He grinned at the thought.

Nafari stepped up beside him, gesturing to the altar. "How many Growers do you think have been sacrificed on that?"

The grin fell. "This church stood for twenty-five thousand years," said Akachi, as if that answered the question. Maybe it did.

"Can you imagine what this place will smell like when it's filled with sweating Growers?" Nafari grimaced at the thought. "The Northern Cathedral will send us supplies, right?"

Akachi couldn't tell his friend how good that casual 'us' made him feel. *I'll get him drunk later, once we're settled.* Though, come to think of it, he had no idea where to get alcohol here. Maybe he could have it delivered from the Northern Cathedral.

"Zalika send supplies?" said Jumoke, returning to the hall. "Some poor bastard is going to have to go get them."

"Excellent!" said Nafari. "Thanks for volunteering."

"We have to tidy this up before we sound the drums," said Akachi. He wanted this place pristine when his replacement arrived.

Would Growers show up tomorrow at the recently reopened church? Did they even know it was being reopened?

"Will the Hummingbirds help?" asked Nafari.

"Not their job."

"We'll help," said the Captain, re-entering the hall. "This is our home too."

"Thanks." Akachi gave her tired smile which she ignored.

That attack was an aberration. It had to be. According to the *Book of Bastion,* Growers were peaceful, docile. Or had the Loa tried to assassinate him as they'd likely assassinated the last several priests sent from the inner rings? That, Akachi decided, made more sense.

Nafari was here with him. Together they'd take on the world. Captain Yejide, though overly serious and kind of scary, seemed a decent sort, if somewhat distant. Breaking the Growers wasn't something she wanted to do, it was something she *had* to do. Responsible for the immortal souls of all Bastion, nahual made hard choices every day.

I'll make a go of this. I'll show Bishop Zalika, throw this back in her face.

First, he'd clean up the church, then he'd clean up the district. He might not be here long, but he'd leave the Wheat District a better place than he found it. This posting would not be his failure. The Growers wanted leadership, they craved order and simplicity. This empty church was more than likely part of the reason the district was in such rough shape.

I'll give them back their gods, show them the path and the light.

This was going to work. It was an opportunity, his chance to earn his way back into the inner rings.

"The kitchen is a mess," said the Human Beard, joining them in the main hall. He looked heartbroken. The rest of the destruction didn't touch him, yet a messy kitchen was apparently an affront to the gods.

"You," said Akachi, pointing at the acolyte.

"Yes, Pastor?"

"I'm not really a—Never mind. Your first job is to clean up the kitchen. Put it in order. Take a look around, make a list of everything we'll need."

"We'll need a cook from the Crafters," said the Captain.

"Well, that hurt," said the Human Beard.

"Add it to the list," Akachi told Jumoke.

"Yes, Pastor," said the boy, rolling up the sleeves of his charcoal acolyte's frock as he left.

"I'll help," said one of the Guards, following.

Akachi turned a complete circle, examining the hall that would soon hold his congregation.

My congregation. He couldn't believe it. He might not be a real pastor, but here he was with a parish of his own and years younger than when his father first earned his.

Did I earn this?

If earning Bishop Zalika's enmity counted, then yes.

Spider webs adorned every corner. The skeletal remains of birds and rats and gods knew what else lay littered among the debris. Smoke stains, twisted snakes of soot, climbed one wall. It looked like squatters lived here for many years, though not recently.

We clothe them. We feed them. We give them homes. We supply everything they could ever need. Why would they want to live in an abandoned church?

Akachi, Nafari, Jumoke, and the seven Hummingbird Guard, spent the last hour of light dragging refuse from the church and piling it in the yard. When the sun dropped below the horizon, Akachi realized he hadn't thought to bring candles. The church was dark and silent. Stumbling with exhaustion, he retired to the pastor's chambers. After making sure nothing dangerous lived in there, he examined the raised slab that was to be his bed. Stone never looked so inviting.

I need a mattress and heavy blankets. For all Bastion's heat during the day, each night the inhabitants saw their breath. Tomorrow he'd send Jumoke and a couple of the Hummingbirds for supplies.

Taking the sacrificial dagger from his pack, he placed it on the writing desk, a stone slab extending from the wall. Even that small distance felt like a weight lifted from his shoulders. It reeked of violence. Even without narcotics in his blood, Akachi sensed the thinning of the veil around it. One did not need to be a nahualli of Father Death to sense its power.

Grimacing, he pushed it to the back corner of the desk with a fingertip.

Collapsing onto the uncomfortable bed, he wrapped himself in the one blanket he'd brought and was asleep in moments.

A colossal snake banded in red, black, and white.

The beginning of the end.

A black stain, starting in the Grower's Ring.

An infection, growing to devour all Bastion.

Fire, the sky blackened by smoke.

The wells filling with thick ash.

Akachi stood alone atop the Grey Wall separating the Growers from the Crafters. He looked down into the Wheat District.

Platoons of Hummingbirds, armoured in jade-green stone, drew swords of obsidian. Southern Hummingbird's elite, the Turquoise Serpents. They were said to be immortal, their swords unbreakable. Akachi stared in horror as the nahual of Southern Hummingbird marched against a mob of Growers, cut men in half, spilled all they were to the stone.

From atop the Grey Wall, Akachi saw something he'd never before noticed. Blood runnels, just like those beneath the sacrificial altar, lined every street. Sanguine rivers, straight and perfect, ran toward the centre of Bastion.

This could only work if Bastion was a bowl with the Gods' Ring at the lowest point. The mathematical precision of such a construct, the sheer scale, staggered Akachi.

This entire city is an altar.

Every ring, the entirety of Bastion, funnelled blood inward.

The rings. The hundreds of thousands of souls. All this endless, seamless stone served one purpose: Feed the gods.

No. It can't be.

It was too much. Akachi reeled, searching for balance and calm. *Cloud Serpent would never—*

Akachi saw a Grower girl down in the street. A brutal scar split her face from above her right eyebrow to the left side of her chin. Baring her teeth in the scar-stretching snarl of a mad dog, she glared up at him. Smoke stained the air around her. Though the Hummingbirds and Growers battled in every alley, none of it touched her. Both sides passed around her, left her space as if unwilling to come too close.

As if afraid.

Kill her. Kill her! He wanted to shout at the Guards on the street, but they couldn't hear.

The clouds over the scarred Grower girl changed. Thin funnels, like the legs of a spider, reached down into every ring of Bastion. Where they touched, death and destruction followed.

The red, white, and black snake coiled around Akachi, crushing him.

The gods are at war, my Heart, Cloud Serpent said, voice like scales on sand. *Hunt the girl.*

Akachi woke to find Nafari standing over him. Jumoke stood at his friend's shoulder.

"Time to rise, Pastor," said Jumoke.

"Go away." He remembered the dream, the scarred Grower girl. *It was real.* He was a nahual of Cloud Serpent, Lord of the Hunt, and his god had shown him his prey. Somehow, she was at the heart of something terrible.

"You all right?" asked Nafari.

"I had a vision."

"A true vision, a dream, or were you smoky?"

"Smoky as fuck," opined Jumoke.

"Please don't use Grower language." Still groggy from sleep, Akachi wasn't ready to talk about it.

That was no dream. It was real. He knew it in his blood, in his bones. Cloud Serpent burned it into him, left no room for doubt. Everything he thought was important last night was now less than irrelevant. Excitement, awe, and raw terror shivered through him.

Cloud Serpent spoke to me!

He'd lived in fear of disappointing his father.

Disappointing his god would be far worse.

"Are you sure you're all right?" asked Nafari, brow crinkled with worry. "You look ill."

Still wearing his robes from the day before, wrinkled and dirty, stinking of sweat, Akachi waved away his friends' concern and climbed out of bed. "Let's see what the Hummingbirds are up to."

Wandering down to the main hall, they found the Hummingbirds already up and bustling about, tidying. Captain Yejide called from the entrance. When Akachi reached her, picking his way through the detritus littering the floor, he understood. The yard was empty, cleared of the garbage they piled out there the previous evening.

"I think the Growers are welcoming you to the neighbourhood," said Nafari, at his side.

"Or they stole it to burn for warmth at night," said Jumoke. "I wish I'd thought of that."

After sending Nafari, Jumoke, and two of the Hummingbirds to get supplies—including candles, mattresses and blankets, food, and more —Akachi wandered into the yard to find a stump to sit on. Two Hummingbirds, the man with the monstrous beard and the woman Nafari had been chatting up, followed him out to stand guard. They ignored him.

Akachi sat, watching the Growers go about their day. Men and women, universally thin, shuffled past, heading out to the fields. Walking in clumped groups they joked and talked, a herd of grey and sweat stains. Some wore subtle accents and accessories. A bracelet of seashells. Bones tied in hair. Some had altered their thobe to hug their form or show a little more flesh. Such modifications, while forbidden, were generally ignored as harmless. Or used to be. Now he wasn't sure. Most of Bishop Zalika's sermons were on the sins of tolerance and the necessity for absolute adherence to the Book.

Some of the younger women batted eyelashes, making no attempt to hide their attention or intentions. Having spent most of the last few years surrounded by the predominantly male priesthood of Cloud Serpent, Akachi decided leaving the Growers their small displays of individuality was probably for the best.

Nowhere did he see the hate and rage of yesterday's attack.

Of course not. These are the good Growers, those who work the fields as they should.

An old Grower hobbled past on his way out to the fields. He used a bent stick as a cane. Technically such use was a crime, but who would forbid a man his needed crutch? His thobe was so dirty as to be more brown than grey.

Dirts. Captain Yejide's word for the Growers.

Akachi pushed these thought away; it was unworthy. Sitting here, in the same robes he wore yesterday, he was hardly a paragon of cleanliness.

Across the street he spotted a young Grower woman lounging against a tenement wall. She studied him, her eyes impossibly bright.

I know her.

He'd seen her before, when he left the Northern Cathedral.

Noting his attention, she nodded, turned, and sauntered down the street, disappearing around the first corner.

Who was she? Was she spying on him? He made a note to mention it to Captain Yejide. Right now, he had to focus. He came out here to think.

The dream.

It wasn't a dream. It was a vision.

He thought he was being sent to the Wheat District because Bishop Zalika hated his father.

That wasn't it at all. Or rather that might have been Zalika's reason, but Akachi knew now he was here because Cloud Serpent *wanted* him here.

Smoke and destruction. The Growers rising up in rebellion.

It was unthinkable, but one did not ignore a vision from the gods.

He remembered the girl from the dream. Was she here in the Wheat District?

He laughed. Where else could she possibly be? He would never forget her features. That scar.

Cloud Serpent, Lord of the Hunt, had shown Akachi his prey.

Returning to his new chambers, Akachi killed off the last of the spiders and cleared away the worst of the webs. After sharing a small room with Nafari for seven years, he felt distant and alone. Though much smaller than what Bishop Zalika enjoyed in the Northern Cathedral, these were the grandest chambers he'd seen since leaving his family estate in the Priests' Ring. Though large, they lacked the beauty and sophistication of his home. Everything was simple stone. A pang of homesickness tightened his chest.

A polite cough from the far side of the curtain he'd hung to separate his rooms from the rest of the church interrupted his thoughts.

"Enter," he said.

Captain Yejide ducked through the curtain. She stood for a moment, angular eyebrow crooked, surveying the room.

When she didn't speak, he said, "A lot of spiders. Only one scorpion."

"You're lucky. The rooms for the Guard are infested. Gyasi chased a red snake out."

Akachi wasn't sure which one Gyasi was, and even less sure how one chased a deadly viper.

Captain Yejide's attention finally settled on him, eyes making no secret of looking him over. A latticework of scars, pale ridges, criss-crossed her arms. Even her face bore scars. She bore his examination, waiting. So utterly calm and composed.

"You popped in to say hello?" he asked.

"Back there," she said, "in the street. Thank you."

Akachi shifted, uncomfortable.

"You aren't trained in battle," she said, eyeing him as if measuring, as if truly seeing him for the first time.

"I'm a nahualli of Cloud Serpent."

"Hunting and war are two very different things. That was brave."

"Brave? I was terrified."

"That's what made it brave. Don't ever do it again," she repeated. "Our task is to protect you. You make that more difficult by exposing yourself to danger."

"Sorry," he lied. *If doing that again makes you look at me like this, I'll do it a thousand times.*

He was about to tell her about the Grower he'd seen watching him when she abruptly said, "We have church matters to attend to."

"Already? I haven't unpacked yet."

"Oh, the impropriety. A Grower came to Lutalo while he stood guard at the church entrance. Apparently, there's a woman in the district who has not surrendered a baby to the church."

He had no idea which one Lutalo was. *Someone let a Grower take a baby home?* "How is that even possible? Was it stolen?"

"I believe she gave birth in her tenement."

"She gave birth in a Grower hovel instead of a sanctioned church?" He shook his head in wonder.

"It happens," said the Captain. "They think they can care for them. They think they can hide them from us." She shrugged. "They aren't terribly bright."

According to the Book, Growers were too ignorant, too stupid, to be entrusted with the raising of children. All Growers were born in church, before the gods, and raised by the nahual in crèches. It was for their own good.

Captain Yejide cocked her head to one side, waiting.

"And?" he asked.

"And we have to go get the child." When he said nothing, she continued. "You have to come. You must take the child into the arms of the gods. You must decide the woman's punishment."

"Right. Forgot." Reading about the duties of a nahual in ancient texts was different than carrying them out. "What is the proscribed punishment?"

"As nahual, you have some discretion in the matter."

Some. "What's typical?" he asked. "What have you seen?"

"The most lenient punishment I witnessed for this crime was fifty lashes in the public square."

How often did this happen that she had multiple experiences to call upon? "Not so bad."

"The woman died a week later."

"Oh."

Captain Yejide shrugged one shoulder. "It doesn't always happen like that. Dirts are usually quite sturdy."

Akachi wasn't sure how he felt about the term *Dirts*. While fitting, it was definitely derogatory. None of the student-priests in the Northern Cathedral ever used it. Then again, none of them had been out among the Growers.

"If you're ready," she said, "we'll go."

"Now?"

"Oh no," she said, "at your convenience, of course. Perhaps a light meal and a nap first?"

"Really?"

She sighed, shaking her head. "Waiting won't make this easier. Better to do it before she forms an attachment with the babe."

An attachment. He imagined someone threatening to take one of his mother's children. She'd have ended worlds. No force in all Bastion could stand before her wrath.

Akachi nodded and followed Yejide out of his chambers. She walked with a confident strut. Although a skirt of hardened crimson leather hung past her knees, covering her ass, his imagination had no trouble picturing it somewhat less clothed.

She would kill you. Focus.

Captain Yejide snapped her fingers, a loud echoing *crack*, as they entered the main hall. The Hummingbird Guard lounging there jumped to their feet and fell in around them like a scruffy-looking honour guard. All were armed and armoured.

The Grower who reported the crime stood waiting in the courtyard. He bowed a few dozen times to Akachi in his desperate need to please.

Akachi blessed him with a quick prayer. "In your next life you'll be reborn nearer the light of the gods."

The filthy man, thobe stained and threadbare, beamed with simple pride and led the way.

Refuse littered the streets of the Wheat District. Most of it was discarded foodstuffs and stank like rotting corn. Scraps of grey cloth, cacked with red sand, twitched in the evening breeze. Here and there the broken remnants of the few farming implements, deemed both safe and simple enough for Growers, lay where dropped. Too stupid to use intricate tools, most of what they had access to amounted to fortuitously shaped sticks. Still, it said something of both the locals and the sad state of this district that such thefts took place.

I'll have to talk with the Hummingbirds patrolling the fields. They're getting sloppy.

Growers eyed their little group from shadowed doorways, though no one sought to impede their progress.

Half an hour walk out from these tenements lay the wheat fields for which the district was named. In truth, there were many Wheat Districts scattered around the outer ring, but since Growers never travelled, they'd never know.

The Grower led them through streets and filth-strewn alleys. Though all Grower tenements were identical—perhaps, by the time the gods were building the outer ring, they were exhausted and could no longer be bothered with detail—many were decorated with small personal touches. Strings of shells hung over some doors, while others bore strips of grey cloth. A few even had splashes of what might have been mud or dull paint. Forbidden as such displays were, Akachi knew most nahual turned a blind eye. The common wisdom was that without such small touches, the Growers were too stupid to find their way home again.

'Sins of tolerance,' Bishop Zalika said when preaching absolute adherence to the Book.

Was she right? Was the Wheat District such a mess because the local pastors were too lenient?

Akachi saw no harm in allowing some small show of personality. And if it helped them find their homes…

The Grower stopped, scratched at an armpit, sniffed his fingers, and then pointed out a tenement. "There."

Captain Yejide snapped her fingers. "Ibrahim. Njau."

Two of the Hummingbirds, one a giant wall of walking muscle, and the man Akachi previously dubbed the Human Beard, approached the entrance. Drawing ebony cudgels, they entered. A moment later, the bearded man returned and nodded to Yejide before retuning inside. Signalling Akachi to follow, she entered the tenement. Another Hummingbird fell in behind them. The other two remained outside, watching the street.

Captain Yejide led him to the back room. As with most tenements, this one was used as a bedroom. A single wide slab of raised stone served as a bed. Two thin grey blankets lay thrown across it. The room stank of sweat. A young male Grower, no older than Akachi, and a girl of similar age, stood with Ibrahim and Njau. The girl wept with great tearing sobs, baby held clutched to her chest. Her body shook with the force of her crying.

Serpent's tongue! Is it already dead?

Had the stupid Growers killed it with their ignorance? Akachi's breath caught. The punishment for killing a child was death on the altar. Fear and excitement swept through him. A chance to truly serve the gods, to see a wayward soul given the opportunity for redemption! *She'll be reborn purified.* It was right. It was what the Book said should happen. Shirking his duty would be a sin of tolerance.

Holding his breath, he leaned closer. The baby lived, somehow managing to sleep through the noise. Though relieved, he couldn't help but feel some disappointment. This would not be his chance to prove himself worthy in the eyes of his god.

At a signal from Captain Yejide, one of the Hummingbirds pinned the young man against the back wall. The youth struggled for a moment before realizing how outnumbered he was. He sagged, unresisting, the fight gone from him.

With the exception of the sobbing woman cuddling the babe, everyone stared at Akachi.

They're waiting for me.

He cleared his throat. "The child must be raised in a crèche. We have come to collect it."

"She's not an *it*," said the Grower youth.

The Hummingbird silenced him with a crushing punch to the kidney. The boy folded, wheezing, and the other Hummingbird kicked him in the ribs.

Frowning, Akachi turned his back on the violence. *It shouldn't have come to this.* "The *Book of Bastion* says all children must be raised in a crèche." It was a slight lie. The Book said all *Grower* children had to be raised in crèches. Since Growers couldn't read, that part was generally left out so as not to confuse them.

"Captain," said Akachi. "Collect the child."

The Grower woman screamed, waking the babe, who immediately added to the cacophony.

"And the punishment?" asked Captain Yejide over the noise.

The woman's wail of despair broke Akachi's heart. This felt wrong. *I have to be strong.* The Book was clear, this was the way. *I have no choice.*

He wanted to say *none*, that this would be punishment enough. He couldn't. Who did Yejide report to, Bishop Zalika? What would she do if he appeared weak, unable to control and punish the Growers of his district? He'd be a failure in the eyes of his father. He couldn't allow that. Akachi was here to do Cloud Serpent's bidding. All this was just a distraction.

The woman collapsed as the Captain pried the crying baby from her. She lay curled on the floor, screaming.

"You should have given birth in the church," Akachi told her. "It's the law. The gods, the *Book of Bastion*—" He stopped. She wasn't listening. "Fifty lashes in the public square," he announced. Glancing at Captain Yejide, he added, "Try not to kill her."

The Captain gestured at Njau and Ibrahim and they lifted the girl to her feet. She hung between them like a broken doll.

Captain Yejide led the way back to the street and Akachi followed. The two carrying the sobbing woman came last. The young man, curled foetal on the floor, crying, they left behind.

"What about the boy?" Akachi asked, once they were back in the cleansing sun. After the stink of the Grower hovel, it felt good. He needed a bath to wash their stench from his hair.

"What about him?" Yejide asked.

"He's probably the father."

"Dirts don't understand such concepts."

"But—"

"Giving birth at the church is the woman's responsibility. She broke the law. She will suffer the punishment."

The Captain handed the baby off to another Hummingbird, a woman with hard eyes. "Deliver it to the crèche. Njau, go with Khadija."

Njau, the one Akachi dubbed 'the Human Beard,' and Khadija broke off from the party. Crèches were never located near where the Growers lived and the nearest was several hours walk out into the wheat fields.

The remaining Hummingbirds escorted Akachi and the crying woman back to the church. The Growers of the district stopped whatever they were doing to watch them pass, eyes heavy. The walk back felt very different from the walk there.

My first real act as Cloud Serpent's nahual in the Wheat District, and I tore a baby away from its mother.

He did the gods' work. The Book was clear.

He still felt terrible, guilty.

It was for the best, for the good of the child.

No one spoke.

After seeing the woman bound and left in the basement to consider her sins, Akachi returned to his chambers. Tomorrow morning one of the Hummingbird Guard would carry out his proscribed punishment.

I couldn't whip a helpless woman.

What kind of person could?

Captain Yejide could.

But who then, really, was to blame for this situation? The Hummingbirds were carrying out Akachi's sentencing. Did that make him responsible? Or was it the woman who knowingly broke the law?

He spent the rest of the morning listening to her screams and sobs until someone stomped down the steps to silence her.

He didn't attend the whipping, but sat in his chambers, writing the sermon for that day. The crack of the lash and the screams of the young mother punctuated every sentence.

NURU – SERPENTINE SONGS

Mother Death speaks through the bones of the earth.

—Loa Book of the Invisibles

Whatever happens next is my fault. She sent Bomani to watch Fadil. She pushed Chisulo to rush to Efra's rescue; not that he needed much pushing.

What if she lost another one of her friends? She wanted to grab him, drag Chisulo to a stop, tell him she was wrong. Except they had to save Efra. It would have been so much easier if the girl had been one of them, with them from the beginning. There'd have been no question of abandoning her. But she wasn't, not really.

It doesn't matter. This wasn't about saving the scarred girl. This was about the dream, the spider. Without Efra, Nuru would never get the tools she needed.

And so you risk your friends for a dream? She hated herself.

Chisulo wouldn't stop anyway, not once he knew what had to be done.

The last of the foku and aldatu Nuru ate before, while she'd been carving the spider, sharpened the world. That was good. She needed it. Her ally lived within. She felt smoky and unreal, detached from the dirt, sand, and stone of Grower reality. The veil between worlds thinned to a translucent sheen. The smoke, her ally, was with her. The viper coiled in her heart, calling promises of cold detachment and easy murder.

Allies existed in the smoke, in the mushrooms and the strange glowing fungus, but they weren't alone. Strange intelligences lurked beyond the veil, waiting, hoping. Promising.

What was the spider? It spoke of a war among the gods. Could she believe it?

She focussed on the moment, the stench of Bomani's death thick in her nostrils. Footprints passed uncaring through the blood and straight to Fadil's. Nuru couldn't look at the corpse of her friend.

As they entered the tenement Omari drew a small flint blade with a makeshift handle of wrapped leather. Where he got it, Nuru couldn't imagine. Owning such a thing meant death. If the Birds found it, he'd be sacrificed for sure. Happy, being a hulking slab of muscle, didn't need a weapon.

Nuru drew the carved viper from its place in her thobe. It was warm. She'd based this carving on Isabis. The scales weren't perfect. The ink, too thick, clumped in ridges in the wood. Her crude tools failed her.

It will work.

Chisulo, Happy, and Omari, seeing the carving, shied away.

"I'll follow along," she promised.

Chisulo nodded, looking like he wanted to say something but couldn't find the words.

"I'll be fine," she whispered.

Once out of the sun, she knelt, holding the carving before her eyes. She focussed on it, let it become her world, her everything. Her ally moved within, entwining with her soul. They were one.

The snake is real. She struggled to ignore the imperfections in the figurine. *My ally and I, we are the snake.* She imagined the way Isabis moved, twisting across red sand. The crudeness of the paint job and the false black of the ink pulled on her focus, threatened to distract.

Focus. Control.

Nuru visualized the jaw opening wide, the vicious fangs dropping into place. She imagined how it would feel to have her belly on ground, no limbs, seeing the world in heat. She closed her eyes, the snake *foku* locked in her mind.

Her ally sang serpentine songs.

She imagined the eyes, green and cold, and hated that she couldn't paint them that way.

It will work.

It had to work. She couldn't fight. If she failed, her friends might die. She heard them continue into Fadil's, felt their steps through the stone against her belly. They were splashes of heat and colour, warm life.

Nuru followed, twisting and sinuous. Deadly.

She heard sobbing and the voices of men.

Efra's still alive. We're not too late. But there was alive, and then there was living. Nuru had seen men and women broken by pain and loss. The Birds' lash sometimes tore more than flesh.

Her ally urged her forward. She slithered along the wall, keeping to the shadows.

In the second room they found Fadil's gang. Except it wasn't Fadil's anymore. Fadil sat in a chair—a real chair!—his eyes wide and staring, his throat a tattered wound. Blood splashed his face and chest.

Did Efra do that?

The rest of Fadil's gang gathered around the girl. Stripped naked, she lay curled on the ground. They taunted and circled her, kicking. Blue bruises painted her ribs. Each time one got close enough, she lashed out and they danced away, laughing. Sefu, that twisted dog-fucker, oversaw the proceedings like a pastor. He shouted encouragement and mockery and offered cruel suggestions.

Where Chisulo hesitated, gauging and measuring, Happy strode past him and punched the nearest man in the back of the neck. The man crumpled, boneless. Omari went right, angling to get at Sefu. The Fingers hated each other. Chisulo finally squared off against another and the two did that thing men do when they know what needs to be done but don't really want to do it. Every time Chisulo advanced, his opponent backed away.

Seeing his size, two of the Fist went after Happy. No man, no matter how big, wants to face two. Happy retreated, huge arms raised, swatting at whoever came within range. He angled to keep them from surrounding him.

Omari and Sefu, stone knives darting and stabbing, circled each other. They were their own world, focussed entirely on killing. Neither saw the deadly black snake slide through the shadows. Gliding past Sefu, she lashed out, sank fangs into an exposed ankle. The Finger screamed, startled and in pain, but kept fighting. He might not know what bit him, but Omari would definitely kill him in an instant, given the chance.

Avoiding the stomping and scuffling feet, Nuru made her way to Fadil's cooling corpse. Someone screamed in agony and she prayed it wasn't one of her boys. She wound her way up the dead man's leg, climbing him like a tree. Her ally guided her, counting the heartbeats.

Timing.

Coiling around Fadil's neck, she lifted her head two feet into the air above him and prayed Chisulo was paying attention.

Nuru knew her snake. She knew her venom.

Sefu collapsed as his heart seized.

Chisulo, for all his many faults, thought fast when he had to. "Look!" he shouted, pointing at Nuru.

She weaved hypnotically, looking from man to man, allowing her attention to linger so they knew they'd been seen. They all recognized the type of viper she'd become. Every Grower knew to avoid them.

Efra rolled over and staggered to her feet. Naked, bathed in a glistening sheen of blood, the tiny girl commanded the room. All fighting stopped. If she was self-conscious, she showed none of it.

"You are Chisulo's now," Efra said. "You join his gang, or you die here." No doubt coloured her voice.

She's terrifying.

Happy's blood was still up. He'd been bruised and bloodied but wasn't ready for an end. "They were going to rape—"

Efra silenced him with a slash of her hand. "Look for tomorrow," she said as if that explained everything.

Whatever her meaning, whatever her intent, it confused Happy enough to slow him.

"Chisulo," said Efra. "Tell them."

Chisulo hesitated.

"Tell them," commanded Efra, "or we're all going to die." She growled in frustration, looking like she wanted to say more, to explain. "How many whippings did you see in the public square last week? How many were sacrificed at church in the last month?"

That's not what she wants to say. There was something else, something she wasn't willing to share. *I'll get it out of her.*

Chisulo shook his head. "Bomani."

"Bomani is dead," snapped Efra. "The only way to survive is to grow."

Chisulo glanced at Nuru, at the snake she had become.

I knew the girl was important! This needs to happen. She did a bobbing dance of a nod; all the viper's body could manage.

Change was coming to the Growers, and it was coming fast. Every week more felt the punishing lash for transgressions ignored for centuries. Men and women disappeared daily, taken in church or dragged away in the night. Even the Birds were scared. She saw it in the way they always kept a hand resting on their cudgels, in the way they travelled in squads where they used to patrol in pairs. The nahual preached obedience in every sermon.

Every day they pound they drums and we go to church. And then they pound their fears into us. Narcotics swam her blood, spoke to her. *The world is coming apart.* The smoke never lied. *The veil stretches. That which is beyond seeks entrance.* And Efra had something to do with this.

Chisulo glanced at Happy and Omari only to discover everyone was looking at him, waiting. *You have to decide.* Nuru knew what he'd decide before he did; he was angry, but not a murderer.

Unlike Nuru.

She glanced at Sefu's rigid body, spine arched in an agonizing death.

He had to die.

As a snake, Nuru knew no remorse. That would come later when the woman returned. Never having killed anyone before, she couldn't imagine how it would feel. For now, she was cold purpose. But Chisulo, she knew, was different, he felt things. He cared. *That's why we turn to him; he's the best of us.*

Sagging, Chisulo shook his head.

He'll let them join us because, even if we outnumber them, he won't chance us getting hurt.

She loved him then, even as a snake. She always had and always would. Bomani might have been the protective friend, but Chisulo was the one she admired, the one she looked up to.

"Are you with us?" Chisulo asked the three men still standing.

They nodded.

"He can't hear you," said Efra. "Answer him!"

"We're with you," they said, glancing nervously at the snake.

Chisulo glanced at Sefu's stiffened body and then to the man Happy punched in the back of the neck who still lay motionless on the floor. "Let's see who's dead and who's…" He breathed deep. "Happy, find Efra some clothes." His gaze lingered on Fadil's men. "She's one of us. Anyone touches her, anyone hurts her, I'll kill you."

They nodded their understanding.

"We don't rape," he said. "We don't murder. We're not animals."

"And we're not Dirts," Efra said. "The Birds underestimate us." She grinned blood. "I have a plan."

Nuru pulled herself back from the snake, fighting the urge to hide here, to cower in reptilian thought. It would never work; eventually the narcotics would leave her system. Pain awaited her. Pain and guilt. *I'm a murderer now.* Her friends needed her. *If I ever lose them, I'll make one last carving, take all the drugs, and stay there forever.* She thought of the spider and shuddered. *Not that one.* As exciting as the prospect of completing the carving was, it terrified her. Much the same way Efra excited and scared her.

The man Happy punched woke and stared about in groggy confusion, pleased to be alive and quick to swear he was with Chisulo now.

Nuru, again herself and smoky with the after-effects of the narcotic melange, collected the carving of her snake. It looked pathetic, inferior ink flaking away to expose the wood beneath. *It's so crude.* Maybe she could touch it up, repair it enough to get another use or two out of the figurine. It possessed none of the life it should. The spider had to be perfect. *I need tools. I need proper paints and brushes.*

She examined Efra. The girl held her bruised ribs, only showing pain when she thought no one was looking. She stayed close to Chisulo, but not too close. Not close enough for her proximity to be noticed. At least not by Chisulo, who tended not to notice such things anyway.

What does she want? What does she really want? Nuru wasn't sure if she should feel protective or scared. Seeing Efra naked, body sheened in blood, reminded her again of the female torso of the spider. They were totally different in build, and yet somehow the spider and the girl shared something.

Efra said she had a plan.

When we are home, I will discover what she intends. Nuru had sorcerous means of discovering deeper truths.

Talking to Chisulo about paints and tools was pointless. She'd tried in the past and he shrugged and explained, in that way men did, what she already knew: They were Growers and Growers were forbidden tools.

Efra won't be like that. The girl would never accept the way things were as an excuse to do nothing.

Things were going to change.

In the distance the drums at the recently reopened church of Cloud Serpent began to beat, calling all good Growers to prayer. Everyone looked to Chisulo for guidance.

Taking in Efra's wounded state, he said, "We'll wait here until the sermon is over and the streets are busy."

AKACHI – THE HUNT IS ON

Sorcery is the sole domain of the nahualli. Anyone else caught practising sorcery will be sacrificed on the altar, no matter which ring they are born to.

—The Book of Bastion

Akachi woke early the next morning before Smoking Mirror surrendered the night and Southern Hummingbird claimed the day. Donning a fresh set of robes, he wandered out into the main hall. He found Captain Yejide there, sparring with the Human Beard. They ignored him, circling each other, feinting and jabbing. The man had forty pounds of muscle on the Captain, but she was clearly faster.

Waiting for them to break, Akachi watched as she slapped her opponent a stinging blow with an open hand, ducked under the counterstrike, and swept the man's legs out from under him.

"You are slow as a pregnant ox," she said, offering a hand to pull him back to his feet.

Grinning, he accepted the hand up. "Sure, but you know that once I get my hands on you the fight is over."

"True. But you need to be faster. Work on your speed with Khadija."

"Yes, Captain."

Seeing Akachi, Yejide turned to face him. "How may we help, Pastor."

"I want to go for a walk."

"Bad idea."

"I need to see my district."

"Too dangerous."

"The Growers need to see me. They need to know the church is open." He hesitated to tell her about the vision.

"I don't like this," she said, crossing her arms.

For a moment he hesitated. As acting pastor, he was in charge. He could command her obedience but didn't want to. *I have to find the scarred girl.* "Captain, I need to do this. Please." He gave her a meaningful look, to let her know that he was asking, but didn't have to.

She studied him, that angular eyebrow creeping up. "We stick to the main streets."

Akachi, not wanting a repeat of their last foray into a filth-strewn alley, agreed.

When they left, the Human Beard took the lead. The Captain walked at Akachi's side. The other woman, Hard-Eyes, he dubbed her, followed a dozen paces behind.

This looks practised.

The sun had barely breached the horizon, but already the day was savagely hot. He wished he'd thought to bring his sun parasol, but knew he'd never dare open it as long as the Hummingbirds shunned such comfort.

Not looking weak is going to kill me.

The Growers wisely kept to the shadows. Akachi, walking in the centre of the street, was soaked with sweat in minutes. The Hummingbirds, in their red leather armour, also sweated heavily. No one complained.

They passed a group of Growers, men and women, gathered around a well, taking turns drinking from the bucket. Tired and dirty, they must have spent the night working in the fields. One of the women raised a tentative hand and he waved back, smiling.

This isn't so bad. Aside from that one attack, which, the more he thought about it the more he suspected it had been planned by the Loa and not by the Growers, the district seemed peaceful enough. Sure, some of the Growers were angry, but there were troublemakers in any group. Once they'd been weeded out, the district would return to normal.

Captain Yejide glanced sideways at him and there was something, some glint in her eye, that shot a pleasant shiver through him. "What did you do to get this posting?" she asked without preamble.

Should he tell her? Would she think he was bragging? "Cloud Serpent chose me."

Her eyes widened. "Truly?"

He nodded, grinning. "That, and Bishop Zalika hates me. You?"

The Captain's lips twitched and Akachi decided it was probably as close to a smile as she was capable. "I was working a crèche and refused to whip an eight-year-old girl," she said, once again scanning the street. "I doomed myself to a lifetime of Dirt postings." She laughed, a humourless grunt. "Should have flogged her."

Akachi couldn't tell if she was joking. "The rest of the squad suffered for your honour?" he asked, trying to subtly let her know he understood and appreciated her stance.

"No. They stripped me of my squad and assigned me this group of drunks and rejects."

"I'm the drunk," said Hard Eyes from behind them. "He's the reject."

"I feel safer already," joked Akachi.

Yejide darted a look in his direction without moving her head.

"You're safe enough."

"Hmm. How about him," he asked, dropping his voice and nodding at the man ahead of them, "the Human Beard?"

"Njau. He killed a Dirt."

"Oh." Akachi made a note to remember the Hummingbird's name.

"The Dirt was raping a boy fresh out of the crèche. Njau beat the man to death."

Akachi noticed a large area of rust-brown staining the road ahead. *Was an animal killed here?* Slaughtering animals was definitely forbidden. Just as all the food of Bastion was prepared by the Crafters, all the slaughterhouses were also in that ring.

"Seems like justice," he said, stepping around the stain. Sand had already got into his sandals and sharp grit chafed between his toes. *Have to remind the Growers that regular sweeping is part of their duties.* He'd work it in to his sermon.

Yejide walked through the stain like she hadn't noticed it. "It was justice. But ours is not to judge. The Hummingbird Guard only carry out the punishment"

The Hummingbird Guard—priests of Southern Hummingbird—were a special kind of nahual, they led no congregations. Southern Hummingbird had no churches in the Growers' Ring. Children were selected from every ring and taken to the Priests' Ring where they were inducted and trained for war.

Captain Yejide continued. "Njau was lashed to the edge of death, forever forbidden to hold rank." This time she did look Akachi in the eye. "I trust him with my life."

"I understand."

"I think not. I also trust him with yours."

"I—"

"You are under my protection. You are my ward as decreed by

Southern Hummingbird. I will die to protect you." She raised a hand to silence him. "This squad, every single man and woman, no matter their faults and crimes, will give their life for you without hesitation."

"I—"

The lifted hand slashed down, cutting him off. "Don't waste them."

"I won't."

"And don't eat Njau's cooking," she said, raising her voice, "unless you have a fondness for dysentery."

"It was only a couple of times," said Njau.

A wagon drawn by two oxen rumbled past, heading into the fields. Outward bound wagons were usually empty, on their way to collect a harvest and deliver it to the Crafters' Ring. This one carried three starved-looking Growers locked into wood stocks built into the bed of the wagon. Thobes stripped away, they wore only stained underclothes. All three bore fresh wounds of recent whippings, their backs leaking blood. One of them, a young woman, arms tattooed with swarms of scampering rats, glared hate at Akachi. Grower gangs and Loa sympathizers often hid tattoos beneath their thobes. What the stylized rodents were meant to communicate, Akachi had no idea. The other two were typical Growers, thin and dirty. They stank of blood and terror. A nahual of Sin Eater sat at the front of the wagon, back ramrod straight. Her robes of immaculate white shone in the morning sun, a beacon of purity at odds with the filth of her charges.

Six Hummingbird Guard, eyes sharp and alert, hands resting on cudgels, marched alongside the wagon. They nodded to Captain Yejide and ignored Akachi.

A penance wagon. He'd never seen one before. These three were being carted to the Sand Wall to be cast into the Bloody Desert. The fall would kill them. Their doomed souls would wander the red sands forever. Or until something out there devoured them.

I wonder what they did to deserve such a fate?

Akachi stopped like he walked into a wall. He stared at the cross-roads ahead. Nothing differentiated this intersection from any other street in the Growers' Ring. Yet he stood, unmoving. The Hummingbirds stopped too. They asked no questions, but he felt their heightened alertness.

This street. He turned, seeing the Grey Wall a few blocks away. This was where he dreamed of the girl. The street faded, and he relived the dream. Again, he saw the scrawny Grower girl, the vicious scar dividing her face. *This was it. This is the spot. She was right here.*

"Are we still in the Wheat District?" he asked Captain Yejide.

"Yes."

She's here, in my parish. I knew it! I am here by the will of the gods. Whatever that scarred Grower planned, Cloud Serpent wanted Akachi to stop it. *I must hunt her.*

"Something wrong?" asked Yejide.

Akachi grinned at her, laughing. "The drums sound," he said.

"And we go to church," finished Yejide, looking perplexed. Every Growers learned the words from birth.

Tomorrow he'd sound the drums and the Growers would come to church. Would the scarred girl be among them? Maybe. It sounded too easy, but it would be foolish not to at least try.

What do I do when I see her? Should he have the Hummingbirds follow her, or grab her right then and there?

What are the odds she works alone? No, she must have friends, co-conspirators. *Grabbing one Grower girl won't solve this, whatever* this *is.*

Akachi needed to understand. Could one girl be the entire reason he was here? *Maybe she's a street sorcerer.* A thrill of excitement ran through him. Finally, a chance to test his skills against this almost mythological enemy. He'd read about street sorcerers, raw but untrained talents, and he'd heard plenty of stories, but that's all they were.

And if she didn't come to church?

Then we'll do this the hard way: I'll stalk her in her dreams.

If he did this, if he cleaned up the Wheat District, perhaps even routed out the Loa heretics, his path to the inner rings would surely be shortened.

"Akachi?" asked Captain Yejide. "Is something wrong?"

He blinked, surprised. *How long have I been standing here, daydreaming?* "Sorry."

Hard-Eyes stood guard, watching the street and passing Growers. Everyone gave them a wide berth.

"What's Hard-Eyes' name?" he asked, nodding in her direction.

"Hard-Eyes," said the Captain. "We just call her Hard-Eyes."

"Really?"

"No. She's Khadija." Captain Yejide never lost her deadpan expression, never cracked the faintest hint of a smile.

"We have to get back to the church."

The Captain nodded, uttered a low whistle, and the other Hummingbirds changed facing. They headed back to the church with Khadija taking the lead.

Akachi talked as they walked. "Captain, I need to find a girl."

A moment of silence, then, "A girl?"

"A Grower girl."

"I see."

Does she look disappointed? "I'm hoping she'll come to tomorrow's sermon."

Yejide gave him a long look. "Are we taking her politely?"

"Politely?"

"Or do we grab her when she enters the church?"

"Neither," said Akachi. He caught a flash of confusion on the Captain's features. "I want you to follow her. I need to know where she lives."

"Ah." She looked away.

Ah? "I need to know who she is working with." *Does she think I'm picking a Grower girl from the crowd for personal reasons?* He'd heard of priests taking Growers for servants or sexual partners. It was frowned upon, but largely ignored. "This isn't... I'm not... She might be dangerous."

That caught Yejide's attention. "Street sorcerer?"

"Maybe. I believe she has ties with the Loa."

The Captain considered this. "I'll have Talimba follow her. He's been trained to fit in with the Dirts. He knows their slang, how they walk and talk." She grunted. "And he's the sneakiest bastard I've ever met. If Southern Hummingbird hadn't claimed him as a child, he'd be a dangerous Finger."

Cloud Serpent, Lord of the Hunt, set him on this path. Akachi would find the girl. Finding her would see him anointed as a true pastor. She was his way out of this filthy district and back to the North Cathedral. Maybe even to the inner rings. He'd do it, and he'd be years younger than his father.

Then he'll respect me. Then he'll love me.

Calming breaths did nothing. Whatever this girl was, street sorcerer or Loa heretic, he'd soon have her.

The hunt is on!

The next morning, standing before the gathered Hummingbirds and his fellow priests, Akachi laid out his thoughts. "The Grower I am looking for didn't show. We sounded the drums and she didn't come." He knew it wouldn't be so easy. Cloud Serpent wouldn't have selected him for something so simple and effortless as waiting for a girl to walk into a trap. In a way, he decided, this was better. A real hunt. Real prey, intelligent and cunning. Excitement sped his heart.

"What if she lives on the outer edge of this neighbourhood?" asked Jumoke. "She might live closer to one of the other churches."

"She lives nearby," said Akachi, confident, but not sure why.

"Or maybe she doesn't live in the Wheat District at all," suggested Nafari.

"She lives here," Akachi repeated.

"Or she never attends church," said Captain Yejide. "It happens," she added. "We pretend it doesn't, but not all the Growers work in the fields. Not all go to church."

"How do they survive?" asked Nafari. "How do they eat?"

"They feed off the others, trade sex and drugs for food. Some have even managed to work deals with Crafters." She eyed the priests. "And then some are Loa and have contacts reaching into the very heart of Bastion."

Nafari looked doubtful but said nothing.

"I didn't think the Loa were real," said Jumoke.

Everyone ignored him.

Akachi rubbed at his eyes, forced himself to focus. *The scar.* He remembered the vision, the brutal line dividing the girl's features. "She is scarred." He drew a line across his face from his right temple to the left side of his chin, passing through his lips. "She will stand out. I want patrols looking for her. Talimba," he nodded at the Hummingbird, "can you blend in, ask around?"

Talimba glanced at Yejide and she nodded. Face expressionless, he said, "I'll find a place. Work in the fields with them. I'll find out where they drink, where they get drugs. If she lives nearby, I'll find her."

"Good. Once you know where she lives, report back. Don't take any chances."

"I'll get changed." Talimba spun on his heel and left without another word.

That Talimba carried a grey thobe in his kit spoke worlds about their intentions. And of how prepared they were.

I can't rely on Talimba to find this girl. Cloud Serpent sent me.

This was Akachi's task. She was out there, not far. He'd stalk her in her dreams. If she was a street sorcerer, he'd face her in battle. *I'll need a couple of days to cure and prepare the narcotics.* Facing an unknown enemy unprepared would be foolish.

NURU – IN SMOKE AND STONE

Temple-trained nahualli believe the veil separates us from a multitude of worlds and realities populated by all manner of strange yet strangely familiar spirits.

They are wrong.

The veil separates Bastion from the rest of this world. The Sand Wall is the physical manifestation of the veil.

Souls are eternal. Nothing truly dies.

When a sorcerer thins the veil, when they make contact with something beyond, they are merely connecting with the souls and spirits of our own dead world. Not only did billions of people die in the Last War, but so did every animal and god that wasn't brought within Bastion's hallowed walls. They are universally desperate, hungry to gain entrance, if just for a moment.

Like the gods of Bastion, they feed off us.

—Loa Book of the Invisibles

Nuru stood over Efra, examining the sleeping girl. So small, such a clenched fist of tension.

Why does she matter?

Soon, she would answer that question.

Efra woke with a groan and squinted blearily up at Nuru. "My ribs feel like they'd been kicked in by a gang of angry… Ah. Fuck."

She rolled over, the course blanket pulled up to he her chin as if it might protect her from the memories.

The basement was dark, but a dim light shone from above, lighting the same set of stone steps every tenement had leading to its basement.

Touching her ribs, Efra winced. "Last I remember, Fadil's gang were somewhere between beating me to death and raping whatever was left." She groaned again, rubbing her temples. "I have this weird memory of the gang storming in like heroes from some story." She stopped, darted an uncertain glance at Nuru. "I remember there being a snake as well, but that part seems even weirder than the rest."

"I'm going to light a candle," said Nuru.

She felt the girl's eyes on her. Efra cowered in her blanket when a warm yellow light filled the basement.

"You're beautiful," said Efra. "Or you would be if you cut your hair and took all the bones out."

Nuru swept the bound hair over her shoulder protectively. "Never."

The bones and braids, like the dark tattoos snaking her flesh, were a part of what she was. It was her story writ in the only language she knew. Each bone meant something, reminded her of a specific moment. Each tattoo told the tale of a hard lesson learned. The bones the nahual ignored. The tattoos would see her flayed.

"It's too hot for a scarf," said Efra.

"That's Isabis," answered Nuru, stroking the sleeping snake.

"Oh."

Interesting, Isabis doesn't bother her. That was rare. Even Chisulo refused to go anywhere near the creature.

Efra studied Nuru. "How'd I get here?"

"Chisulo carried you. I dressed you." Nuru coughed a soft laugh. "Though I did have to convince Happy I didn't need his help."

"Thanks."

"How do you feel?"

"I think I'm going to puke."

"You already did. Several times. Blows to the head can do that."

Shrugging aside the blanket, Efra staggered to her feet. She stood, weaving drunkenly. "Chisulo carried me?"

Nuru remembered the sight of the petite woman cradled in his strong arms. "It's who he is," she said. "He needs to take care of people. He needs to feel people can trust him, that they can rely on him."

"Why?"

"It's who he is," Nuru repeated.

Turning to her table she retrieved a fire-hardened wood spike. Omari found it at Fadil's and the surviving gang members said she used it to kill the Fadil. Knowing Efra would want it back, Nuru cleaned the gore from it.

She held the spike out in offering. "This is yours."

Flashing a look of gratitude, Efra made the spike disappear into the folds of her thobe.

"Can you make it upstairs?" Nuru asked.

Efra nodded and led the way. She moved slow, one hand brushing the stone wall for balance. Nuru snuffed her precious candle, lay the snake on the floor, cooed to it to behave, and followed her up.

In the room above, they found Chisulo, Happy, and Omari sitting on overturned boxes and drinking from wood mugs.

Efra hesitated at the top of the stairs, uncertain.

Nuru stopped behind her.

Seeing the two women, Chisulo gestured at the remaining box. "Sit."

Though Efra was part of the gang, attended meetings in this kitchen, she'd never before been offered a seat.

"It's only because Bomani's gone," she said. "Shouldn't Nuru get the box?"

"Nuru never sits," said Chisulo. "Go ahead." He looked hollow, wrung out.

She sat.

With narrowed eyes Omari studied Efra. "That's Bomani's."

Efra gave him a flat look. "Bomani is dead."

Omari came out of his chair, flint dagger appearing as if by magic. "I'm going to open you—"

"No," said Chisulo. "You're not."

"She—"

"We don't hurt our own. Ever."

"But—"

"Ever." Chisulo took a deep breath. "And she's right. He's gone."

Omari collapsed back onto his box and glared hate at Efra.

"Where are the men from Fadil's gang?" she asked.

"I put one in charge of running Fadil's corner," said Chisulo. "He knows a Grower who has a patch hidden in one of the wheat fields where he harvests erlaxatu."

"And you need his connections."

Chisulo nodded.

"But they aren't here." She gestured at the table. "You don't really trust them."

"No."

"But I'm here."

"For now," said Omari.

"And you've finally offered me a place at the table."

Efra looked from the Finger to Happy to Chisulo, and glanced over her shoulder at Nuru, who still stood at the top of the stairs.

Efra returned her attention to Chisulo. "You don't trust me because I'm not one of you, because I didn't grow up in the same crèche. You see the way I stay on the outside. I keep to myself. You want to see if I can do it, if I can fit in. If I can be one of you."

"Can you?" asked Nuru.

"I can fake it."

Nuru snorted amusement. "At least she's honest."

"I need time. I've been alone...forever." Efra shrugged. "There's a cost—a danger—to belonging."

Chisulo sat forward, the overturned box creaking. "And that is?"

"Vulnerability. When Bomani died, it hurt you. All of you."

Chisulo flinched.

"It still hurts," said Nuru. "It will for a very long time."

"It doesn't hurt me," said Efra. "I survive because I can do anything to anyone. Nothing *ever* hurts me." She touched her scar, her bruised ribs. "Except being kicked and cut."

"I don't think you're as hard as you claim," said Nuru.

"You don't exactly look like you've been thriving," added Omari.

"And you're not great with people," said Chisulo.

"Efra," said Nuru, "I need your help. Will you help me?"

Efra turned on the box so she could see the street-sorcerer.

She's wondering if she should ask what I need help with.

"What are you thinking?" Nuru asked.

"I'm wondering if I should ask what you need help with."

Honesty, again.

"You can."

Now she's wondering if this is a test. Which, of course, it was.

"I'll help you," said Efra.

"Good," said Nuru. "Let's go for a walk. We need to talk, and it smells like balls in here."

"Should I come?" asked Chisulo.

"So I can bring the stench of balls with me? No thanks." She glanced at Efra. "You feel up to walking?"

She grimaced. "I'll manage."

Once out on the street, Nuru grabbed Efra's hand. Growers staggered about their business. Everyone was bent, exhausted. Most looked so tired they barely paid attention to where they were going. Even the youths, those fresh out of the crèche, looked bone-weary, old before their time.

They're working us to death.

They walked the first block in silence, hand in hand.

A train of massive wagons, each drawn by four oxen, rumbled down the street on their way to the gate to the Crafters' Ring. Piled high, they were loaded with tight-bound sheaves of golden wheat, bushels of bright fruits and vegetables, and cages of clucking chickens. The Birds were everywhere, red armour glowing in the sun. She overheard them talking about how there'd been a riot in a neighbouring district.

"You think the Dirts stink now," said one, "you should smell 'em when they been lying dead in the sun for a couple of days."

Squads of Birds walked or rode with each wagon. Nuru couldn't imagine what it would be like to ride.

Between a row of tenements, she caught sight of the gates through the Grey Wall. The larger of the two, a colossal wooden thing which somehow lifted itself into the wall, was for the wagons. A smaller gate, off to the side, provided the inner rings with entrance to the Growers' Ring. A squad of Birds stood at each gate. They searched each wagon before allowing it to leave the Growers' Ring.

This close to the gates, it wasn't uncommon to see Crafters. Their orange and brown clothes stood out in the grey world of the Growers.

They travelled in small groups, sometimes shepherded by a Bird or two, sometimes, very rarely, alone. They never went far from the wall. Growers knew to avoid them. Except for the whores. It was easy to pick out the whores. Their thobes were clean, their hair less greasy. And they were fatter and softer than the rest of the Growers. The whores were the real gateway. Every illicit item, every narcotic beyond the euphoria-inducing erlaxatu grown in secret fields, every tool in the Growers' Ring, came in through the whores. They traded sex for the forbidden.

What wonders lay beyond the gate? What magic did they work to turn wood and stone, animals and plants, into tools and food?

There, coming back through the gate, was a convoy of returning wagons bearing the simple farming implements required by the Growers to work the menageries and fields. These were the only tools allowed in the ring, and even then, the nahual made it clear Bastion owned everything. Anyone caught bringing such things back to their tenements was either lashed in the public square, or sacrificed to the gods, depending on what they stole.

Another wagon rolled past, bringing with it the stink of ox sweat and dung. Neat rows of hard-bread—a basic staple for Growers—sat stacked on long shelves. A whore once told Nuru that she'd eaten a soft-bread, a gift from her Crafter lover. It was, she said, the most delicious thing she'd ever tasted.

Nuru walked at Efra's side, still holding her hand. The woman ignored everything, seemed to stare at things Nuru couldn't see.

"Why are you holding my hand," Efra asked.

"If men see this, they'll think we're together. They'll leave us alone."

"We are together."

"I mean together, like lovers."

Efra considered this for a moment, lips pursed. "Oh." Efra glanced at the her. "Any time I want release, I get a man. Even scarred, volunteers are easy to come by. They're not too picky, I guess." She laughed. "Chisulo." She flattened her nose with a finger and made a comical face mocking the look he got any time he was concentrating on something. "Maybe I'm not too picky either." She glanced at Nuru. "Are you like that? Do you prefer women?"

"I need help getting some stuff," said Nuru, ignoring the question.

"What stuff?"

"Stuff that'll get us killed if we're caught."

"What stuff?" Efra repeated.

"That simple? No other questions?"

"What else should I ask?"

Nuru studied her for a moment before shrugging. "I need tools. Crafter tools. I need stone-carving tools."

"The nahual say working in stone is evil."

"Yet they sacrifice us with obsidian knives."

"True. What else do you need?"

"Proper paint brushes and paints." Nuru glanced around, checking no one was close enough to overhear. "I need colour."

"For what?"

Tightening her grip, Nuru walked another block in silence.

"Did you not hear," asked Efra, "or are you ignoring the question again?"

With her free hand Nuru fished the incomplete carving out of a pocket hidden in her greys. It looked like a woman who was in the process of being eaten by a spider trapped in red stone.

Efra leaned closer to examine it. "She's beautiful. Looks like you."

"Don't be ridiculous."

"Can I touch it?"

"Never." Keeping it sheltered from sight, Nuru put the carving away. "It isn't finished. I can't do any more without real tools and paints. If it isn't perfect, it won't work."

"Work?"

Nuru leaned close and whispered, "I'm nagual. We use carvings as a focus. We can become what we carve. Jaguars. Eagles. Coyotes."

"What was the carving?" asked Efra. "I never saw anything like that in the menageries."

"It's a demon. I think."

"Demons devour souls," Efra said, no doubt repeating something a priest once said. "They're evil."

The nahual loved to preach about the dangers of consorting with evil spirits and demons.

Nuru gave a half-shrug. *They lie so much we can't tell the falsehoods from truth.* Ignorance was a form of control. "Unless the nahual are lying to keep us weak."

"That makes sense. Will it work?"

Nuru squeezed Efra's hand again and nodded. "If everything is perfect."

"And for that you need tools and paints."

"And drugs. Foku to help me remember the dream, for absolute focus. Aldatu to alter my senses, to help me see other realities."

Efra studied Nuru from the corner of her eye, measuring.

She's wondering if this will be useful, if she can use me toward whatever it is she wants.

Nuru saw a whore approach a Crafter as he cleared the gate. Draping herself across him, she licked his neck and whispered in his ear. The two went off together toward the nearest tenements. No one lived there. No one wanted to be close to the wall, or the Birds at the gates.

"What lives do the Crafters return to when they leave us?" Efra asked.

Nuru studied her, waiting.

"The drugs will be difficult," said Efra.

"Difficult?"

"I think the Artist can get them for us."

The Artist lived on the border of Chisulo's turf and traded tattoos for food and narcotics and favours. He'd done all of Nuru's tattoos. He also had the most unbelievably dreamy eyes. No woman in the Wheat District hadn't fantasized about him at least once.

"You know him well?" asked Nuru.

Efra shrugged. Tugging the right sleeve of her thobe back, she exposed a rectangle of black tattooed into the inside of her wrist. The flesh was raw and red. This was recent work, no more than a day old.

"What does it represent?" Nuru asked. She'd never seen anything like it.

"Futility. The absence of purpose."

The answer was too quick, too smooth. Practised to sound casual. *She doesn't think like that*, realized Nuru. The tattoo would be something real, not a vague idea. "Don't lie."

Efra flashed a quick grin, stretching the scar. "I had a dream."

Nuru kept her face carefully blank. Having had her own dreams recently, she desperately wanted to know. "About?"

"Smoking Mirror spoke in smoke and stone."

Smoking Mirror. Father Discord.

"What does that mean?" Nuru asked.

"Doesn't matter. We'll need something to offer the Artist in trade. Or we take what we need."

"We can find something. And the tools?"

"Impossible."

"Damn."

"But I know how to get them too."

Efra stopped without warning, forcing Nuru to stop too.

Across the street, another Grower slowed for half a step and then kept walking. He disappeared around a corner.

Something isn't right. He moved wrong, stood too straight. No slope to the shoulders. His greys were dirty, yet he didn't seem tired. And his eyes, too alert.

Is he following us?

"You can't say something like that and then not explain," said Nuru. *What do I do?* Had she imagined it?

"Crafters," said Efra.

"We fuck Crafters for the tools? Won't work," said Nuru. "No Crafter is dumb enough to smuggle tools for sorcery. It's death if they're caught."

A ragged look, sharp and wounded, crossed Efra's eyes. "I'll kill any Crafter who touches me."

"So?"

"We're going into the Crafters' Ring and taking it."

Nuru only half listened.

I need to know if he's following us.

She dragged Efra after her, the girl wincing at the pain in her ribs. "Come. I think someone is following us."

Efra didn't flinch, didn't look around in an attempt to spot who-ever Nuru was talking about. *She's not dumb.* Instead, she held on to Nuru's hand and followed.

Nuru kept her pace steady, not giving in to the urge to run and hide.

Guilty Growers run.

"Are you sure?" asked Efra.

"No."

"Should we split up?"

What if the man followed Efra instead of her? No doubt the girl got into all manner of trouble when not with the gang. *Getting away gets me nothing. I need Efra, and I need her help finishing the carving.* "He looked dangerous," she said.

Efra's eyes narrowed. "I just spotted him," she said. "There's something wrong."

"We should run," said Nuru.

"No. We're going to kill him."

"We'll lead him back to Chisulo, get help."

"No," said Efra. "That would mean leading him to our home. We're going to kill him."

"We need to know who he is. If he's with a rival gang—"

"He's not with a gang."

"Then we need to know who he is."

"No," repeated Efra, "we don't. We need to kill him."

"He might be a street sorcerer trying to get my—"

"He's not a Grower."

"But then—"

Efra squeezed Nuru's hand tight, silencing her. "We're going to kill him."

Nuru caught movement in the corner of her eye and knew Efra was right. Growers didn't move like that.

"Look," she said, louder than necessary, and doing her best to sound annoyed. "I'm not going to get drunk with you and your man."

Efra blinked and said "Fine." She oozed vapid petulance. "So, what *are* we doing tonight?"

Still holding her hand, Efra led her toward the next intersection. As they reached the corner she whispered, "Keep walking. Keep talking."

Once around the corner and out of sight, Efra stopped and waited. Drawing out her fire-hardened spike, she pressed her back to the wall.

She's crazy. We need to run!

Nuru continued, slowing her pace, carrying on a one-sided conversation. She checked over her shoulder. Efra stood hunched, favouring her ribs, wincing with each movement.

She can't fight now. She just suffered a vicious beating!

The man came around the corner. He didn't move anything like a Grower. He reminded Nuru of the cats in the menageries.

Efra drove the spike up and into his belly. He blocked the thrust with an arm like thick ebony. The spike spun away to clatter in the street. He didn't look startled or scared.

Too calm.

His forehead met Efra's nose, smashing her down. Her knees hit stone. He struck her, a short, frighteningly efficient punch shattering her nose and spraying blood down the front of her thobe. She made a wet choking sound and he hit her again over her right eye.

Nuru froze. *Run.*

Efra hurled herself at the man, driving her shoulder into his groin. Fists struck her fast and hard. She sank her teeth into his thigh, still pushing forward.

Run away.

He only made noise when Efra tore out a chunk of flesh with her teeth and even then, it was just a grunt. His foot slipped on something and he went over backward. Punching and clawing, Efra crawled on top of him.

Run and get help.

Using her weight and joints against her, he rolled Efra off, somehow ending above her, grinding her face into the grit and stone of the street. He had her right arm bent behind her back, the wrist twisted up near the base of her skull. The joint would pop. The bone would break. He pulled it higher, his knee pinning her, and she screamed in raw animal pain. With sickening inevitability, the bone slid in its joint.

And came free.

He broke her!

A broken Grower was a useless Grower. Useless Growers died.

Run. Get away.

If she did, Efra would die. Either here on a street, or on an altar in a church.

Retreat was death.

Retreat was what Growers did.

Nuru sprinted at the man atop Efra, tackled him from the side, crashing them both to the ground. He countered Nuru's every move before she finished it. Calm like stone, he fought with deadly efficiency, each movement small, tight, and fast. Nuru had seen dozens of fights, but never one like this. No, that wasn't quite right. She once saw a Bird smash two Growers. They hadn't stood a chance.

He's a Bird. She knew she was right.

He spun her until somehow, he was behind her, legs wrapped around her belly, squeezing like a constrictor, one arm around her throat, crushing it closed. He held her wrist with his other hand. She couldn't move, couldn't strike at him. Efra, one eye swollen closed, blood drooling from her nose, an arm hanging limp, collect her wooden spike and staggered to her feet.

Nuru's world went dim.

Efra stabbed the man in the side of the throat. When she yanked the spike free, he made a wet gurgle and spewed blood on Nuru. Efra stabbed him again and wood struck bone. He twisted away. Slick with blood, the spike was torn from her clumsy grip.

He gagged and clutch at the holes in his neck. Blood soaked the sand around him, a growing stain. Efra stepped back, face expressionless, head tilted to one side, watching.

He gasped, red bubbling from the ragged wounds in his throat. His lips moved, trying to force out words. He sputtered something that might have been a threat and was still. He stared at Nuru, unmoving, unblinking.

"We have to go," said Efra as Nuru woozily regain her feet.

"What happened?"

"I killed him."

"Your arm."

"We have to go." Her voice sounded funny, nasal.

Nuru wanted to lie down in the street and sleep. "Your face."

Still staggering and unsteady, Efra grabbed the street sorcerer's hand and set a fast pace. She breathed through her mouth and spat blood every few paces. Her right arm swung wrong and Nuru wanted to puke.

He was a Bird. Why was a Bird following them? Did the nahual somehow know about her dream? She prayed not. Maybe their little gang war caught someone's attention. If so, Chisulo's gang was doomed. Dead.

No. That Bird was following us. If they knew where we lived, they'd have caught us all there.

That made sense. Or she thought it did. Her brain felt jellied and slow. The thought of Chisulo in danger hurt. *I have to protect him.*

"Hurry," said Efra, dragging Nuru into an abandoned Grower tenement; they were everywhere.

Once out of sight of the street, Efra, one-handed, struggled out of her thobe.

After Nuru rang out as much of the blood as she could, she turned it inside out and helped Efra put it back on. Nuru reversed her own thobe and used the hem to wipe the worst of the blood from their faces. Efra groaned and bared her teeth, hissing, when the street sorcerer accidentally brushed her nose. Her bloodshot eyes watered. Her arm swung with every movement.

Damp and clammy, blood and sand chafed Nuru's skin. She stepped back to examine Efra.

"Your face says everything I don't want to hear," said Efra. "I'm fine." She laughed, teeth red, and spat blood. "Maybe not." A crack showed in the stone of her and she sobbed, "He fucking *broke* me!" She steadied herself against the wall, drooling blood onto the floor at her feet. "I'm fine," she repeated.

Nuru understood: Broken Growers died. They starved to death in abandoned tenements just like this one.

"Don't leave me," said Efra. "I don't want to die here. Alone." She swallowed more blood and then puked it all up, spattering the floor red.

"You're not alone." Efra wobbled and Nuru caught her. "Lean on me. I'll get you home."

"Home."

Nuru led her through the streets. Efra, eyes clenched against the searing sun, stumbled often. Nuru never let her fall.

"Blind me, Smoking Mirror," Efra whispered. "Please, Father Discord, I beg you." Her arm swung, grinding bone on bone. Her nose leaked blood down her throat and she gagged often, stopping to cough and spit blood. Each breath came as a wet choking gasp. "No. No. No," she moaned.

"What?" asked Nuru, leading her into another filthy alley.

"I left my spike." Tears came to her eyes, the first time Nuru ever saw her cry.

"We can't go back," said Nuru.

Efra leaned heavily on Nuru. "Smoking Mirror spoke in smoke and stone," she muttered.

What part did Father Discord play in this? Nuru couldn't begin to guess the will of the gods.

They staggered from alley to alley, avoiding the main streets. Efra became increasingly heavy as her legs gave out.

"In the end," muttered Efra, fading in and out of consciousness, "just me. Me and the Obsidian Lord."

She wasn't making sense. Another dream?

Nuru hooked Efra's good arm over her shoulder and manoeuvred her into another alley. "Keep moving."

Efra's head hung forward, drooling blood from her shattered nose. "I'm sorry. I'm sorry I'm sorry."

"We're almost there," soothed Nuru, her arms shaking from the effort.

Don't think about how far it is. Just keep moving.

"He's planned it all," whispered Efra. "He knows me. Inside. I hear him. He *wants* this!"

"We're almost—"

"Hearts of stone. Shards of obsidian buried in the meat of our souls."

"Keep moving."

"It's how they mark us, how they *claim* us."

"Almost there."

By the time they got home, Nuru carried half Efra's weight. Chisulo, Omari, and Happy all sitting in the kitchen, leaped to their feet when the women entered.

"What happened?" demanded Chisulo.

"We were attacked," said Nuru.

"Who? One of Fadil's?"

"No, I—" Efra, alertness returning, squeezed Nuru's hand hard, interrupting her. "I don't know."

Happy stood and walked forward to lean over Efra.

She glared up at him. "The fuck you want, you fucking ox?"

A huge hand grabbed the top of her skull and held her motionless.

With his other hand he took hold of her nose. She tried to scream, tried to kick and claw and fight. He ignored her. Happy pulled her nose straight and she screamed in agony. Then he shoved her arm back into the socket. When she stopped screaming he leaned in to examine her and she tried to kick him. He batted her foot away with a hand like a bear's paw.

"Better," the big man grunted. He wandered away to collapse back onto his box.

"Cunt," said Efra. Her voice sounded normal and she drew an experimental breath through her nose.

Chisulo paced circles around the table, fretting and worrying about things he couldn't control. Omari tried to spin this as a reason Efra shouldn't be in the gang, and was ignored.

Nuru grabbed Chisulo's arm as he passed and dragged him to a halt. "Go get her a new thobe. I'm going to clean her up and then take her to the baths."

Happy stood.

"Not you," said Nuru.

"In case trouble," said Happy.

"You just want to see her naked."

He shrugged.

"No," said Nuru.

She shooed Chisulo out, told Omari to watch the street for suspicious people, and then sent Happy to fetch something to numb Efra's many pains. Everyone did as instructed without argument and in moments Efra and Nuru were alone.

"You're really the one in charge here," said Efra.

"Only when I want to be." *I don't think I want to be any more.* Not after Bomani.

Efra studied her, deep bruises ringing bloodshot eyes

"I see you thinking about that," said Nuru. "We can discuss it later." She glanced toward the stairs. "I'm going to get something for you to drink."

Collecting one of the wood mugs, Nuru descended into the basement, leaving Efra on the ground floor. She shuffled in the dark, careful not to step on Isabis. Not bothering to light one of her precious candles, she worked by feel. At the table she found her pouch of cured ameslari fungus. Selecting a nugget, she rolled it in her fingers until it warmed and softened. Offering a quick prayer to her allies, *Open Efra's dreams to me so I may see the truth of her*, she ate it, chewing fast and swallowing. It tasted like dead rat rolled in sand. The rat had not been skinned.

After filling the mug with cider and dosing it with egia she returned to Efra. The girl sat scratching at the stone table with a ragged fingernail.

Nuru placed the cup in front of Efra. "Drink. It'll numb you a bit."

"Smells like apples." Efra drank. "This is awful."

"So I hear. Drink."

She drank more.

"Who was that in the street?"

"I don't know," Efra answered. "He was a Bird, wasn't he?"

"Why do you think a Bird was following us?"

The egia in the cider would loosen Efra's tongue, reduce her inhibitions, and eventually put her into a deep sleep, receptive to Nuru's sorcery.

Efra opened her mouth to speak, and then closed it. She blinked at the table.

She wants to tell me something but hesitates.

"The gang needs to grow," Efra finally said. She snapped her mouth closed with a look of surprise.

Where countless millennium had softened Bastion, rounded her every corner, the ameslari made everything pillowy like a rabbit's soft belly. A deep desire to curl up on the stone floor and sleep filled Nuru and she fought it with her training. She needed to be awake and focussed, ready when the egia finally took Efra to the edge of the veil.

Efra managed a lazy half grin. "Things are changing. More guards on the wagons. Whippings in the public square every day. Growers disappearing. The end." She winced with the last word as if she hadn't meant to say it aloud. "Hey, my nose doesn't hurt anymore." She drank more. "Why did you send Happy to get stuff for my pain when this works great?" She giggled and twisted her nose and immediately looked regretful.

"So we could talk."

"About the end?"

Nuru nodded.

"The bones in your hair rattle like...like... Like death," said Efra. "Can I touch your hair?"

"No."

"When we were kids, no one got tossed from the wall. Now it's scores every day. Sacrifice on the altar was rare, an event. Now it happens so often no one even comments on it. There will be war. There has to be. We can't go on like this." She scowled at the mug and took another drink.

Nuru waited, intent.

Dust danced gold in a sunbeam shining through the open window, wrote ancient and long forgotten hieroglyphs on her eyes. She could read them, receive messages from Bastion, were she to focus on them long enough. But doing so would cost her the growing connection with Efra.

"You're gorgeous," said Efra. "Beautiful eyes. I bet Happy—"

"What do we do?" asked Nuru. She shifted, slouching in her thobe, uncomfortable with being the centre of attention.

"Whatever we have to. We survive. And I want to fuck Chisulo. I think he'd be good."

Nuru's jaw tightened.

"Is that okay?" Efra asked. "Is he yours?"

"Not mine."

"Good. I like his shoulders. And his nose. It was broken once, right? Like mine? Except no one put it back into place." She drank more cider. "This isn't so bad."

"Can I trust you?"

"To fuck Chisulo?"

Nuru stared at her, waiting.

"Oh." Efra looked around the room, gnawing on the inside of her cheek. "I wanted to leave you when that Bird came after us, but I couldn't because of the spider demon and Smoking Mirror." She blinked. "Fuck."

"Smoking Mirror?"

"It's nothing."

"Father Discord is never nothing."

Efra laughed at that. "The Birds are going to come with huge obsidian knives as long as I am tall and butcher everyone. He showed me in a dream."

Nuru's heart raced but she kept her face calm. "Oh?"

"Smoking Mirror said that the gods are at war."

Nuru froze. Those words. The spider used those exact words. Could Smoking Mirror and the spider be on the same side? Was this spirit—or whatever it was—a servant of Father Discord? "I knew that," she said.

"The spider told you, eh? I think some of the gods seek to depose Father Death. Smoking Mirror said things have been the same for too long and that the city is stagnating. Dying. What do you think the spider thing is?"

"Banished spirit. Maybe a demon of some kind."

Smoking Mirror speaks to Efra, shows her the future. Or a possible future. Did that mean he sided with the Growers? It certainly seemed that way. And Efra said, 'because of the demon and Smoking Mirror.' Did the god want Nuru to complete the carving?

If Father Discord backs Efra, then she's even more important than I realized.

"Anyway," said Efra, "we have to control the Wheat District." She opened her mouth wide, peeling back her lips. "My mind feels slippery, like wet clay. Each thought slides off it and out my mouth."

"The Wheat District?" probed Nuru.

"Just kidding."

"Oh good, I thought—"

"We're going to take the entire Growers' Ring. We need it all. It's obvious. All the food for Bastion is grown here. Whoever controls the food controls Bastion."

Impossible! We couldn't even take one district. "How?"

"Chisulo is perfect."

Nuru, worried Efra was going to start talking about fucking him again, hesitated to ask. *I need to know.* "Perfect for what?"

"Happy is stronger. Omari is faster. Bomani was more dangerous. You're smarter *and* you're a sorcerer. And yet you all turn to Chisulo for leadership." Efra swirled the froth in the mug around and took another sip. "Sure, when you want you can give orders and they'll all do what they're told, but this isn't Nuru's gang. Everyone knows it's Chisulo's. People turn to him. People like him. He has…charisma. He's a natural leader."

"You're part of this gang and yet you didn't mention yourself."

Efra grinned at her, eyes softening, losing some of their obsidian edge. "If people would follow me I'd have this district within a week, the ring in a month, and by this time next year I'd rule Bastion. But no one will. I'm too short." She breathed deep and let it out. "And, as has been pointed out, I'm not good with people." Licking her lips, she stared up at Nuru. "I think I'm not right in the head. That's probably why Smoking Mirror chose me. I can do things."

"What kind of things?" Was she a secret sorcerer? It was certainly possible to hide one's talents.

"Things that need doing. Things that people like you and Chisulo will hesitate to do."

Remembering the way Efra attacked the Bird, Nuru let it drop.

Use Chisulo's natural leadership to take the district. It sounded insane, and yet if the Growers would unite behind anyone, it was Chisulo.

Best not to tell him. It'll scare the hell out of him. She set aside the thought for later. Right now, she needed to get Efra back on topic before the egia took her away.

"Somehow, it's all connected," said Nuru. "You. The carving. Smoking Mirror."

The timing could be no coincidence.

"Smoking Mirror showed me the end," said Efra. "There will be war in the streets. The fields will burn, the wells fill with ash. The Birds are going to kill us all."

"When?"

"Soon. Real soon."

"I meant when did Smoking Mirror show you this?"

"The day Bomani died. Well, the night before." She held up the wrist with the black rectangle tattooed into it. "I got this done that morning. The Artist did it. He's got nice eyes and a great ass." She tilted her head to one side in contemplation. "Or maybe it's a nice ass and great eyes."

Nuru sat in silence, thinking. What did the black rectangle mean? Was it a marker? Had Smoking Mirror claimed the girl as his own? Would priests recognize it, and if they did, how would they react? If Efra was lucky, they'd merely flay off the offending flesh and lash her to the brink of death. These days it seemed more likely they'd sacrifice the girl on the altar, or throw her from the wall.

Smoke in the skies. Ash in the wells. The Birds are going to kill us all. Nuru realized she believed everything Efra said, and not just because of the egia. *I have to finish this carving.* Efra was somehow pivotal.

"I need stone-working tools and paints," said Nuru. "You said you knew how."

Efra grinned at her and emptied the cup. "This stuff is really good. Where'd you get it?"

"I made it."

"You should trade it for stuff."

"No. How are we going to get tools?"

"We're going to the Crafters' Ring. We're going to take them. We'll probably have to kill a few Crafters."

Nuru remembered the dead eyes of the Bird Efra stabbed in the neck, and her chest tightened. *He was going to kill us.* It didn't make her feel better. And Fadil's corpse. Somehow Efra had killed the gang leader before they arrived. *She killed two people in as many days.* Was that the thing Smoking Mirror knew Efra could do where others would hesitate? What about Nuru? She killed Sefu. *Am I any better?* She wanted to blame it on the snake, but it had been her choice.

"Probably?" asked Nuru.

Efra thought it over, rubbing at the scar where it crossed her lips. "Maybe. Do you think Chisulo wants me?"

"I think he likes you."

"Fine, don't answer."

"You have a plan?"

"I was going to crawl on top of him and start grinding until he got the message. That always works with men."

"Good luck," muttered Nuru. "I meant about getting the tools."

"Oh. That. The Crafters come to fuck Growers all the time. There's a place by the gate where you can meet them. They usually pay with drugs and food. The Birds ignore it."

"You've done this?"

"No. You and I are going to wait there. We'll blow kisses and look horny and hungry—we're skinny enough. We'll get one each. We'll take their Crafter clothes, and walk into the Crafter Ring." She scratched again at the table. "I feel smoky from the tips of my toes right through my forehead." Lifting the mug, she found it empty. "Oh," she said, tilting the mug so Nuru could see. The bottom was flaked and chipped, scummed with apple-scented froth. "You drugged me."

"I did." The ameslari peeled her soul like a flower opening to the morning sun.

"Why?"

"I had to know if I could trust you."

Efra scowled at the table, clearly trying to remember everything she'd said, trying to figure out if she'd come out of this looking trustworthy. Finally, she gave up and said, "So?"

"I still don't know."

"No one ever does. Not really. You think you do, but you don't. Not until you're tested. Not until *they're* tested." Efra yawned and stretched, groaning at the deep ache in her ribs.

"You're wrong," said Nuru.

"I'm not. When people are afraid, scared for their lives, they become like me. Until you've faced death, you don't really know yourself. Until you've killed…. I can *feel* the smoke."

"You can?" Nuru asked, surprised. The smoke was one of her allies, a creature of sorcery. Did the girl possess some talent?

"It's in me. Coiling about my soul."

"That's my ally."

"What's it doing?"

"Helping me get to know you. You were saying," prompted Nuru, "until you've killed?"

"It's so easy to take a life."

Maybe it was. But what came next, the guilt and shame, wasn't. "It shouldn't be."

"But it is."

The smoke carried Efra away. The girls' eyes unfocussed and she stared at nothing. There, but not there. The ameslari in Nuru's blood thinned the veil between the two women.

We're a world of walls. Walls between the rings. A wall between us and the rest of the world. She studied the sitting woman, gaze tracing the jagged scar. *A wall between you and me.*

Nuru dismantled the wall and stepped into Efra's dream.

Efra dreamed of Smoking Mirror, an obelisk of obsidian, standing in the middle of the street. It was as wide as she was tall, and four times her height. She saw herself reflected in its surface, warped by imperfections in the stone, wreathed in smoke.

Nuru understood the tattoo, the black rectangle. Efra wore Father Discord etched forever into her flesh.

"I can't do this," Efra told the god.

Then you'll die, said Smoking Mirror. *Everyone you know and love will die.* He spoke in smoke and stone.

"I don't love anyone."

He laughed at her, mocking. *Witness.*

A man in the red, white, and black robes of a nahual of Cloud Serpent stood atop the Grey Wall separating the Growers from the Crafters. Young and gaunt, his long hair hung knotted with snake skulls. Behind the priest the sky twisted with serpentine clouds.

It rained ash. Fat greasy flakes fell from the sky, coated everything. What little colour the Growers' Ring possessed disappeared beneath a blanket of grey. The horizon burned, the fields afire, lighting the clouds of smoke from beneath.

Nuru turned her attention to the obelisk. In its surface she saw the streets of the Wheat District. In the distance, a squad of Birds marched in tight formation. There were more than she'd ever seen, more than she would have believed possible. They wore strange armour, green like jade, glistening like polished stone, and carried obsidian knives as long as her outstretched arms.

That's impossible! Sharp as it was, obsidian shattered easily.

A mob of Growers, ten times the Birds' numbers, poured from every street. The Birds cut them down with methodical precision. So much blood. Even in the smoky reflection of the towering obelisk, the streets ran like a red river. Bastion drowned in blood.

That, Nuru realized, wasn't quite true. It was cleaner, neater. Planned. Spilled blood ran from the centre of each street to fill gutters she'd never noticed before. They lined every lane and alley. The blood flowed toward the heart of Bastion, toward the Gods' Ring. The scale—the forethought—stole her breath.

With those terrible long black knives, the Birds slaughtered the growers, cutting them in half, splitting them open, spilling their innards splashing to the stone. Blood fell and gutters ran deep. The Birds fought as one, perfect synchronization, flawless timing. They moved as if each were a part of a single massive seething beast.

They're organized. Trained. Where the Birds fought in perfect rows, the Growers were chaos.

Behind a curtain of ash and smoke, the sun, a dull red disk, fell. Efra stood in the obelisk's shadow. Instead of looking small and vulnerable, she seemed protected.

Helpless, the priest up on the Grey Wall witnessed all that happened below.

He looks terrified, appalled.

Guilty. Had he somehow caused this?

He's so young. It was difficult to judge, but he looked about Nuru's age. Certainly, no more than twenty. Attractive too, in a wiry kind of way. The skulls of snakes rattled in his hair.

How did one become a priest? Was it a position you were born into, or did you earn it? Was everyone in the Priests' Ring a nahual? She had no idea, no understanding of how things worked beyond the Grey Wall.

The nahual watched with sad eyes, the clouds behind him twisting in rage. Was he her enemy?

All who dwell in the the inner rings are. Souls entwined, Nuru wasn't sure if that was her thought or Efra's.

Seeing the Birds butcher the Growers with their impossibly long obsidian knives, protected by their strange armour of green stone, Nuru's thoughts reeled with possibilities. What other marvels were the Crafters capable of?

Obsidian knives and green stone armour. But the nahual forbid the use of stone in sorcery! They claimed that only the Loa heretics worked in stone. Yet more hypocrisy?

The Birds were invincible. To fight them, she knew she needed what they had. Efra was right, taking the Growers' Ring was not enough.

We need to take the Crafters.

Was that enough?

She wasn't sure.

The only way to truly be safe is to be in control. That felt more like Efra than Nuru.

All the power lay in the centre of Bastion.

Take it all.

Efra sank deeper into the dream world. Tempting as it was to follow, to see the innermost workings of the girl's mind, Nuru wasn't prepared for a deep dive. The primal depths were no place to venture when not braced with the proper narcotics. And a mind like Efra's... Nuru shuddered to think what she might find.

The obsidian obelisk saw her.

When she tried to leave Efra's dream world, it held her there. Terror flooded Nuru. She was helpless, powerless. The scrutiny of a god seared away her sorcerous defences, flayed every shred of her emotional armour, and laid her soul bare.

She is my Heart, said Father Discord.

His names ran through Nuru, a litany learned in church: The Obsidian Lord, God of Storms, God of Strife, Lord of the Night Sky, Enemy of Both Sides, We Are His Slaves, He by Whom We Live, Lord of the Near and Far, Father of the Night Wind, Lord of the Tenth Day, The Flayed One, the Jaguar God. On and on. He was older than Bastion, remembered a world of green and blue. Oceans and lakes and forests spanning entire continents. He remembered damp jungles and the taste of his first blood sacrifice. He remembered pyramids of stone that stood for thousands of years and were now long gone, lost to the endless red desert.

Nuru saw all of this in the stone of his voice.

Protect her or Bastion falls.

AKACHI – SCALE OF ATROCITY

The third ring is the seat of the Senate. From here the rules and laws of Bastion are made. Such rules and laws shall be enforced by the Hummingbird Guard, the nahual of Southern Hummingbird. All citizens of Bastion requiring legal redress may travel to the Senators' Ring to have their case heard. All legal and political matters fall under the purview of the Senate.

—The Book of Bastion

After dismissing the others, Akachi returned to his chambers. He collected his tools and the hawk carving he was working on and went to sit in the sun. Captain Yejide followed, and sat nearby. For two hours he worked, nicking out the tiniest notches of wood, little more than dust sometimes. She ignored him, lost in her own thoughts, as she watched the Growers go about their toils.

When he paused, she shuffled closer and leaned in to examine the hawk. "It's beautiful."

Even on this hot day he felt a flush of heat light his face. "I...uh... Thanks," he managed. It'll be even better after I've painted it." He turned the hawk in his hand, examining it from every angle to distract himself. "Almost ready."

"Really? Looks perfect to me." She hadn't moved away.

"Not yet. I'll need to eat foku for the final sessions. It's the only way to get every detail." He glanced out toward the Sand Wall, though at this distance he couldn't see it. The scale of Bastion humbled him every time he came even close to comprehending it. "If I can, I'll visit the menageries one last time. I'd like to see a real hawk again." He hadn't been since he was an acolyte. He remembered his last trip, a month spent with a class of would-be nagual and peyollotl, practitioners of totemic magic. They were there to eat foku seeds and study animals. He'd been stunned by all the life. So much green. Colossal menageries housed every kind of animal and bird and lizard imaginable. And so many animals running free! Herds of cows wandering open fields, flocks of birds swooping and hunting. And he remembered the first hawk he saw, riding the hot winds blowing above Bastion, king of the world and free. He knew someday he would carve the perfect hawk.

"You look far away," said Yejide.

"Sorry. You ever been out into the fields, ever visited the menageries?"

She shook her head.

He hesitated. *Nothing ventured, nothing gained.* "Can I take you someday?"

"Someday."

"Someday," he agreed. Akachi glanced around, making sure no one was within earshot. He felt foolish. *Should I say something?*

"Yes?" she asked, studying him.

"This is a blood-tailed hawk," he said, displaying the carving.

"Mm hm."

"You can't tell yet because I haven't started painting, but the tail will be—"

"Blood red?"

"The rest of the body is a mix of orange and brown. They're gorgeous."

"Gorgeous, eh?"

Something in the way she said it made his heart stutter.

"You're a nagual?" she said. "A shape-shifter?"

He wanted to brag that he was talented in several fields of sorcery, but worried it would seem childish to this woman. He nodded, confused. *Why did she change the subject?*

Yejide glanced at the hawk in his hand. "Have you ever been a bird?"

"My first carving was a falcon. It wasn't very good. I was still learning to carve and my narcotics mixes were never perfect." He pictured the falcon, the rough finish, the flawed feathers.

"Flying, what was it like?"

"Ah, the Bird wants to know what it's like to fly," he said, intentionally using the derogatory Grower slang for the Hummingbird Guard.

Her eyes narrowed but held a playful glint.

"It's beautiful," he said. "On my third flight I climbed higher than ever before. I could barely breathe." He dashed an embarrassed grin at her. "Higher than I was supposed to; my teacher was furious. I saw Bastion, the rings. All the life in the world lay beneath me. And beyond the Sand Wall, the Bloody Desert. No matter how high I flew, there was nothing but red sand. Forever."

"How did it feel?"

"It was freedom, and it was a prison. You walk through your days, thinking yourself free. From up there you see the walls. We ignore them because they're always there, but they're always there." He struggled to put the feeling into words. "Birds don't know walls. They fly over them like they're nothing. But the man in the bird, he must return to his flesh. The flesh is a prison. The walls are a prison. The desert is a prison." He was dangerously close to quoting the *Book of the Invisibles*.

"Loa blasphemy," Yejide said, winking.

"But are they wrong about everything?"

"Can anyone be wrong about everything?"

Akachi sounded the drums every day and preached to the Growers who shuffled, stinking and exhausted, into his church. He scanned their filthy faces for that scarred girl. She never came.

Each evening Captain Yejide joined him in his chambers and sat in comfortable silence while he worked at his desk curing mushrooms in preparation for his dream-walk, or writing his sermon for the next day. Sometimes she polished her leather armour to a lustrous red shine. Sometimes she stretched lithe limbs in the most distracting ways and the sermon had to be finished later, after she left.

He thought about her constantly. His stomach knotted whenever she was away. What did she think of him?

Yejide wasn't at all what he imagined his perfect girl to be. Before meeting her, his dreams were populated by soft bodies, full breasts, and well-rounded hips. She was none of that.

For one thing, she's a woman, not a girl.

So, she wasn't his dream girl and he thought about her all the time. He wanted her more than he ever wanted anybody.

Each evening, after Yejide left, Akachi ingested a blend of narcotics and hunted the dreams of the Wheat District. He found nothing. Somehow the scarred girl evaded him. Either she didn't dream, was a powerful sorcerer, or had help from one.

One night, as he prepared his narcotics, Captain Yejide strode into his chambers to report they'd found Talimba dead, murdered.

"How?" Akachi asked, unsure why it mattered.

"Stabbed in the throat. He must have been outnumbered, taken by surprise."

"How can you be sure?"

"They're Dirts. Talimba is Hummingbird Guard."

Akachi accepted this without comment. Having seen the Hummingbirds fight, he understood the Captain's confidence. Could this be a coincidence? Talimba was looking for the scarred girl when killed. Had he found her?

"He had long hair caught in his fist," said Yejide. She held up hair tangled in rat bones.

"Lots of Dirts do that," said Akachi. "It's decoration, an attempt at individuality." Unlike the tattoos, most nahual tolerated such small sins.

"How did they know he wasn't a Grower?" asked Yejide.

"I don't know." *Should I tell her about the dreams, about Cloud Serpent's message?*

The scarred girl he saw in his dreams didn't have long hair with bones tied into it. She looked like any other filthy Dirt.

"They left him to bleed out in the street. His death cannot go unpunished."

"It won't," promised Akachi. "I need the hair." He could use it to track the dreams of the person it came from.

She handed it to him without question. "I'm taking Gyasi and Njau. I'm going to question the locals. Maybe someone saw something." Her expression said success was unlikely.

"Should I—"

"No. Stay." Shoulders set, she spun and left.

He wanted to tell her to be careful. He wanted to tell her he was sorry about Talimba, sorry he put the man in danger. He said nothing. Not until she was gone.

Then he said, "Fuck." The course language, so typical among the Growers, shamed him.

He stood motionless for several minutes, wondering what he

should do.

There were dangerous narcotic blends he'd eschewed in his search. It was one thing to ghost the streets, peering into dreams. It was another to open one's soul to the will of the gods and allow them to guide you. Any error in the preparation and he might brain-burn himself.

Cloud Serpent watches over me.

Akachi collected his supply of ameslari fungus, a powerful hallucinogen allowing a trained user to slip into the dream world, and spent the next three hours preparing it, blending the fungus with equal parts foku seeds and jainkoei. It was a dangerous mix, but he needed the jainkoei to open his soul to the guidance of Cloud Serpent, and without the foku he might miss some critical detail.

In the past he'd been looking for the scarred girl. It was time to try something different. This time he'd search out whoever killed Talimba. With their hair, it would be easy to find them.

When finished he glanced out the nearest window, gauging the stars. It was late. The Growers would be in the deepest realms of sleep, their spirits wandering the dream world. The ameslari was a dangerous ally, wilful and difficult to control. If he could confront the murderer in that unfixed reality, soul opened to the will of the gods, he had no doubt he could crush them. He might even be able to dig through their mind and look for memories of the scarred girl.

Akachi was completing the mixture, grinding it into a smokeable hash in which he'd included shavings of the hair, when Captain Yejide coughed politely at the entrance to his room.

"Come in."

She entered. "Pastor, you are needed."

Pastor?

She turned and left without waiting for a response.

Stretching his legs, working out the kinks from sitting cross-legged for hours, Akachi followed. He found Nafari, Yejide, and the entire Hummingbird squad awaiting him in the main hall. Gyasi stood hunched, one hand pressed to her belly. Blood seeped between her fingers. She looked pale. Nafari stood at her side, worried and trying to offer support.

A Grower knelt on the floor, surrounded by hostile glares. Filth caked the man's grey thobe, his hair a stinking, tangled mess. He looked up as Akachi entered and spat blood on the floor. He looked to be missing a few teeth. Akachi got the feeling these were recent losses.

"What happened?" Akachi asked.

If she'd been hard before, Captain Yejide was hewn from ebony now. "We were questioning this Dirt when he stabbed Gyasi."

"Is she going to be okay?"

"Fine," said Gyasi, through gritted teeth. She didn't look fine.

Growers weren't supposed to have weapons. "What did he stab her with?"

"A damned sharpened stick."

"Njau," said Akachi. "Go wake Jumoke. Get him to the nearest Lord of the Root's church as fast as you can. Find the resident nahual and bring them back here to see to her wounds."

Njau neither blinked nor moved. Akachi wondered if maybe the man was deaf.

Yejide nodded and Njau left.

"Captain," said Akachi. "Is this man involved in…" He wasn't sure what to call it.

"I don't think so. He panicked because he was smoky and had er-laxatu and a weapon hidden in his greys. I already questioned him." She lifted her right fist, the knuckles of her leather gauntlets bloodied. "He's just a stupid Dirt."

The kneeling Grower glared up at Yejide. "Fuck you, Bird cunt." He drooled blood between missing teeth.

With an impressive economy of motion, the Captain punched him in the face silencing any further outburst.

"Gyasi will live?" Akachi asked.

"Most likely."

"No way some smoky Dirt is killing me," said Gyasi.

"He attacked a nahual," said Nafari.

Akachi blinked at his friend. "We'll see how she—"

"He stabbed a nahual of Southern Hummingbird, Akachi. You know the penalty for striking a priest."

Akachi nodded. A chance to do his holy duty, to shepherd a damaged soul to the gods so they might redeem it!

"Death," said Captain Yejide.

"Sacrifice on the altar," said Akachi. He glanced at the stone altar, the blood runnels to direct the spilt life to the gods at Bastion's heart.

How many generations of Growers has it been since this altar tasted blood?

Suddenly he remembered the dream from his first night in the church. The streets lined with gutters running deep with blood. The ranks of Southern Hummingbird's elite, the Turquoise Serpents, their obsidian swords and green stone armour.

That wasn't a dream.

He realized that everyone was staring at him. For a moment he wondered why, and then understanding dawned.

I have to kill this man. Me. As the ranking priest in this parish, however nebulous that rank, it fell to Akachi to sacrifice this Grower to the gods. *He'll be reborn. He'll be reborn a better man to live a better, purer life.*

Aside from squishing spiders or crushing the odd scorpion, Akachi never killed anything. Prior to the journey to the Wheat District, he'd never even been in a fight.

And now I have to bleed a man for the gods.

If this man went unpunished, gods alone knew how the stupid

Growers might react to Akachi's leniency. Would they think it was acceptable to attack priests? This Dirt hadn't simply raised his hand against a nahual, he tried to kill her. To strike at a priest was to strike at the gods.

Akachi glanced at his friend. Nafari hovered near Gyasi, concern and anger writ clear on his features.

Captain Yejide studied him, awaiting his judgement. Was that pity in her eyes? Concern?

But sacrifice is a beautiful ceremony! At least that's what his teachers said. Sending a man to his god was the most holy event.

But it was one thing to read about his responsibility for the souls of his parish. Listening to lectures on sacrifice, reading ancient tomes on exactly where to cut. What if he did it wrong? What if the man suffered needlessly?

"I've never... Does this have to be public?"

"The fight was seen by few," said Yejide. "But word will spread." She reached a hand toward Akachi as if to offer comfort and stopped herself, returning it to her side. "Sacrifice this man now," she said. "The Growers will know he was taken and never returned. They'll understand. Later, when you've sacrificed a few and are both skilled and comfortable with the act, you must do them in public."

Skilled and comfortable. His heart beat hard in his chest. He didn't know what to feel. His stomach writhed at the thought of killing a man, yet he was excited about the opportunity to do his holy duty, to prove himself worthy in the eyes of his father, and his god. How old had his father been when he first sacrificed a man? Akachi had no idea. Father never talked about it.

This will make me a true priest, a real pastor, no matter what Bishop Zalika says.

Akachi closed his eyes, sought calm, tried to open himself to the will of the gods. *I wish I had some jainkoei in my blood.* Even just a little erlaxatu would take the edge off. He remembered his teacher's warnings on becoming dependant on the narcotic tools of their calling. Many nahual brain-burned after falling to the lure of the narcotics.

There was no calm.

If the gods spoke, he was deaf to their words.

"Captain," he said, "take him to the altar. Nafari, fetch the sacrificial dagger from my chambers."

Captain Yejide and Hard Eyes—Khadija, Akachi reminded himself —grabbed the Grower and dragged him to the altar. The man struggled until Khadija clipped his chin with a short punch.

With a quick nod, Nafari dashed off. When he returned, he held the obsidian dagger pinched between two fingers, as far from himself as possible. Face pale, he looked ill.

"I'm sorry," said Nafari. "I puked when I picked it up. It's..." He shook his head, at a loss for words.

"Jumoke will clean it up when he gets back."

Akachi accepted the dagger. It infected him with its sickness. Fighting the desire to collapse onto his knees and retch the stain from his soul, he turned to face the altar. Yejide and Khadija held the man down.

"The straps are gone," said Yejide.

"But then—"

"We'll hold him."

Akachi approached, the foul black knife in his fist. Its infection crept up his arm, snaked through his veins. He swallowed bile. *It's poisoning me.*

"I'll tell Jumoke," he said, forcing calm, "to fetch new straps when he returns."

Though dazed, the Grower understood. "I'm sorry," he said, eyes wide with fear. "Never again. I beg mercy. I..."

He struggled. Between the Captain, Khadija, and whatever beatings he'd suffered, he was helpless.

"Please." The Grower pleaded with his eyes, tears falling.

A tear trickled into the man's ear.

"I'll leave," said the Grower. "I'll go to another district. No one will know you didn't sacrifice me." Words poured out now, a torrent of terror. "I heard of priests doing that, letting people go if they promise to disappear. You don't have to kill me I'm so sorry I panicked I didn't mean to stab her—"

Captain Yejide twisted his arm until his words choked off in a screech of pain. "The only way you could have heard such rumours is if the stupid Dirt in question stayed around to talk about it. The punishment for striking a priest is death." She wrenched another scream from him. "You're lucky we can only kill you once."

"I wouldn't stay," he screamed through the pain. "I'd leave! I swear!"

Khadija punched him silent. The Grower lay limp. Only the rise and fall of his chest told Akachi he still lived.

Akachi approached the altar. The pulse of the artery in the man's neck caught his attention.

There.

Deep bowls, sunk into the stone of bastion, forever stained from previous sacrifices, waited beneath the altar to catch the precious blood and funnel it to the waiting gods.

We must feed them with our sinners.

The circle of life and death was crucial to the existence of Bastion. Corrupt souls had to die so they might be purified and born again, given another chance.

This isn't death.

No, that wasn't true. It was death, but it wasn't the end. All who died within the rings of Bastion were reborn.

A nahual's most holy duty.

The most beautiful ritual.

Man and god, connected.

The endless cycle of rebirth without which Bastion would wither and die.

The obsidian dagger hung heavy in his fist. The arm, numb, felt like a weight of dead flesh.

There would be a spurt at first, a great gout splashing the floor. There were runnels down there, too. The gods did not waste the gift of life. The Grower would struggle, ever weaker. Akachi remembered his teacher's description of how the eyes would stop moving and became dead like polished stones. The old nahual spoke in reverent tones. He said it was the deepest honour to shepherd a soul to the gods. 'The body will tremble and twitch to the end,' his teacher said. 'The meat resists losing the soul. But eventually the meat must die. The meat always dies.'

An unconscious Grower. Meat.

It wasn't beautiful.

It was a nightmare.

Blood got everywhere.

It sprayed the wall and fell in the dirt. It got in Akachi's hair and spattered his face. He tasted the man's soul on his lips. Blood soaked his robes until they clung to him, heavy and rank.

After, staring at the meat, he didn't feel honoured. He felt like he cut a helpless man's throat.

The vision. Blood running like rivers in the streets. The Turquoise Serpents wielding obsidian swords.

Could sheer scale of atrocity absolve Akachi of sin? If cutting a man's throat meant even worse things were avoided, was he innocent? Or at least not guilty?

He returned to his chambers. Stepping over the puddle of Nafari's vomit, he stripped off his bloody robes and tossed them aside. Everything stank. Wrapping the sacrificial dagger in one of the sheets from his bed, he hid it at the back of the closet.

I am a murderer.

No matter how many times he told himself he did the will of the gods, he knew what he was.

His pouches of prepared narcotics still hung around his neck. He never took them off. They had to be attuned to his body, to his heat. Akachi removed a half dose of dried erlaxatu and ate it. Not the best way of ingesting the euphoric, but he didn't have the energy to mess about with the pipe. It would take the obsidian edge off his soul, and that's all he wanted.

Yejide.

She helped me kill a man.

He remembered how she held the Grower still while he cut the man's throat. Unlike Akachi, she hadn't flinched at the blood. She remained cold and hard, unmoved throughout the process.

It wasn't her first.

She's killed before.

He laughed mockingly at himself, at his pathetic naivety. Of course she had. She was a Hummingbird Guard.

He tried to imagine how many throats he'd have to cut before it failed to touch him. The erlaxatu found his blood and he felt some of himself fall away. His worries, the tension, the knot of disgust in his belly, sank into a murky swamp of gelid euphoria.

The mortar and pestle caught his eye. The mix of ameslari, foku seeds, jainkoei, and hair, still sat in the marble bowl. He'd forgotten it when Yejide came to get him and left it unfinished and unattended. Sloppy. His teachers would have berated him, told him to toss it and start again.

It will be fine. A few hours in the mortar should have little effect. He couldn't find it within him to care.

Collecting the white marble mortar, Akachi returned to his bed. He sat, cross-legged, and finished grinding the contents. With the grinding complete, he took the pipe from its place in his belt and filled the bowl. Reaching to the table beside his bed, he collected one of the lit candles and put its flame to the pipe. The hair stank as it burned.

Akachi inhaled, pulling fire into his lungs.

Warmth enveloped him, sank slow and deep into his bones.

He inhaled again, holding the smoke in his lungs until his vision collapsed like a crumbling tunnel, he released serpentine clouds, thick coils of smoke.

His thoughts crawled out of the centre of his head and trickled down his spine like a line of marching ants. His eyes lost focus and his chambers faded to a dim fog and then to nothing. The jainkoei emptied him.

Cloud Serpent show me your will. I beg of you.

He left his body behind.

NURU – AN UNCOMFORTABLE TRUTH

The Last War is something of a misnomer. Dozens of wars were fought after the birth of Bastion, as those surviving gods battled for supremacy. This was a world of a thousand pantheons, ten thousand gods. Far too many to feed from the few surviving mortal souls. And so they cast out the losers, culled their own numbers.

Those that survived are the most dangerous, those most willing to betray their own.

We don't have the gods we need. We have the gods we deserve.

—Loa Book of the Invisibles

Nuru worked in the basement, curing a new batch of narcotics, harvested fungus, and dried leaves Omari collected for her. There was little the Finger couldn't acquire through trade or theft. From the saliva of poisonous frogs to dried mushrooms, he found it all. Some things, however, like Crafter stone working tools, were beyond his abilities. She puttered, touching everything, attuning it to her heat, reminding her allies that she loved and needed them and would call on them soon.

She'd already arranged everything needed for the spirit walk she planned for her friends. It was time to bring them together, to knit them as one. The wounds left by Bomani's death were still raw. It was time to heal them, to make her friends whole.

Efra spent most of the last three days sleeping in Nuru's room, only rising to eat and drink. The bruising around her eyes faded, though she still looked exhausted. She'd risen an hour ago and now sat with Chisulo, talking at the table in the main room.

Nuru had been listening to their conversation, but when the volume suddenly dropped, curiosity drove her from the cool safety of her basement. Ascending the stairs, she stopped where she could see the two, but was unlikely to be noticed. She stood wreathed in shadow.

Earlier she'd taken Efra a mug of cider dosed with some herbs that would dull her many pains without clouding her thoughts. The mug still sat, untouched, in front of the girl.

Efra sat in Bomani's place and Nuru's chest tightened in grief.

Leaning on the table, left arm taking her weight, the girl examined Chisulo with those intense eyes. The other hand rubbed unconsciously at her scar, caressing it where it bisected her lips.

"You feel all right?" Chisulo asked, voice soft.

"My head hurts, but my teeth aren't loose anymore." She looked him over, making no attempt to hide her attention. "Otherwise…"

"Happy should have warned you before he—"

"No. He did it right."

Sitting across from her on his own over-turned box, Chisulo towered over Efra.

She's so small.

She had this presence that made her seem bigger, but she was tiny.

Tiny and mean. Had Nuru suffered the beating Efra took, she'd still be in bed whimpering.

"You should drink that," Chisulo said, gesturing at the mug. "It tastes like dog's ass, but it'll numb the pain."

"She already drugged me once."

Chisulo laughed. "You get used to that. She does it to all of us. Next thing you know, you're telling her everything."

"How can you trust her?"

"She knows me. I've told her pretty much everything in my head."

"Do you love her?"

"Of course I do."

Nuru's breath caught.

"Like a friend," he added.

They'd known each other too long, their entire lives, really, to be anything other than friends. It still hurt.

"She knows your secrets?" asked Efra.

"All of them."

"Do you know hers?"

"Nope."

"Doesn't that bother you?"

"Nope."

Nuru wanted to hug him, to touch that stubbled scalp.

"What about Happy and Omari?"

"She knows their secrets too. Sometimes she finds these mushrooms—they taste like cat turds—and we sit around chewing this leathery shit and talking. Everything gets out. She brings out all our worries, everything that's bothering us. She cleanses us."

"Does anyone know her secrets?"

Kind of focussed on that, aren't you?

"She's a street sorcerer," answered Chisulo.

Efra glanced at the mug. "I'm worried that now that she knows me, she'll poison me." She looked away.

For a moment Nuru saw the scared girl behind the brutal façade.

What does she think she shared that she's worried I might kill her?

Had Efra somehow managed to hide something even more terrifying than the fact Smoking Mirror spoke to her and the Birds were going to kill everyone?

Nuru shuddered at the memory of being held helpless before the god.

Without hesitation, Chisulo reached across the table and grabbed the mug. He took a long swallow and returned it with a grimace. "Dog ass. But I think this dog was dead for a week before she harvested the butt."

Efra sipped at the drink and stuck out her tongue. Then she finished the rest. "I need numb." Eyes on Chisulo, she bit her bottom lip, teeth worrying gently at the ridge of scar. "Did she tell you what I said?"

"She never tells," he said. "Ever. I think it's part of what she is. There's a…" He hunted for the word, forehead crinkling in concentration. "…a spirituality to her I don't understand."

"I don't understand any of you."

"You will. She told me she has more of the mushrooms. She's been waiting for you to heal enough. We'll all—"

"Except her."

"No, she eats them too. She leads us, takes on spiritual journeys, helps us get past… things. We'll do it soon. Bomani—" He paused, swallowing his grief. "We need to heal."

Efra studied Chisulo, eyes drinking him in, measuring everything. And there was something else in that look, something predatory. Something Nuru didn't like at all.

"Those mushrooms," he said, "she calls them allies like they're alive and have a will of their own. She explained it once, but I didn't understand."

"Like the smoke?"

"The what?"

"Nothing."

"With Bomani's—" He drew a calming breath. "With Bomani gone, she'll bring us all together soon."

"Should I leave for that?"

"If you're one of us, you'll stay."

She scratched at the stone table with a much-chewed fingernail, and then reached out to place her hand on Chisulo's. He grinned back at her.

"You make it sound like it's my choice," said Efra.

"It is," said Nuru, coming the rest of the way up the stairs. Chisulo pulled his hand away and looked everywhere but at her. "The basement is ready. Chisulo, gather everyone and bring them down."

"Is Isabis down there?" he asked.

"If you don't sit on her, she won't bite you. Go find Omari and Happy."

Chisulo nodded and ducked from the tenement.

Efra studied her. "Do you want me to stay?"

I need you *to stay. It's different.* "Yes."

"Can I come sit with you downstairs while we wait?"

Nuru hesitated. No one ever came down unless invited. "Yes."

Turning, she retreated to the basement.

Half an hour later, Chisulo returned with Omari and Happy in tow. Descending the steps, they found Nuru, Isabis sleeping around her neck, and Efra already in the basement. Efra flashed him a nervous smile. Two sputtering candles filled the basement with stinking smoke. With the on-set of night, the temperature would plummet and they'd see their breath. Luckily, Nuru's narcotics had a way of keeping one warm.

"Everyone, strip down to your underclothes," commanded Nuru, leading by example.

Again, Chisulo looked everywhere but at her. It made it easier for her to examine the hard lines of him, but still hurt. *We're friends. Can't think of him that way.*

"Nice," said Happy, grinning at Nuru and waggling eyebrows.

She ignored him.

Chisulo, she saw, was watching Efra strip from the corner of his eye. Efra started lifting her undershirt off, exposing ribs, bruised and purple, when Nuru said, "Leave that on or Happy will be too distracted to participate."

The big man grunted disappointment. Though Chisulo clearly shared the sentiment, he kept quiet.

"Sit in a circle," instructed Nuru, sinking down to sit cross-legged.

She leaned forward, placing a bowl of hollowed wood in the centre of the group. Dried mushrooms filled the bowl. "Stop trying to look down my shirt, Happy."

He grumbled a wounded complaint.

"Take one nugget," said Nuru. She waited until everyone held a leathery mushroom. "Eat it," she commanded. Everyone did. "Right. Now close your eyes."

Nuru closed her eyes and hummed, swaying back and forth like Isabis did when she sang to her. Cracking an eye open just a hair, she examined Chisulo. He hadn't closed his eyes. In fact, he sat staring at her as if entranced. She read the love, yearning, and regret on his face.

"Chisulo," she said, "close your eyes."

"Sorry." He closed his eyes.

Time ran thick like tree sap.

Nuru stopped humming and everyone opened their eyes, waiting. "One at a time," she said. "Take two more nuggets, tell us an Uncomfortable Truth, and then eat them."

Everyone nodded agreement.

She felt loose, like soft clay mud. She remembered playing by a lake where the crèche nahual taught the kids fishing. The crèche master, an eternally angry priest of Her Skirt is Stars, had been furious at how filthy Nuru got. She remembered the sting of the lash, the rattle of snake spines in the old man's jade-green robes.

It's time.

Too many pressures weighed on her. No doubt her friends suffered equally under their own burdens.

We need An Uncomfortable Truth. It was one of the first lessons in spirit walking she'd learned.

She had to go first. But what to share?

Should she tell Chisulo how she felt? She knew he had feelings for her too, and not just friendship. But she also saw the way he looked at Efra.

We've been friends too long.

Should she tell everyone about the spider carving? She hesitated. That was her secret. Only Efra knew, and that was one person too many. She could tell them some of it. They needed to know.

Decision made, Nuru took two nuggets. Rolling them around in the palm of her hand, she worked them like hard mud.

"Difficult times are coming," she said. "I'm carving something I don't think I should carve, and it scares me. But I believe Efra. I believe *in* Efra. We fight or we die. We need whatever allies we can make." She ate the mushrooms.

Nuru nodded at Happy and the big man grunted. He stared at his huge hands, palms up, before selecting two mushrooms. He made fists, and then opened them again.

"Bomani was crazy," he finally said. "He was mean as a scorpion. He was a sun-crazed snake. He shouldn't have gone to Fadil's alone, but I wasn't here. I was off chasing a pair of tits like I always am. I should have been here for him. I should have been with him. All I know is, he died on that asshole's turf. He probably brought it on himself. Maybe he was drunk. Maybe he was smoky; he usually was." Happy shook his head, a slow back and forth. "Bomani started fights for fun. But he was my friend. I miss him." He ate the mushrooms, tears spilling from his eyes.

It was my fault. I told Chisulo to send him. She couldn't speak the words, her throat refused to cooperate. That truth was too uncomfortable. Anyway, her turn was finished. Swallowing her guilt and stifling her own tears, Nuru glanced at Omari.

The Finger collected two mushrooms, rolled them across the back of his knuckles. "Bomani scared me. When he got drunk, he wanted to fight. I was always afraid I'd get dragged into it." He looked to his friends, but avoided Efra. "I'll fight if I have to, but not because someone called someone else's girl a camel's ass. Half the time, I thought he was going to come after *me*. I'd make some joke about him, about his temper, and his eyes would change. It's like he had to make a conscious decision not to beat me to death. He had to think about it."

Happy nodded agreement but said nothing.

"He never did," said Omari. "Maybe he always had a reason not to." He sighed. "I didn't like Bomani. Never did, even when we were at the crèche. But he was my friend. If I was in need, he'd beat stone to dust with his bare hands to help me. I wasn't there when he needed me. I miss when we were kids and would play in the fields when no one was looking." Omari ate his mushrooms, chewing furiously.

Nuru nodded to Chisulo.

He took two mushrooms and stared at them in his hand. "An Uncomfortable Truth. How about, these things taste like dried cat shit? Is that uncomfortable enough?"

The narcotics in Nuru's blood, combined with her sorcerous training, laid him bare, wrote his thoughts like tattoos on his flesh.

All his truths were uncomfortable. Nuru in her underclothes made him uncomfortable. Should he talk about that? She was so beautiful it hurt. But they'd been friends their entire lives. He dared not chance ruining that.

It was what she wanted, and it filled her with unspeakable sadness. She could never have him.

I love the way you see me, even if I'm not truly as you see. He was blind to her flaws.

There was more, she saw. His feelings for Efra, a confused maelstrom of fear and lust and a desire to protect the girl, also made him uncomfortable.

"If I have to eat two of these," Chisulo said, "Happy should have eaten four."

They laughed—except Efra, who looked confused—but it was the polite laughter of friends.

"Why am I always last?" He glanced at Efra, so small, so hurt. So strong. "Oh. Sorry. Not last."

Would she do it, would she share an Uncomfortable Truth? She seemed to waver between moments of brutal honesty she'd be better off not sharing, and the rather frightening, self-centred behaviour she often displayed.

And then Nuru saw it. All this was Chisulo's evasion.

He blames himself for Bomani. It's eating him up inside.

But she couldn't tell him it was her fault. The Uncomfortable Truth had rules, and she'd already shared.

I'll tell him later.

"I don't want to lead," he said.

"You have to," said Efra. "It has to be you."

Everyone stared at her in shock. No one ever spoke when someone was in the middle of an Uncomfortable Truth.

"If anyone gets hurt," said Chisulo, "if one of you dies, it'll—" He swallowed his pain. "It'll be my fault."

"I've known you my entire life," said Omari as if it explained everything.

She breaks an unspoken rule, and changes everything. Somehow, this was Efra. That idea, that she was a force of change, summed her.

The Finger cleared his throat. "These mushrooms are really dry." He laughed, a cough of sadness. "Ever since we met at the crèche, you've been my friend. We look to you for leadership because you have something we don't. I don't know what it is, but I will follow you. If I die following you, it will have been my choice. You can't take responsibility for our choices."

Happy grunted agreement.

"Dying at your side is about the best death I can imagine," said the Finger. "But I'd still rather not die, so don't make any stupid decisions."

Chisulo glanced at Happy and the big man nodded.

He turned to Nuru, and she said, "What Happy said."

"If you had any idea how scared I am," said Chisulo, "you'd run screaming instead of following."

"That's why we follow," said Happy.

Bomani is dead because of me. She wanted to say it and couldn't.

Chisulo ate the mushrooms. "These taste like sweat-soaked donkey balls."

Nuru gestured at Efra and the girl took two nuggets of mushroom.

"I'm getting tired of you drugging me," Efra said.

Again, everyone laughed that polite laugh. She looked confused like she hadn't meant it as a joke.

"I'm pretty sure I can trust you," she said. "Except Omari. He doesn't like me." The Finger shrugged and grinned. "What I don't know is if you can trust *me*. I'm so used to being alone, to being all that matters. If I stay like that, I'll die. I have to learn to change." She sighed, picking at the stone floor with a ragged fingernail. "I'm going to make this gang a lot bigger. We're going to take the Wheat District and then, if we're not dead, the Growers' and Crafters' Rings. We'll see how far we get before the Birds come to kill us all."

"Kill us?" asked Chisulo.

"Smoking Mirror showed me. He said the gods are at war. I think Bastion is dying, stagnating. He wants to stir things up. He wants change. We're going to do it. If we don't, we're going to die."

"I told you she was crazy," said Omari.

"You're going to lead the gang," said Efra, ignoring the Finger. "You're going to lead two rings by the time I'm finished." She showed no hint of uncertainty.

"Me?" Chisulo glanced at Nuru and she nodded. "I can't even lead this damned gang!"

Efra turned fierce eyes on Chisulo and for an instant Nuru thought she was going to crawl across the floor like a hunting tigress and attack him.

He wants her to.

"I think," Efra said, "I'm going to have to teach you to be a little more like me. But I also need you to teach me how to be more like you."

"You can do it," said Chisulo.

She stared at him, unblinking. "Maybe."

Efra ate the mushrooms and sat chewing. Her eyes never left Chisulo.

"That was very honest," said Nuru.

"I planned all of it," said Efra. "Is it still honest, or does forethought make it manipulative?" She smiled that scar twisting smile. "I honestly don't know."

"I change my mind," said Omari. "She's way past crazy. I like her."

Laughter passed through the room, a ghost sweeping away tension and leaving unity in its path.

Or a semblance of unity. Nuru felt more outside her group of friends than ever before.

A buzzing like a swarm of bees ran from deep inside her forehead, down the base of her skull, and followed her spine to her tail bone. Isabis woke up and stared at her. It winked and blew her a kiss.

"Mushrooms," Chisulo said.

Everyone nodded, grinning.

Efra looked up, met his eyes. "Later," she said, "I am going to fuck you."

"Your Uncomfortable Truth is over," said Omari. "You can stop now."

Efra, who'd been focussed on Chisulo, suddenly turned to stare at something behind Nuru. "Who is that?"

AKACHI – SMOKE, EPHEMERAL AND FREE

The Bankers are responsible for overseeing the distribution of wealth and goods—including everything made in the Crafters' Ring—in Bastion. Among their responsibilities is seeing that the Growers, who are neither intelligent nor educated enough to understand even the most base concepts of economics, are provided with food, water, and clothing.

—The Book of Bastion

I am smoke.

The blend of narcotics infused Akachi. His chambers faded, unreal, a dull dream of ancient stone rounded by unimaginable time. There were sketches of the city in the oldest copies of the *Book of Bastion*. They showed sharp corners, defined edges. Doorways and windows looked smaller. The bloody desert ate Bastion one grain of sand at a time. It wouldn't stop until she'd been devoured. Would the gods make a new city for man? Could they? Did they still have that power? Certainly they hadn't shown anything like it in tens of thousands of years.

Akachi pushed aside the distraction. *Cloud Serpent, show me.*

He stood in the Growers' Ring, surrounded by identical tenements. Even so, there were enough markings—Grower efforts to personalize their homes in some pathetic way—for him to know where he was.

I'm a few streets from my church.

The warring Hummingbirds and Dirts of his previous vision were gone. Night, Smoking Mirror's domain. The great ocean of stars punched holes in the sheet of night. An owl call shimmered the air. All else was silence. The storm he dreamed on that first night was gone too, like it had never been, like it was nothing more than the hallucination of a smoky mind.

No, it was more.

The sky was clear like it had been every day of Akachi's life.

A murmur of voices tickled his awareness, more imagined than heard. Ahead, the entrance to a Grower tenement beckoned. The voices, too low to understand, came from within.

Akachi hesitated. *It'll stink.* He imagined the stench of sweaty Growers, flavoured by whatever they ate, crammed into too small an area. How many lived in there? Even though there were empty tenements everywhere, the Dirts huddled together like rats.

You have to go.

Akachi stepped toward the entrance and stopped when he noticed the blood runnels lining the edge of the street. He turned a complete circle, looking down every lane, every litter-strewn alley. Gutters everywhere.

No, they're gutters for rain.

It hadn't rained in centuries. The gods filled the wells from underground springs, pulling water from the very deepest bowels of this dead world to wet the crops and fields. Rain was something near mythical.

And they weren't for waste or effluent either. The Growers, like everyone, shat into holes in the floor of their tenement. The waste fell away into the sewers beneath the city. What became of it, Akachi had no idea. He'd never given it much thought. Except for the ubiquitous red sand, the gutters were clean. Well, as clean as anything in the Growers'

Ring.

Holding his breath, Akachi entered the Grower home. Daring a tentative sniff, he released it.

It doesn't stink at all. At least no more than any place where people congregated. He stood in the first room. Windows, perfect circles in the endless stone of Bastion, let in enough starlight to see the room in a monochrome of greys. In any other ring, this would have been the kitchen, but Growers were too stupid—too helpless—to prepare their own food. A raised segment of stone provided them with a surface to eat the food provided by the Crafters. Overturned boxes surrounded the table, no doubt stolen for the lazy Growers to sit on. This alone was enough to earn whoever lived here scores of lashes.

He passed through the kitchen into the room beyond. Mattresses of straw stuffed into crudely sewn-together thobes, lay on the stone bed. Taking anything from the fields for personal use was forbidden. *More lashes.* Misuse of supplied items, such as clothes, was forbidden. *These people will be lashed to the bone.* Assorted detritus and knick-knacks, badly carved shapes depicting voluptuous women, littered the floor. Several men shared this room, he guessed.

Again, he heard voices.

They're downstairs. He glanced to the nearest window, saw the stars beyond. The basement would be pitch black. Unless they had candles. *More whippings.*

Akachi moved to the top of the stairs. Down below he saw the wavering yellow of tallow candles. The basement stunk of burning fat. He paused to listen. Several men and women conversed in hushed tones. A thrill of fear ran through him. He was here alone, facing an unknown number of Growers. He blinked and laughed, though he was careful to keep it quiet.

This isn't real.

The vision was so detailed, he forgot he was hallucinating. The nahualli who taught him the art of the pactonal to control his narcotic-induced dream travels would have smacked him in the back of the head. He focussed on his lessons.

I am in the dream world. I am the master of this reality.

Akachi stood motionless, felt the cold night air blowing in through the window. He centred himself.

I am smoke, ephemeral and free.

He rose up off the floor until his feet hovered a hand-span above the stone. He hung there, existing and not existing, building the reality he desired in his thoughts.

I am the will of the gods given flesh.

Akachi floated down the stairs. At the bottom he found the basement lit by two tallow candles. Five Growers, three men and two women, sat in a circle. The guttering candles turned their faces into demonic pits of ever-changing shadow. He watched them talk and eat mushrooms, and understood. *This is a crude version of a huateteo's spirit trance.* One of these Growers was a street sorcerer with at least one ally. The woman with the snake tattoos and the long tatty hair wound with rat skulls seemed to be leading the group, though looks could be deceiving. He listened. *She's binding them together, strengthening their bond.* So close to his church. When he woke from this vision, he could have the Hummingbirds here in minutes.

His own narcotic-shaped reality intruded upon that created by the street sorcerer and shared by these Dirts. Untrained, she couldn't hope to match him. *I'll trap them here in the dream until I can send Yejide and her squad to collect them.*

Akachi wrested control of the reality from the street sorcerer without her noticing. It was easy. In this hallucinated reality Akachi was god. As long as he controlled his thoughts, as long as he remained focussed, he could do anything. Though dream walking hadn't been the focus of his studies—he would never qualify as a true pactonal—he had no doubt he knew a thousand times more than this ignorant Dirt street sorcerer. The rest of them would be utterly helpless.

I am master of this reality.

A sputtering candle flared, illuminating the group and he saw the jagged scar dividing the face of the girl at the back.

Akachi grinned. *I have her.*

NURU – HISTORY WILL DEVOUR US

The Book of Bastion is a much censored, much rewritten, history. Entire chapters have been carved from the text, their pages burned and forgotten. New chapter are written, added as gospel. The names of the rings change as the city changes. The lives of those in each ring change as we sink deeper into an idea gone wrong. We weren't always this fractured civilization.

Forgetting the past doesn't change it. Dead gods wait beyond the Sand Wall, billions of damned souls, ghosts of the Last War.

Our history will devour us.

—Loa Book of the Invisibles

Efra stared over Nuru's shoulder, brow wrinkled. "There's a man," she said. "But he's not really there."

"Hallucination," said Chisulo. "It's normal. Can't hurt you."

Omari glanced past Chisulo and laughed. "I see him too."

"Shared hallucination," said Nuru. She'd created this alternate reality with her allies in the mushrooms. She ruled here.

Happy looked up from his hands. "I see him too. Made of smoke. His feet don't touch the ground."

Nuru turned, the need to look crushing her confidence that there was nothing there. At least, nothing real. A wiry young man wearing the red, white, and black banded robes of a nahual of Cloud Serpent, hovered at the bottom of the stairs. Tangled in snake skulls and tied back in tatty braids, his hair hung to his knees. Tattoos of entwined snakes wreathed thin arms.

Not nahual, nahualli. A sorcerer priest.

Nuru stood. "Everyone get away from the stairs!" She slid Isabis from her neck, lowered the snake to the ground. Her eyes never left the nahualli.

"We're dead," said Chisulo, standing. "They found us."

"We have to stop him from leaving," barked Nuru, unsure how to do that in this dream world. While she'd created this reality, unlike this church-schooled nahualli, she had no training in sorcerous combat.

Omari, surprising everyone, leapt to his feet and charged, roaring. No hesitation.

Just like Bomani would have.

The nahualli collapsed, smoke swirling and twisting, and became a massive viper banded in red, black, and white. The snake filled half the basement, coils writhing, spilling down the steps.

The viper struck Omari. Fangs, dripping smoke, sank into his flesh. It lifted him from the ground and tossed him aside. The Finger spun into the wall. He hit like a wet rag hurled at stone and slid to the floor.

Once again, the young priest stood at the bottom of the stairs. He advanced on the Growers, calm as death.

I can't do that! I can't fight him!

She had an idea: In this world thought and perception were reality. If she robbed the nahualli of one of those, it might weaken him.

"Back!" screamed Nuru. "Snuff the candles!"

Happy rolled over and tried to crawl toward a candle. He moved like his limbs didn't work. Nuru crushed the nearest one in her fist and smelled burnt flesh.

Time slowed.

The nahualli's presence filled the basement, choking Nuru's lungs, suffocating her thoughts.

"Be still," the priest said.

And they were still.

The other candle was a thousand strides away, and no matter how hard Nuru tried to convince herself it wasn't true, that the candle was right there within reach, her body refused to move. It was too far. She'd never make it.

No point in trying.

He beat me. The fight drained from her. *He came into my reality and crushed me.* She wanted to cry, to curl up on the floor and hide away from her failure. She brought her friends here, made them vulnerable, and then failed to protect them.

This is all my fault.

Bomani was but her first failure.

"Growers obey," said the nahualli. It was truth. They were helpless in the presence of his sorcery. He was the eyes and fists and will of the gods.

Efra rose to her feet. Hands raised in an awkward fighting stance, wrists turned to face the nahualli.

"No," said the priest.

Nuru, immobile and helpless, watched her scream and charge the incarnate will of the gods. As Efra passed, Nuru saw that rectangle of perfect black tattooed on the inside of her right wrist.

"It can't be," said the nahualli, seeing Efra's wrist.

Then he was gone.

Efra stood where the nahualli had been, face distorted in a scar-twisting feral snarl.

Whatever held Nuru came apart like ash in the wind. "We have to get out of here," she said. "Before he comes back for real."

"We're dead," said Chisulo, climbing shakily to his feet. "We're smoky and hallucinating. No one escapes the nahualli of Cloud Serpent. They are the *Hunters*."

Rising, Happy went to collect Omari. He scooped him up, held him like a sleeping baby. Shards of dust ran from somewhere within the Finger's robes.

His flint dagger. It shattered when he hit the wall.

Everyone, Nuru included, turned on Chisulo, desperate for leadership.

The walls pulsated, the very stone of Bastion breathing. *I am a living rock*, it seemed to say. The city was alive; she felt its laboured inhalations in her bones. She looked at the steps leading out of the basement, worn and shallow. *Bastion grows old.* The floor beneath her sighed with the weight of millennium and Nuru wanted to lie down and sleep. She wanted water.

"I can't," said Chisulo, shaking his head, pupils huge. "I am so fucking smoky."

"We're only a few streets from the church," urged Nuru. "We have to go."

No one moved. Everyone waited for Chisulo's order.

He stared at Nuru, eyes pleading. "It's too much. I can't do this."

"We should go to Fadil's," she said.

"No," said Efra. "We can't trust them. They might turn us in so they can get Fadil's turf as well as ours."

Ours. And just like that she was in the gang for real. Chisulo liked it, Nuru could tell by the grateful smile he flashed Efra.

"Did you promise to make me the leader of the entire Grower's Ring, or did I hallucinate that?" he asked Efra.

"We have to go," Nuru said. "We'll find an abandoned tenement."

Everyone stood frozen.

Omari, cradled in Happy's big arms, made a wounded, broken sound and everyone moved, all talking at the same time. What was that? Was it real? What should we do? We have to help Omari. We have to run away.

Nuru, frustrated, pulled the group together. "We're only a few streets from the church. The Birds will be here any moment. We're leaving *now*."

Efra twitched and flinched at the things that were no doubt moving and darting in her peripheral vision. Nuru was accustomed to the hallucinations, but remembered what it was like the first time. Even now she felt like someone watched out for her. As if on cue, millions of tiny eyes opened in the stone, followed her every movement. Catching sight of the hand she burnt snuffing the candle, she realized it didn't hurt. Pain, she knew, would come later.

Nuru met Happy's eyes. There was something tender in them she never saw before. The way he carried his friend. He nodded at her.

Efra, standing on far side of the big man, said, "You're not as dumb as I thought."

"You scare the shit out of me," he answered

"An Uncomfortable Truth is over," cut in Nuru, holding her burnt hand to her chest. "Focus."

After finding Isabis and draping the viper around her neck, she herded them up the stairs and through the house. She remembered the crèche nahual doing something similar when they were children. She had to stop Happy from trying to bring his box even though he carried Omari.

"This looks bad enough," Nuru said. "We don't need to be seen with forbidden items."

"It's comfortable."

"Why aren't Growers ever allowed to sit?" asked Efra. "We stand in the fields. We stand in church. We stand at home. We only lie down when sleeping and fu—"

"Focus!" snapped Nuru.

'She's angry," said Chisulo, sidling up beside Nuru. "Always so angry."

No. Scared.

Happy gave his box one last look of heartbreaking longing.

Up here, the walls no longer watched Nuru. She didn't miss the staring eyes, but did regret the loss of feeling like something looked out for her.

Once Nuru got everyone outside, Efra stopped and stood with her head tilted back, admiring the endless expanse of stars.

"How long were we down there?" Efra asked.

Nuru waved her to silence and set off. Thankfully, they followed.

Night was good. All the Growers were asleep. As long as they avoided the Birds they'd be fine.

After two blocks she realized she'd lost Efra and Happy. The two had stopped half a block back and were once again staring up at the stars.

"Stay here," she told Chisulo and Set off to fetch them.

"The stars promise endless wisdom," Efra said as she arrived. "If we could just understand their message."

"Hey," said Happy, "even though I can see my breath, I'm not cold."

"We have to go," prodded Nuru, trying to get them moving again. They ignored her.

"For the first time in forever," said Efra, "I feel like I belong. I told everyone my crazy plan and you didn't kick me out of the gang."

"We have to get off the street," hissed Nuru. "Move!"

"I like you," Efra told Happy. "But touch my nose again and I'll kill you."

Happy grunted an unconcerned laugh.

Nuru punched Happy in the shoulder.

"Look," he said, finally noticing her. "Stars."

"Stars," agreed Efra.

"If you don't start walking," Nuru told the big man, "you'll never see another set of tits."

Happy left.

"What won't I see?" asked Efra.

"Tomorrow."

"Oh." Her brow crinkled in thought. "But we never see tomorrow."

"Move or I'll punch you in the ribs."

"Right." Efra followed Happy.

This time keeping a close eye on them, Nuru led them through cluttered alleys, often pausing whenever someone stopped to stare at something only they could see. Terrified as she was, she had to admit this was the most beautiful night ever. The stars were bright and alive, singing and dancing. She knew it would all change when the mushrooms wore off, but decided to enjoy it while it lasted. Smoking Mirror was going to tear everything apart and she and Efra would play their part in that. But after, they'd build something new. Something different. Change was everything. Father Discord knew that. She did too. That thing she was carving, it was definitely going to change things, whatever it was.

I'm going to do it, I'll save the Growers. I'll save my friends.

Friends. Like that's all they were. The boys were there in her first memories. Chisulo... Her heart hurt. Even Efra, hard and brittle, scared and angry, had fought to save her from the Bird. Smoking Mirror must have picked the girl for a reason.

A shiver of fear ran through Nuru.

That nahualli of Cloud Serpent showing up in the basement, and the way Efra defeated him, proved it was all real. The tattoo staining her wrist connected her to Smoking Mirror.

Things have been the same for too long.

Could eternal gods grow bored?

It was time for change. She felt it in her blood. The nahual needed reminding that they did not, in fact, rule Bastion. The gods were at the centre. The Priests' Ring was the second, not the first.

Seeing Efra slow, Nuru poked her in the ribs to get her moving again.

Spotting an abandoned tenement, entrance thick with dust-clogged webs, Nuru herded her friends inside. She hustled them all straight into the basement. Uncoiling Isabis from around her neck, she let the snake free to go exploring and kill any pests she found.

This home had been long unused, if the dust and debris were anything to judge by.

After kicking aside some garbage, Happy lay the Finger out on the floor. Omari groaned and twitched. Blood leaked from his ears and nose. The big man fussed over his friend, singing in a soft voice. Chisulo sat alone, staring at his hands. He looked haunted, like he lost something.

Efra sat beside him. He didn't seem to notice.

"Chisulo?" said Efra.

"Hmm?" He glanced at her, eyes hollowed.

What will she do? Did Efra understand what Chisulo needed?

"Will you hold me?" asked Efra.

Yes, she does.

Chisulo needed to be needed, but did Efra do this out of compassion, or manipulation?

Nuru felt her jaw tighten as Chisulo put an arm around Efra and she lay her head on his chest.

Happy singing to Omari. Chisulo and Efra sitting together.

Nuru never felt so alone.

"In this smoky world," Efra said to Chisulo, "you are real. You are stone."

"I feel more like smoke," he answered.

"I'm going to give you the entire ring. Maybe more." Efra looked up into his eyes. "Maybe all Bastion."

Nuru turned away.

AKACHI – WAR AMONG THE RINGS

Culture, like religion, depends on the indoctrination of children before they are able to question or think for themselves. It is critical that the formative years of a Grower's life be spent in an environment controlled by the church.

—The Book of Bastion

Akachi woke in the church courtyard, sprawled in red dirt, filthy and bruised. His mouth tasted like the bottom of a Grower's foot. He pushed himself into a sitting position with a groan. The sun sat low on the eastern horizon.

Wasn't I in my chambers? He couldn't remember. A mix of narcotics still swam his blood. *Did I eat erlaxatu before using the mixture?* Stupid. Dangerous. There was a price to communing with the gods. He'd read about nahual who spent too much time basking in the presence of divinity. It was addictive, to be so connected with your god. Mortal souls could not bear the full brunt of their light. It burned.

He remembered the brain-burned priest, the week spent caring for him when Akachi was an acolyte. He remembered wiping the man's face after meals and his ass after each shit.

"I know what I'm doing," Akachi told the dead plants littering the courtyard. "This is Cloud Serpents' will. I must find the—"

The girl. He'd seen her. A Grower basement. She wasn't far from here.

Akachi rose and turned to head into the church, only to run into Captain Yejide as she hurried out.

"Where were you?" she demanded, eyes fierce. "I thought you left, alone. We've been looking for you. Khadija and Gyasi are searching the basement." She scowled at the flattened area of dead vegetation. "Ibrahim was on guard. How did you get past him? Did you sleep out here?"

Too many questions. "I think so."

She looked bewildered. "Why?"

"I… I don't know. I spirit-walked last night, looking for whoever killed Talimba. I found her. She's a street sorcerer. I found the girl too, the one with the scar."

"You faced a street sorcerer alone? Where?"

"Two blocks from here." He glanced at the rising sun. *Serpent's tongue! I lost hours lying in the dirt.*

"I'll get Njau and Lutalo. We go now."

"Lutalo?"

Yejide shot him an angry look and disappeared back into the church. She returned with the two Hummingbirds, armed and armoured. Lutalo was a short, wiry man, veins like snakes standing out on his arms. A wispy scraggle of beard grew from his chin but left the rest of his face nearly hairless.

"Lead the way," she said.

Akachi pointed and set out, Yejide at his side.

"The street sorcerer," he said, "she was nothing." He felt awful, his stomach twisting with bile. "Wait."

Akachi stopped to puke into the gutter running alongside the street. The Hummingbirds stood, waiting with ill-concealed impatience.

He stared at the gutter, glanced around. Thin vomit sluggishly trickled toward the centre of Bastion.

Blood running like a river in every street. He shook off the vision. Growers passed, pretending they hadn't seen a nahual retching in the street like a common addict.

The basement. He was in his element there, the only trained nahualli in the room. Through the narcotics they shared an alternate reality. One he controlled. When everyone froze at his command, the scarred girl attacked.

He saw the tattoo on her wrist, a black rectangle. He'd seen it only once before, in the oldest copy of the *Book of Bastion* the Northern Cathedral held. That black rectangle was Smoking Mirror's truest name.

That tattoo was enough to get her, and every Dirt who'd seen it, thrown from the Sand Wall.

"The scarred girl isn't alone," said Akachi, straightening, wiping his mouth. "She's backed by a power." He resumed walking.

Even though Yejide wasn't a nahualli, she understood there were many powers, from the allies found in narcotics, to all the many branches of sorcery. "Another street sorcerer?" she asked. "Or a Loa nahualli?"

"A god."

She shook her head in vehement denial. "Impossible."

"Smoking Mirror backs the girl. She bears his mark. No way a stupid Dirt knows his most secret symbol." He glanced at Yejide. "And she walked through my sorcery like it was nothing."

Captain Yejide picked up the pace and Akachi hurried to follow.

Spotting the tenement from his dream, he said, "This is it."

Signalling Lutalo to stay with Akachi, she and Njau entered the tenement, cudgels drawn.

Akachi glanced at Lutalo but the short Hummingbird ignored him, stroking that scruff of beard and watching the street and passing Dirts.

He considered following the Captain. As nominal pastor, he outranked Yejide. If there were rebellious Growers inside, however, this became a policing matter which put her in charge. And it would be embarrassing if he tried and Lutalo stopped him.

Akachi waited, pacing. Local Growers crossed the street to avoid the nahual. The morning's wagons, loaded with raw foodstuffs, rumbled by on their way to line up at the gate to the Crafters' Ring. A squad of Hummingbirds travelled with each wagon. A penance wagon with a half dozen Crafters, still wearing their orange and brown, rolled past on its way to the Sand Wall.

Even the Crafters are acting up.

Captain Yejide returned, Njau following. She didn't look happy.

"Well?" he asked.

"No Dirts. There's a fermentation still, and some crude tools in the basement, paper and ink, small shards of flint for carving. Even a couple of old glass jars."

"Tools for sorcery."

Yejide nodded.

"Where would they go?" Akachi asked.

She made a show of looking around. Maybe one in five tenements was inhabited. "They could be anywhere." She gestured at a cobwebbed entrance across the street. "We'll never find them. We don't have enough people to conduct a search." She examined Akachi. "Unless you ask the Bishop for help."

"No."

That angular eyebrow crept up.

"Cloud Serpent sent *me*," he said. "If Smoking Mirror—"

She cut him off with a look. "We're exposed here. Let's return to the church."

Back at the church, Akachi didn't have to wait long before Yejide strode into his chambers. She stood, arms crossed, waiting.

He remembered his vision, the street gutters running with blood, always flowing to the centre. *The gods are at war.* Should he tell her?

"If Smoking Mirror is backing this girl," he said, "we aren't just facing some rebellious Dirts."

"Maybe you underestimated the street sorcerer," Yejide suggested, still looking for a saner explanation. "Maybe the scarred girl is a sorcerer." She sat on the edge of the bed. "How much jainkoei did you take?"

He shrugged. *A lot.* "What was required."

"You know how dangerous it is. Opening yourself to the gods like that." She put a hand on his knee. It was warm. "I don't want you brain-burned."

"I'll be careful." *Unlike last night.*

She gave his knee a squeeze. "You do that. We have to figure out our next step. Talimba was the only one trained in how to pass as a Grower. He knew their culture, how they talk, the slang. With him gone, we'll have to look at other means of gathering information."

Other means. When he closed his eyes he saw blood, the still corpse of the Grower he sacrificed on the altar. *Cloud Serpent will lead me.*

"We need more Hummingbirds," Yejide said. "We should talk to Bishop Zalika."

"No." Akachi drew a deep breath. "She sent me here to fail."

"Asking for help is not the same as failing."

"It is." He couldn't tell her about his father. He couldn't explain what it was like to be the heir to the High Priest of Cloud Serpent. Everyone expected great things.

If I tell her, it will change everything. He liked that she didn't know. She expected nothing.

"How is Gyasi," he asked to change the subject.

"Healing."

"Good. We're going to work the streets. You, me, Njau, and Khadija will be one group. Nafari, Gyasi, Lutalo, and…" He struggled to remember the other Hummingbird's name. *It's that big one, the wall of muscle.* "…Ibrahim will be the other. We're going tenement to tenement. Someone saw something. That scar sets her apart. She can't hide from me."

"Why do you think *you* have to do it?" She examined him. "Why did Zalika send you out here to fail? Why did she assign you a squad of Hummingbird rejects?"

"She hates me." It wasn't a lie, but it also wasn't the entire truth.

His last dose of jainkoei still coloured his reality. His thoughts felt smoky and unreal as though at any time, all this could end and he'd wake up somewhere else, as someone else.

Yejide touched him once, a caress on the cheek. "I'll see you in the morning." She hesitated, hand still on his face.

Should I say something? Should I do something?

"Goodnight," she said, and then left.

He almost said, 'wait.' He almost said, 'stay.' He almost said, 'Don't go.'

He said nothing.

Later. Next time he'd say something.

Yeah? What are you going to say?

What was a proclamation of love from a boy to this warrior wo-man of Southern Hummingbird?

That night he dreamed of battle, of facing a powerful sorcerer, and woke knowing he needed something with which to fight.

He had to arm and armour himself.

Akachi knew what he needed: He already had Gau Ehiza, the puma spirit-animal, carved. The cat would give him speed. Indar Handia, the bear spirit-animal, would give him strength. Bihotz Blindatua, the pangolin spirit-animal, would armour him.

Cloud Serpent made it clear the scarred Grower is important. She bore Smoking Mirror's sacred name on her wrist. The only way she could have known what it was, was if the god shared it with her. Could she be a Loa High Priest? Had he misjudged her in their brief meeting? It was, he knew, possible for a truly powerful nahualli to hide themselves from lesser practitioners.

She charged through my sorcery like it was nothing.

The implications were stunning. The tattoo.

What gods opposed Smoking Mirror? *Cloud Serpent and Southern Hummingbird for sure.* Where did the allegiance of the other gods fall?

This is impossible! How could he understand the intentions of gods?

The vision. The Turquoise Serpents slaughtering Growers in the streets.

That wasn't just an uprising. That wasn't Southern Hummingbird's elite called out to quash some minor district riot. That was war. Cloud Serpent said the gods were at war, but for the first time Akachi truly appreciated what that meant.

"War among the rings."

With the population of each ring shrinking as one moved inward, the Growers outnumbered all the others combined. Akachi recalled the penance wagon filled with Crafters. Who would they follow? Would the Crafters, the second most populated ring, the makers of all food, equipment, and weapons, side with the Growers?

I have to reach my father. Maybe he already knew far more than Akachi. *He must. He's Cloud Serpent's High Priest.* Was his father in danger? Should Akachi send warning?

He's fine. He has the very best protecting him. But the best were all Hummingbird Guard. Could Akachi be certain Southern Hummingbird and Cloud Serpent were united? He shook the thought off. *I'm going in circles.*

War among the gods.

War among the rings.

He felt small.

It was too much.

He couldn't do this, not alone.

Captain Yejide. What he felt for her, he never felt before.

Maybe I'm not alone.

AKACHI – STONE SORCERY

Written after the Last War, the Book of Bastion details rules of survival for a long dead era. Chaos and strife threatened the very existence of humanity, and so the city's founders sought structure and control.

Structure leads to stagnation.

Control leads to abuse.

—Loa Book of the Invisibles

Akachi woke dripping with sweat. Through the window he saw a sky in the first stages of shedding the puma black of night and becoming the eternal bowl of blue he saw daily. The city wavered in the heat, the air roiling and twisting above the red-stained grey stone of Bastion.

How hot before the stone melts?

Rising, he pulled on a clean set of robes and contemplated the day ahead: A door-to-door search for the scarred girl. It would be dangerous. The memory of the attack when they came out to the Wheat District was still fresh. Faces twisted by rage, bared teeth and savage snarls. They wanted to kill him. And today he was going to walk into their territory, in search of a girl who may well be a ranking Loa, with fewer Hummingbird Guards than he had that first day.

I have to be ready. This time he would not be caught helpless and unprepared.

Not knowing what he might face, Akachi decided on a more physical approach. Collecting the tools of his trade, he sat cross-legged on his bed and took an hour to prepare a mixture of narcotics consisting mostly of foku and aldatu. Selecting the completed carving of Gau Ehiza, the puma spirit-animal, he tucked it in his belt. Perhaps Gau Ehiza was not as strong as the bear he was still working on, it was still much stronger than Akachi. It was also a great deal faster.

With the narcotics finding his blood and thinning the veil between worlds, he locked his control tight, careful to let no hint of his reality-twisting power escape. His allies awaited his call, pressed against the veil separating his reality from theirs, stretching it just shy of snapping.

Akachi headed for the main hall.

As always, the Hummingbird Guard were already up and about. He found Captain Yejide, Njau, and Khadija waiting.

"Nafari and the others just left," said Yejide as he joined them.

Njau and Khadija stood impassive and silent. Seeing him, they spun and exited the main entrance without a word.

"Everything all right?" Akachi asked.

"This isn't a good idea," said Yejide. "It's dangerous out there. The three of us are insufficient protection."

"I can't hide in the church. Cloud Serpent has shown me my prey. I must find her." He flashed a quick grin. "And this time I am ready for trouble."

She examined him, eyes narrowed.

"We will go door-to-door asking after the scarred girl," said Akachi. "Someone *must* have seen her. The scar is too distinctive."

"They'll lie," said Yejide. "We will learn nothing and you will be exposed to attack."

"I do my god's bidding."

Captain Yejide nodded grim acceptance. Not that she had much choice. "Stay close. We enter no homes; I don't want us cornered. If I tell you to run, you run. You don't wait for me. You don't turn back to see if we are following. You don't do anything stupid or heroic. You run."

There was no mistaking the worry and concern in her eyes. *I'm not just her ward. She cares.* He wanted to touch her, to hold her, to tell her it would all be fine, that they did the gods' will.

"Of course," he lied. No way he would leave her behind. He would never abandon her to danger.

Yejide leaned in close to study his eyes and he smelled the warmth of her, felt her sheer physicality like a wall.

She's an extension of Bastion. Her connection to the last city ran deep in her blood. It defined her somehow.

"You're smoky."

"If we are attacked, I will not be helpless."

"What did I just tell you about running?" she demanded.

Akachi shrugged, grinning sheepishly.

"What am I going to do with you?"

He had several suggestions but kept them to himself.

Shaking her head, she led him from the church.

Out in the street the full fury of the sun bent its will against Akachi. Fleeing back to the shade suddenly looked a lot more appealing. He'd suggest they come back and do this on a cooler day, but there weren't cooler days. Not anymore.

Discomfort is nothing. I do Cloud Serpent's will.

Growers shuffled about their filthy lives, moving even slower than usual. Shimmering mirages turned distant streets into bright wavering mirrors like the sun reflected off water. Flocks of birds wheeled lazy circles in endless blue skies. Was it cooler up there? Did they enjoy breezes that never reached the choking streets of the Wheat District?

The carved hawk in his belt beckoned, promised freedom from this stifling heat. He wanted that, to fly far above the concerns of both man and god, to dive and turn, to escape the stench of Dirts. He could become the hawk, return to his home in the Priests' Ring in a few short hours. He imagined the surprise on Mom's face as he burst through the door and pulled her into a big hug. Father would be at the Cloud Serpent High Temple. Imagining his reaction, when he returned home to find his son had fled the Growers' Ring and abandoned his responsibilities, killed the dream. Father would never forgive him.

I cannot fail. I will not fail.

All morning Akachi, Yejide, Njau, and Khadija went door-to-door, asking if anyone had seen the scarred girl. Yejide and Njau always positioned themselves between Akachi and the Dirts, ready should someone attempt to lunge at him with a weapon. No one did. Khadija remained behind him, covering his back.

Teams of lumbering oxen dragged massive wagons loaded with grains inward to the Crafters' Ring, or hauled penance wagons out to the Sand Wall. They moved grudgingly, often suffering the lash of the driver.

Any hotter and Bastion will grind to a halt. He remembered the vision, smoke and ash. *Or burn.* Casting a glance out toward the distant fields, Akachi saw only a haze of red dust blurring the horizon.

Every tenement was the same. Dirts eyed him with suspicion, but bowed their heads in meek obeisance. No, they hadn't seen such a girl. Yes, if they did, they'd report her to his church immediately.

"It's not possible," grumbled Akachi as they approached another block of tenements. "The Wheat District isn't that big. Someone *must* have seen her."

"They're lying," said Yejide. "If you want the truth from these Dirts, ask Bishop Zalika for more Guards. We'll return in force, drag them from their homes and bring them back to the church. Strap them to an altar and the truth will shine through the dirt-stench of their lies."

She was right. He saw it in the surly glances, the ill-concealed loathing.

The people of this district are too far gone. Yet he hesitated. The memory of opening that man's throat, of bleeding him on the altar, haunted Akachi.

What if we grab someone who honestly doesn't know the girl, has never seen her? Yejide wouldn't hesitate to break a few Growers to get what she wanted.

Cloud Serpent sent you here to do his will. Why are you hesitating? Held before the will of his god, what was the life of one Dirt worth? What of a thousand?

I am a nahual of the gods of Bastion, a sworn shepherd to all her people.

Even the lowliest Grower.

Leaving another tenement and heading into the street toward the next block, Akachi saw a clump of four Growers. Unlike the others, these moved with purpose, angling to intercept Akachi and his Hummingbird retinue. One of the Growers raised her face and a shock of recognition ran through him.

Yejide saw them too. "Akachi," she said, voice sharp. "Stay behind us." She glanced back, checking the street behind them. "It looks clear. If I say run—"

"I'm not running," said Akachi. "I've seen her before. I saw her when we left the Northern Cathedral and again when I sat outside, carving."

"You should have said something," Yejide growled.

"I wasn't sure." Which wasn't quite true. He'd been about to and then there was that whole fiasco with the Dirt baby born outside of the church.

Cudgels drawn, Yejide, Khadija, and Njau moved to block the Growers' approach, Akachi behind them. They stood ready, relaxed but poised for violence.

The Growers slowed and stopped before the Hummingbirds. They showed no fear. Up close, the girl with the impossibly bright eyes was even more beautiful, soft and curved, with flawless skin.

The whites of her eyes shone like a fire lit her from within. Those gorgeous eyes fixed on him and stole his breath. His thoughts, a moment ago sharpened by foku, slowed to the sludge crawl of thick mud.

"She's unarmed," Akachi said, trying to calm the Hummingbirds. He couldn't bear to see this woman hurt.

"She's got something in her hands," said Yejide. "Stones of some kind."

Stones…something…a series of lectures. Akachi couldn't remember, didn't care.

"I would speak with the nahual," said the young woman, voice soft like silk.

"Speak," said Yejide, keeping herself between Akachi and the girl.

"I would speak to the nahual," she repeated, "in private."

Akachi wanted that. Alone. Just the two of them. That perfect skin. The curves her thobe did little to conceal. Those eyes. He drowned in them, sank deep, and disappeared, all concerns and worries washed away.

He opened his mouth to tell Yejide to step aside when the captain said, "No."

"It's fine," said the woman, soft, full lips promising everything. "I'm not going to hurt him."

"It's all right," said Akachi. "Step aside."

"No," said Yejide.

"Captain," said Akachi, "I am in charge here. Step aside. I would speak with this—"

Without warning Yejide lashed out with her cudgel, striking the woman on the temple with a vicious scything swing. Bone shattered, the occipital cavity caving in and rupturing her left eyeball.

The woman fell.

Akachi knew an instant of stunned confusion. Why had he ignored Yejide's warning? Why had he commanded her to let this woman pass? Why had the Captain ruined that perfect face?

Cudgels appearing from under thobes, the three Dirt men hurled themselves at the Hummingbirds. Akachi retreated, dazed. The hard slap of ebony on flesh. The hiss of wood parting air. Someone grunted in pain. The Hummingbirds advancing, the fight moved past the woman with the broken skull, leaving her and Akachi behind.

With a grunt, she pushed herself back to her feet.

Perfect once again, flawlessly beautiful, the young woman grinned at Akachi, raising her right hand toward him. She bore no weapon, but her hand wasn't empty. She held what looked like a shard of raw stone, a crystal tainted deep red, like old blood. There was something in her other hand too, another chunk of crystal, though he couldn't see what.

Such perfect skin. Such bright eyes. She was his dream woman in every way.

Crystals. Stones That mattered, meant something. Struggling, his thoughts finally coughed up a single word: *Loa*.

The woman stepped toward Akachi and he stood waiting, wanting to flee, wanting to touch her. Wanting her to touch him.

Yejide must have seen something in her peripheral vision, because she spun and shattered the woman's right knee with her cudgel. The Captain's opponent tried to take advantage of her distraction and tackle her, but she neatly side-stepped his charge. As he passed her she struck him hard in the back of the skull with a hollow *thock!* He pitched forward and fell motionless to the street.

The young woman regained her feet, knee whole. She lunged at Yejide, trying to touch her with the shard of red stone. Avoiding the hand, Yejide broke the elbow with her cudgel. In rapid succession she shattered both the girl's knees, caved in her trachea, and struck her in the temple. She moved like a jaguar, perfect balance, absolute economy of motion.

The beautiful woman fell, gagging and choking, and Akachi's thoughts cleared.

She's using crystal magic. Forbidden by the gods as tainted sorcery, it was the sole purview of the Loa. Stone sorcery. Crystal magic. Mother Death.

She's a Loa assassin.

Khadija disarmed her opponent, broke his collarbone and one of his ankles, and kicked him in the face. She turned in time to see the young woman again rise to her feet. Hard Eyes struck from behind, breaking several ribs. The Loa assassin crumpled once again. Stepping forward, Khadija raised her cudgel to deliver a skull shattering blow. The assassin reached out and touched the blood-red stone to the exposed skin of Khadija's leg beneath the hem of her armoured leather skirt. The softest caress.

In an instant Khadija suffered a dozen wounds. The side of her skull caved in, the occipital bone shattered, and her left eye burst. Her knees and elbows broke as if struck by invisible cudgels. Her throat collapsed, trachea smashed flat. She pitched forward, face slamming into the unyielding stone of Bastion, gagging through her crushed throat, the back of her skull misshapen.

The beautiful woman, once again flawless, pushed back to her feet, unhurt. Bright eyes brimming with madness, she smiled at Akachi. This time, instead of lust, he knew only fear.

Crystal sorcery, the blackest of arts. He knew next to nothing of it, could barely remember the lectures he sat through back in the Northern Cathedral. It had all seemed so unreal, so far away, like the stories of the earliest days of Bastion.

Yejide, who'd turned to help Njau dispatch his opponent, saw the woman rise. "Break her!"

She and Njau circled the Loa assassin, smashing her, breaking bones, and crushing her skull. Each time she rose again, flawlessly beautiful, unharmed. Each time her eyes shone brighter, glowing with utter insanity. The bloody shard of stone pulsed with foul energy ravaging the world around her, twisting Akachi's guts into a tight knot of terror.

The assassin lunged at Njau and he managed to block her arm with his cudgel. The two fell, the woman on top, struggling to touch him with the stone.

Stone sorcery. Different kinds of crystals did different things. Akachi racked his brain trying to remember the lectures on Loa sorcery. He recognized the crystal in her left hand: violet amethyst. He couldn't remember its sorcerous properties. Her right hand... the deep red crystal... adrenalin and fear scattered his thoughts.

Garnet!

Yejide kicked the woman off Njau and leapt back to avoid being touched.

"The stones," Akachi yelled, "get them away from her!"

Yejide lashed out with her cudgel, striking the assassin's hand and pulverizing the bones. The woman screamed but somehow didn't drop the stone. It remained clutched tight in her broken fist. Yejide and Njau attacked, crushing bones, beating her to the ground, yet she healed even as they broke her. She rolled, darting a hand out toward Njau and he jumped away, narrowly avoiding her touch. Yejide struck her in the hand again and still the stone remained locked tight in her ruined fist.

We have to remove the hand. But the Hummingbirds of the Growers'

Ring carried no cutting weapons.

Akachi dragged the carving of a puma from its pouch behind his belt. Every hair seemed real, the eyes glowed green. It was easily one of his best works.

Blood singing with the blended narcotics he ate before leaving the church, Akachi caressed the veil between worlds. It bent at his touch, stretched to snapping. There, on the far side, prowled Gau Ehiza, the puma spirit-animal, the archetype of the perfect hunting cat.

Akachi called the spirit through the veil. It pounced, entering him, infusing his soul. The scared and confused boy was gone, replaced with raw, predatory intelligence. Opening himself to the spirit, welcoming Gau Ehiza to his soul, Akachi *became* the puma. Inky black fur burst from his flesh. His limbs bent and twisted, joints cracking and reforming. It was agony. Great fangs filled his mouth and he tasted the air on his tongue.

Prey everywhere. Warm meat, alive and terrified.

A woman wrestled with the woman he cared deeply for and a protective, possessive rage filled him. Black light, reality twisting sickness, stained the air around his enemy's fist. It was wrong. The gods forbid such sorcery for a reason. Such stones were the tools of Mother Death, God of Earth and Rock. She sang through crystals, her light, the hard glint of diamond.

The Loa sought to topple Father Death from his place at the head of the Pantheon, to replace him with Mother Death, the god who had once been his wife. If they had access to such stones, could draw on her power, she must be closer to gaining access to the city than the nahual knew! He had to report this to Bishop Zalika. He had to get word to his father!

The Loa assassin, healed once again, struggled with Yejide as Njau angled for another killing blow.

It won't work. You can't kill a servant of Mother Death. At least not while she held a shard of garnet in her fist. Freed from adrenalin and fear, he remembered the stone's properties. It was used to heal wounds by storing the damage in the stone. Those stored wounds could be released from the stone onto anyone it touched. Every time they hurt her, they were building her power.

Akachi attacked, powerful jaws closing around the woman's wrist. He bit down, shaking her like an angry child shakes a doll. Blood filled his mouth, hot and salty. The delicious taste of life.

No wonder the gods craved the precious fluid! Bones snapped and broke beneath his teeth. Sweet marrow!

Shaking her again, he bit through her wrist. The hand fell away, stone still clutched tight. Akachi swallowed blood and flesh.

Something touched the side of his skull, cold and hard.

The other stone. She had two. He'd been so focussed on figuring out the garnet he forgot the other.

The Loa assassin grinned in victory. "I've got you," she whispered into his feline ear.

He saw the raw shard of violet amethyst in her other hand and remembered: *The stone of self-destruction.* It made people weak, susceptible to addiction, depression, and self-destructive behaviour. *She touched me.*

Akachi sank his jaws into her throat. Blood rushed to fill his mouth, hot silk, thick and salty. He savaged her, a growl rumbling deep in his chest as the bones in her neck collapsed beneath his teeth. Raw animal hunger and fear won out, washed Akachi away in a torrent of need.

He couldn't stop himself. The puma was hungry, and he was weak.

Akachi fed on the corpse, aware of Yejide and Njau keeping a safe distance. The streets were empty of people, the Growers having fled. Need sated, he found himself and drove Gau Ehiza back through the veil. He sat in the street, red with blood, and watched it trickle toward the nearest gutter and flow toward the heart of Bastion.

The gods always get their share.

Gore soaked him, splashed his face, ran from his hair. His clothes stuck to him, drenched.

"Akachi?" said Yejide, voice tentative.

"I'm fine."

"Did… did she touch you with the other stone?"

"No," he lied. "It was close though."

"You…" She trailed to silence, teeth worrying at her lower lip in uncertainty.

I killed a woman, tore her throat out with my teeth. "When a nagual becomes the animal, they *become* the animal. I haven't eaten since yesterday morning. Just forgot, too busy. The puma was hungry."

It was true, and it was a lie. He could have stopped the cat, had he wanted to. He'd been trained, knew the dangers. He'd been taught how to drive animal spirits out and reclaim his body.

I didn't want to. I wanted to feed. I wanted blood.

He'd wanted to escape himself and the puma spirit offered him that.

I'm fine.

Amethyst.

"I'm fine," he said. "Help me up. Take me home."

He caught sight of the mauled and partially devoured corpse and bent to vomit raw meat and blood to the street.

"Get me home," he repeated.

He needed ameslari, something to dull the memory. He needed something to distance himself from the horror of what he'd done.

I'm fine. She barely touched me.

Captain Yejide helped him back to his feet, held him up with an arm under his shoulder. Njau went to Khadija, gently lifted her shattered remains. He showed no expression, face hard as stone.

Hard, like Khadija's eyes.

NURU – THEIR ENEMIES ARE OUR ALLIES

The nahual decry all use of stones and crystals in sorcery and yet the Hummingbird Guard bear obsidian weapons that store the souls of those slain. The Lord thinks he stole that stone from Mother Death. He is wrong. She shall return to reclaim what is hers.

—Loa Book of the Invisibles

Nuru kept them in the basement for three days. Each night she sent Chisulo out to scrounge for food and water. He returned with crusts of bread, rinds of cheese, and skins of musty tasting water. It wasn't much, and no one wasn't hungry, but it kept them alive. They managed to feed Omari some drops of water but were unable to make him eat. The already wiry Finger shrank before their eyes.

The pain in her burnt hand faded but remained a dull background ache, a reminder of her failure. The Cloud Serpent nahualli was never far from her thoughts.

Isabis found, killed, and ate a rat and promptly curled in a corner, belly distended, to sleep. Efra suggested they cut the snake open and then eat both the rat and the snake. One look from Nuru put that idea to rest.

Happy refused to leave Omari's side. Nothing, not starvation, not

Nuru, not the very gods of Bastion could move him. "Omari and I will leave together," he said, if pushed.

Efra paced the confines of the filthy basement like a caged panther in the menageries. Her bruises went through a murky rainbow of hues, from red to blue to purple to green, and finally to yellow. By the third day she no longer favoured her ribs and looked ready to storm the world above. Nuru wondered how long before frustration got the better of the girl and drove her from the basement and away from the group. When she told her they wouldn't force her to stay, Efra gave Nuru a wounded look and went back to pacing.

Omari remained unconscious, but he groaned and twitched as if haunted by terrible dreams. Having used the last of her supply, Nuru sent Chisulo in search of ameslari so she could attempt to dream-walk into whatever world tormented the Finger. The fungus had always been difficult to acquire, even for someone with the right contacts, and Chisulo had never been that person. He returned empty-handed and apologetic. He took it hard. His failure to help his friend cut him deep. Nuru saw it in the beaten hunch of his shoulders, the way his attention often strayed to Omari. She didn't have the energy to talk him out of his self-imposed gloom.

It hurt that she couldn't at least try. Helplessness crushed her, a feeling she loathed.

For three days Nuru watched Efra and Chisulo pretend the other didn't exist but continually steal looks when they thought no one noticed.

Is she weighing his usefulness, or does she genuinely care for him?

She wasn't sure which bothered her more.

Efra confused her. She seemed to bounce randomly between cold self-interest and a desperate yearning to belong.

Which will win?

On the fourth evening Efra approached Chisulo. He lay on his side, pretending to sleep. She kicked him in the ribs.

"Would you gather everyone together, please?" she asked.

Chisulo groaned and rolled over to glare at her. "Why did you phrase that as a question?"

"That's what you're supposed to do," she said. "You all do it. When Nuru asks you to go get food, she's not really asking."

"Actually," said Nuru, "I am."

"Actually," snapped Efra, "you're not. Everyone gather round."

"Giving orders now, are you?" Nuru asked.

Efra turned on her. "Someone has to."

She isn't wrong. Chisulo didn't look ready, and the last decisions Nuru made got Bomani killed and Omari badly hurt. She glanced guiltily at the Finger. She should have been able to protect her friends. *I may have got him killed, too.*

"Now," said Efra, "if you'd please all fucking gather round."

Nuru, Chisulo, and Happy did as requested, though they didn't have to move far. They all sat while Efra remained standing. Chisulo's eyes never left her.

Is he falling for her, or is he falling for her need?

"We've waited long enough," said Efra. "It's time to start *doing* again."

Truth be told, Nuru felt impatient too. When the initial rush of terror passed and the Birds failed to come storming down the steps, she figured they just might survive. A distant fear, she discovered, was less terrifying than having a nahualli show up in the middle of a huateteo spirit trance with your friends.

Something has to change or we'll lose Omari.

"Do what, exactly?" asked Chisulo.

"Do we share everything?" asked Efra, staring at Nuru.

Everyone else nodded, so Nuru did too.

"Nuru has been carving something," said Efra.

"Oh fuck," said Nuru.

Happy and Chisulo turned curious looks in her direction.

"What?" asked Chisulo.

"Show them," said Efra.

Nuru removed the incomplete stone spider from its pouch and set it on the floor before her.

Happy squinted at the carving and then up at Nuru. "The girl part looks like you."

"Don't be ridiculous," snapped Nuru. It was far too beautiful, too perfect.

Chisulo leaned in to scowl at it. "What *is* that?"

Nuru resisted the urge to snatch it up and hide it away. "It's nothing."

Efra shook her head. "It's not nothing. Nuru can make it work."

Make it work? The girl had no idea what she was talking about, what was involved in being a nagual. The thought of completing the statue excited Nuru, infected her dreams, plagued her day and night. It also terrified her. *For this to work, I have* become *the spider creature.*

"Not real," grunted Happy.

Nuru realized what he meant and was surprised he knew that much about sorcery. "He's right. Only carvings of real creatures work. This... It was a dream, a hallucination. A nightmare."

"It is real," said Efra, ignoring Nuru's glare. "We've all heard the nahual preach about demons."

"Demons are evil," said Chisulo.

"So the nahual tell us," said Efra. "But seeing as those are the folks hunting us, maybe their enemies are our allies."

Didn't I say something like that?

Chisulo looked doubtful but remained silent.

"Nuru needs proper tools and paints to finish it," continued Efra. Seeing they were staring at her in confusion, she spelled it out to the men. "She needs Crafter tools. She needs Crafter paints."

"Impossible," said Chisulo.

Happy grunted agreement.

Efra stared down at them. "We're going into the Crafters' Ring to get them."

Chisulo's mouth fell open. "You're insane."

"Listen," barked Efra, "don't speak. We're all going. We're going to stay there. I've thought this through, all of it. The Birds are looking for us. We can hide here for a while, but not forever. Eventually we have to move." She looked at each in turn, daring them to argue. "That nahualli walked into our dreams. He stepped in and controlled the reality Nuru's mushrooms made for us. He *saw* us. All of us. He knows what we look like." She drew a calming breath. "Remember his robes? Red, white, and black. He's a nahualli of Cloud Serpent, Lord of the Hunt. He'll find us. Maybe he'll come to us in our sleep, kill us in our dreams."

"Can they do that?" Chisulo asked, turning to Nuru.

She glanced at Omari. "Yes."

"He will search the Growers' Ring until he finds us," said Efra, "because he dares not let us go."

"We're not that important," said Happy.

"Wrong," said Efra. "We are." She pointed at Nuru. "She is. That carving is."

Everyone stared at Nuru.

Efra nodded toward Chisulo. "And he is. He's a natural leader. He's perfect. I can get the District to rally behind him. The whole ring, eventually."

All eyes turned on Chisulo and he put his face in his hands, muttering something under his breath.

"We're Growers," said Efra. "The Birds call us Dirts. They can't imagine us anywhere but in the dirt. Growers don't leave the ring. Ever."

"The *Book of Bastion* says if we leave the ring we're to be thrown from the Sand Wall," Chisulo said into his hands.

"Right," agreed Efra. "It's forbidden." She grinned, stretching the scar. "So we're leaving."

"It won't work," said Chisulo.

"It will. I have a plan."

"How?" asked Happy.

"The whores who wait at the gate for Crafters to come fuck them for trinkets, food, and narcotics. Nuru and I are going to pretend we're whores. We'll lure them in, one, maybe two at a time. Ox-brain and flat-nose here," she nodded at Happy and Chisulo, "will be waiting. Once we have enough Crafter clothes, we go."

"How are we going to find a Crafter as big as Happy?" asked Nuru.

"We'll figure it out."

Chisulo lifted his face from his hands. He looked ill. He eyed Efra like she was either a venomous insect, or his only hope at salvation. "No Grower has been in the Crafters' Ring. We don't know what it's like. We don't know how things work there. We don't know how they walk, how they talk. How are we supposed to fit in?"

"Crafters come here all the time to fuck Growers," said Efra. "They don't walk different. They're just like us except they have nicer clothes and smell better."

Happy sat up. "Smell better?"

"Yes."

"What do the girls smell like?"

Efra shot him a look and he sat back with a dissatisfied grunt.

"Crafter homes are going to be just like ours," she said. Her brows furrowed as she considered the other ring. "Maybe a little nicer, with actual chairs, like the priests have."

Happy let out a groan of pleasure at the thought.

"We'll claim an empty tenement in the Crafters' Ring. Once we're settled, we'll find the tools we need."

Efra snarled in frustration when no one leapt up to agree with her.

She expects everyone to do as she suggests, without question. She sees an answer, believes it the only answer, and is confused we haven't figured it out already.

"Look," said Efra, holding her hands up to stall arguments. "You know how the Growers who work the farms are supplied with whatever tools they need?"

"I wouldn't call a collection of conveniently shaped sticks 'tools,'" said Chisulo.

The rest nodded. The crèches where the children were raised were all out in the fields, far from the gates and the more heavily populated tenements. As soon as the kids could walk, they were handed crude implements and taught to farm.

Efra ignored Chisulo. "It's going to be just like that for the Crafters. Except all the tools are made right there. They'll be easy to get. It'll be just like walking into the tool shed and taking a rake."

"The Birds count the rakes," pointed out Nuru. "They keep track of who took one and who returned one. Anyone who fails to return something gets lashes."

They all nodded again. As children, they'd all been whipped for losing or breaking farming tools.

"It'll be easy," said Efra. "They're Crafters. They need tools constantly, every day."

Nuru had her doubts. She'd never talked to a Crafter, never been closer than a score of strides. No matter what Efra said, they seemed different. Less tired. Happier. Less sweaty. And they *did* walk differently from Growers. They walked like they belonged.

Efra paced. "We have to do it now. The longer we wait, the more chance they find us. If we can take enough Crafters today, I say we leave before sunset."

Chisulo glanced at the unconscious Finger. "What about Omari?"

"If he doesn't wake in time, we'll have to leave him." She gave a half shrug. "It's a shame but..."

"Efra," said Nuru. "Do you think Chisulo would ever leave one of his friends behind?" Efra frowned, thinking it over. "He won't leave Omari. Just like he wouldn't abandon me or Happy. Just like he won't abandon you."

Efra darted a glance at Chisulo and he nodded. "Idiots." She sighed. "Fine. We're not all going until rat-face-stink-breath-small-balls is awake."

"Good," said Chisulo.

"All?" asked Nuru. "We're not *all* going until he's awake? You make that sound like some of us are."

"You and me," said Efra. "We're going. We're getting Crafter clothes today and then we're going through the gate. We're going to find the tools you need." She made a helpless, frustrated fluttering gesture with her fingers. "Omari might be unconscious for a while. We aren't wasting time just because he's useless."

"Wouldn't you be better off taking Happy or Chisulo?" asked Nuru. "What if there's trouble?"

"If there's the kind of trouble requiring a big, dumb man, we're already in more trouble than we can handle. Do either of these monkeys know what tools you need?"

She goes from insane to scary smart way too fast. "You and me," agreed Nuru. It was happening. Bastion, in its strange and roundabout way, was providing her with the tools she needed.

Efra turned on Chisulo. "If we don't come back, it's because we found a really nice place to live and decided we didn't need you after all."

Is she joking? Once again, Nuru had no idea.

Chisulo looked uncomfortable, like he asked himself the same question. Happy had a huge grin. Either he knew, or just enjoyed the thought of Efra and Nuru being together.

"Here's the plan," said Efra. "There are a lot of empty tenements near the gate." Growers didn't like living that close to where there are so many Birds, and the continual wagon traffic was annoying. Ox shit everywhere. "The Crafters use those tenements when they cross over to fuck Growers. Nuru and I will select two Growers and bring them back to one of the empty homes." She pointed at Chisulo. "You are going to follow us. Stay well back so they don't get spooked. Once we're inside, you come in and help us dispatch the Crafters."

"Dispatch?" asked Nuru.

Efra hesitated. "Bang them on the heads. Tie them up in the basement. And remember, we need their clothes, so not too much blood." She glanced at Nuru, eyes narrowing in thought. "I have an idea for that. You and me, we're going to see the Artist first."

"Why?" asked Nuru.

Efra offered her a hand and pulled her to her feet. "I'll tell you on the way."

She's hiding something, or doesn't want to tell me what she has planned because she knows I won't like it.

"One moment." Nuru went to the corner where Isabis slept, told the snake she'd be back soon and not to bite Chisulo, and gave it a kiss goodbye.

"Do I get a kiss?" asked Happy.

"Go ask Isabis." She returned to Efra's side and the girl grabbed her hand again.

"You're going to follow us, right?" Nuru asked Chisulo.

He nodded. "Won't let you out of my sight."

"Let's go," said Efra, "it smells like balls in here."

AKACHI – SHE SPEAKS IN STONE

In the first centuries after the formation of Bastion the city was torn apart by strife. Gods battled for supremacy, warring to fill the positions of a nascent pantheon. The losers were forever banished from the city, barred entrance by the impregnable Sand Wall, a work of colossal sorcery. The Bloody Desert is home to countless lost souls, demons, evil spirits, and defeated gods.

The decision to enact the struggle solely in the realm of the mortals—for the gods to choose Obsidian Hearts—often referred to as their Heart's Mirror—to fight for them—was the only choice possible.

—from The Book of Bastion

Amethyst. The stone of self-destruction.

Akachi swept the room with the straw broom Jumoke picked up on his last trip to the Northern Cathedral. Usually this was the acolyte's job, but Njau and the youth had gone again for more supplies. It was danger-ous to send them alone, but Captain Yejide was unwilling to leave fewer than two Hummingbirds with Akachi. Lutalo and Ibrahim, Akachi had been informed upon rising from bed, left early in the morning, chasing rumours of the scarred girl.

Yejide sat in the centre of the hall, legs crossed, working on her leather armour. Having already done whatever maintenance the skirt and shirt required, she now worked on the helm, checking the stitches, and buffing out any marks or stains. She'd been quiet since their return, the loss of Khadija no doubt hitting her hard.

Was it my fault?

First Talimba, and now Khadija. The Hummingbirds were being picked apart. Each time someone died, they were doing Akachi's bidding. Did Yejide blame him for their deaths?

Akachi swept an area he already went over twice.

The assassin, that flawless beautiful skin. Those bright eyes, shining as if lit from within.

She used Loa sorcery.

The whole encounter seemed unreal. Khadija crumpling, bones shattering, skull caving in. The wet *pop* as her eye burst.

He remembered the cold stone against the side of his skull. *She touched me with the amethyst.*

After returning to the church, Akachi smoked a blend of erlaxatu and a dash of zoriontasuna. He probably had more than he should have, but he needed to escape, to put the horror behind him.

I ate *a woman!*

Remembering the taste of her flesh and blood twisted his stomach.

When he woke, mind numbed to dull stupidity, he dug out his copy of the *Book of Bastion* and read what he found on crystals and Loa sorcery. There wasn't much beyond the fact that stone magic was the province of Mother Death, and forbidden. He wished he had a copy of the Loa *Book of the Invisibles*, but no one was allowed to remove them from the library in the Northern Cathedral. The Loa text went into much greater detail on the stones, their alleged powers and uses in dark sorcery. He'd read the book once, but that was years ago. Not being dosed with foku at the time, too many details now escaped his memory.

He hated himself for lying to Yejide about the Loa assassin touching him, but didn't want her to worry.

The Loa called Amethyst the Stone of Destruction. In the hands of a sorcerer, it could twist a man's soul with the need for self-harm. It was never as simple as suicide. The stone provoked a slow descent into ruin.

I'm a failure.

And in so many ways. Everything was falling apart.

He'd confronted the scarred girl and her street sorcerer in the dream-world and somehow been bested. All he managed to do was alert his prey that he was after them. They were gone, having fled their tenement, and could be anywhere. Had they left the Wheat District? Though Growers were forbidden from leaving the district they were assigned, it was impossible to actually keep track of them.

If they've left, I have truly failed.

Assigned his parish, Akachi couldn't leave. In a way, the Growers had more freedom than he. If they left the district, likely no one would pursue them. If he abandoned his parish he could be stripped of what little rank he had. He might spend the rest of his life rotting out here among the Growers, serving some pastor. He might even be cut from the church, forced to return to the Priests' Ring a failure, a pariah.

He'd have to face his father.

They couldn't have left. They had to still be here, still within his reach. Cloud Serpent would…

Cloud Serpent would what, make sure the hunt wasn't too challenging?, he thought, mocking himself.

I will hunt them wherever they flee. Damn Bishop Zalika. He was a nahual of Cloud Serpent. His god showed him his prey. Nothing else mattered.

He wished he believed it, wished he still felt the stone-cold certainty he'd known when Cloud Serpent first showed him the vision.

Doubt ate at him, gnawed at his faith. This was too much, too big for one man. He should admit he wasn't up to the task and report what he knew to the Bishop and his father, let them deal with this.

Except what did he really know?

All he had were guesses and assumptions. Would they even believe Cloud Serpent spoke to him? Would they laugh? He imagined his father's look of disappointment.

Cloud Serpent sent me here. That had to mean something.

Think, he berated himself. *Think this through.*

The *Book of Bastion* said Loa sorcery—the use of stones and crystals—was the sole domain of Mother Death. The Book also stated that, with Mother Death trapped beyond the Sand Wall, Loa sorcerers were crippled, near powerless. The stones were a conduit for her power, and the Sand Wall severed that connection.

Yet that Loa assassin used the garnet to heal herself over and over and killed Khadija. That stone *definitely* had power. The amethyst...

Akachi shook the thought off.

I'm fine.

Really? The garnet had power but the amethyst didn't?

He pushed his doubts away, though they still lurked in the dark shadows of his mind. He craved jainkoei, to once again feel the will of the gods in his blood. Maybe he should return to his chambers. He darted a glance at Yejide. He'd only smoke a little.

Focus!

If the *Book of Bastion* was correct—and it must be—then Mother Death had some way of channelling power through the wall.

Or she's already inside Bastion.

If she had somehow entered the city, Loa sorcery, their filthy crystal magic, was operating at full strength. No nahualli had faced a real Loa sorcerer since Mother Death's banishment. He had only the vaguest idea of their capabilities. How much of what he'd read was true? Could they really turn into dragons and demons and elephants? Were there crystals that turned rock to dust?

Mother Death is inside Bastion.

That was a terrifying thought but made more sense than the ancient death god somehow finding a crack in the perfection of the Last City. She had to be inside.

The assassin attacked during Akachi's door-to-door search for the scarred girl. That couldn't be a coincidence. Were the Loa trying to stop him from finding the girl? Was she Loa?

No, that felt wrong. When he found her in the dream world there'd been no Loa there to protect her, just that street sorcerer, and she'd been helpless. He'd seen no sign of stones or crystals, not a hint of Loa sorcery. They'd just been five filthy Dirts hiding in a basement. The Loa, the ancient enemies of the true nahual of Bastion, would be better organized, better prepared.

He remembered the tattoo, a black rectangle inked into the flesh of her wrist. That was Smoking Mirror's truest and oldest name. No way she could have known that unless Father Discord shared it with her. The scarred girl wielded it like a weapon, held it before her like a talisman, and walked through Akachi's sorcery.

Smoking Mirror backs the girl.

If that was true, and the Loa assassin's attack had been as much about protecting her as it was about killing Akachi, then Smoking Mirror must also be backing the Loa.

Father Discord works to bring Mother Death back into Bastion.

And there could only be one reason for that: Smoking Mirror sought to topple The Lord from the head of the pantheon, and replace him with his banished wife, The Lady of the House.

But why?

Smoking Mirror, like all of the gods, had many names. Father Discord. Lord of the Night Sky. The Obsidian Lord.

Obsidian. Stone. Obsidian was the only crystal magic not forbidden in Bastion. The tecuhtli, practitioners of death magic, and nahualli of Father Death, made use of it, as did the Hummingbird Guard. But Smoking Mirror was its master.

Mother Death, she speaks in stone. That line was oft repeated in the Loa *Book of the Invisibles.*

Was there some connection between the two gods? The Last War was history beyond ancient. Twenty-five thousand years in the past, the *Book of Bastion* was thin on details. At least in more recent copies. Perhaps older versions held more. There was, Akachi remembered, one of the very first copies in the Northern Cathedral, in Bishop Zalika's personal library. As an acolyte he'd had no access to the book. As a nominal pastor... He doubted his questionable rank would change anything. But if he brought proof to Zalika that her god was under attack, that Smoking Mirror worked to return Mother Death to Bastion, she would *have* to help him.

The scarred girl—the tattoo on her wrist—is my proof.

The god had marked her with his truest name.

Once Akachi had her, he'd bring her to the Northern Cathedral, show Bishop Zalika. He'd try and bring her alive, but if she died, Zalika, a powerful tecuhtli and the ring's highest ranked Priest of Father Death, would have no difficulty questioning her corpse. Then he could plead his case, beg access to the ancient book.

Akachi stopped sweeping.

Smoking Mirror must have opened a path for Mother Death. She's in Bastion. Otherwise Loa stone sorcery wouldn't work. He plans to bring down The Lord, replace him with Mother Death.

He knew he was right. Cloud Serpent sent him here to stop this.

This wasn't at all about finding some Dirt girl. The gods warred, plotted against each other. Such a power struggle could see the end of the Last City, the final extinction of all mankind.

Find the girl, and I'll find Mother Death.

The visions: The fields burning. The wells filling with ash. The Turquoise Serpents marching against an army of Growers. It was all real. Or would be real.

Unless I stop it.

More than ever he desperately wanted to drown himself in the will of the gods, to ingest so much jainkoei they spoke directly into his blood.

Ibrahim, the huge Hummingbird, strode into the cathedral hall and stood waiting. His face showed equal measures of disdain, disappointment, and disapproval.

Captain Yejide stood, donning her leather helm. "Report."

"We found a Dirt who said he knew the scarred girl. He led us to the leader of some local gang. We were attacked by a mob of Growers and he escaped. Lutalo and I were forced to split up during the pursuit. Did he return with the Dirt?" He delivered his report in a flat, emotionless monotone.

Akachi's heart kicked. *They're still here!* They hadn't left the district! He could still catch them. "Where—"

"Why did you split up?" asked Captain Yejide.

"We lost sight of him. Lutalo stayed to search the tenements while I continued on. When I returned, Lutalo was gone. I assumed he found the Dirt and brought him back to the church."

"He hasn't returned," said Yejide. "How long ago did you split up?"

"An hour. Maybe two."

"We should go look for him," Akachi said.

"No," said Yejide, looking unhappy about the decision. "Too dangerous. If he hasn't returned, it's because he found trouble."

"Then we should definitely go!"

"Our assignment is to guard you," she said as if that settled the matter.

"He could be hurt."

"He knew the risks," she said. "Gyasi is wounded. Njau is with Jumoke. Taking you into the street with just Ibrahim and myself is too dangerous."

"I will go alone," said Ibrahim, glancing at his Captain, waiting for her decision.

She studied him, mouth set in a hard line, and nodded once.

Ibrahim spun and left.

Returning to his chambers Akachi ground and smoked erlaxatu. He didn't do it for sorcerous reasons. He didn't do it to centre his soul. He did it for the one reason his nahualli teachers warned him about: He did it to escape.

One more failure.

He didn't care.

Akachi smoked until he *was* smoke.

Then he slept.

Akachi woke when Captain Yejide sat on his bed. His thoughts ran thick and gritty like blood in sand. Yejide looked tired, angry.

He felt like he needed a thousand years more sleep. Through the window he saw it was still night, though he had no idea of the time

Yejide glanced at the pipe he left on the table and looked away. Black burnt ash spilled from the bowl.

That was sloppy. It was supposed to stay with him at all times. He should have cleaned it right away and returned it to its place in his belt.

Akachi said nothing.

Captain Yejide shifted. "When I was standing guard outside, the local nahual of Precious Feather approached me with news. Some of the Hummingbird Guard attached to her parish were attacked while on patrol. Three were killed, beaten to death. She also said there was open rioting in the Oak District. That's bad. They harvest lumber and have access to flint-bladed axes. She told me Bishop Zalika has called for the Turquoise Serpents."

Southern Hummingbird's elite soldiers hadn't set foot in the Growers' Ring in ten thousand years.

Blood in the streets, running thick in gutters, flowing to the heart of the city. The vision was coming true.

"You should take your squad and leave," Akachi blurted.

She gave him a funny look, part annoyance and a little of what might have been weary fondness. "The Hummingbird Guard never abandon a post. Unless so ordered."

"So I could order you away? I could order you to safety?" Where was the distance he found in the erlaxatu? He wanted that, wanted it so bad. *I want to be numb.*

"Bishop Zalika gave us this assignment. Only she can command us to leave."

Shit. Another failure.

"Has Lutalo returned?" he asked.

"No. Ibrahim found no trace of him."

"What do you think happened?"

"I think the Dirts got him." She gave him a long, hard look. "We're being picked apart and are massively outnumbered."

"We're going to find the scarred girl and we're going bring down the Loa," he said as much to convince himself as her. "It may cost me everything, but I will not fail Cloud Serpent." He met Yejide's eyes, tried to pour certainty into his words. "I can't fail my father. If I have to risk brain-burn to win, I will." *I won't fail again.*

"I know." She didn't seem happy or proud of his bravery.

Yejide left then, and he wondered if he'd failed at something else, something he didn't understand.

Akachi sat alone, eyeing his pipe and selection of narcotics.

NURU – COLLAPSING NIGHT

Where there is inequality, there can be no justice.

— Loa Book of the Invisibles

Out in the street, still clutching Nuru's hand, Efra led her through filth-strewn back alleys. Each time they approached an intersection, Efra pulled her to the wall before scanning the streets ahead for Birds.

"I don't remember it being this dirty when I was a kid," said Nuru, frowning at heaped refuse. Most of it was torn greys and food scraps. The alley stunk of rotting fruit.

"It wasn't."

"Why are we going to see the Artist?"

"The bones in your hair are too scary. We have to cut them out. You need to look like a Dirt whore."

Nuru stopped, dragging Efra to a halt. "My hair? No."

"Yes."

Nuru scooped her hair over her shoulder. Knotted with bones and small animal skulls, it was a symbol of what she was, of *who* she was. "No."

Efra glared at her. "Which do you want more, carving tools and paints, or hair?"

Nuru glared at her. Finally, she sagged. "The tools."

"Then it goes." Efra pulled her into motion. Setting a fast pace, she hauled her toward the next street. "Anyway, we need your hair."

"For what?"

"You'll see." Efra winked. "Always have a backup plan."

The Artist, with his gorgeous eyes and hair always falling forward to curtain his face, was sitting at the front entrance to his tenement when they arrived. Every woman in the Wheat District fantasized about those fingers and smoky eyes.

"Efra" he said, eyes lighting in a way that made Nuru's heart do a little stutter and gave her just the smallest stab of jealousy.

Efra nodded like she hadn't seen the look and pushed by him, pulling Nuru into his home.

"Come on in," he said as they passed.

Where every Grower tenement was identical inside, the Artist's was different. Strange symbols covered the inner walls. A mural depicting a woman being thrown from the Sand Wall covered the ceiling. Painted in black ink, it was old and faded, the paint flaking away in places.

The Artist followed them in.

"Did you paint that?" Nuru asked.

Eyes following Efra, he said, "When I first came here."

The detail was stunning. She had no idea that many shades of black and grey were possible. "It's beautiful."

Efra glanced at the ceiling with an utter lack of interest.

Art doesn't touch her.

"I'm guessing you aren't here because you have the ink," the Artist said to Efra. He seemed only nominally aware of Nuru.

Poor man is smitten. He had no idea what he was up against.

"No," said Efra. "We need your help. I want you to cut her hair."

Now the Artist did turn to examine Nuru. "You're a street sorcerer."

She nodded.

"The only reason you'd cut your hair is if you're hiding."

"Don't ask," said Efra, "and I won't have to lie."

The artist gave her a long look that would have melted any other woman and she said, "Save the hair. You're going to make something out of it."

Shrugging, the artist circled Nuru, examining her hair. Stopping in front of her, he asked, "You ready?"

"No."

"You don't have to—"

Efra interrupted the Artist with a raised hand. "Yes she does. The whores at the gate don't have bones in their hair."

That earned a raised eyebrow from the Artist.

"Don't ask," repeated Efra. Turning on Nuru she said, "You want the tools? This is how we get them."

The spider. The dream. Nuru closed her eyes and nodded.

Collecting a shard of sharpened flint, the Artist moved to stand behind her. "You're sure?"

"Yes," said Efra, "she's sure."

Nuru nodded again, not trusting herself to speak.

She felt his fingers in her hair as he untangled bone after bone, carefully setting them on the table. It would have been nice, erotic almost, is she hadn't known what would follow. She felt naked, stripped of identity.

Why couldn't Efra understand that hair was more than just something that grew on your head? Why couldn't she understand it might have meaning to Nuru?

Or does she know and not care?

The nahual of Her Skirt is Stars who ran the crèche Nuru grew up in had cut the children's hair short, given them all exactly the same blunt look. Even then she'd known it was a subtle hint, control. You're all the same. The day she left the crèche, Nuru swore that from that day on, she alone would decide her appearance.

Taking a deep breath, Nuru made a decision. "Do it."

The Artist hacked away Nuru's long braided hair with a jagged wedge of flint and spent another few minutes fussing over his work until Efra told him to hurry up. That little shard of broken stone was a death sentence. By allowing them to see it, he was saying he trusted them with his life. He sliced away stray hairs and then brushed it out until it hung about her shoulders in tight curls. Finally, he stood back to examine his work. Making small sounds like an annoyed chicken, he spent several more minutes arranging it before finally surrendering. As instructed, he lay out the long ropes of cut hair on the table.

The Artist eyed the hair. "So what are we making with this? Otochin fetish? Art?"

"Garrotte," said Efra.

"Oh. Of course." He gnawed the inside of his cheek for a moment, thinking. "Wait here." Then he disappeared into the back room.

Nuru watched him leave, then turned on Efra. "Garrotte? Why?" she demanded.

"I lost my spike, we have no weapons. It's stupid to go into a situation like this unprepared."

"We aren't killing them."

"Unless we have to."

"We *aren't* killing them."

Efra shrugged and Nuru couldn't tell if it was acceptance, or dismissal.

When the Artist returned, he carried four short sticks of ebony that fit comfortably in his fists. Tucked under his arm he had a longer stick that was bent, with both ends connected by a strip of rawhide, and straight stick with a chunk of knapped flint attached to one end.

"What are those?" asked Efra, moving closer to examine the objects.

The Artist lit up at her interest.

"Sit with me," he said, sinking to sit cross-legged on the floor.

Efra sat across from him, entranced. Nuru remained standing, watching the two.

"These," said the Artist, placing the four smaller sticks on the stone floor, "will be the grips for the garrotte. He held up the long stick with the knapped flint and the bent stick with the rawhide for Efra to examine. "This is a bow drill." He turned it, plucking the rawhide to make a thrumming note. "In the inner rings there are things like this, with wood bodies, where the strings are tuned for making music."

"Why?" asked Efra.

He blinked at her and shrugged. "The Hummingbird Guard also use something like this as weapons, but never in the outer ring." He darted a quick glanced at Nuru before returning his attention to Efra. "We're going to use it to drill holes in the handles so we can attach your friend's hair."

Efra picked up the stick with the sharpened flint. "How did you attach the flint?"

"That's filtered tree sap mixed with ash. It hardens when it dries."

Efra placed the drill stick back on the floor. "These are tools. How did you make them?"

"People have been making tools for millions of years."

"All of this..." She gestured at the gathered implements. "You shouldn't display stuff like this. You can't trust people."

"Are you going to report me to the nahual?"

"No."

"So I'm safe."

"Idiot."

The Artist drilled holes in the ebony handles. After twining Nuru's cut hair into long braids, he attached each end to the wood handles, tying it through the drilled holes. When finished, he offered a garrotte to each girl.

"Ebony is strong," he said. "It won't break. And the hair, wound like that, will have more than enough tensile strength to choke a man."

"Good," said Efra. "What's tensile strength?"

"The ability of an object to withstand load." He sounded like he was repeating something from memory.

"Thank you," said Nuru, knowing Efra wouldn't.

Eyes on Efra, the Artist appeared not to have heard.

"Now, how about clothes?" said Efra. "The whores always have clean thobes and ours are filthy."

The Artist sighed and wandered off to return moments later with two sets of clean greys. They were exactly as if they'd come from the Crafters' Ring, unmodified, and designed to fit both men and women. Badly.

He turned his back while Nuru and Efra stripped off their old thobes and donned the new ones. The course material chafed her skin. Geys always took at least a week to become comfortable. The women hid the garrottes in the long loops of fabric.

Efra examined Nuru. "Better stay away from Happy." She turned to the Artist, her face a frown of concentration. "Thank you," she enunciated carefully like the words were new to her. "We owe you for this. We won't forget. *I* won't forget." She turned to leave and then stopped. "I don't know how I will pay you back, but I will."

He shot Nuru a crooked half-smile. "There is no debt." Glancing at the entrance, he added, "The Birds have been searching the tenements.

They've been asking about a scarred girl. Stay safe."

Efra nodded and dragged Nuru back out into the street.

Nuru looked around but couldn't see Chisulo anywhere. *Now, when I wouldn't mind catching a quick glance to make myself feel better, he hides like a Finger.*

Efra didn't seem the least concerned.

Once they were well away from the Artist's, Nuru said, "He likes you."

Efra grunted.

"Do you like him?"

"He has nice eyes."

"Do you like Chisulo?"

"He has nice shoulders." She tilted her head, thinking as she walked. "I like his squished nose too. And his lips, the way he smiles. And his ass."

"Not what I meant."

Efra sighed, a sound somewhere between wistful, and annoyed. "I know."

"Do you feel something for him?"

"Lust."

"Anything else?"

"I don't like the way he makes me feel," said Efra. "It's scary. I feel vulnerable." She darted a glance at Nuru. "Vulnerable is bad."

Nuru realized where Efra was leading her. "We're going to the gate *now*?"

"Why wait?"

"I—"

"Pretend to be the kind of girl Happy likes. Stick your tits out. Act smoky."

Nuru thrust her chest out and Efra laughed.

"Like you're doing any better," muttered Nuru.

"I have the scar."

"I think they prefer tits."

"Some men want something different."

"Yeah, but—"

"These men and women come through the gate to fuck Growers. That pretty much tells us they're looking for something different. They'll be curious, as long as I don't act scary."

"Can you do that?"

Efra shrugged.

This close to the Grey Wall, it towered above the two women, a constant reminder of the gods. Were it later in the day, it would throw them into shadow. Nuru marvelled at the impossibility of it. One hundred strides tall, the nahual said it took over one million strides to walk all the way around. If one was to walk at a brisk pace for eight hours a day, the journey would take twenty days. Walking the length of the Sand Wall, she recalled, would take well over a month. Not that anyone ever did. At least not Growers. She wondered what the world must look like from up there.

Someday. Someday I'll leave the dirt behind and walk the Sand Wall. She'd never left the Wheat District. What were the other districts like? Was it all like this?

Efra squeezed Nuru's hand. "There are men coming through the Bird cordon at the gate. Act sexy."

Efra led her across the path of two Crafter men. It was hard to judge their age. Where Growers became increasingly bent as they aged, broken by the hardships they endured, Crafters got fatter. And balder.

The two Efra selected were typical of the few Crafters Nuru ever saw. The older, bigger man wore shirt and pants of orange, the sleeves cut short. The younger, a head shorter than Nuru, wore similar clothes but in a faded brown. Where Growers went barefoot and the Birds wore sandals strapped tight all the way to their knees, the Crafters wore floppy slabs of thin leather that slapped the ground as they walked. Nuru squinted at their feet. Nothing but a single loop of leather over their big toe kept the sandals from falling off.

The Crafters beamed smiles of white teeth when they spotted the girls. Or one did. The younger Crafter smiled nervously.

What are we doing? This was a mistake. She never should have let Efra talk her into this. Only her hunger to see the spider completed kept her moving. Glancing over her shoulder, she prayed for even a glimpse of Chisulo. Nothing. He was doing a masterful job of staying out of sight.

"Girls," said the older of the two Crafters. Hair thinning, he looked kind, but his eyes betrayed a hunger Nuru didn't like. He had thick fingers, rough with callouses, and was rounder than any Grower. A lot of it was muscle.

So they do still work. Maybe they were more like Growers than everyone thought. But then why were Crafters allowed to pass through the Grey Wall where Growers weren't?

Nuru waited for Efra to take the lead. The girl froze, squeezing her hand hard enough to hurt.

Nuru had no idea what to do. Was there some agreed upon process for this? Looking around, she saw several Growers—alone or in pairs—talking to other Crafters who came through the wall.

"First time?" asked the older man.

Nuru nodded.

"That's fine. You understand what we want?"

She nodded.

"Fine, fine. In trade we have sweets."

Checking over his shoulder, making sure no one was paying attention to their transaction, the Crafter removed a small leather pouch from a pocket. The Birds at the gate saw everything, ignoring the transaction. The pouch had leather ties and designs worked into the surface. She'd never seen anything like it. Opening it wide enough to give her a glimpse within, he held it under her nose. Black lumps looking suspiciously like polished pebbles lay at the bottom.

"Anise," he said.

Nuru leaned in to sniff and blinked in surprise. Nothing, not even the ripest fruit had ever smelled so sweet. Her mouth watered.

"And perfume," he said, putting the pouch away and waving a bottle the size of her smallest finger at her. The liquid within was light brown, like muddy water.

Why would anyone fuck a Crafter for this shit?

It occurred to her that she should haggle. She looked to Efra for guidance, but the girl just squeezed her hand again and nodded.

Looking up and down the street, she saw no sign of Chisulo. *Where is he?* Chisulo always took instructions too literally.

The Crafter misunderstood. "Don't worry. As long as we don't bring anything useful through, the Hummers don't care."

Hummers. So the Crafters had their own name for the Birds. Interesting. The word 'useful' caught her attention. *What else might they have that we don't?* She couldn't imagine. That little leather pouch, shown so casually, was already beyond her experience.

"Your friend is pretty quiet," said the Crafter. "That scar, is she right in the head?"

Like you care. Nuru nodded.

"Fine. Fine." He looked a little disappointed.

"We have a place!" blurted Efra.

"She speaks!" The older man turned to the younger. "Which do you want?"

The youth glanced up at Nuru, looking her over like he was selecting a piece of fruit. She wanted to hit him, to tear aside the veil of lies and show him the world of her power.

"I want the small one," he said, nodding at Efra.

"Fine, fine. That's good. I'll take the brains of the operation." He winked at Nuru. "I don't suppose you're hiding a mean streak? Got a little fight in you?"

He turned away, missing the cold look of death that crossed her features.

"Follow us," said Nuru. "Our place is really comfortable."

"Dirt hovels are never comfortable. Anyway, I come pretty often. I have a couple of rooms I rent for this."

Rent? What did that mean?

"Trust me," he said, and she knew she didn't. "You've never seen anything like this."

"Our place—"

"No." He gave her a long, searching look. "If this isn't what you want, there are lots of other Dirt girls who do."

"Let's go with them," said Efra.

"Yeah?" The Crafter stared at Nuru, waiting.

She nodded. *Come on Chisulo, just let me catch a glimpse of that squished nose.*

"Fine. Fine." He offered her a hand and she stared at it until it returned to its usual place. "Fine," he said again. "Let's go."

The older man set a fast pace. The younger, walking at his side, stared at everything like it was the most amazing sight to behold.

Nuru scanned the streets. Still no sign of Chisulo. *You better be following us.*

The old Crafter led them to a nearby set of tenements. When he spotted one with a washed-out stain of brown over the entrance, he grunted, "This one," and entered. The younger Crafter followed, with

Nuru and Efra entering last. A tall Grower, all bone and sagging skin, sat on an overturned box far enough inside to be out of the sun.

"You know these two?" the big Crafter asked, gesturing at Nuru and Efra with a meaty thumb.

The old Grower looked them over, gaze lingering on Nuru. "Nope."

The Crafter nodded, apparently satisfied, and led them through to the back rooms.

Heavy curtains of some thick material, lined bright in colours, hung over every entrance, deadening the sound. She'd never seen so much colour in one place. The windows, too, were covered. Candles, purest white and perfectly straight, provided the only light. Pots of burning incense filled the air with cloying sweetness. When he swept the curtain aside to allow Efra and the young man to enter, Nuru saw the walls within were lined with the same fabric.

He led Nuru to the next room.

She entered and stood staring. "What is that?"

"A bed."

"No, on top of that."

"A mattress." He laughed, enjoying the moment. "A *real* mattress, not a thobe stuffed with rotting straw."

He followed her in, allowing the heavy curtain to fall into place. The room was full of a quiet that was unlike anything Nuru ever heard before. It felt like the rest of the district disappeared, ceased to exist. Crossing to the bed, she touched the mattress thing. It was soft and squishy and covered in another fabric which shimmered in the candle-light.

"What's inside?" she asked, squeezing the mattress.

"Down."

For a moment she thought it was a command, that he wanted her to kneel and pleasure him, but he looked distracted and not at all interested in sex.

Noting her attention, he added, "And before you ask, the fabric is called silk. Yes, it's soft. If you try and steal it—even a little—the nahual will bleed you dry."

"I'm not a Finger."

"A what?"

"A thief."

"No, you're a whore." He pointed at a bowl of water set out on the stone table. A folded square of fabric, again different, again strange and new, lay beside it. Flower petals floated in the water.

Nuru crossed to sniff at the water, stalling, waiting for Chisulo to come charging into the room. She touched the fabric and it was soft and deep. She lifted it and brushed it against her face.

"You use it to scrub yourself," said the Crafter.

"What about you?"

"I take baths every day."

Every day? Growers were allowed into the bathhouses once a week. Trying to slip in more often earned lashes in the public square. No one cared if they went less often or not at all.

"Stop standing there staring at me and clean up," said the Crafter.

Chisulo, where are you?

Nuru touched the wood handle of the garrotte tucked into her thobe.

I can't do it.

Turning back to the bowl, she dipped the fabric into the water, wrung it out, and then scrubbed her hands. Desperate to see Chisulo, angry at him for waiting until the last second, and terrified of what she might have to do if he didn't show up, she kept glancing at the entrance.

What if he doesn't come?

If she said she changed her mind, would the big Crafter let her go? What if he didn't? Could she try and kill him? If she screamed, would anyone come to investigate? Probably not, she decided.

Efra slipped into the room and Nuru's heart jumped and then fell in disappointment.

Why was she here? Had she changed her mind?

The Crafter turned the moment she entered, scowling at her. "Don't tell me this is going to be a problem. I don't have time to waste on scared whores."

Efra glanced at Nuru who now stood behind the Crafter. *Jump him now while he's distracted*, her eyes said. Nuru stood rooted.

"Um," said Efra.

"Get back in there and take care of my boy."

Your boy? Did he somehow own the youth? Come to think of it, the two did look kind of similar. She struggled with the concept. Had this man somehow found his son in the Crafter Ring and figured out their connection based solely on some shared features? She'd heard about that happening with Growers, where two people would meet and look so similar everyone figured they had to be related. Whatever the truth, there was some connection between the two.

"Something happened," blurted Efra. "He's not moving."

No, no, no. Nuru's heart dropped into her belly. *She killed him.* She couldn't imagine how Efra dispatched the boy so fast.

The Crafter knocked Efra down in his rush to get into the other room and she landed badly, cracking her head on the wall.

Nuru scrambled to her side. "Are you hurt?"

Dazed, Efra blinked up at her with bleary anger. "Go fucking get him!"

Nuru hesitated. "You're—"

"They'll kill us if he escapes."

"But—"

"No choice. Go!"

Efra was right. If the Crafter got out and told the Birds, she and Efra would be sacrificed on the altar. If, that is, the Birds didn't kill them right then and there. Cursing, Nuru scrambled to her feet and chased after the man. Dropping one end of the garrotte, she entered to find him kneeling over the boy, keening like a wounded goat.

She leapt at his back, but he turned, his elbow catching her in the cheekbone and sending sparks arcing across her vision. Stunned, she stumbled and fell. He screamed something and punched her in the chest. Blows fell, one after the other. A few she caught on her arms, but he was twice her weight. She went down under the onslaught, every instinct screaming at her to curl up and protect herself, but knowing he'd beat her to death if she did. He wailed and screamed, incoherent rage and loss.

One hand still gripping the wooden end of the garrotte, she rolled away and lashed out with it. The chunk of wood at the other end struck him a glancing blow, opening a gash on his forehead and spilling blood into his eyes. He kicked her again, this time connecting with her ribs. It felt like he shattered something.

Blindly, she lashed out. He caught the other end of the garrotte and tore it from her hand. Wood clattered on stone as it he tossed it away.

"Going to kill you," breathed the Crafter. He knelt over her, trapping one of her arms and crushing her beneath his weight. "Fuck the priests' justice. You killed my boy. Going to fucking kill you."

Huge hands wrapped around her neck. He lifted, and then brought the back of her head down hard on the stone. She lost everything.

World gone.

She heard a voice, distant and boxy. "No, not yet."

Someone smacked her, open handed, across the face.

An eye opened. She couldn't focus. Hands around her neck, squeezing. No air. Her body kicked, twitched with the need for breath. Fading.

"Not so fast."

Hands loosened allowing the tiniest sip of air. Just enough to bring her back. Then he crushed her throat closed in his fingers. She clawed at him. He didn't care.

Buzzing filled her ears. Collapsing night.

"No fucking escape."

A sucking intake of breath tore her throat and was gone. She kicked, weak. Her body bucked with need. Fading.

"Not done with you, fucking whore."

Black.

The hands around her neck loosened. Air rushed into her, a screamed inhalation.

Bubbly choking, but this time not her.

Nuru cracked open a bruised and swollen eye. The Crafter still straddled her, but Efra stood behind him. She had a knee against his back and her garrotte looped around his throat. Teeth bared with effort, she growled low and feral as she pulled.

The Crafter hooked a finger under the garrotte and struggled to get more in there.

She's weak. Her arms will give out.

Efra's strength faded fast.

But both hands clawing at the garrotte left the Crafter exposed. With her free hand Nuru punched him in the groin. It was an awkward blow but got his attention. She hit him again. When he adjusted his weight, trying to twist away, she pulled her other arm free.

She remembered the fight with the Bird, the blow that took the wind from her. She knew exactly where he hit her. She hit the Crafter there. She hit him over and over, driving her knuckles into the centre of his chest, just below where his ribs met. When he dropped a hand from his throat to try and ward away her attacks, she abruptly changed tactics and grabbed his arm with the fingers caught under the garrotte.

Yanking it free, she screamed, "Choke him you fucking bitch!" at Efra.

Efra twisted the garrotte tight, turned so she held it over her shoulder, and put her entire weight into it.

Nuru fought to keep the Crafters' hands entangled.

Finally, his eyes rolled up and he hung limp from the garrotte.

"Bitch," grunted Efra through gritted teeth.

A moment later her arms gave and the Crafter pitched forward to land on Nuru. Rolling him off, Nuru crawled away. Every breath hurt. Everything hurt.

She knelt, tears streaming, shaking. Her gaze twitched from the youth to the big man, attention lingering before darting back. "You killed them."

"We had to." Efra rubbed her head where it had hit stone. She scowled at Nuru. "Why are you crying?"

She couldn't take her eyes off the boy. "He was just a kid!"

"You killed Fadil's man, that shit-stain Sefu. I don't remember that bothering you."

Nuru glared at her, eyes stinging. "When I killed Sefu I was the snake. When a nagual becomes an animal, she *becomes* that animal."

"I don't—"

"When I was the snake, it filled my thoughts. For a snake, killing a man is nothing. I'm not a snake. I cried for hours that night."

Efra studied the young man's corpse and shrugged.

She feels nothing.

"You're not a snake," Efra said. "But I kind of am." She turned to

Nuru. "Stay there."

Limping to the curtain, favouring her ribs and grinding her teeth against the pain, she peered through. "The old Grower is gone." She returned to Nuru, pulling her to her feet. "Where is Chisulo? What about all that 'People can depend on me' crap?"

"Something must have happened." Nuru stared at the corpses.

"What would keep him away?"

Nuru shrugged, wiping her eyes.

"You look weirdly normal with your hair cut short and tattoos hidden," said Efra. "Just another Dirt girl."

Except I'm not. "Birds," said Nuru.

"What?" Efra hurried back to the curtain and checked through a crack in the fabric.

"The Cloud Serpent nahual we saw in the basement. He must be looking for us. He saw you, your scar. He saw Chisulo's squished nose. They're distinctive. Everyone knows you're with us by now. Someone must have said something."

"If the Birds have Chisulo, it's only a matter of time before he tells them what we're doing."

"He wouldn't."

"You drugged me and I told you everything. You think a nahualli can't do that and more?"

She was right. Of course she was right.

Efra peeled off her greys, unwrapping layer after layer of her thobe and dropping it to the floor. Bruises ranging in colour from dark blue to a slurred yellowish purple covered her torso. "Hurry up. We have to change."

"If they have Chisulo, all this is pointless."

"He'll be fine. Smoking Mirror wouldn't let anything happen to him." She grinned at Nuru. "I need him. Anyway, we're still alive. Even without him, life goes on."

"No, it doesn't."

"Yes," said Efra, "it does."

Efra struggled with the boy's corpse, trying to remove the clothes.

"We have to wait," said Nuru.

"No, we have to leave." Efra stalled her argument with a raised hand. "If the Birds have him, we can't help. They'll search the tenements near the gate. I promise you they know about the Crafter whorehouses. If something else happened, if he was delayed for some reason, we'll find him when we get back."

"Get back?"

"We're still going. You and me."

The spider. The demon, if that's what it was. She wanted it. She wanted to finish the carving. She *needed* to. That's what this was all about. She couldn't forget.

"We are coming back?" Nuru asked.

"Of course. But if we don't get out of here now, we might see the other side of the Sand Wall."

Nuru cursed under her breath and then stripped off her greys. The boy's corpse kept drawing her eye, the bulging, staring eyes, the red wound around his neck where Efra garrotted him with Nuru's hair.

I didn't want this.

What happened to Chisulo? Where was he? Sick with guilt, sick with worry, she followed Efra's lead with numb obedience.

Neither woman had ever worn anything other than a Grower's thobe before. The Crafter clothes—shirt and pants—were awkward, felt strange and restricting. The fabric was soft and strong, unlike anything they'd seen.

Efra tried to adjust the brown shirt so it didn't chafe her armpits.

"Stop fidgeting," said Nuru. She turned Efra in a circle, examining her. "I think it's on backward."

"How can you tell?"

After squirming her arms out, Efra turned the shirt around. It looked better.

The youth's clothes were big on Efra, but passable. Nuru disappeared into the man's shirt.

In the end they settled for rolling up the sleeves and legs at the wrists and ankles. It would have to do.

And still Chisulo failed to arrive, Worry built in Nuru's gut, a tight, nauseous tension. She wanted to call this off, tear the dead man's clothes off, and climb back into the familiarity of her thobe. Everything about this was wrong. But Efra wouldn't let her. The spider wouldn't let her.

Chisulo will be all right. He has to be.

"Right, then," said Efra. "Let's go."

"Sandals," said Nuru.

A few minutes later, when they could walk without tripping, the sandals smacking the stone as they shuffled about, Efra decided they were ready. "Now?"

Nuru stopped her with a hand on the shoulder. "We look like we lost a fight."

Efra showed bloody teeth in a savage grin. "But we didn't."

AKACHI – THE STONE OF SELF-DESTRUCTION

Sin Eater ruled the pantheon for two thousand and thirteen years before her Heart's Mirror was assassinated by Loa heretics during a Crafter uprising. In the resulting seasons of wither, one fifth of Bastion's population was lost to starvation and war. For seventy-nine years the gods' Hearts battled for supremacy, with Father Death's Heart finally emerging victorious and claiming the title of Heart's Mirror. The current Heart's Mirror is the eyes and voice of The Lord. She is seven thousand six hundred and eighty-three years old.

—The Book of Bastion

Alone in his chambers, Akachi set aside the pipe, pushing it to the far corner of his desk. It rolled to one side and lay still, accusing and abandoned.

No.

He would not escape his failures by fleeing into the narcotic bliss of erlaxatu. Much as he wanted to. Such cowardice would shame him. How could he face Yejide knowing he'd abandoned his responsibility? How could he face his father?

But what could he do?

He needed to be proactive, to make things happen.

I need to find that scarred girl and the street sorcerer.

"I found them once," he whispered. "I'll find them again."

How?

He'd been dream-walking when he discovered them last time. The street sorcerer was no threat, but the scarred girl, backed by the power of a god, shattered his sorcery.

Once again, the pipe and narcotics drew his eye.

"I wasn't ready for battle."

He'd confronted them, secure in his superiority, confident his knowledge and sorcery were enough. But preparing oneself for war in a smoke reality was different than pursuing a victim and crushing an ignorant Dirt street sorcerer.

What if he tried again? What if, this time, he went in prepared for a fight? His allies, spirit animals, servants, and peyollotl charms, would serve him as well in that reality as they did here. He couldn't hope to defeat a god, but Smoking Mirror hadn't actually manifested. Father Discord remained in the Gods' Ring. Only some infinitesimal shred of his power reached out to the Growers' Ring. Now that Akachi knew what he faced, he could be ready.

He remembered sinking his teeth into the Loa sorcerer's wrist, the salty explosion of blood, the meat of her, the delicious fat. The way she gagged, trying to suck a breath past his fangs in her throat. That moment when her body gave its final twitch and stilled.

The boy in him rebelled, stomach churning at the memory. The puma animal spirit, an ally never far from his thoughts, craved flesh, revelled in the beautiful savagery of feeding.

Would that work? If he surprised the scarred girl as she surprised him, could he bite off the arm carrying Smoking Mirror's sacred mark? The more he thought about it, the more sure of success he felt. This time he would kill the lot of them in the dream world. They'd never awaken, their souls having fled. He'd have ended Smoking Mirror's madness, caught his prey as Cloud Serpent commanded.

This, he decided, was much better than escaping into the smoke of erlaxatu and abandoning his responsibilities.

Grinning with excitement, Akachi set about gathering his narcotics.

Once he had everything heaped on his desk, he sorted through it all, setting aside those he needed.

Jainkoei to open his soul to the will of Cloud Serpent. If he had more of that in his blood last time, perhaps his god's presence would have counteracted Smoking Mirror.

Aldatu, so he could access his nagual powers, become his spirit animals.

Foku to sharpen his senses so he missed nothing.

Ameslari, of course, so he could enter the dream world, bend its mutable reality to his will.

He paused to consider his choices.

It's not enough.

He'd been unprepared last time and wouldn't do that again. Another failure would be too much.

The erlaxatu drew his eye. Just one. Half a bowl.

"No."

He turned away. He wouldn't be weak. The amethyst was nothing. The stone of self-destruction carried no power. Crystal magic was a laughable farce without Mother Death's influence.

Unless I'm right, and she's inside Bastion.

It couldn't be. The gods would never allow it. No way she could penetrate the sorcery writ deep into the Sandwall. There had to be another, more sane, option.

He eyed the heaped narcotics. Was it enough?

Selecting a dose of gorgoratzen, he added it to the pile. *Don't want to forget anything.* He wanted every moment of his final victory written forever in his blood, engraved in his mind.

Pizgarri to keep me alert, to aid in concentration.

He added that too.

Those narcotics he could ingest by eating he devoured, chewing fast and hard, grinning at the foul taste. Black saliva spilled from his lips, stained his chin, and he wiped it away with a careless sleeve.

Those requiring inhalation he hurriedly ground up and crushed, heaping it together in a chaotic blend on his desk. He laughed, contemplating the apoplectic fit his teachers back at the Northern Cathedral would have at such careless handling.

It doesn't matter.

Victory, a successful hunt, was more important than suffering through what would no doubt be an epically bad comedown.

Cloud Serpent watches over me.

Shoving the blend into the bowl of his pipe, he realized there was too much. He'd have to refill the bowl three times to get it all. Lighting the pipe with a candle, he inhaled deep, holding the smoke in his lungs until the need for air forced him to exhale. Over and over, each inhalation held until the world collapsed around him.

Eyes open. Hyper-focus. Crisp clarity.

The texture of Bastion's stone screamed at him, sawed at his thoughts like a jagged knife in tender flesh. He heard Yejide's slow deep breaths from two rooms away. She slept.

I could enter her dreams.

Would she like that, or would it be an invasion?

What was she like in there? Who was the real Yejide, the one she never showed to the world?

No, he decided. He would not intrude.

He heard Njau's steady pace as the Hummingbird patrolled the church. Beyond his window the stridulating of grasshoppers changed until they sang in infinite harmonies. One hundred thousand voices, each with its own note, and he discerned them all.

After smoking the last bowl, he tossed his pipe aside and lay down on his bed. The down-filled mattress, acquired through seemingly magical means by Jumoke, floated him like soap bubbles on water.

He lay motionless, staring at the ceiling, examining the stone as he never had before. The foku brought it into impossibly sharp focus and the gorgoratzen locked it indelibly in his mind. He would remember this ceiling until he drew his last breath.

I need to relax.

His lungs and throat felt like they'd been pulled inside out and scoured by one of those sandstorms that periodically pummelled Bastion's great Sand Wall.

Dream walking was achieved through a state of detached reality, oneness with everything. Inner peace. But excitement tumbled through him. His thoughts jumped and skittered, racing from one topic to the next. The curves hidden under Captain Yejide's armour. The way she smelled. Was Nafari in Gyasi's room? Akachi's friend had been oddly quiet on his relationship with the Hummingbird, but the two were always together. Sometimes, when Captain Yejide talked, he got the feeling he was missing some deeper context. There was something in the way she looked at him. Two days ago, he would have said that she liked him, was maybe even interested in him. But after yesterday, that look had to be pity. She saw him kill and half devour a woman.

She must be disgusted.

He missed her strength and wished she was here with him. Someone to talk to. Someone to listen. The hunt. The gods. The stone of self-destruction. He coveted Nafari's easy way with women.

So alone. Such crushing responsibility. He couldn't do this. He was going to fail.

Fail his father.

Fail his god.

Fail Yejide.

Fail everyone.

Why did Cloud Serpent choose me?

The gods are at war, my Heart, Cloud Serpent said during that first vision. *My Heart.* What did that mean? Was it simply a proclamation of love? That didn't feel right. It was familiar, too. There was some mention of Hearts in the Book of Bastion, but Akachi couldn't remember it, couldn't concentrate.

If only I'd read it while dosed.

Hearts, and the Heart's Mirror. Obsidian Heart. My Heart.

His thoughts skittered and jumped back to Yejide.

Too much pizgarri, he realized. It kept him awake, stopped him from achieving the trance-state he needed to dream walk.

Again, the pipe caught his eye. Erlaxatu would counter the pizgarri, allow him to relax.

Rising, Akachi fetched his pipe and the bag of erlaxatu from his desk. Returning to the bed, he sat cross-legged to smoke.

I'm not weak. This isn't an escape. I need this.

The erlaxatu took his edges away, rounded him like the wind-worn stone of Bastion.

This isn't self-destruction. I'll find the scarred girl and the street sorcerer. I'll end this tonight. I will not fail my god.

The jainkoei peeled Akachi's soul and the searing light of the gods flayed him like a sand storm stripping flesh off a corpse.

He closed his eyes and fell into nothing.

NURU – POWER COMES WITH A PRICE

Bastion has been in a state of decay since its first day. Steps wear shallow. Hairline cracks—ignored by all—mar every surface. Millennia of wind and sand round every corner, widening windows and doors. Every year an increasing number of homes lie empty. Half the warehouse districts in the outer ring have been abandoned for centuries. The fields nearest the Sand Wall have grown wild, unchecked, for thousands of years.

The Last City of Man is dying.

—Loa Book of the Invisibles

Nuru and Efra strode hand in hand. The Crafter sandals, dangling from the loop hooked over Nuru's toe, made dry *thwack* sounds as she walked. Efra managed to be slightly quieter, but stumbled often. They headed toward the pedestrian gate in the Grey Wall. At this time of day only a few wagons, loaded with vegetables and bleating animals, were lined up at the main gate. Drying clods of ox dung, swarming with flies, littered the street. Later, under the watchful eye of the Birds, Growers would haul out wood carts to be filled with the collected dung. They were supposed to drag it all back out to the fields, but there was a surprising demand for dried shit, which could be burned for heat. Desert nights were cold, and Growers not allowed more than a single grey sheet.

A squad of Birds lounged at the gate. They watched everyone, Grower and Crafter alike, with equal suspicion.

This is stupid. It'll never work. She glanced at Efra. Her face was a mess, the flesh around her eyes and right cheek swollen.

Nuru wasn't doing much better. Her bottom lip was split, a scab forming. It felt like it might start bleeding again if she tried to talk. The only blessing was that, with her head tilted forward, the height of the sun threw her face into shadow.

"We're a mess. This will never work. We should turn back now."

"Too late," said Efra. "They've seen us."

Nuru squinted at the gate. Sure enough, the Birds were all staring at them. "Can you run?"

"In these damned sandals? No. We're going through."

As one, the Birds stood. They moved toward Nuru and Efra.

"I'll tangle them," mumbled Efra. "You run."

Nuru squeezed her hand tight. No one outran an entire squad of Birds.

The Birds jogged past the two women without so much as a glance. Looking over her shoulder, Nuru saw another Bird limping out of an alley.

"Trouble. More Birds coming."

If someone hurt a Bird, all the other Birds in the neighbourhood got together and busted heads until they found the sinner. Then they made an example out of whoever had been stupid enough to raise a hand against them. Most of the time the poor bastard never made it to a church where he might throw himself on the mercy of a nahual.

"They're distracted," said Efra. "We go now."

Dragging Nuru by the hand, she hurried them toward the gate and the lone Bird still there. The man stopped them with a raised hand, but his attention kept straying to the rest of his squad who gathered around the injured Bird.

"Did you leave any contraband behind in the Growers' Ring?" demanded the Bird. "You have in your possession all objects, artefacts, crafts, and tools you entered with?"

Nuru nodded.

The Bird took a long look at the two women, scowling when he caught sight of Nuru's face. "Did a Dirt do that?"

Nuru shook her head.

"Fucking Crafters." He turned and pounded on the pedestrian gate with his fist.

Again, checking over her shoulder, Nuru saw the injured Bird limping toward the gate. The rest of the squad sprinted off into the alley he staggered from. *Big trouble.* Something had them riled up, and an angry Bird was a violent Bird.

Something about him looks familiar.

The gate swung open just enough to allow Nuru and Efra to squeeze through and the Bird impatiently herded them on their way. On the far side she saw a long tunnel through the stone of the Grey Wall. She slowed. *I had no idea it was so deep.* She imagined the wall being a foot or two thick, maybe an entire stride, but this would take a minute to traverse at a brisk walk.

Efra pulled her forward.

The length of the tunnel, the crushing feel of being surrounded on all sides by stone, slowed Nuru. Torches hung every few paces, lighting the tunnel and staining the air with smoke. She'd seen them in churches, during rare late-night masses, and assumed they existed only there, the right of nahual. *The Birds are nahual of Southern Hummingbird,* she reminded herself. It was easy to forget the head-bashers were actually priests; they didn't act anything like the nahual of the other gods. But then those other nahual didn't worship Father War.

Two squads of Birds awaited within, one at each end of the tunnel. These looked very different from those who patrolled the Growers' Ring. Even in the smoke-filled tunnel, she saw their armour was brighter, looked better cared for.

One of the Birds stepped forward. She gave Nuru and Efra a cursory glance, tutted disapproval, and waved them toward the gates at the far end.

Nuru walked hand in hand with Efra, waiting for the inevitable command to stop.

At the far end they were met by the second squad. These barely noticed them. One opened the door to allow them through and slammed it behind them.

Both Nuru and Efra stopped. They blinked in the sun, blinding after the dark of the tunnel.

"We're in a different world," said Efra.

Looking around, Nuru agreed. Being a street sorcerer, she was accustomed to existing in different states of reality. She understood the laws governing each were different. Through the careful use of narcotics, the veil separating them could be pierced, allowing those rules to leak into her reality. But this... How could this reality exist so close to hers? She felt like, in crossing the tunnel, she walked into an altered state. Could that be true? Could the rings of Bastion be separate realities? Was there something in the smoke filling the tunnel? Her mind reeled at the implications.

Is each ring its own reality?

"I didn't know there were so many shades of brown and orange," said Efra.

The Crafters, all of them, wore those colours and only those colours. But no one ever wore both. Did that mean something? Those in brown did seem younger. After the grey of the Growers' Ring, it was staggering. Some of the women wore wrapped thobe-like sheets of orange or brown, but most wore shirts and pants. They all wore sandals like those the girls took. Crafters went about their business, the soft *thwack thwack thwack* of sandal-clad footsteps a background hum.

Outside one large open-air building, fat children herded small animals in pens or fed them grain. Carcasses of slaughtered animals hung everywhere. Nuru had never seen so much meat. Men and women worked at long tables, chopping and preparing.

The buildings were different, too. Not only were they not identical tenements—each was shaped differently depending on its purpose—but many were painted, splashed with colour. Strange lines and swirls adorned many an entranceway. The Crafters defaced Bastion!

"That's forbidden," whispered Efra.

Except clearly it wasn't. Not for the Crafters. The patrolling Birds, working singly or in pairs instead of entire squads, paid the blasphemy no mind.

The people were so different from the Growers, bigger, stronger. No one looked malnourished. Many of the elderly had paunches and moved as if they hadn't been broken by a lifetime of hard labour.

"Children," said Efra. "They're everywhere."

"The local crèche must lend them out to assist with labour."

It didn't look like most were working, however. They ran screaming and playing. They got underfoot and were ignored by the adults.

Nuru turned a full circle, trying to understand. Grower children were born in the church, taken from the woman who gave them birth, to be raised in a crèche. They lived there, working the crèche's practice fields, learning their assigned jobs, until they turned twelve. Nuru hadn't seen anyone under the age of twelve since leaving the crèche. Rumour had it the kids were always placed in districts other than the one they were born in.

"I don't see a crèche," she said.

A woman, voluptuous and soft, unlike any Grower Nuru ever saw, exited a Crafter home and collected a child, scooping him into her arms. The child babbled. Only when he called the woman Mother did Nuru understand: Crafter children were not taken at birth to be raised by the church. They were raised by their mothers, a word she barely knew, had only heard in sermons regarding Her Skirt is Stars, Precious Feather, and Mother Death. She watched in stunned silence as similar scenes played out all around her.

Tears came. She cried and she didn't know why.

Efra, unmoved by the strangeness of the Crafters, grabbed the sleeve of a passing man. "Tools," she said. "Where can we find tools?"

The man stopped, annoyed until he caught sight of her face. "Are you hurt? We should get you to a hospice."

Hospice? Nuru had no idea what that was, but it sounded bad. When Growers got hurt, they lay in their tenement. Many died, their gaunt corpses collected each morning by the nahual of The Lord, owl-feather cloaks dragging behind them with the hiss of a thousand snakes. The *Book of Bastion* said, 'Work a day, earn a day's food.' The church forbade sustenance to those who hadn't earned it. Those lucky enough to have friends to bring them food and water had some chance at recovery, but not many were willing to risk the lash.

Efra ignored his question. "Tools," she repeated. "Where?"

"Well, what kind?" He waved a hand at the street, flustered by her bluntness.

"Tools for carving stone. Paints."

He blinked at her in confusion. "You can't do both."

Efra growled. She pointed at Nuru. "She does the carving." She pointed at herself. "I do the painting."

"Oh! Sorry! I thought—never mind. Silly." The Crafter nodded at a nearby building. "That's paints for this district."

Now that she looked at it, Nuru realized the swirling symbols did kind of look like a stylized paint brush.

"For carving tools," said the Crafter, "you'll have to go to Sulaiman. He's two streets that way." He pointed deeper into the ring.

Efra nodded and set off, Nuru in tow, toward the building with the brush.

The Crafter watched them leave, a look of confusion clouding his face.

"How do we get paints?" Nuru asked Efra.

"Don't know."

They entered, Nuru marvelling that any part of Bastion could be so different from the endless tenements she knew. Where each Grower tenement had a single identical round hole in the wall to allow in light, this place had several huge square holes that let the sun fill the room. Nuru caught a glimpse of the basement as they passed the stairs. Pure white candles lit the lower level bright as day.

Glass jars of paint, sorted by hue and brightness, filled the shelves lining every wall. Nuru's glass jar, stolen hundreds of years ago and passed from sorcerer to sorcerer, was her prized possession. Or it had been, until she left it in their tenement when they fled the nahualli. The loss still pained her, but going back to get it would be stupid. There was more glass in this one building than in all the Growers' Ring.

So many colours. Nuru had never seen so much variety, didn't know that many colours existed. And yet the world of the Crafters was orange and brown. What were all these paints used for?

A woman approached, her clothes spattered in colour. "Can I help you?" She smiled, friendly and open.

No fear. No bent subservience.

"We need paint," said Efra. "And brushes." She glanced at Nuru. "For detailed work. Very small detail."

The woman nodded. "Colours?"

Efra raised a questioning eyebrow.

Nuru coughed, considered the spider with the woman's body. "I need black. Shiny black. Glistening black like a scarab."

The woman nodded again.

"I need paint that won't chip or fade." Nuru paused, waiting for the woman to complain or protest. When she didn't, the street sorcerer continued. "I need red. Dark like blood. Hints of purple."

The woman led them to an entire wall of reddish-purple paints.

Nuru searched the selection until one bottle caught her attention. She knew instantly it was the right red for the eyes. Lifting the bottle from the wall, she held it up and the woman again nodded.

Next, they were led to a wall of blacks, from matte to glossy, from hints of purple to blue to red.

"I never knew there were so many blacks," said Nuru.

The woman gave her a strange look, brows furrowing in confusion.

This time it took Nuru longer to find the perfect black. When she did, it shone and shimmered like the shell of a death scarab in the sun.

"You have scrips and permissions?" asked the woman.

"Scrips?" asked Nuru.

"To pay. And your permissions, signed by a Master Crafter and your priest."

"Of course," said Efra. "But we need brushes too."

The woman hesitated, then turned to lead them back to the front where the brushes were. As they passed the stairs to the basement, Efra grabbed her by the shirt, spun her, and sent the Crafter toppling backward with a hard shove to the chest.

"Efra!"

Ignoring Nuru, Efra followed the paint woman down. Nuru hurried after.

The woman lay bruised and groaning at the bottom. She'd hit her head, but was already regaining her wits.

Spotting a basket of dirty paint rags, Efra grabbed a fistful and stuffed them into the stunned woman's mouth. "Hold her down," she ordered Nuru. She wandered deeper into the basement, searching for something.

Nuru dropped her knees on the Crafter's shoulders, pinning her. "It's all right," she said. "We aren't going to hurt you."

The woman groaned, her eyes widening as she realized what happened. She fought, but the blow to the head left her weak. Nuru held her down.

Efra returned with a length of orange fabric. "Flip her onto her belly. It'll be easier that way."

It took both of them to roll the struggling woman.

Efra knelt on the woman's back.

"You're going to be fine," Nuru soothed, trying to reassure the Crafter. "We're just going to tie you up."

The Crafter woman whimpered in fear.

"I'll tie her feet," offered Nuru.

"Don't bother."

"But she'll be able to get up the stairs—"

Efra flipped the fabric over the woman's head, looping it around her neck. She leaned her weight back, choking the Crafter. The woman thrashed.

Nuru stared in horror, shock stalling her thoughts. *Not again.* "No!"

She grabbed Efra's shoulder, tried to drag her off the Crafter.

Efra clung tight, refusing to budge. "Quiet," she snarled through gritted teeth. "Let go of me!"

She shoved Nuru away and the Crafter drew a wheezing breath in the momentary respite. That breath choked to silence as Efra redoubled her efforts.

Less than an hour ago that had been Nuru, strangled by the big Crafter, allowed sips of breath, just enough to stop her from losing consciousness. Knowing she was dying. Helpless. Her throat ached.

"Efra, you can't do this."

Efra watched her through narrowed eyes.

"We can tie her, we don't have to kill her," pleaded Nuru.

"We do. She'll tell. Don't be stupid!"

"We'll be gone!"

"Still need tools," Efra ground out.

The Crafter kicked and bucked, almost dislodging Efra.

"Hold her legs!"

Nuru hesitated, uncertain. Efra was right, they did still need to get tools. What if the woman escaped her bonds and reported them to the Birds? They'd be waiting waiting at the gate. The nahual would torture them until they told where Chisulo and the others hid. Her friends would die. They'd all die. The nahual would bleed them on the altar. She'd never finish the spider.

"Now!" snapped Efra. "Before someone comes!"

Panicking, Nuru dropped onto the woman's legs, helping pin her.

They choked her to death.

Nuru, still raw from the dead Crafter boy and seeing children run free, cried the entire time.

After, when the tears stopped, she sat beside the corpse. Her head hurt, a pressure building behind her eyes. Balanced on an obsidian edge, she felt ready to crack. One more horror would shatter her.

What is she turning us into?

Before biting Sefu, she'd never killed anyone. Never even hurt someone. That's not the kind of person she was. Between her friends, and her reputation as a street sorcerer, people mostly left her alone. Bomani dealt with those who didn't.

Bomani.

I miss him so much. His absence was a gaping wound in the fabric of her reality.

Now, three people lay dead.

Everything she'd ever been taught, every word the nahual crushed into her since birth, every story and parable, came back to weigh upon her. She knew her place, and it wasn't here.

"I'm done," said Nuru. "No more. This... killing. The gods forbid it!"

Efra stared at her, incredulous. "How many times have you seen someone lashed to death in the public square? How many skulls have the Birds broken in the last week? How many people do you know who've been sacrificed on the altar for doing something Crafters and nahual do every day? How many penance wagons have you seen in the last month? The nahual kill. The Birds kill. And you tell me killing is forbidden? I'm done with one set of rules for them and another for us. Fuck the gods." Her words built, gaining momentum. "No one tells *me* what to do. Not anymore. If we're good Growers, we're dead Growers. That spider demon thing, it's an ally. A powerful ally. You're going to make it, and I'm going to help." She stood, hands on hips. "Now get up."

Nuru pushed herself to her feet, anger propelling her forward. "This is wrong."

"There is no such thing as wrong."

"There is! And just because the nahual spill blood, it doesn't mean we're justified in doing the same."

Efra stepped close, scar stretched in a snarl. "Yes, it fucking does. This is a fight. This is a war, just like the nahual preach about. You don't win a war by being meek and subservient and peaceful. You win a war by killing your enemy." Nuru retreated and Efra followed. "The priests are our enemies. The Bankers, the Senators, the Crafters. They're *all* our enemies. Look around you. See the way the Crafters live, how much better they have it. Food. Clothes. Tools. They even get to raise their own children!" Efra stopped, and swallowed, her eyes bright with rage and pain. "Everyone has it better than the Growers. Everyone. And they only have it good because we have it bad. When we try to change that, they will fight to stop us. All of them." She gestured at the dead Crafter woman. "What is her life worth when held against the survival of the Growers? Would you sacrifice her to save Chisulo?"

Nuru couldn't answer. There had to be a limit. At some point the price was too high. Wasn't it? "You don't understand," she said. "Power comes with a price."

"Oh, I understand," said Efra, turning away and heading up the stairs. "The nahual have the power, the Growers pay the price. It's time *they* paid."

Nuru followed her. Even here in the Crafters' Ring the steps were worn shallow by the feet of thousands of generations.

She's too quick to violence, too sure of her reasons. Nuru's own doubts weren't gone, far from it. *I have to control her. She's dangerous.* But Nuru needed her. What made Efra dangerous made her useful. No one else would have dared this mad dash into the Crafters' Ring.

Smoking Mirror chose her. There had to be a reason. Or was that it? What if the god chose her because she could kill without hesitation? What did that mean for what was to come? Did the god see a future where Efra's willingness to violence was advantageous, where it was necessary?

I can stop her from killing again. I'll be ready.

And maybe Efra was right, at least in part. Maybe war was the only way. After all, Nuru became a street sorcerer because she wanted power, because she wanted some shred of control. That Cloud Serpent nahualli wandered into the smoke-world she created for her friends and took over. She was nothing. He crushed her will, commanded her to be still, and she obeyed.

Never again. The next time she met that priest, things would end differently.

Maybe there was no such thing as *wrong,* just like Efra said. The pounding of the drums, the whip, fear of sacrifice, and the promise of being reborn closer to the gods in the next life. Maybe all these things were a means to an end: Control. Maybe teaching Growers of right and wrong was a way to get them to imprison themselves.

What about Chisulo? They followed him, at least in part, because he had such a clear idea of what was right. He never bowed, never bent. You could trust him. *If Efra is right, what does that make Chisulo? A fool?* And what did that make Nuru and her friends for following him?

I didn't follow Chisulo here, I followed Efra.

Here they were, in the Crafters' Ring, where no Grower had ever gone before. Either it would change everything, or get them both killed.

Bruised and beaten as Efra was, Nuru couldn't imagine anything killing the girl.

Back in the street, surrounded by bustling life, the murder felt unreal. A nightmare. Tremors of horror ran through Nuru and she wasn't sure if she wanted to vomit or cry. It felt like the after-effects of badly blended narcotics. Her stomach twisted and the world seemed too bright, too crisp to be real.

A man made to pass them, to enter the painter's abode.

Efra stopped him with a hand on his chest. "She's busy," she said.

He glanced at the sun, high above. "An early lunch?"

"Yes," said Efra.

After he wandered away, Nuru asked, "What's *lunch*?"

Efra shrugged, grabbed Nuru's hand, and set off.

Crafters, in their infinite shades of brown and orange, crammed the streets, hustling about their inexplicable business. She let it distract her. Anything was better than thinking about the people she helped kill.

Allowing Efra to pull her through the streets, she saw an entire block of buildings with freshly slaughtered animals displayed in the windows. Hanging upside down, flesh and fur removed, they looked cold. The dead Crafter woman lying among her beautiful paints, she too would grow cold like this. Nuru imagined her hanging alongside the rabbits and goats.

The buildings of the next street were all open to the air, lacked front walls of any kind. Huge wood tables sat in front of each. Lumps of pink and brown covered the tables, swarmed with fat green flies. A wagon with a squad of six disinterested looking Birds stood nearby. Crafters scooped stuff from the table, tossing it into the back of the wagon. A strangely familiar scent, sour and staining the back of her throat, reminded Nuru of meal time back in the crèche.

She remembered finding a dead rabbit in the field she'd been assigned to work as a child. Nuru, Chisulo, Happy, Bomani, and Omari had already fallen in together, formed a tight-knit group. They skinned the little corpse, impaled it on a stick, and cooked it over an open fire. It was half burnt, and half raw when they ate it, and she would never forget the flavour. When the crèche nahual, snake spines woven into her hair and robes, caught them, Bomani took the blame. He said it was his idea, that he cooked it and bullied the others into eating it with him. The priest dragged the boy into the crèche courtyard and whipped him bloody before all the gathered children. Bomani lost consciousness before he made a sound. Not one whimper. When he woke, he grinned at his friends. Even at eight years old he was the craziest Grower she ever met.

I'm going to cry again. "The flies are beautiful," she said.

Efra glanced at the tables. "That's meat," she said. "They're loading a wagon to take it to the Growers." She pointed out another area where Crafters carefully wrapped meat in brown paper. "That one is bound for the inner rings."

Huge roasts. Entire legs of lamb. Strips of strange meat, salted and left in the sun. Tubes of bright pink, joined together, made long chains. Nuru had never seen so many different kinds of meat before. Strips of chewy goat were all that ever made it to the Growers.

A second group loaded each package into another wagon. They worked with exaggerated care. A single Bird loitered at this wagon, watching.

At another building across the street, a Crafter woman approached one of the open tables. She handed something to the man at the table and pointed out a slab of red meat. The man wrapped it in the brown paper and gave it to her. She wandered off like it was nothing. No one stopped her. The Birds in the area didn't even notice.

I want meat. I want rabbit again.

Efra pulled her into another street. A train of wagons, some loaded with brightly coloured fabrics, some bearing what looked like complete suits of Bird armour, rumbled past. Once again, a single Bird travelled with the wagon.

They don't fear the Crafters. She couldn't imagine why not. The Growers had nothing, while the Crafters could make their own weapons and armour. Glancing around, she realized none of the Crafters were armed. None even carried the tools of their trade unless they were actively working on something. Were they not allowed to remove the tools from where they worked? Even here, she realized, there were subtle levels of control.

The crèche nahual's sermons on Bastion returned to her. One hundred and seventy thousand strides between the Sand Wall and the Grey

Wall. Only fifty-six thousand strides lay between the Grey Wall and the Wall of Lords which separated the Crafters from the Senators' Ring. Half expecting to see the Wall of Lords from here, she looked west. Heat hazed the distance, made it wobbly as if she'd eaten ameslari fungus. She saw nothing of the wall separating the Growers and the Senators. The scale of Bastion made comprehension impossible.

Turning away, Nuru studied the Crafters. Now that she paid attention, she saw the dashed looks of concealed hate and loathing as Bird-guarded wagons wended their way to the Senators' Ring. The brightest fabrics. The choicest cuts of meat. Nuru understood. The Crafters made everything that fed and clothed all of Bastion, but the best of their efforts were taken inward.

So dazzled by their myriad shades of orange and brown, she hadn't considered why they didn't wear other colours. *Like us, they have no choice.*

They ate better. They had better clothes. They were, apparently, allowed to raise their own children, a concept so strange Nuru couldn't wrap her head around it. They had access to tools, at least with permission from a priest and scrip—whatever that was. Though looking around, that permission was clearly given freely. And yet discontent simmered beneath the surface. She couldn't understand why. *They have so much more.*

The Crafters' Ring seemed like a dream-world, a vision in a narcotic-induced hallucination. She wanted to grab one of the many fat, soft women, shake her, and scream, 'You still have your baby!'

She wanted to wreck it all, bring down the Grey Wall and show the Crafters how good they had it.

That's not me. I'm not like that.

AKACH – HE SPOKE IN DUST AND BONES

Obsidian is a stone of souls. Each life an obsidian edge takes is trapped within. The souls are the smoke in the glass.

Before a sacrificial dagger is bequeathed to a nahual, it must be brought to the Gods' Ring to be exorcised of souls lest it become too stained with death. Upon the death of that priest, the dagger must once again make its journey to the gods to be cleansed.

—The Book of Bastion

Akachi stood in the grand hall of the Northern Cathedral. Pillars, ornate swirls of stone twisting like tortured snakes, reached up to support the arched ceiling fifty strides above. All part of Bastion. All part of that one flawless stone comprising the entire city. Row upon row of stone pews faced the grand altar at the head of the hall. Every day, thousands of nahual from every sect gathered here to listen to Bishop Zalika's sermons. As an acolyte he'd often smuggled in a small cushion to sit on. While the awe of those early days was gone, murdered by the contempt of familiarity, he still felt some thrill at being here again. This hall was for the nahual. The only Growers who ever saw the inside of the Cathedral were those about to be sacrificed to the gods. He couldn't remember how many live sacrifice lectures he'd sat through, the guilty party strapped to an altar in front of the class, gagged and restrained, while the nahual talked through the finer details of the art.

Art. The memory of the Grower he sacrificed in his church, haunted him. The look in the man's eyes as he realized he would not escape, that there would be no tomorrow. The way that looked changed as the blood drained away and the doors to Father Death's underworld opened before him.

A cold wind blew through Akachi's robes, raising goosebumps. Turning, he saw a door at the far end of the hall that he didn't remember.

Not in the Northern Cathedral, he reminded himself.

'The dream world has its own logic,' one of his teachers once said. 'You must listen. What you see is not what is. The truth often lies buried in symbolism.'

Approaching the door, he saw stairs spiralling down into darkness.

The scarred girl isn't down there. She couldn't be. They were a day's walk from the Wheat District. Why had his allies in the smoke brought him here? Was there something Cloud Serpent wanted him to see, or were other forces at work? What if a Loa sorcerer had penetrated Akachi's dream? This could be a trap.

What if the trap is one of your own creation? What if you've been betrayed by your own thoughts and the influence of the stone of self-destruction?

No. The amethyst was powerless without Mother Death's influence and she remained beyond the Sand Wall as she had for a tens of thousands of years.

You don't believe that. The Loa assassin had power.

Come, the door seemed to tease, *or are you a coward?*

Akachi descended the steps, down, down.

Hours passed.

Ever deeper.

Days.

The air grew cold and Akachi huddled in his robes.

Hunger and thirst came and passed.

Years.

The flesh melted from him, decaying and peeling away to expose the muscle below. That muscle rotted and ran off him in vile white streams of putrescence. His eyes dried up and fell from their sockets like raisins. His brain putrefied and leaked from his skull, and still he descended deeper.

Centuries.

By the time he reached the first floor, he was bone, a skeleton held together by gristle and a fraying will power. Though he had no eyes he saw the world in a smear of grey. Though he had no ears he heard the hollow *tock tock* of his bone feet on stone.

A colossal chamber opened before him. Hundreds of lit torches lined the walls, giving off a harsh white light. Tens of thousands of statues stood scattered chaotically about the room. Those closest to him were crisp and detailed, the work of masterful artistry. Those further away became crude, the work of savages and madmen. Some he recognized. Smoking Mirror, a twelve-foot-tall monolith of jagged obsidian. The coiled rattlesnake statue of Feathered Serpent stood three times Akachi's height, feathers cresting its rearing head. Southern Hummingbird, constructed of many types of stone somehow fused together, showed a warrior decorated in bright green jade feathers wielding a curved snake like a weapon and clutching an obsidian mirror in his other hand. It looked like it might suddenly burst into action.

Akachi wended his way through the statues, brushing stone with bone fingers, as he passed. With each contact he felt a dizzying flash and saw the gods as they were, ancient and selfish, wrapped in jealousy. They craved worship, begged for his attention. He continued deeper into the chamber.

He walked for days, touching statues and dreaming their forgotten pasts.

He saw the statue of a bearded man with black hair whose name was something like Lord of Ghosts and who claimed to be the Father of Gods. Having heard so many similar claims, Akachi moved on.

A two-sided statue, a beautiful woman on one side, the other a terrible monster, she wore snake scales like a tight-fitting dress. She was ancient, gave birth to monsters and gods.

The King of Gods. The Mother of Gods. She Who Birthed the World. A thousand gods, a thousand grand claims.

Some gods were horrors, tentacled and insane, nightmares carved in stone. Most were men and women. Many could have walked the streets of Bastion without drawing attention beyond their strange garb.

They made us in their image.

And yet a thousand gods claimed to have made man. They couldn't all speak truth.

Over and over he saw the same gods, twisted, changed in some way, but sharing aspects of others he'd seen. Sometimes they had more or less less limbs or eyes. Sometimes crows rode their shoulders or hawks. Sometimes wolves followed along behind them, sometimes jaguars or bears. Yet they always shared features, boasted the same achievements.

And there, at the far end of the Hall of Gods, standing before a set of stairs descending even deeper, was the last god, carved in red and black hematite.

Akachi approached, reached tentative fingers of bone toward her.

Chandraghanta. Ambika. Kālikā. The Fullnes of Time. Sekhmet. Kālarātri.

The Destroyer.

She Who Ends the Universe so it May Be Reborn.

Mother Death.

She was beyond beautiful. Blue-black skin and eyes of midnight, each with a star trapped within. Sometimes she had four arms, sometimes as many as ten. He couldn't focus, couldn't make her be one thing. But she was always voluptuous, always curved and proud.

She looks no older than I.

Akachi's thoughts reeled. What was this place? What did it mean?

Some of these gods he knew. Others he recognized as being trapped beyond the Sand Wall, demons haunting the Bloody Desert. Yet each time he touched a statue, he knew something of them. Did that mean some aspect of each god still resided within Bastion? Was this how the Loa assassin was able to use crystal magic?

This is the dream world. I'm not in Bastion. Not really.

Was Mother Death guarding the stairs?

No, that felt wrong. Had she been placed there as a mockery?

Mother Death seemed to wink at him as he moved beyond her to the waiting stairs.

Akachi descended deeper.

Forever down. Deeper into the rank guts of a dead world.

Thought became anathema to existence.

Contemplation eroded sanity.

Empty.

One calcifying bone foot in front of the other. Ever down.

Akachi stood blinking at a purple sun for years before some semblance of self returned.

This is the underworld, the land of the dead.

He'd descended into Father Death's domain.

He remembered when he first came to the Northern Cathedral, how he'd half believed The Lord and all his lands existed beneath the great church.

Standing atop a hill, a scene of unspeakable war greeted him.

Millions upon millions of dead fought, seething against each other in colossal armies. Mountains roared across the twisted landscape, crashing into each other like warring elephants. Rivers of blood, thick with corpses both fresh and decayed, swept past. Prides of black jaguars prowled the landscape, bringing down their prey. They dragged the corpses to the shores to be tossed in the red rivers. A searing wind whipped shards of obsidian in flesh-shredding tornadoes, flaying the dead. A cacophony of screams struck Akachi with concussive force, staggering him.

This isn't right.

This was supposed to be a place of respite. Father Death purified souls, prepared them for rebirth. The Lord was under attack.

A host of Loa sorcerers, armed with hematite weapons, fists gripping strange crystalline stones, cut through a phalanx of nahualli armed with obsidian swords, dressed in stone armour of jade.

Southern Hummingbird has sent her elite to aid The Lord.

He saw men and women he knew. The nahual who taught him how to achieve the pactonal trance state. The man died of old age in Akachi's third year as an acolyte. The old woman who'd been his nanny when he was a child fought alongside the shambling corpse of a Hummingbird Guard. He saw Talimba, Lutalo, and Khadija battling back to back, surrounded by Loa.

He saw the beautiful Loa assassin with the brilliant eyes. She glowed bright. A thousand stones, sunk into her flesh, throbbed with vile sorcery. She wielded their power, crushing her enemies. Magical shields blazed around her, deflecting both physical and sorcerous attacks. She spread madness like a plague. Temple-trained nahualli tore their own eyes and tongues out in an effort to escape. With a stone embedded between her perfect thighs she summoned monsters and nightmares, demons and myths. The stones burned hot, cooking her flesh, but a garnet sunk between her breasts healed those wounds in an instant. The hand Akachi had bitten off remained missing, the wrist an ever-bleeding wound.

The gathered hosts were nothing before her.

She turned them against each other, spread chaos wherever those bright eyes looked.

This isn't real. The Loa aren't attacking the underworld.

It couldn't be real.

Oh gods, the drugs. He'd taken no precautions, mixed them with no thought to how they might interact. He was trapped here in this nightmare. He tried to remember his descent to the underworld. How long had it taken? Thousands of years? Longer? How long before the drugs wore off?

Or had he brain-burned?

Was this what it was like for those drug-addled nahualli the acolytes cared for? Did they stumble through their days deaf to the real world, trapped in imagined hells?

What if this never ends?

What if it was real?

How much time had passed in the real world? Minutes? Hours? Was Captain Yejide standing over his comatose body at this very moment?

Wake up!

"Wake up!" he screamed, his voice disappearing as if devoured by sand.

A seething flock of owls and bats, draped in thick spiderwebs and crawling with spiders, flew down out of the north. Arriving at the scene of battle, they coalesced into a giant of a man, stripped of flesh, bones red with blood and shreds of raw meat. He wore a cloak of owl feathers draped over his vast shoulders and a necklace of eyeballs that seemed to see everything.

Awe staggered Akachi to his knees.

The Lord has come!

The pitiful Loa were doomed. Their attack on Father Death's domain seemed laughable now that the god had arrived.

The Lord towered over the girl with the bright eyes.

"Your mistress is banished. Why have you woken me from my slumber." He spoke in dust and bones.

The girl laughed, mocking. "She was right, you are a fool."

With a wave of Father Death's hand, the Loa sorcerers fell to ash, their souls snuffed. Only the girl remained, surrounded by the countless millions of The Lord's dead. She stood proud and beautiful, stones melded into her flawless flesh, curved and perfect. Unafraid.

She grinned. "We *wanted* you to come."

The god hesitated. "Wanted?"

"In the Gods' Ring the others might fight at your side. Here you're alone."

Father Death's own dead attacked him and Akachi understood. The same stone she'd used to make him fall in love with her when first they met, had been used to enslave the dead of the underworld. The battle had been a farce, a lure to bring The Lord from the Gods' Ring. The dead mobbed him, tearing Father Death apart, breaking his bones and grinding them to dust in their teeth. Southern Hummingbird's elite with their ancient obsidian swords cut his legs out from under him. They hacked him into smaller and smaller pieces and the other dead fed on him.

Akachi knelt, transfixed, until the god was gone.

This isn't real. I didn't just witness the death of a god.

Then, the girl with the bright eyes saw him and he loved her. Dark and twisted, it was a love that left no room for self.

"I'd cut myself a thousand times before I hurt you," he told her.

Endless aeons of dead worshipped her and she became the newest of Bastion's patchwork pantheon. She became Face Painted with Bells, Mother Death's beloved daughter.

Akachi retched, vomiting up partially chewed mushrooms and the last dregs of whatever he ate for dinner. His stomach twisted and heaved until there was nothing left in him, until he felt like he'd spewed his internal organs onto the floor. Dry tearing sobs wrenched from his smoke-tortured throat and he coughed thin yellow drool into the puddle of hot vomit. Tears ran from stinging eyes, blurring the world. The morning sun screamed through the window, sawed at his thoughts, bathed him in sour sweat.

Hawking and spitting the last of the bile, he wiped feebly at his chin and crawled to the darkest corner of his chambers to curl up on the floor. Shivers racked his body, contorting him in muscle-clenching spasms.

He was colder than he'd ever been.

Not real. Not real. Not real.

Everything he'd seen had been a fever dream, the result of the unbalanced narcotics he'd so carelessly ingested.

Still think the amethyst had no power? He cackled mad laughter at the thought.

He'd taken in an obscene quantity of narcotics, given no thought as to how they might interact, and then smoked a bowlful of eraxatu. He was lucky he wasn't in a damned coma or a brain-burned husk!

What was I thinking?

The scarred girl. The street sorcerer.

Making his father and his god proud.

Making Yejide proud.

I failed. Again.

It was too much. He couldn't face her like this. She'd see his weakness. She'd know him for a failure.

Crawling to the bed, Akachi dragged the sheets off to hide the vomit on the floor. They stank of rank sweat. Jumoke would clean up. He trusted the boy not to speak of this.

Pushing to his feet, he stood, limbs shaking, feeling like he'd collapse to the ground at any moment.

I can't face her like this.

Collecting the erlaxatu and his pipe, still filled with the ash of the last bowl he smoked, he retreated to the bed. The shivers faded after the first bowl. After the second he could stand steadily. A tiny dose of pizgarri woke him up enough he could function. The world became sharp-edged and harsh with detail. A small amount of Kognizioa kept his thoughts from stumbling over each other and becoming tangled.

Half an hour and another pipe of erlaxatu later, he felt something approaching normal. His eyes no longer stung, and the pain in his skull faded to a background throb.

That wasn't real.

He'd simply bungled his narcotics and paid the price. He was lucky it hadn't been worse.

NURU – A WORLD OF STONE AND SAND

Located next to the gods, the priests are responsible for interpreting their will. While the Senators provide law, and the Bankers economics, the word of the nahual is final. To them falls the care of each and every soul in Bastion. Without nahual, chaos would rule and the city would crumble. It is only by the grace of the gods that humanity survived the Last War. In all things we must bow to their will and wisdom.

—The Book of Bastion

Carrying a collection of obsidian-tipped carving tools in a small and intricately carved wood box with leather hinges, Nuru and Efra left the tool-maker. The box fit in the pocket of Nuru's Crafter shirt. The Crafter lay in a back room in a growing pool of blood, throat cut by one of his own tools when Nuru's back was turned. Efra wanted to search the building for obsidian in fragments large enough to be used as a weapon, but Nuru, terrified of being caught, hurried them out. After that, they found a woman who stocked orange and brown clothes. They left the woman dead in the basement, skull smashed while Nuru was searching for a shirt large enough for Happy.

Nuru walked in a stunned daze, appalled at what they'd done. She cried after killing Sefu, spent the night hating herself for taking a life.

That was nothing. She'd played a part in murdering five people in a single day. It didn't matter that Efra had done the killing; somehow, Nuru should have stopped her.

She planned this.

From the very beginning Efra knew she was going to kill these Crafters and hid it from Nuru. She'd lied, shrugged away Nuru's concerns of violence like they were nothing.

But now they had the tools, the paints, and Crafter clothes for their friends. Could they have done with without killing anyone? They'd spent the entire day at this. What if someone got loose and reported them?

She did what she had to do to guarantee our success. Nuru thought it over. *I would have got in the way. My unwillingness to kill might have jeopardized everything.*

She loathed herself for justifying Efra's actions.

Efra said that they were at war, and that the only way to win a war was by killing your enemy. Was that true?

The carving. Was it really that important? Was it worth five lives?

She glanced at Efra. The girl seemed unaffected by the violence.

How did she do it?

Smoking Mirror talks to her, shows her things.

Had Efra seen something so terrible it justified her actions? Was that even possible?

The day died, the sun sinking low. Soon it would be cold and dark. They got lost several times while tracking down everything they needed and Efra pointed out the few abandoned buildings she saw. There weren't nearly as many as in the Growers' Ring, at least not in this district, but there were plenty to choose from.

"Crafters never enter the Growers' Ring at night," Efra said.

"No?" Nuru didn't feel like talking.

"We'll stay in one of the abandoned buildings I saw, go home in the morning."

"Hungry," said Nuru. She couldn't remember the last time she ate.

"Me too, but every time a Crafter gets food they hand over something. We don't have whatever it is. If we get food, we'll have to kill the Crafter."

"Not hungry anymore." *I will not murder someone so I can have a crust of bread.*

The Crafter tenement was strange. It smelled different from the Grower homes she was accustomed to, spicy and sharp. There were four bedrooms instead of the usual two, and all of the rooms were much bigger. At least Nuru assumed they were bedrooms. She couldn't imagine what else the empty space could be used for. What would have been the eating room in the Growers' Ring, included rows of shelving here, and stone counters as well as the usual table. Even that table was different, twice the size of the ones she knew. What did they keep here? Did they own things beyond their clothes and sandals? Why keep it in the eating room? Did Crafters prepare their own meals instead of eating whatever they were given at The Provider's church?

The floor around the table was scuffed in oddly parallel lines and she understood. Chairs. The Crafters sat on real chairs when they took their meals. The luxury staggered her.

The big Crafter they killed had a room in the Growers' Ring with a mattress, and soft fabrics. She'd been so stunned at the time it hadn't really sunk in. Was that commonplace for all Crafters? Did all their beds have mattresses? Were all their eating tables surrounded by real chairs? She wanted to go in search of an inhabited Crafter home, see how they lived.

That night Nuru sat staring into the dark, unable to sleep. She couldn't get the dead out of her mind. She kept seeing them. Empty eyes, slack faces. She imagined the way they fought, the way they clung to life as Efra choked it from them or hammered at their skulls with whatever blunt object came to hand. She saw the blood.

Tears came and she shook, sobbing.

Efra examined her, eyes two sparks in the night. "They had to die," she said.

Nuru laughed without humour and turned away.

The next morning, as the sun crested the eastern horizon lighting the world in blood, they left for the Grey Wall. Efra talked about small nothings. What she was going to eat when she got home. How she looked forward to kicking Chisulo's ass for abandoning them. Maybe Omari had awoken and they could all come to the Crafters' Ring.

She acts like nothing happened. Nuru fingered the wood box in her pocket.

"I've never seen so much finely crafted, perfectly edged obsidian before," said Efra.

Nuru said nothing.

"I saw a nahual's dagger once, at a public sacrifice. Can't remember what the Grower did, but it angered the Birds something fierce. They'd beaten him bloody already. I think, by that point, cutting his throat was a mercy."

Nuru grunted.

A pair of Birds passed.

"Notice how the Birds in the Growers' Ring only have cudgels?" said Efra. "They have obsidian knives here."

Why here? Were the Birds more afraid of Crafters than they were of Growers? Seeing as the Crafters made all the weapons and armour for the Birds, they could, Nuru supposed, decide to keep some for themselves.

Efra definitely would.

"We had to kill them." Efra said, darting a concerned look at Nuru, measuring her response. "Never leave someone behind who might later make things difficult."

"Difficult," said Nuru. "We're leaving the ring. What could they have done? We could have tied them up. We didn't have to—"

"You would risk our lives—Chisulo, Happy, and Omari's lives—for some *Crafter*? They're not one of us."

"We can't kill everyone."

"We can. The rings will be at war. Growers are unarmed, uneducated, and taught subservience from birth. We're going to die, a lot of us." She glared at Nuru. "You want to keep your friends alive? Be ready to kill whoever gets in our way. Don't hesitate. It's us against them, and they have all the weapons."

"You're crazy."

Efra laughed at that, unhurt by the harsh words. "I'm the kind of crazy that will get us through this."

"Chisulo isn't like that. He won't just kill."

"He will if you tell him to."

Nuru sagged. *She's right.* Chisulo would do whatever she suggested. His charisma and reputation led the gang, but as often as not it was her decisions that everyone followed. Decisions like sending Bomani to spy on Fadil when Omari would have been a smarter choice. Hell, even Efra would have been better.

"I can't do it anymore," said Nuru, hating the pleading weakness in her voice. "Too many people have already died because of me. This is *wrong*."

"Wrong," said Efra, mocking. "Pull it together, we're almost at the wall."

The Birds outside the gate waved them into the Grey Wall with a cursory glance and no real interest.

Nuru squinted in the murky torch light. Smoke stung her eyes.

Only a couple of the torches had been lit, and a Bird was in the process of lighting the rest. It was dark and cold within the wall.

The guards on the Crafter side nodded to them as they passed. Hand in hand, Efra and Nuru walked the length of the tunnel.

The squad at the Grower's side watched their approach.

"Good day, Crafters," said a woman.

"Good day," said Nuru, voice tight.

"Business in the Growers' Ring?"

A flash of panic swept through her. What business did Crafters ever have with the Growers? Sometimes she saw them inspecting wagons, and if a wheel ever broke, several came through to fix it. Otherwise, as far as she knew, they only ever came to fuck Growers. Was that something you could say?

"For fun," blurted Efra. "We heard about a Grower with a huge cock." She giggled. "A Grower with a grower!"

The Bird grunted, clearly unimpressed. "Search them."

"Yes, Captain," chorused two Birds, stepping forward.

Was this normal? The Birds hadn't paid much attention to them when they left the Growers' Ring. Were they more anxious about Crafters *entering* the outer ring? It made some sense. Tools must be closely monitored. *Don't want the Growers getting anything dangerous or useful.*

"Captain," said the Bird searching Nuru. "Found something." Pulling the wood box from her pocket, he opened it and displayed the carving tools and brushes within.

This couldn't be happening, couldn't be real.

Bastion wanted me to have these tools.

It couldn't end like this.

She was a fool. The Birds, nahual of Southern Hummingbird, were closer to the gods, more a part of the great city than any filthy Dirt could ever dream to be. She'd been lying to herself, pretending this might end in some way other than death on the altar.

The one searching Efra found the paints and the extra Crafter clothes.

The Captain turned back to Nuru. "Take them."

An instant of terror ran through her, the need to flee. Inside the wall, a squad of Birds at each exit, there was no escape.

She darted a nervous glance at Efra. Would she try and fight her way free, kill a dozen Birds on her way out?

Efra collapsed to her knees, hid her face in her hands and sobbed.

It's an act, Nuru realized.

Two of the Birds grabbed Nuru, one on each side, fingers like talons digging into her. Two more hooked hands under Efra's arms and lifted her. She hung limp, letting them take her weight.

"The sentence for smuggling tools into the Growers' Ring," said the Captain, "is to be cast from the wall." They started carrying the girls back toward the Crafters' Ring.

Terror surged through Nuru. *I don't want to die in the Crafters' Ring!* At least in the Growers' Ring there was some chance, no matter how slim, of escape.

"No!" said Nuru. "We're Growers."

That stopped everything.

"Impossible," said the Captain.

"It's true. We're from the Wheat District," said Efra.

One of the Birds raised a torch and the squad gathered around to examine them.

"Let's see the bottoms of your feet," commanded the Captain.

Nuru kicked off one of the awkward sandals and showed the callused and scarred sole of her foot.

"Well I'll be thrown from the wall," said the Captain. She glanced back toward the gate into the Wheat District. "Bring them."

The Birds carried the two women back to their home ring. The guards outside turned in surprise as those escorting Efra and Nuru pushed them, blinking, into the morning sun.

For the first time, the lack of colour struck Nuru as strange. Theirs was a world of stone and sand, grey and red.

It's intentional. It's control.

"Captain Dziko," said a small, mean looking man with a big nose and an angry mouth.

"Tariq," the Captain answered with ill-concealed distaste.

"Who are these two?"

The Captain gestured at Nuru. "Growers, apparently."

The man scowled at the girls. "No. No way a Dirt was in the Crafters' Ring."

"They say they're from the Wheat District. They must have come through *your* gate."

Tariq looked ill.

The Captain displayed the tools and paints. "And they stole these," she said. "What's the nearest parish?"

"Cloud Serpent. New nahual—"

The Captain lifted a hand, silencing him. "Send two of your men to fetch the nahual."

"No need," said Tariq. "One of the Guard assigned to him is camped out in a Grower hovel across the street."

The woman glanced at the endless rows of tenements. "Poor bastard. He must have really pissed off the nahual."

All the Birds nodded in commiseration.

"He's an alright sort," said Tariq. "Funny, too. One time he said he caught two Dirts fucking during a sermon. They were doing it standing, and—"

"Not interested," snapped Captain Dziko.

Tariq shrugged like it was her loss. "Wambua, go get Sulo, you lazy Dirt-fucker."

The Bird shot him a look of purest hate and departed for the nearby tenements.

Tariq, watching him leave, muttered, "Stupid cunt," loud enough for everyone to hear.

The other Birds laughed or smirked, except for the Captain.

It never occurred to Nuru that there might be tensions and division within the Birds. They always presented as united in front of the Growers.

They know we're going to die, cast from the Sand Wall. The thought tore an odd mix of emotions from her. Fear, and a longing to see what the world looked like from atop the tallest wall.

Beyond the Sand Wall, endless desert. A dead world. She couldn't comprehend the scale. Bastion was huge, it was everything, everywhere. As a child she dreamed of walking beyond the walls, of the freedom. *You'll get your chance.* It was, however, unlikely she'd survive the fall. She'd heard sermons about the few who did. Inevitably they lay wounded and screaming in the red sand. Few lasted more than a day. Heat and dehydration took everyone.

Nuru stifled a laugh. *For the few heartbeats it takes to fall, I'll be free.* The nearest Bird elbowed her in the gut. She doubled over and crumpled, wheezing, to her knees.

"Here he comes," said Tariq.

Eyes watering, Nuru heard the gritty sound of sandals on stone as Wambua brought the other Bird over to the squad.

"Sulo," said Tariq. "We caught that scarred Dirt cunt you've been looking for. You didn't mention that the other one was such a stunning piece of slash. Keeping her for yourself, are you?"

"Get her up."

Nuru lifted her head. *I know that voice.* She stared, uncomprehending, at Chisulo. He wore the red leather armour of a Bird, right down to the strapped sandals. A cudgel hung at his hip. Never before had she been so happy to see a squished nose. She bared her teeth at him in a snarl to cover her surprise.

"Dirt cunt knows you," said Tariq.

"Use that word again," said Captain Dziko, "and I'll cut you one of your own."

Tariq swallowed, muttered something that might have been 'sorry' and stared at the ground. His face flushed red.

"I'll take them back to the church," said Chisulo. "I'll need those tools, too" he added, speaking to the Bird holding them. "The nahual wants to see what they went to collect."

The Bird handed them over without question.

"What would Dirts do with tools anyway?" asked Tariq. "They're too stupid to use them."

Chisulo gave a shrug that somehow said, *Not my place to question.* "Let's get moving," he said, turning to Nuru and Efra.

"Alone?" asked the Captain.

Chisulo made a show of examining the girls. "Bind their wrists. Two little Dirt girls won't give me any trouble."

"Didn't you hear?" asked Tariq. "Dirts dragged a member of the Guard into a tenement basement and beat him to death. Cracked his head."

A look of guilt crossed Chisulo's face and was covered by a growl of anger.

"I'll walk back with you," said the Captain.

"Should I come too?" volunteered another Bird.

She flashed him an annoyed look and suddenly everyone was binding Nuru and Efra's hands. It was weird, because it really shouldn't have taken that many of them, but no one wanted to look like they weren't busy. Even Tariq made a show of overseeing things, offering pointless suggestions and advice.

"Umm," said Chisulo when they finished.

"Lead the way," said the Captain, gesturing toward the Wheat District.

Pushing Nuru and Efra out in front, Chisulo set off. He walked slowly, limping slightly. The woman matched his pace, looking calm and comfortable.

"My name is Dziko," said the Captain, once they left the other Birds behind. She walked so close to Chisulo their shoulders touched. Efra glared death at the Bird like she wanted to kill her.

"Sulo," said Chisulo.

"You're with the nahual in that reopened church of Cloud Serpent?"

He nodded.

"Whose porridge did you shit in to get that posting?"

He coughed a sputter of laughter. "More than one." He had that easy grin in place.

Efra, jaw clenched, eyes blazing hate, looked like she wanted to strangle the woman and hadn't yet decided what she'd do to Chisulo. It wouldn't be pleasant.

Nuru listened as Chisulo and the Captain blathered on like they didn't have a care in the world. The Bird bitch kept touching him, a hand on his shoulder as she laughed at some stupid joke. She even said how much she liked his shaved head and ran a hand over his stubbled scalp.

He doesn't have a plan, Nuru realized with a start. *He's stalling.* What did he think was going to happen? The church wasn't that far. Half an hour at most.

"What's the young nahual like?" Dziko asked.

"He's all right."

"Maybe after," Dziko said, "you and I—"

"I have to pee," said Nuru.

"And I'm going to puke if I have to listen to you two flirt," added Efra.

Everyone stopped, turning to stare at her.

"What?" she demanded. "Just fuck already. Look." Hands bound behind her, she gestured to the nearest tenement with her nose. "In you go. Have a fast one—I can't imagine him being capable of much else— and we'll wait out here."

"The stupidity of Dirts," said Captain Dziko, "never ceases to amaze me."

"I'm going to piss myself," said Nuru. "Please, just let me go inside. Pick the building. Come in and watch. I don't care. Just let me pee!"

Dziko glanced at Chisulo.

"I don't want to spend the next half hour with a whining Dirt who stinks of piss," he said.

"Fine," said Dziko. Picking an abandoned tenement, she pushed Nuru toward the entrance.

"We'll come too," said Chisulo, shoving Efra in front of him. "Just in case they've somehow set a trap or there's someone inside."

Dziko slid her cudgel from its loop in her belt and held it ready. Chisulo drew his too, though he looked a lot less comfortable with it. Dried blood and hair matted the end. Keeping Efra before him, just like a paranoid Bird would, they followed Nuru and Dziko into the tenement.

Dziko slowed, looking around.

"Never been in a Dirt tenement before?" Chisulo asked.

Efra rolled her eyes.

"No," said Dziko. "Never been in this ring before. I work the tunnel through the Grey Wall. Entire days where I don't see the sun."

"The waste room is in the back," said Chisulo, as if giving a tour. "They shit into a hole in the ground. They're supposed to throw food waste in there too, but they're too damned lazy."

You're a little too good at this. Did Chisulo enjoy being a Bird?

As the Captain turned away, he pushed Efra aside and stepped forward, cudgel rising, ready to strike Dziko from behind. The Captain spun away from his attack, her own cudgel held at the ready.

"You have to watch your shadow," she said. "You were back lit."

Chisulo advanced.

"Loa assassin?" she asked, retreating, keeping an eye on all three of them.

Chisulo bared his teeth. "No." He faked an attack, trying to draw her out, and she ignored it.

"Then what? The nahual wants her, but not for sacrifice?"

"Nope. I'm just a stupid Dirt."

Dziko blinked in surprise and then laughed. When Chisulo attacked, cudgel lashing out to crush her skull, instead of retreating, she stepped in and straight kicked him in the gut. He folded, and she kicked him in the knee, buckling it.

Hands tied behind her, Efra threw herself at the woman. Dziko side-stepped her charge, but Nuru hit her from the other side. The Bird went down, tripping over Efra. Nuru dropped on the Captain, sprawling across her torso, and immobilizing the arm holding the cudgel. Dziko punched her fast and hard with her free hand, squirming to get free.

Struggling to her feet, Efra kicked Dziko in the side of the head. She had to do it three more times before the Bird stopped moving. She was lining up for another when Chisulo's hand on her shoulder stopped her.

"No," he said. "No need."

"Not dead yet," panted Efra.

"She's out. She can't hurt us." A look of utter guilt and misery crossed his rugged features. "If you keep kicking her in the head, she'll die."

"That's the plan."

"No!" He pushed her away. "Turn around so I can untie you. Nuru, watch Captain Dziko."

Relief surged through Nuru. He wouldn't let Efra kill the Bird.

"Captain Dziko." Efra spat on the unconscious woman before turning.

Chisulo untied Efra and Nuru and bent to use the same rope to bind the Captain's hands.

"We have to kill her," said Efra, rubbing her wrists. "She's seen us."

More dead. "No," said Nuru. "They've all seen us. What do you think will happen when she doesn't return?"

"She needs to die." Efra rounded on Chisulo. "It's us against them. There's going to be a war. I've seen it."

Chisulo turned a questioning look on Nuru.

She hesitated and then nodded. "She's right. But we still don't need to kill the Bird."

Nodding at the rough knot, Chisulo stood. He didn't look happy. "The Birds are looking for a scarred Grower girl. Only Efra. No mention of a street sorcerer. No mention of a Grower with a crushed nose. No mention of the biggest Grower anyone ever saw. Just her."

"The Cloud Serpent nahualli wants her," said Nuru. "Smoking Mirror talks to her. She's important." Though she still didn't understand how.

"You're wrong," said Efra. "It's you that matters. You and that carving."

Nuru shook her head in denial. "We can't fight them. We have to run. We have to hide."

"No," said Efra. "That's what Dirts do. If we want to be something more, we have to act like something more." She turned on Chisulo. "Where were you? You said you were going to stay with us."

Chisulo hung his head in shame. "I got jumped by two Birds. Some squealer pointed me out to them, told them I knew a girl with a scarred face. It got violent." He lifted the leather armour to show bruised ribs beneath. "But the locals saw what was going on and stepped in. They threw rocks and shit at the Birds and I used the distraction to run. I hid in a tenement and they had to split up to search." He swallowed. "I killed one."

"Good," said Efra. "That's one less Bird we have to fight later." She glanced meaningfully at the Captain.

Chisulo ignored her. "We fought and I took his cudgel. Cracked his skull. I stole his armour and weapons and left him in the basement." He looked to Nuru, eyes haunted. "I've never killed anyone before."

"It gets easier," said Efra.

Does it? wondered Nuru. *When?* Did she even want it to? Shouldn't murder remain difficult?

Chisulo looked doubtful.

Efra flashed a quick grin. "You got the tools and the paints."

"Took me forever to come up with a reason they should hand them over," he said.

Efra snorted. "That's because you're dumb as sand. You forgot to get the Crafter clothes."

Chisulo cursed.

"Don't worry about it," she added, voice softer, touching his arm. "We're going to do it. We're going to hide in a basement, and Nuru is going to finish her spider thing."

"Happy will have to do the food and supply runs," said Nuru. "No one is looking for him and the Birds know what Chisulo looks like."

"How long do you need?" asked Efra.

"I need narcotics first. Jainkoei. Foku. Aldatu.

Chisulo whistled. "That won't be easy."

"I know who can get it for us," said Efra. "The Artist. He knows everyone, and everyone knows him. If Happy tells him I need it, he'll give it to us."

Chisulo's eyes narrowed. "Why would he do that for you?"

"Because he's in love with her," said Nuru. "But don't worry, she feels nothing for him. I saw it."

"I wasn't worried."

"Right."

"Can I hit the Bird one more time before we go?" asked Efra.

"No," said Chisulo. "We're better than that. Surviving means nothing if we surrender our humanity."

"*You're* better than that." Efra thought it over, rubbing at the scar where it crossed her lips. "I don't know how much humanity I have to lose. Does that make it more precious, or less?"

"More," said Chisulo.

"I knew you'd say that. But held against survival, what was it really worth?"

Nuru wondered if perhaps Smoking Mirror chose the girl specifically for that lack of humanity.

AKACHI – DEAD OR BROKEN

Perception is causal, defining. Each point of perception collapses its own reality.

The nahual bring those realities together, bind them into a working civilization.

The nahualli, however, learn to infiltrate and control those myriad realities.

—The Book of Bastion

After spending a day in bed, telling anyone who asked that he didn't feel well, Akachi rose the next morning feeling strangely reinvigorated though slightly detached from reality. Needing to act, to move, to show his father and his god and Yejide he wasn't a failure, he immediately dosed himself with foku and got to work carving new animal spirit allies. They were almost finished and he took them out to the courtyard to work in better light. Detail was everything.

The foku kept him sharp and alert.

The erlaxatu kept him calm and balanced.

He studied the figurines. The bear, Indar Handia, was the size of his thumb, paws and claws raised, so detailed it looked alive. Bihotz Blindatau, the pangolin, with its many over lapping plates of scale-like armour. He'd already completed Gau Ehiza, the puma caught in mid-sprint, muscles bunched, limbs extended.

Yejide stood nearby, arms crossed, attention on the street. Sweat dripped from her tightly braided hair, followed her sharp jawline and then her fine neck, to disappear into her armour. The days got hotter and hotter. In all his nineteen years, Akachi couldn't remember it ever being this brutally scorching. It felt like the gods sought to burn the world clean and start again.

The Captain never talked about Lutalo, or Khadija. When Akachi asked why, she said the dead weren't the responsibility of Southern Hummingbird. He thought he understood.

Each day the sun was a blistering rage from the moment it peeked over the horizon until Smoking Mirror chased it away. The Dirts shuffled slower and looked a little more bent. The heat turned them into wizened strips of dried leather. Every day more dead were found sprawling in fields where they fell, or stinking in their tenements. Those the sun didn't get, died in the cold of night.

"Are these like the others," asked Yejide, gesturing at the carvings, "for focus as a nagual?"

"Yes, though they work for peyollotl's totemic magic as well." Seeing her look of confusion, he added, "A peyollotl can turn the carving into a real creature. You have limited control of it, which can be dangerous, but a skilled practitioner can see through the creature's eyes, hear what it hears, taste what it tastes."

Hot blood! The crunch of bones and cartilage cracking beneath his fangs! Akachi flinched at the memory. "There are legends of ancient nahualli creating huge fire breathing lizards, flying lions, and all manner of fantastical creatures, but that's just myth, stories for children." Stories the Book of Bastion recounted as if fact.

"The puma I understand," Yejide said, "but why would you want to become a pangolin. They're slow and dumb as Dirts."

"Armour."

"They're beautiful." Stepping closer she leaned in to examine the carvings and Akachi inhaled the scent of her hair. "You're really good at this. Have you used carvings like these before?"

Akachi nodded again, pleased. "A couple of times, but never anything so extreme, so... physical. Nahualli study all the branches of sorcery, but most are drawn to just one. Some few have a talent for two."

"You're good at all of them, aren't you?"

Even in the sweltering heat Akachi felt a blush of warmth cross his face. "My teachers said I was a natural nagual, though I'm also a passable pactonal. They said I lacked the social awareness to be a good huateteo, and was too grounded in the now, too tied to earthly worries, to ever be much of a tezcat. And of course only a nahual of Father Death can become a tecuhtli."

"What's it like, when you become the creature?"

He shied from the question, distracting her with details. "We take various narcotics to prepare our minds. Some thin the veil separating us from the world of spirit animals. Others open the door to the dream world."

"The world of spirit animals is different from the reality of dreams?"

"Very," answered Akachi, relieved to be on safer ground. "Spirit animals are closer to gods than the allies you find in smoke and mushrooms. They are the purest form of the animal, undiluted power." He struggled to find the words to explain. "Each puma you see in the menageries is an extension of the original puma, the animal spirit defining it. When you learn their true names, you can open yourself to them. If they like you—and it's rare—they will help you. Gau Ehiza is the essence of what it is to be a puma."

"So, if I was a nahualli, I'd now be able to contact the puma spirit animal because you told me its name?" Yejide's eyebrow rose to a sharp peak. "All nagual do is memorize a bunch of names? I'm less impressed than I was."

Laughing, Akachi shook his head. He felt better than he had in days. "It doesn't work like that. Gau Ehiza is the name *I* was told in a smoke dream. The spirit animal would tell you a different name, would be something different for you. When we're studying, we have to live with the animals of the spirit we're trying to contact for several weeks. During that time, you must maintain a steady state of unreality, taking carefully measured doses of bihurtu. If the spirit animal likes you, it will share with you one of its infinite names."

"So if I wanted to contact Gau Ehiza…"

"You have to first live among the pumas. Naked. Without weapons. You have to be one of them."

"Sounds dangerous."

"It is. Many nahualli acolytes die, get mauled, bit, poisoned, and eaten." He flinched at the last word.

"How many spirit animal names do you know?"

"Six."

This time, when Yejide leaned closer to examine the bear, Akachi kissed her on the neck. She tasted of salt. He did it without thought, without planning.

She flashed a quick smile that stuttered his heart. "I was wondering how long that would take. What does the bear give you, a furry back?"

She didn't kill me! "And terrible farts."

"You already have those."

Akachi set the bear on the bench. "This is Indar Handia. From her I get strength." He showed her the pangolin. "Bihotz Blindatau. From him I get physical protection." He set it beside the bear and lifted the puma. "Gau Ehiza gives me speed. I will be strong and fast and armoured next time I meet the enemy." He reached a tentative hand to touch Yejide's arm and she didn't move away. "I'm not supposed to tell you any of this."

She put her hand on his. "Your secrets are safe."

He decided not to mention the large doses of bihurtu he spent the last few days preparing or that he took some every night in case the Loa dared come for him in the church.

They aren't coming. They've already achieved what they wanted. The Loa assassin carried two stones. They wanted him dead or broken. She'd failed to touch him with the garnet, but succeeded with the amethyst.

I will not self-destruct.

He hadn't slept well in days. Though the foku kept him on an obsidian edge, sometimes his thoughts wandered. Scenes of endless blood and death tormented him in waking dreams. Bastion was a sacrificial altar. Ancient and senile gods fed on the last remnants of humanity, who they bred like pigs. The gods bickered and fought among themselves like spoiled, mad children, triggering some cataclysm and feeding off the ensuing orgy of violence. Over and over the cycle continued. Those visions weighed on him, a damp blanket muzzling his thoughts.

"You okay?" asked Yejide.

Akachi blinked. "Yeah. Haven't slept well."

"I know." She leaned back to study him. "You look awful."

"Thanks." He wanted to tell her of the dream walk, of The Lord's death at the hands of the Loa assassin. *She wouldn't believe me.* And he'd have to explain the amount of narcotics he had taken, and was, in fact, still ingesting every day.

"You were skinny to begin with," she said, "but you're damned near skeletal now."

"When this is finished, I'll sleep for a week."

"This?" asked Yejide. "What do you mean?"

Good question. He wasn't sure how to answer.

"Trouble," said Yejide, stepping away, putting a more socially acceptable distance between them. The woman who stood chatting with him was gone, replaced by the Captain.

Akachi stood too. A Hummingbird strode toward them. She didn't look happy, her face bruised and puffy. Blood ran from her nose and her lips were cracked and swollen.

"Captain Dziko," said Captain Yejide.

"Captain Yejide." The Hummingbird entered the courtyard, walking with a confident strut at odds with the beating she'd clearly suffered. Stopping before Akachi, she offered a quick bow. "Pastor, that man you sent to the gate was a Grower."

Akachi blinked in confusion. "What man?"

Captain Dziko scowled. "You didn't send a Hummingbird Guard to wait at the Wheat District Gate for a scarred Grower girl to come through disguised as a Crafter?"

Yejide had spread the word to the Hummingbird Guards in the district to keep an eye out for a scarred Grower girl, though Akachi hadn't sent anyone to the gate. *A Grower would never—*

Dziko's words sank in. *Disguised as a Crafter.*

The scarred girl must have help. *She must have contacts high in the church. If she can travel between rings at will…* Was she even a Grower? He remembered the way she looked in the street, thin and dirty. She had to be.

"What happened to you, Captain?" asked Yejide.

Captain Dziko eyed Yejide. "I was escorting him here with the prisoners—two Dirt girls—when they jumped me."

"Were the prisoners bound?"

"Hands behind their backs."

"So you were taken by a Dirt and two tied up girls?"

Dziko ground her teeth. "Essentially."

"Hmm," said Captain Yejide.

"Why go to the Crafters' Ring?" mused Akachi, uncomfortable in the growing tension. Clearly the two women knew each other. "If they were trying to escape, why return?"

"They brought back a selection of high-quality carving tools and paints," said Captain Dziko, touching a swollen cheek and wincing.

"Sorcery," said Akachi. "They've brought back the tools to arm street sorcerers, to close the gap between them and real nahualli. What kind of tools?"

"Stone carving tools, paints, and brushes."

Crystal magic. Loa sorcery.

"They also had several extra sets of Crafter clothes," added Dziko.

"Then they were planning on returning to the Crafters' Ring at some point." Akachi's mind reeled at the implications. Growers and Loa sorcerers moving freely between the rings.

"There's more," said Captain Dziko. "Tariq's squad found one of the Hummingbird Guard dead in a basement."

"Lutalo," said Yejide, bowing her head. "He's been missing for days."

"They cracked his skull and left him there to die."

"Animals."

"Captain Yejide," said Akachi. "Please see Captain Dziko has an escort back to the gate."

Yejide nodded and led the woman into the church.

Though Akachi hadn't dosed since last night, the dregs of bihurtu still swam in his blood. If he stared for too long at one of the carvings, he felt his spirit allies reach out to offer aid. *Not yet. Not yet.* He itched to loose them, to feel their animal savagery in his veins. Instead, he returned them to their pouch. This was the kind of holy fight acolytes dreamed of.

A just cause, the knowledge he did Cloud Serpent's will.

The visions will guide me.

Existing every day in such a state, with the veil between realities stretched so thin, was dangerous. Every day he risked brain-burn.

It's worth the risk.

Akachi considered returning inside to dose again with foku and zoriontasuna; he needed to think clearly, and to feel the presence of his god.

Captain Yejide exited the church with Captain Dziko and Ibrahim following. "We'll escort her back to the gate. We're going to make sure the Guard they found is Lutalo." She stopped an arm's length from Akachi. He wanted to reach out to touch her, to reaffirm her strength and solidity. "Stay inside the church until we return."

"Yes, Captain."

A look crossed Yejide's features, concern and worry, intermingled with something else.

"I'll be fine," he said. "I have my carvings. I'm ready."

"We'll be many hours. If we don't return—"

"If you aren't back before sunset, I'm going to tear down every tenement in the Wheat District until I find you."

She blinked onyx eyes, looked away, and finally nodded. Turning, she marched out the front gate, Dziko and Ibrahim following.

I will never understand that woman.

Her concern he understood. *She's worried about the drugs.* Yejide might not be a nahualli, but she knew enough about what was involved. She understood that when he said he was ready, he admitted to being dosed. She knew the dangers.

She's afraid I'll brain-burn.

How much more worried would she be if she knew he'd been touched with a stone of self-destruction?

He shook the thought off. *I'm fine. Loa sorcery is weak.*

But was it? He already suspected Mother Death had somehow infiltrated Bastion. What if the insidious crystal magic of the Loa now worked at full power?

If that was true, could the battle in The Lord's realm have been a true vision?

No! It was just a narcotic dream. The Loa hadn't slain Father Death and conquered the underworld.

Keep telling yourself that.

Captain Yejide returned late in the evening, as the sun fell, bleeding light through the ever-present haze of red dust like a leaking corpse. Finding Akachi in his chambers, reading at his desk, she sat on the edge of the bed.

"Captain Dziko gave me detailed descriptions of the Growers. They were wearing Crafter colours, but they could be wearing anything by now. The street sorcerer has changed her appearance. She cut her hair and looks like any other Dirt." Yejide drew a deep breath and let it out in a long sigh. "While I saw to Lutalo's remains, Dziko took her squad and Tariq's into the tenements near the gate. They went door-to-door with the descriptions. There was some violence and they cracked a few heads." She gave a dismissive shrug. "Dziko is angry at being bested by Dirts. Anyway, they found some people who knew them. Your scarred Grower belongs to a gang. One of the members recently visited a Dirt known as the Artist. Apparently, he does tattoos for the locals. He gets ink from somewhere. He must have contacts. At the very least, he might know who this scarred Grower is."

"I want their names."

Yejide agreed. "It's late. In the morning we'll question this Artist, find out what he knows."

"I'm coming."

"Too dangerous."

"I'm coming," he repeated.

"The Dirts are getting worked up. Several threw clods of shit at Dziko." She smiled, a small quirk in the corner of curved lips, at that. "The Captain's handling of the search was clumsy. It didn't need to escalate to violence. And now..." Yejide studied Akachi. "We're a broken squad. Lutalo, Khadija, and Talimba dead. Gyasi wounded. Maybe we should leave the district. I'll escort you to the Grey Wall gate. From there you'll be taken back to the Priests' Ring." She drew a calming breath, clearly agitated. "We'll report back to Bishop Zalika, weather our punishment, and move on to our next assignment. But you'll be safe."

Akachi rose from the desk and sat beside her. He placed his hand on her arm, feeling the corded strength, the ridges of scar. "I can't. I was sent here for a reason. I can't disappoint my god. I can't disappoint my father. I will see this through."

Captain Yejide stood. "We'll visit the Artist at first light." Eyes narrowed, she studied him. "Get some sleep."

Then, she left.

NURU – A JUXTAPOSITION OF OPPOSITES

Though cast from Bastion, Mother Death has not been complacent. When she returns she will do so with an army of dead and banished gods at her back.

—Loa Book of the Invisibles

On Chisulo's orders, everyone stayed in the basement. They ate and slept there. Much as Nuru complained about the smoke and flickering candlelight, she did her carving there too. They only ventured to the ground floor to use the shithole. As much as possible, they wanted this to look like an abandoned tenement. It was, he said, an imperfect plan. Better plans, however, escaped him.

With the Birds scouring the streets for a Grower with a squished nose and detailed descriptions of both Efra and Nuru, Happy had no choice but to do all the scrounging and scavenging. Nuru saw that leaving Omari wounded his soul, a betrayal of his promise to his friend, but she didn't have the energy to talk him around. He also made regular trips to the Artist for her narcotics. Each time, upon returning, he rushed to the Finger to check if anything had changed. Nothing did. At least not for the better.

Omari could have done this. The Finger had a knack for stealth.

Bomani used to joke that it wasn't so much that Omari was a good Finger, more that he wasn't worth looking at. Omari would feign anger and punch him and Bomani would laugh all the harder.

Nuru made several attempts to wake the Finger. Desperate, she even tried reaching him through his dreams. Upon waking she said, 'I couldn't find him,' and cried for hours.

Omari grew thinner and thinner. In the last day he stopped twitching. The Finger lay motionless, chest barely moving with shallow breaths, skin a grey sheet stretched over bone. He looked like sunken fruit, rotting from the inside.

You're going to be so hungry when you wake up.

Happy returned with what supplies he managed to scrounge, beg, borrow, and steal. He shared the food around, husks of vegetable matter and crusts of hard bread, making sure everyone got more than he.

Your heart is too big, my friend.

Efra scowled at the food Happy laid before her. "I'm tiny. You're huge. Take more food. Idiot."

Happy demurred until she threatened to kick his balls in the next time he slept.

Nuru carved. She ate mushrooms and she carved. She smoked stale seeds and some nasty fungus smelling like rancid bellybutton snot, and she carved. She screamed when she slept, torn by nightmares, and woke wild-eyed and hallucinating.

The Artist gave Happy candles and everyone agreed they were Nuru's to use as she needed. Chisulo, Happy, and Efra lurked in the shadows like wraiths. Nuru, sitting in a flickering pool of smoky yellow light, claimed the centre of the room. No one wanted to disturb her. She talked and ranted, twitched at things no one else saw. She carved with her impossibly small tools, tiny shards of obsidian mounted on perfectly shaped ebony handles. She talked to the woman spider emerging from the red stone, in a ceaseless flow of narcotic madness.

"Stop this," Chisulo said, when she paused to wolf down scraps of food. "You're killing yourself. It isn't worth it."

"I can't."

She didn't want to. The carving devoured her, ate her every thought. In her dreams it spoke in rot and decay, promised to save her friends. Nuru had no choice. They were doomed. A nahualli of Cloud Serpent hunted them. The Birds were looking for them and knew what they looked like. It was only a matter of time before someone turned them in.

Hour by hour the carving changed. She shaved away breaths of stone exposing eight legs, impossibly thin and fragile. The torso, that of a young woman, curved and yet firm, took shape. This creature, this foul spider, jagged legs jutting up past the woman's head, was wrong. Deeply wrong. She felt it in her bones, in her blood. It was horror given form. It was flawless.

It was their only hope.

When she finished the face, Chisulo again tried to stop her.

"Look at it," he said, crouching before her, blocking her light.

She wanted to hit him, to send him away. Instead she peered at the carving. The woman was as beautiful as the spider was terrible.

"She's beautiful," she said. "Perfect."

Glancing over his shoulder he saw Efra sleeping, wrapped in a grey blanket. He leaned closer and whispered, "It's you. The face. The nose." He hesitated. "The body."

"No. I'm not that... I'm all flaws."

"I've seen you naked often enough to know. You're a beautiful wo-man." He flushed in embarrassment, looking everywhere but at her.

She studied the carving, trying to see it. "No. You're wrong."

"Let me destroy it," he begged. "We'll find another way."

"There is no other way."

"We'll get into the Crafters' Ring somehow, hide there."

"They know now. They'll be watching the gates."

Chisulo growled in helpless anger when she sent him away.

She returned to her work, lost herself in the creation.

When hunger or exhaustion forced her to set it aside, she communicated in grunts. She ate without noticing the food, eyes staring at nothing.

Then she began painting.

The spider changed. The body glistened black, caught the shivering light of the candles and took on a life of its own. The eyes, bloody and red, saw everything.

Chisulo turned away, saying he could watch no more. It hurt, but she couldn't stop.

The nahualli would find them, would open their veins or throw them from the wall. They needed this.

When he thought her asleep, she heard Chisulo talk to Happy in hushed tones. "I'm failing her. Now, after all these years, I'm letting her down because I'm afraid."

But Happy was lost in his own misery worrying for Omari.

She hated herself, hated that she couldn't stop for her friend. She hated that she didn't want to.

Through slitted eyes she watched as Chisulo sat staring at the floor, drowning in helpless rage. Efra dropped down to sit beside him. She leaned against him, her head on his shoulder.

"You have something I don't," she said.

"And that is?"

"It's the thing that tells you something is right or wrong."

Chisulo darted a guilty glance at Nuru.

"I know when things are right and wrong for *me*," continued Efra.

"But you know when things are right and wrong. It's funny, because they're just ideas. Right and wrong aren't real. They don't exist without someone to decide which is which."

Efra leaned away so she could look him in the eye. The contrast of her beauty, her smooth skin, intense eyes, and that ragged scar, fascinated Nuru. Everything about the girl was a juxtaposition of opposites.

"They aren't real," she said, "but because everyone pretends they are, they *become* real.

"We aren't pretending."

"You are, you just don't know it."

"So this thing I have, is it good or bad?"

"I think it might be good for those around you, but bad for you."

"Fantastic. You're worried it can be used against me? You think that, because I have a code, I can be manipulated."

"You're not quite dumb enough for that."

Nuru stifled a laugh. *Not quite.*

Chisulo said nothing.

She probably thinks that was a compliment.

"I worry it will get you killed. When you should be saving yourself, you'll save someone else instead."

"You worry about me?" He grinned, a momentary crack in the days of misery. "That's you thinking about someone else. There's hope for you yet."

"I worry about losing you because of what it will mean for *me.*"

"Oh." He looked thoughtful. "So losing me would be inconvenient?"

She gave him a long look. "Yes," she said. "Inconvenient."

"I can never tell if you're joking."

"I know."

"Chisulo," said Happy. He knelt at Omari's side, hunched over the

Finger.

Leaving Efra, Chisulo joined his friend, kneeling beside him. She followed, standing with one hand on his shoulder.

"He's dying," said Happy, voice cracking. "We're going to lose him."

Nuru sat up.

"No," said Chisulo. He punched the floor in frustration, tearing the skin of his knuckles.

Happy stared at him, eyes like wounds, needing hope and seeing none. "Maybe we can take him to a priest."

"A priest did this to him," said Efra, from behind Chisulo.

Happy glared at her. "A different priest. Lots of churches to choose from."

"Might as well hand yourselves over."

"If that's what we have to do to save him."

"So the nahual can bleed him on the altar?"

Happy growled, low and threatening.

"I have an idea," said Efra. If she noticed the big man's rage, she paid it no mind. "The Artist. He knows things. He…" She searched for the word. "He crafts. He's not what he seems."

"What can he do?"

"Drugs. Medicine." Efra shrugged. "I don't know. Maybe nothing."

Rising, Nuru staggered over to her friends. "I'm finished." She held up the carving.

"We're going to go get the Artist," said Efra. "We'll bring him back here."

"Is that safe?" asked Happy.

"Safer than trying to carry Omari there," she snapped.

"Is it night?" asked Nuru. She hadn't left the basement in days, and they'd hung heavy curtains, layers of grey cotton, over the entrance to muffle any sounds they made.

"Day," said Chisulo.

"Shit."

Chisulo ground his teeth in helpless anger. "We can't do *nothing!*" He stood. "I will go fetch the Artist." He stared down at the sunken husk of a friend he'd known his entire life. "First Bomani, and now Omari. I won't let it happen."

"I'm coming," said Efra.

"I'm coming too," said Nuru. "I need to see the sun again." Glancing at the carving, she flinched. "And I want to see if he knows what this is."

"What if he won't come?" asked Happy. "Everyone knows the Birds are looking for us. He might decide it's too dangerous"

"He'll come," said Nuru, glancing at Efra.

AKACHI – THE SMOKE IS THE SOULS

As is the gods' will, the central ring shall remain forever closed to humanity. Only Heart's Mirror, the voice of the head of the pantheon, may enter into that ring to converse directly with the gods.

—The Book of Bastion

Akachi woke with a start. He was still dressed, and sweat soaked both his robes and the sheets. His heart felt like a hummingbird trapped in his chest. The sun sat high in the sky. He'd slept through the morning.

A Hummingbird has my heart. He laughed at the thought, a dry choked cough.

Not bothering to change his robes, he went to his desk. Selecting a mixture of foku seeds, jainkoei, and bihurtu, he prepared the previous evening, he filled the bowl of his pipe. This particular combination wasn't taught in the schools. He'd realized he needed something more if he was to best this scarred Grower and her street sorcerer. Specially if the Loa were on their side. It could not have been coincidence that the day he planned on going door-to-door searching for her, the Loa assassin attacked.

The feel of that cold stone, a raw shard of violet amethyst, still haunted him.

It barely touched me. Little more than a caress.

"I'm fine," he said, eyeing the narcotics littered about his desk.

He needed deadly focus, to open himself to the will of Cloud Serpent, and the ability to reach through the veil of worlds and channel the power of his spirit animals. He couldn't remember if he'd mixed in some pizgarri as well to help keep him awake. Should he do that now?

Smoke it. See how you feel. Decide after.

On his desk a candle burned, though only a thumb's length remained. He had no recollection of Jumoke entering his chambers to light the candles. The rest had long since burned out. His hand shook, splashing hot wax on his arm, as he used the candle to light the pipe. The pain was dull and distant, a small penance. The wax dried fast, tightening the skin beneath. The first inhalation, drawn deep into his lungs, filled him with the light of the gods. Exhaustion, weariness, doubt, meant nothing. His blood no longer slouched through his body. It roared in a torrential swirl of life.

Akachi felt real, more real than he'd ever been. Every colour shone with an intensity and lustre that welled tears of joy in his eyes. The stone of Bastion, ancient and wise, sang songs of eternity. This ringed bowl of life held everything. Crying, he hunted through his narcotics until he found the ameslari and jainkoei. Cloud Serpent loved him, trusted him. His god gave him purpose and reason. Cloud Serpent gave him everything his father never did. Acceptance. Understanding.

Akachi wanted more.

Wolfing down several mushrooms, he refilled the bowl of his pipe.

Bastion is a bowl funnelling blood to its centre. Bowl of life. Bowl of blood. Bowl of my pipe. Beautiful symmetry.

Amethyst, the stone of self-destruction.

No, I do this because I must.

Today they would go to the Artist. He would tell Akachi where to find the scarred girl. Today it would all end. *The Loa want me to doubt.*

He smoked the mix to ash, tasted the sour bile of his own spit. *Should have cleaned it first.* He'd forgot.

The veil between realities stretched so thin he could tear it with a careless thought.

Remember your training.

His training said it was dangerous to smoke without thoroughly cleaning the pipe between sessions.

Akachi locked his thoughts down. He visualized a sturdy ebony box with a close-fitting lid. His imagination went in there. He would be stone until he needed to be otherwise.

Hunting about the floor, he found a set of robes that wasn't too stained and ripe. He put them on. Banded in blood red, pure white, and night sky black, he felt better.

He found the sacrificial dagger, still bundled in a set of his robes at the back of the closet. Uncrumpling the clothes, he displayed the knife.

The smoke is the souls.

He took it in his hand, felt its foul weight. This dagger had taken a great many lives since last it made the journey to the Gods' Ring to be emptied. So much violence. Death permeated Akachi, strangled his thoughts like ropes of dust-clogged spider webs in Bastion's deepest basements.

That Grower I sacrificed, his soul is in here, awaiting purification and rebirth. What was it like to be a soul in stone? Were they aware?

"Don't worry," he told the souls within the dagger, "when this is all over I'll make sure the knife returns to the Gods' Ring. You'll all be re-born."

Akachi strode from his chambers and walked the halls of the church. Windows, perfectly shaped gaps in the endless stone, let in plenty of natural light. How long had it been since Talimba's death? A week?

Akachi wasn't sure, the narcotics skewed his sense of time. He ran his fingertips along the wall as he walked, feeling the texture of the stone. Shivers of pleasure tingled up his arm and climbed his spine into the centre of his skull. Such a simple thing, to touch the stone that gave them all life, and yet so few bothered.

We are blind. Eternity dulls us.

What of the gods?

Could they forget? Could gods go mad? How long would it take?

In the main hall he found Nafari waiting with Captain Yejide and the remaining Hummingbirds.

Gyasi stood near Akachi's friend. She looked pale and still walked with a slight hunch like it pained her to move. And yet here she was, ready to do her duty. She might be bent, but never broken. Ibrahim, the huge Hummingbird, stood silent, arms crossed, tight-bound rage. *He is obsidian.* Something changed in him after Lutalo's death was confirmed; Ibrahim was brittle now. Akachi tasted it in the fabric of the worlds.

Only Njau, huge beard hanging down his chest like a black curtain, seemed unchanged, unbent by his time in the Wheat District. Whatever he felt, it was locked so deep Akachi saw no trace of it. *The Hummingbird ideal.*

Even Yejide, strong as she was, looked worried. The last week frayed her hard edges. Not softening her, but rather leaving her jagged and sharp. *She's tired.* Akachi realized she probably hadn't slept any more than he.

Jumoke puttered about the hall, dusting and cleaning.

"I gathered everyone like you asked," said Nafari.

I did? Akachi had no memory of the request. Still, it made sense.

Nafari examined him with worried eyes.

I'm okay, my friend.

"I'm fine," said Akachi. "I needed to prepare in case there is trouble. Last night. My dreams." He hadn't actually slept, but had hallucinated the entire night. The streets ran with blood. "We're going to visit the Artist. I will question him and he will tell us where this street sorcerer is, where the scarred Dirt is."

A sliver of Akachi's imagination escaped its box. The narcotics in his blood thinned the veil of realities to transparent. A smoke-twisted shadow of Gau Ehiza, his puma spirit animal, prowled around Akachi, shoulders rolling with muscle, eyes green diamonds of hunger.

Eyes wide, Yejide retreated before the vision.

Akachi locked his control tight. *She worries about me.*

The stone of self-destruction.

"How much?" she asked.

"Enough," he said.

"What have you taken?"

Unable to remember, he evaded the question. "Only that which I need." He wasn't sure if he lied.

"You have to stop," said Yejide, her eyes deep wells of fear and concern. And maybe love. "It's too much. The cost—"

"Will be worth it. Today we will finish this. Today I will have answers." He felt it in his blood.

"Talimba mentioned this Artist in one of his early reports," said Yejide. "The man is much respected in the district. We must tread carefully or risk angering the Growers."

"Fuck the Dirts," said Akachi and her eyes widened. "Tattoos are forbidden. Art is forbidden. This man has sinned and must pay." Foku roaring in his veins, the pieces snapped together, tight fitting like the wood puzzles his father used to bring back from the Crafters' Ring. "The scarred girl bears a tattoo marking her as a worshipper of Smoking Mirror."

Those who didn't already know, gasped in shock.

"Who," asked Akachi, "do you think gave her that tattoo?"

"We must question the Artist," agreed Nafari. "But Captain Yejide is right. The man is loved. The Growers outnumber us, thousands to one."

"They beat Lutalo to death," said Ibrahim.

"They will pay," swore Akachi.

He'd been distracted. Captain Yejide. The Dirt mob who attacked them on the way out. The damned Loa assassin with her bright eyes and pathetic stones. Too long he allowed others to carry the burden that was, in truth, his to bear.

"The Artist will answer my questions," said Akachi.

Jumoke remained silent.

Out in the street, the sun scorched everything to bone and ash. Akachi stood, arms raised to its purifying fire.

Burn me clean.

"Let's get moving," said Yejide. She squinted in the light, sweat pouring off her.

Glancing around, Akachi saw all the Hummingbirds sweat profusely. Nafari's robes stuck to him. Akachi felt nothing. He was dust riding a beam of purest light, floating wherever the will of the gods took him.

The Growers remained indoors, hiding from the sun's rage. Eyes like shards of obsidian glinted in the dark, followed his group's progress.

"I'll bring you the sun," he told them.

"I've never felt it so hot," said Nafari, wiping sweat from his brow. His hair was plastered to his skull. "There are so many Growers here. They must have been let out of the fields. It's too hot to work."

His friend was right. The Growers might not be out on the streets, walking the alleys where they so carelessly threw their garbage, but the homes were packed. A filthy, sweating Dirt lounged in every entrance, peered from every window.

"Akachi." Nafari stood staring out toward the distant fields. The Sand Wall was out there, though too far away to be seen. He pointed.

Akachi saw a colossal pillar of smoke rising into sky. There was, he realized, more than one. Ash stained the horizon. The dream. The spider, legs of smoke touching down in each ring, with the Growers' first.

The fields are burning.

Akachi, Nafari, and the Hummingbird Guard, stood staring.

"Should we…" Yejide didn't finish her sentence.

"Others will deal with that," said Akachi, though he couldn't imagine who, or how.

He turned his back on the smoke. His prey wasn't out there.

I am a nahualli of Cloud Serpent, a priest of the hunt.

"Lead on," he commanded Yejide.

"Ibrahim," she barked, "out front. Njau, in the back. Gyasi, with me."

The Artist lived a few blocks from the Grey Wall and the gate. They walked, Akachi aware of the eyes following him. His sharpened senses saw every grain of sand, every granule of blood red. No shadow spoiled the world. Noon, the sun shone directly above them.

In the Last War, the final battle where man and god fought beside and against each other, humanity was brought to the very brink of extinction. Today it felt like the sun might finally burn clean this dead world.

Why is there no god of the sun?

Every god ruled over several aspects of the world. Each god had so many names, most had been forgotten by all but the most devout historian.

Smoking Mirror was the night sky and wind, storms and jaguars, obsidian, discord, beauty, and a thousand other things. Father Discord.

Father Night. His names went on and on. Even Cloud Serpent, god of the hunt, ruled over dozens of aspects of life in Bastion, from debtors to several types of justice and stalking cats.

But no god claimed the sun. No one ever spoke of it. Suddenly, that seemed very strange.

Had the god of the sun died in the Last War?

That would explain the orb's relentless fury, its daily attempt to bake the world. What other aspects of this reality lost their controlling gods? Feathered Serpent was god of the daytime wind and sandstorms, but there was no god of sand, no god of the Bloody Desert. Was this why it seemed like Bastion was caught in an eternal war with the blood-stained sands?

Could gods be reborn like mortal souls? Were the gods of Bastion merely biding their time until new gods were born? What of the Heart's Mirror, worshipped by all as the Voice of the Gods? Were they trying to make her into a new god, just as the girl with the bright eyes had, worshipped by the dead, ascended to become Face Painted with Bells?

That wasn't real!

If that's what they were trying to do, what did that mean for all the previous Heart's Mirrors? Were they failures?

The gods are at war, my Heart, Cloud Serpent said. *Hunt the girl.* The god spoke in sand and scales.

My Heart. What did that mean? It sounded formalized, like part of a ritual. Had Cloud Serpent chosen him for something more than hunting the girl?

"We're here," said Captain Yejide.

The Artist's tenement looked like all the others.

Akachi started forward and Yejide put a hand on his shoulder, halting him.

"Ibrahim," she said. "You and Njau in first. Njau, signal when it's clear. Search the basement. I don't want any surprises. Gyasi, eyes on the approaches. Check alleys."

"Be careful," Nafari said to Gyasi before she left. She flashed him a smile and for an instant was someone Akachi never met.

We change each other. Had he changed Yejide? She used to smile like Gyasi just did; he hadn't seen that in days. Not since he started dosing himself in preparation for what was to come.

That fraying. It's my fault.

What effect did she have on him?

He considered the changes in them both. *I think she makes me stronger, but I weaken her.* Was it her caring that weakened her, or her worry he did himself harm? *You're dodging the blame.* If he loved her as much as he thought he did, shouldn't he do whatever was needed to make her happy, to make her strong?

I will. Once this is over.

Amethyst. He pushed the thought away. "Yejide."

She turned to face him.

Akachi wanted to apologise, to explain. "This will all be over soon."

Only after the words were out did he realize how that might sound. His thoughts swam in narcotics. Foku fought to pull his attention to the perfect gutters lining the streets. Bihurtu stretched the veil of worlds so thin he saw his spirit animals circling impatiently, ready to come to his aid. Jainkoei peeled his soul, exposed him to the gods. He felt them all around him. Their will drove him, made him dance like a marionette. He was a twig caught in the raging torrent of divine need. He couldn't think what to say to Yejide to make it right. There wasn't enough of him left.

"Soon," he repeated, hoping she understood.

Yejide looked doubtful.

Gyasi returned from a nearby alley, walking with one hand pressed to her side. "All clear. Too hot for Dirts to be out causing trouble."

Glancing past Akachi, Yejide said, "Njau is waving us in." She turned to Gyasi. "You come in too. Get out of the sun."

"I'm fine," said Gyasi, but she followed them in.

NURU – I AM THE END

At the end of the Last War, the surviving gods swore to save what remained of humanity. With the formation of Bastion, an eternal cycle of life, death, and rebirth was created. After each death, a person is reborn in proximity to the gods based upon how piously they lived their previous life. Even the lowest Grower can be reborn closer to the heart of Bastion by living a true and pure life in service to city and god.

—The Book of Bastion

Nuru gathered what narcotics remained. She examined the shrunken pile of dried seeds and leaves and leathery mushrooms. The spider sat on the floor where she placed it. It felt like it was watching her. Red eyes. Blood. Hunger. Its legs were barbed and sharp, knees jutting up past the woman's head. The girl part was pretty, in a fragile way, and entirely terrible.

That's madness. No such creature existed. *It won't work.* But if it did? What if she *became* that? The carving terrified her.

"You ready?" asked Chisulo.

Nuru blinked up at him. He'd once again donned the armour he stole from the Bird. The cudgel, their only weapon, hung from a loop in his belt. He even wore the sandals, though the straps looked wrong, sloppy.

Chisulo shrugged. "In case there's trouble."

"By now the nahual knows there a Grower dressed as a Bird."

"Maybe it'll be enough to make them hesitate. You'll pretend to be prisoners. Or something."

"Or something," said Efra.

Nuru wasn't sure if the girl found humour in the statement or was mocking Chisulo. She delivered everything with the same lack of emotion. *Almost everything.*

Nuru turned back to her stash of drugs. Gathering them together, she shoved the entire lot into her mouth and chewed. Some, she knew, were more effective if smoked. She didn't have time to prepare the mixture properly. The comedown, after, would be ferocious. She'd likely be bedridden for days while her mind and body recovered. But if they were venturing out, she wanted to be ready for anything. Hopefully she could get more from the Artist.

Swallowing, she collected the spider and returned it to its pouch. "Let's go."

Chisulo led them up the stairs and into the blinding sun. Eyes slitted, she staggered under the savage weight of its heat. Efra followed.

From the basement she heard Happy call, "Hurry!"

Once on the street, Chisulo stopped. "The fields," he said, staring outward.

Columns of twisting smoke reached up into dark clouds like the legs of a spider.

Ash choked the sky, a spreading cancer.

The fields which grew the food for all Bastion were on fire. Nowhere out there was free of smoke.

That's the future burning. She saw it. *This is the end.*

"We have to move," said Chisulo.

Pushing them all into motion, he set a fast pace.

Efra jogged to keep up. Nuru's longer legs let her match his stride, but she stumbled often. She felt weak, drained. She hadn't eaten more than a few crusts of stale bread in days. Her stomach felt like it had collapsed in on itself. Spasms of nausea ran through her.

Sorcery came with a cost. It burned her from the inside, devoured her. This weak, she had no idea what would happen if she pushed hard. A vision of greasy ash dancing pirouettes in the wind caught her attention. Distracted, she tripped over something and fell to her knees. She was still watching the swirling ash, knowing it was her, when Chisulo pulled her to her feet. Blood trickled down her shins.

"Are you hurt?" he asked.

"No. I'm dead." She looked at him, saw his skin burn and peel away like parchment held to a candle. He was bone, burnt and black. "I am the end, the destroyer of worlds."

"You're smoky," said Chisulo. "What did you take?"

"Everything."

Efra appeared at her side, small and real like stone. That scar, dividing her face, it halved her. Good and caring on one side. Pure selfish evil on the other. *She wants to be better and doesn't care what it costs.*

Hooking an arm under Nuru's armpit, Efra kept her upright.

"Lean on me," the girl said.

I will.

Chisulo, abandoning all pretence of being a Bird, took the other side. The three staggered through the streets. Having fled the brutal sun, the tenements were crowded with cowering Growers.

"They're all here," said Efra. "Who is fighting the fires?" She kept glancing over her shoulder, eyes bright, showing no hint of terror. If anything, she looked excited, like she expected this.

"No one," said Nuru. "They're all hiding."

"From the fires?"

"From the end."

"This isn't the end," said Efra. "It's the beginning."

"Only for some." Nuru examined the girl, watched the two halves of her face do battle for her soul. "You knew. You knew this would happen."

"I saw the spider's legs," she said, gesturing at the distant swirling columns of ash. "Eventually they'll touch every ring."

"There it is," said Chisulo, pointing. "The Artist's place."

A bellow from behind stopped them. Turning, they saw Happy running down the street toward them. The sky behind him grew dark as the clouds of ash spread. Moment by moment more of Bastion fell into shadow.

Dead world. Stained. A false night crept over the city.

"No," said Chisulo, voice falling flat, shoulders slumping in defeat. "He wouldn't leave Omari unless—"

"Unless he's dead," said Efra.

He can't be. Squeezing tight like the coils of a constrictor, the walls of Bastion closed in on Nuru. She couldn't breathe.

Omari. Her whole life. Her friend. Her thoughts stuttered and collapsed. In turning to face the lumbering Happy, Chisulo and Efra released her. Nuru slid to the ground. She stared at the stone beneath her. Red sand dusted everything. The stories the nahual preached every day since her birth ran through her thoughts. Red sand, the dried blood of billions. She didn't even know what 'billions' was, just that it was more than all of Bastion. Tears fell, pattering into the sand.

Turning it back into blood.

Happy arrived. He stopped. Eyes red, he said nothing. He shook his head.

Chisulo took the big man into his arms and held him. Happy made a low moan of broken misery, forlorn and alone. Unable to watch, Nuru focussed on the uncaring stone. This close, she saw tiny cracks, miniscule chips and divots. They were everywhere.

Not so perfect.

Had it ever been, or could Bastion age and die?

"We're here," said Efra, pointing at the Artist's tenement.

Ashen clouds drown the world.

AKACHI – TRAFFIC IN SIN

The proper mix of narcotics will open a nahualli to the will of the gods. In our stable state we are blind to their light, deaf to their wisdom. In thinning the veil, we become receptive.

But stare wide-eyed at the sun for too long and you will go blind.

The gods are too much for us. Their purest light will burn us clean, leave us hollowed and empty.

—The *Book of Bastion*

The Artist lived alone. Though, like any Grower, he slept on a single blanket on stone, his tenement brimmed with sin. A magnificently detailed mural of a woman being thrown from the Sand Wall covered the ceiling. It reminded Akachi of the tapestry in Bishop Zalika's chambers, and looked to be several years old, judging from its chipped and faded state. Wood bowls of paint lined the table. Akachi couldn't imagine how this man created these colours. Sheets of heavy paper depicting scenes from public lashings to portraits of Dirt faces, lined and haggard, littered the floor. An open bowl of black ink, dried to a hard crust, sat on the stone table beside a row of sharpened feathers and what looked to be porcupine quills. Burnt stumps of slumping tallow candles lay scattered everywhere.

"Gyasi," said the Captain. "Search the basement for contraband."

Gyasi left without a word.

The Artist stood beside the table, studying Akachi. Meeting his eyes, the man nodded greeting. "You are the new nahual in the church of Cloud Serpent."

"I am."

"You're young."

The Artist had at least a decade on Akachi. It was hard to judge with Growers; they aged so fast.

"You traffic in sin," said Akachi. "Tattooing is forbidden. Art is forbidden. Tools are forbidden."

"Crafters make tools." He glanced at Akachi. "You bear many tattoos. The Gods' Wall is a beautiful piece of art."

Akachi swallowed. It was impossible. This Grower could not have seen the wall separating the priests from the gods. Someone, some careless nahual, must have told him of it. "These things are forbidden to *Growers*."

"And yet nahual ignored such things for years. Generations. I've made no attempt to hide. Everyone knows me as the Artist." The Artist examined Akachi with knowing eyes. He showed none of a Dirt's fear or subservience. "Why now?"

Akachi pointed at the ceiling. "Defacing Bastion is punishable by death."

"Only in the Life Ring."

How did he know the original name for the Growers Ring? Only the oldest copies of the *Book of Bastion* still bore than name. *We'll discover this truth too.*

"I have questions," said Akachi. "Questions you will answer."

"Not offering me a deal, priest? Not even forgiveness if I cooperate? Perhaps a commuted sentence, lashings instead of bleeding out on the altar?"

"Cooperate, and you'll be sacrificed to be born again. Though another chance is more than you deserve. Otherwise, you'll be thrown from the Sand Wall."

Glancing at the mural above, the Artist laughed, mocking. "Can't get much further from the gods than I already am."

One of the papers littering the floor caught Akachi's attention. Foku-honed obsidian-sharp memories stabbed through his thoughts. He bent to collect it. A charcoal sketch, it somehow conveyed weight and reality. The eyes, infinite shades of grey, were alive.

"You're very good," said Akachi, turning the paper so the Artist could see. "I particularly like how you captured the scar." He turned it again so he could further study the piece. "Otherwise, she'd be a real beauty."

"She *is*. There is no otherwise."

The Artist was right. Somehow, the girl *owned* the scar. It should have marked her. She should have been embarrassed, self-conscious of her flaw. She wasn't. She looked like she either didn't know she was scarred, or didn't care.

That makes her strong.

"You understand," said the Artist. "I see it in your eyes." He smiled a sad smile. "I'd like to draw you as you are right now. To show you. So you can see yourself in this moment."

"Dirts don't draw."

"Dirts. You never used to call them that."

He's guessing. But he wasn't wrong. Akachi remembered the first time Yejide used the derogatory term, his own uncomfortable embarrassment. He remembered the first time he said it.

I grew to hate them, to loathe their laziness. What changed, he wasn't sure. *The longer I was among them—the longer I was away from the comforts of home and the beauty of the inner rings—the more I hated them.* He felt like they stole something from him. *I was happy in the Priests' Ring.*

"You don't like them," said the Artist.

"They're filthy. Lazy. Stupid."

"No. That's what you tell yourself to justify your hate. It's what you're trying to make them. What they are is people, just like you."

You're wrong. Akachi remembered his vision, ranks of Turquoise Serpents wielding obsidian swords. Blood in the streets. Blood running in gutters, a fast-flowing river of spilled life.

The fields burned. There would be panic, hoarding, a war for food. The only things growing in the inner rings were flowers and trees, their purpose beauty rather than survival. The inner rings would starve.

Was I sent here to make all this happen, or to stop it?

"Your eyes," said the Artist. "You're riding the edge of brain-burn. You've done a bad job of mixing your narcotics. You've been sloppy, and you've taken too much."

"What would you know of such things?" demanded Akachi.

The Artist shrugged. "So many questions. No answers. That's life, young nahualli."

Akachi raised the picture of the scarred Grower. He shook it, paper making sharp snapping sounds. "Where does she live? What is her name? Who is she?"

"I don't know where she lives. Her name doesn't matter." The Artist grinned perfect white teeth. "And she is the beginning."

"Captain," said Gyasi, coming out of the basement. "I found something." She held a marble bowl with a close-fitting lid, something no Grower should possess. "There's dozens of these down there. Mortars. Pestles. Plants hanging from the ceiling. Mushrooms growing in pots of horse dung. Glowing fungus on the walls." Gyasi lifted the lid and held the bowl out for inspection.

A small amount of liquid, creamy yellow shot with swirls of blood red, swam in the bottom. Akachi recognized it immediately. Etorkizun, the sap from a rare tree. Mixed with the blood of a nahualli, it was used by tezcat, practitioners of divinatory magic.

"You're a street sorcerer."

"Your terminology belittles everything they do," said the Artist.

"They?"

"You're running out of time. Best ask your questions."

Running out of time? Stupid Dirt thought he could smear etorkizun on his eyelids and see the future.

Akachi drew the sacrificial dagger. It numbed his arm, cold and foul. The weight of countless souls clogged the air, made it difficult to breathe. He felt it move in his hand, hungry.

"That dagger hasn't been to the Gods' Ring in a long time," said the Artist.

"Shut up." Akachi didn't want to hear it. Couldn't. When had he lost control of this? "Tell me what I need to know. I don't want to hurt you."

"Then don't."

Why doesn't he look scared?

The etorkizun. Had this strange Dirt caught some glimpse of a future where he got out of this unscathed? Didn't he know how fickle such visions were, how open to interpretation?

He thinks I can't do this, that I don't have it in me to cut him.

The Artist was wrong.

"Ibrahim, hold him."

The big Hummingbird dragged the unresisting Artist to the table, pinned him there.

The Artist studied Akachi.

He's looking for weakness.

"I have to do this," explained Akachi.

"No, it's a choice."

"It's not. Not really. I have to."

"Educated," said the Artist, "is different than intelligent."

Akachi frowned. What did that mean? "Tell me about the girl."

"No."

Akachi let the obsidian ask the next question.

"Stop," said Yejide. "He's dead."

Akachi blinked. Gore splashed his arms to the elbows. Foku smashing through his veins, he remembered everything in perfect detail. Every cut. Every hiss of parting flesh. The Artist's blood soaked him. His robes hung sodden and hot. He stunk like an abattoir, meat left long in the sun.

Looking at the floor, he saw the art there, sprayed red. The picture of the girl—Efra, he now knew—was spattered in gore. Only now did he notice the narrow gutters. The blood on the floor trickled outward to the walls where it was funnelled out to the larger gutters in the street. He watched the flow. *The floors must be slightly convex.* He admired the perfection. Was it the same everywhere? Even standing here, knowing the floor must have some curve, he couldn't detect it. He had no memory of gutters in the other rings.

I wasn't using so much foku back then.

His past, everything before leaving the Northern Cathedral and taking residence in the Wheat District, seemed muted, unreal.

If you don't take a little foku every day, gods know what you'll miss. He needed to be sharp, to be alert. What if he missed something crucial because he was dull, distracted? He wanted to rush back to the church and dose up. Maybe he should include gorgoratzen and koznizioa into his daily regimen, at least until this was over. *Dangerous. Too dangerous.* He ground his teeth in frustration. *I need to be better.*

Fumbling with his pouch, Akachi spilled foku seeds into the crimson-stained palm of his hand. *Just a few more.* Yejide slapped his hand away, spilling seeds to the floor. They floated in blood like those little wood boats his father used to bring back from the Crafters' Ring. He remembered going to the river and racing his friends.

"We all had boats," he said. "Mine was blue."

"Akachi," said Yejide. "We have to go."

Akachi turned his back on the horror that was what remained of the Artist. "Why?"

"What the Artist said."

He replayed the last hour in his mind. Blood. Weak flesh. Screams. "He never begged. Never asked me to stop."

"At the end," said Yejide, "he laughed. Said he was stalling. Keeping us here until it was time."

"I remember." He eyed the seeds in the blood. Noticing one stuck to his bloody hand, he licked it off. *Salty.*

"He was no nahualli. Whatever he thought he saw, he was wrong."

"The girl is coming," said Yejide. "The Artist set a trap. He let you torture him."

He remembered. "That's right! Efra will be angry because I tortured a gentle, harmless man." Akachi glanced at the corpse. *I did that. I cut a gentle man.* Murdering that Dirt, the man he sacrificed on the altar in his church, stained him, lessened him somehow. This was worse. A thousand times worse. *I wilfully tortured a man, every cut designed for maximum torment.* As a nahual of Cloud Serpent, his knowledge of the human body was extensive. Hunting, he was taught, often involved asking hard questions.

He hated himself.

I had to. The gods...

He needed more jainkoei. He needed to feel the will of Cloud Serpent in his blood.

"He said she has the street-sorcerer with her. We have to go," repeated Yejide. "*Now.*"

"I bested that street sorcerer once. It was easy. I will crush her." He looked around. "Where is Nafari?"

"He went outside. This..." Yejide gestured at the corpse, at the blood painting the walls. "This disgusted him."

"And you?"

"I am trained in torture. I first cut a man when I was eight."

Eight. What did it take to make a Hummingbird Guard? Akachi had never before thought about it. And it wasn't an answer. Not really.

Nafari stuck his head in the entrance, face wan, dripping sweat. "Someone is coming!"

"Let's see the end of this," said Akachi, moving to join his friend in the street.

Captain Yejide, Ibrahim, Njau, and Gyasi followed.

For a moment Akachi thought he'd lost track of time in the Grower's tenement and night had fallen. Looking up, he saw world-swallowing clouds of ash blanketing the city. The sun, a dim circle of crimson, lurked behind a billowing haze of smog turning the smoke a diseased yellow like rot.

Eternal Bastion lay wreathed in shadow.

NURU – QUEEN OF THE RED DESERT

The Rada Loa are the oldest entities in existence, the very first intelligences of this reality. They birthed the first gods, are the distant ancestors of the failing deities currently plaguing humanity. They are the essences upon which the frame of this world is built, elemental in nature, ancient beyond reckoning. Only one of the Rada Loa remains, her true heritage forgotten by false priests and upstart gods.

From the moment this reality birthed life, death was born.

Mother Death, The Lady of the House, is the true master of Bastion.

Mother Death is the last Rada Loa.

—Loa Book of the Invisibles

"Trouble," said Nuru.

Everyone focussed on her and she pointed at the Artist's home. A gaunt young man in robes of banded red, white, and black exited the tenement. The white bands were splashed with gore. His hands dripped blood. Long hair, twisted knots entwined with the bones and skulls of dozens of snakes, fell to his knees in tight braids.

Nahualli. More real than stone. Eyes like the smoky depths of obsidian. The world shook around him, wavered with the stretching of the veil separating Bastion from a thousand other realities.

He stopped in the street, looking around as if wondering how he got there. Four Birds exited behind him.

"I'm done running," said Chisulo, drawing the cudgel.

Happy cracked his knuckles. Grunting agreement, he wiped tears from granite eyes.

Efra, small and unarmed, stood at Nuru's side. "Growers run. We're not Growers anymore."

"Nuru?" asked Chisulo.

She drew the stone spider from its pouch.

Ash fell from the sky, thick flakes choking the air, coating everything in greasy smears of grey.

Efra laughed. "That's our colour."

The nahual, wearing the blood-spattered robes of a priest of Cloud Serpent, spotted Nuru and grinned with bright teeth. Another young priest, ruggedly handsome, stood with him.

The Artist is dead. Nuru knew it. The nahual killed him looking for her and Efra. Something inside her broke, snapped like a dry twig.

Nuru knelt in the road, and placed the spider carving before her. For a mad moment she was reminded of playing in the fields as a child, kneeling in the dirt. Ash settled on her shoulders, clung to her face like grey tears.

Passing Nuru, Efra kept moving, Chisulo and Happy at her side.

Four Birds, armed and armoured, red leather smeared cinereal, stood with the priest.

"Shit," said Chisulo. "Six in total."

Happy eyed the Birds, two women and two men. "I don't hit women."

"Well they're going to hit you," said Efra.

The Birds fanned out on either side of the nahual of Cloud Serpent—*Nahualli, church-trained sorcerer,* Nuru corrected. She recognized him from the basement. He'd been gaunt the first time. Now he was etched sharp on bone, eyes hollowed with exhaustion and bright with a narcotic madness she suspected she shared.

The Birds stood, cudgels held low, waiting. The other priest stood back like he didn't want to be involved. He looked nervous, like he might break and run at any moment.

Efra slowed as she approached.

This felt wrong. Somehow, Nuru had expected everyone to sprint screaming into a fight. This was all too deliberate. The Birds looked calm, ready. The nahualli, on the other hand, looked oddly wide-eyed and innocent, a child seeing the world for the first time. Reaching out an open palm he caught a flake of ash. He licked it, frowning in distaste.

He's smoky. Totally prepared for us.

Well, so was Nuru. The priest was in for a surprise.

Last time, in the basement, the nahualli defeated her. This was different. That had been a dream, an alternate reality achieved through narcotics. This time... This time it was real.

This time I have the spider.

Efra stopped a half dozen paces from the nahualli.

Seeing him this close Nuru realized how young he was. *No older than me.*

"The Artist?" Efra asked.

"Dead. I had to use him to find you."

"Did you?" She looked around. "Here I am. I came to you. Are you sure you didn't torture a good man for no reason?"

He blinked, glassy eyes shot with red. He looked haggard, exhausted. "It is the gods' will."

"There," said Efra, "we agree."

"That armour," said one of the Birds, a man damned near as big as Happy, teeth bared in a snarl. He nodded at Chisulo. "Where did you get it?"

"I took it from the last Bird I fought."

"How many of you jumped him? Filthy cowards."

"I was alone."

"Liar."

Chisulo shrugged. He didn't look happy, didn't look proud at besting a Bird.

"I'm going to break your skull like you broke his," said the huge Bird. Anger cut his features, but he was calm. Cold.

"I'm sorry," said Chisulo, and Nuru knew he meant it. This was not some empty apology, he genuinely regretted killing the man. "I didn't mean to." His shoulders sagged. "I was scared."

"Scared," said the gaunt nahualli, tasting the word. There was no mockery in him. Leaning to one side, he tried to see past Happy's bulk. "What is your street sorcerer doing?"

"Preparing," said Efra. "You're all going to die."

"Kill them," said the woman who was clearly in charge.

Nuru recognized the differences in her uniform. *She's a Bird Captain.*

The Birds advanced, the priests remaining behind. The nahual she'd never seen before looked ill. His robes were spattered and stained with puke. The stench came off him in waves, rode the hot breeze.

The Cloud Serpent nahualli knelt, just like Nuru, and laid carved animals on the ash-stained stone before him.

We're going to play together. The thought, and the accompanying visual, was so insane Nuru giggled.

Two of the Birds—a man with a huge beard and a woman who walked like her ribs were busted—went after Happy. The other two, the massive Bird and the Captain, faced off against Chisulo.

No one thinks Efra is a threat. They'd learn.

Where Chisulo retreated, swinging his cudgel to keep his opponents back, Happy roared like an enraged bull-elephant and charged. The male Bird swung low and Happy took the blow on his thigh. He punched the Bird in the chin, crumpling him to the ground. For a big man, he was surprisingly fast. The woman hit him in the side and he grunted. He suffered two more vicious attacks, his left arm taking most of the damage, as he bent to collect the man's dropped cudgel. Then he turned with that deceptive speed, struck her on the temple with his cudgel. She dropped, boneless, the shape of her head wrong.

The other priest, the one who looked like he puked on himself, screamed and sprinted to the woman. He dropped to his knees at her side, weeping.

Efra stood rooted in place. Screams of pain and rage echoed off nearby tenements.

She'll run now. Self-preservation will drive her. Fighting Birds was stupid. It was death.

Already the man Happy punched had regained his feet. Somehow, even though Happy held the cudgel, the Bird managed to back the Grower up, ducking and weaving under the big man's attacks.

The kneeling Cloud Serpent nahualli twitched and shook, eyes rolled back in his head.

Chisulo caught one of his opponents, the large Bird, just below the ear with a wild swing. The man wobbled and fell, but Chisulo's mad attack left him exposed. The Captain knocked his cudgel away, spun, and smashed his left knee with her weapon. He screamed, hobbling backward.

He's going to die. We're all going to die.

To Nuru's surprise, Efra took two running steps and kicked the kneeling nahualli in the face. He fell backward, sprawling awkwardly in the street. Something fell from his robes, skittered across stone. Something black. It glittered like a smoky mirror. Efra bent to collect the obsidian dagger. Soft leather, stained and brown, damp with new blood, wrapped one end. The Artist's blood.

The huge Bird on the ground groaned and pushed himself into a sitting position. He sat, back to Efra, a stride from the girl. She cut his throat before he knew she was there, left him gagging and clawing at the wound.

She is death.

The Bird Captain had Chisulo down and was dismantling him. She smashed bones and joints with expert precision.

Efra ran, bare feet silent on stone. She stabbed the woman in the side, two quick jabs. The obsidian passed through leather like it was cotton. The Bird turned, swinging her cudgel in a skull-splitting arc. Efra ducked under it and stuck her in the belly. The Bird's own momentum tore the wound open and she splashed the street at her sandalled feet red with spilled gore. The woman, one hand holding herself in, kicked Efra in the gut. Efra's knees struck stone and she wheezed, fighting for breath. The Bird Captain loomed over her, pouring blood and not caring.

Nuru watched, helpless.

She going to smash her brain all over the street.

The cudgel swept up.

Growers cower.

Growers flinch away.

Growers run.

Efra drove herself from the ground. Coming up inside that swing, she stabbed the woman in the throat. Even haemorrhaging blood, the Bird disarmed her, sending the dagger skittering away, kneed her in the gut and caught her on the side of the head with an elbow. Efra collapsed to the street, dazed. The Bird Captain staggered, struggling to stanch the wound in her throat and hold in her ravaged belly. Blood spurted past desperate fingers. She retched and coughed, spraying a red mist. Sinking to the ground, she sat, and then fell to one side. Her legs twitched and kicked.

Chisulo pushed himself to his feet. Chest heaving, teeth bared in a snarl of pain, he limped toward the nahualli. The priest grinned with madness. Carved animals lay scattered, forgotten on the ground.

The nahualli changed. His chest and shoulders swelled to twice their size. Muscles rippled over impossibly huge arms. Glossy black fur shimmered in the sun. Armoured plates folded out of his flesh, covering him. Inch long claws, curved like hooks, grew from his fingertips. Green cat's eyes surveyed the street.

Spotting the woman Efra stabbed laying motionless in a growing pool of her own viscera, he roared. The sound was full of pain and loss.

Seeing Efra, the priest stalked forward, a hunting cat. Gone was the skinny youth. This was some kind of hallucinated monster mixing aspects of a puma, a bear, and what looked to be pangolin scales.

Chisulo pushed past Efra. "Get behind me."

No! Run! But Nuru knew he wouldn't.

The spider.

She shouldn't have been watching her friends die, she should have been focussing on the carving, letting the narcotics do their work. But she couldn't look away.

The nahualli laughed, a mad half-sob of agony.

"It ends," said the priest. "Smoking Mirror has failed. Your punishment is death."

Chisulo snarled in challenge. "Run," he said over his shoulder to Efra.

He charged the priest. With a yell, he brought the cudgel down on the nahualli's monstrous arm. Ebony snapped with a *crack* like desert thunder. The priest backhanded him, lifting him off his feet and sending him spinning away. He landed, rolling. Chisulo rose again, grimacing in agony. His right arm hung useless, shards of shattered wood embedded in his knuckles. He advanced.

"Run!" Nuru screamed.

Chisulo ignored her. She knew he would. He would never abandon a friend. Never.

Nuru saw Happy slamming a Hummingbird's head on the stone street, massive fingers wrapped around the man's skull, the ground beneath red with blood.

She saw the other priest kneeling over the woman Happy brained with a cudgel. He cried, screaming in soul-torn anguish.

She saw the woman Efra stabbed. The Bird lay still, eyes wide, dead.

She saw the carving before her. Red eyes. Flesh so dark it ate light.

Give yourself to me, said the carving. *I'll save your friends.*

Lost souls. Banished gods. Demons. The nahual spoke of such things, read from their book. Nuru had listened. She remembered every story, every word. With the exception of the handful of gods at the heart of Bastion, the old gods were either dead or banished or both. Ancient deities with strange names. Mama Oclla, Apophis, and Tâmtu, Red Smoking Mirror, who she remembered was also referred to as The Flayed One. Banished gods stalked the Bloody Desert, hunting those souls cast from the Sand Wall, devouring or enslaving them.

Focus on the carving.

She hadn't blinked in an eternity. Tears streamed from her eyes, fell from her chin to wet the sand, turning it back into blood.

Blood.

Blood red eyes.

Chisulo said it looks like me. Nuru couldn't see it. The carving was beautiful where Nuru was all flaws.

It's perfect. She'd captured every detail, every nuance. She knew its rage at being banished from Bastion.

Nuru saw the nahualli rear up like a huge bear covered in armoured plates. He'd shed all sign of humanity, shredded the veil between worlds. His allies possessed his flesh.

He's too powerful.

Seeing Chisulo rise, the nahualli leapt, too fast for the eye to track, and landed atop him, pinning him.

Efra turned to stare at Nuru, eyes wide with desperate fear. *Do something*, they said. *Save him.*

She does know fear. I was wrong.

Behind the girl, the nahualli lifted a huge bear-like paw and smashed it down on Chisulo, caving in his chest and shattering ribs.

The nahualli stood. Chisulo lay broken at his feet.

Chisulo.

He was there in her earliest memories. He'd been there for her every triumph, comforted her after every failure. Every choice he made was to the betterment of others. He walked through life like making the world a better place was easy, like the right choice wasn't really a choice at all. She loved all her friends, but Chisulo was the best of them. He made them better people. Even Bomani, with all his rage, knew to follow Chisulo without question.

He can't be gone.

The nahualli towered over Efra. The tiny girl turned to face him, alone.

Protect her or Bastion falls, Smoking Mirror said of Efra.

Nuru gave herself to the spider. She called to it, let it fill her. The spider became her everything.

Nuru learned the truth.

This spider was no ally. It was not a lost soul or a demon.

The spider was a god.

Lady of the Dead. The Queen of Bastion. Lady of the House. The Falcon. The Great Mother. Eldest of the gods, her names went on forever, each stranger than the last. Nephthys. Nebthet. Mother of the Universe. Kālarātri. The Black One. The Destroyer.

Betrayed by her husband, The Lord, she'd been banished from the city she helped build.

For twenty-five thousand years she fed off the paltry souls tossed from the Sand Wall. She waited and she plotted, ever diminished, for her chance, for her gateway back into Bastion. Ancient and powerful, she warred against the other dead gods, brought them to heal. She bound them to her will, bound them to her purpose.

She is Lady Death, Queen of the Red Desert.

Nuru's carving was the first crack. Mother Death's influence seeped into Bastion.

But Nuru was the gateway.

Starved to the point of non-existence, The Queen was still a god. She crushed Nuru.

Mother Death could have ended that tiny, ignorant soul then, fed off it to give her some infinitesimal strength. She didn't. Countless millennia in the desert made her careful. She had returned to Bastion, but she was weak. If the other gods found her now, it would be nothing for them to once again banish her. Even a powerful nahualli might manage it.

She needed souls.

She needed sacrifices.

She needed worshippers.

She must feed. She must grow in strength, hidden from the eyes of her enemies within the city. This mortal flesh would be her vessel. She'd wear it when possible, hide deep inside it when she needed to retreat.

This girl would be the mother of a new religion. The Growers, beaten and subjugated, were ripe with dissent, ready to worship new gods promising freedom. The Loa, the tattered remnants of her religion, worked for generations to prepare them.

There would be war, the blood of thousands would spill, run deep in the streets. Her Loa stood ready to block the runnels funnelling it out of the Life Ring. She'd drink every drop spilled here.

The Life Ring was perfect. Rarely did the gods in the centre cast their gaze so far from the beauty and pageantry of their realm. They were petty and foolish, bickering constantly, playing games with the souls of man to entertain themselves. They were also, after thousands of years trapped in the city of their own making, quite mad.

Mother Death was no more sane than they, just hungrier. Angrier.

Nuru knew all this. Though she teetered at the edge of nothing, she still existed. She wailed and screamed and fought for control, but she was a tiny soul consumed by the Great Mother.

A thousand times older than Bastion. Mother Death saw the rise and fall of civilizations. She remembered a world green with life and light, where plants and animals and people blanketed the earth.

The Destroyer was no ally. She wasn't here to aid Nuru. Nuru's cause was nothing to her. Mother Death wanted to break the eternal city until nothing remained of the old ways but smoke and stone.

She would remake Bastion to sate her ancient thirst. The Last City would truly become the sacrificial altar it was always meant to be.

Alone, Nuru cried, helpless.

I did this.

That first narcotic-induced hallucination had been a lure, bait. The vision was a trap, and Nuru, desperate for power, terrified of weakness, rushed blindly into it.

I killed them all.

AKACHI – ECHOES OF LIFE AND STONE

The tasks of the nahual of Cloud Serpent differ in every ring. In the Priests' Ring they hunt renegade priests, and stalk their ancient enemy, the Loa heretics. In the Bankers' Ring they bring debtors to justice and pursue those who would disrupt Bastion's economy. In the Senators' Ring they search out instigators and rebels, bringing political dissenters and revolutionaries to trial. In the Crafters' Ring they hunt saboteurs and those who seek to bring down the tools and machinery of civilization. In the Growers' Ring they battle the ever-growing influence of the Loa, and seek out those who have fled the inner rings to hide among the filth.

—The Book of Bastion

The scarred girl gutted Yejide, his love. It should have been impossible. No Dirt should have been able to end the Captain. Akachi screamed in agony at the loss. He knew no thought but death.

A flat-nosed Dirt got between Akachi and the girl he hunted. He killed the man, punched the Dirt in the chest with a bear-like fist, shattering ribs. The Dirt stared past him, forever unseeing, freed from a life of toil and pain.

Eyes like polished stones.

Ibrahim lay dead, throat open to the sky. Akachi saw a big Dirt smash Njau's head against the stone of Bastion until bone gave. Akachi's sacrificial dagger clutched in his fist, Nafari charged the big man, screaming. Gyasi lay dead behind him. Nafari stabbed the Dirt in the gut. He stabbed him in the chest. The huge Grower punched him in the face, shattering those handsome features. Nafari fell, dropping the knife. Collecting it, the Dirt shoved it through Nafari's heart and then collapsed atop him.

Bodies littered the street, Hummingbirds and Growers. So much blood. The gutters ran fast and deep. Roiling clouds of black and grey soiled the sky, leaching colour from the world. Fat flakes of ash fell like desiccated rain.

Bastion is dying.

Yejide, disembowelled, throat slashed wide, lay sprawled in the sand. Gone. Taken from him by this Dirt girl.

The scarred girl stood before Akachi.

"Why?" he growled.

She didn't flinch, didn't move. "You killed my friends." Tears cut streaks in her ash-stained face, followed the ridge of her scar. She pointed at the house behind him. "You killed the Artist. He was kind to me." She gestured at the flat-nosed Dirt whose chest Akachi crushed. "You killed him. He was my hope."

Hope? Curiosity drove him to ask. "For what?"

"To save Bastion. To save myself." She grinned up at him and it was terrible. "You killed him before he could make me better. And so, I remain what I was."

Akachi hesitated. *Smoking Mirror backs this girl.*

Movement, behind her.

The wretched stench of death filled the air, obliterating the harsh tang of blood and violence. To Akachi's heightened senses, it was overpowering, choking.

Black, glistening and huge. Evil. Dainty steps sent waves of revulsion rushing through Akachi's gut.

A colossal spider, twice his height, danced forward, movements jerky yet somehow graceful. The front half was the torso of a woman in the flush of youth, skin blacker than anything he'd ever seen. She was beautiful. She was terrifying. Red eyes examined him with disdain. He recognized her from the basement.

The street sorcerer.

Akachi's years of study under various memory-enhancing narcotics bubbled up a deep-buried recollection. It was in History class. They studied Bastion's oldest texts, reading about the first days after the Last War. Some of the founding gods schismed, banded together and fought to wrestle control of the city from the others. Defeated, they were banished from Bastion. He remembered the tapestry in Bishop Zalika's chambers.

"Mother Death," he said. "The Destroyer of Worlds."

The spider skittered forward. It stood over the scarred girl, protective.

Mother Death stared down at Akachi. "Worship, or die."

Blood and worship; the gods fed on both.

A wash of narcotics roared through Akachi's blood. Yejide was gone. He couldn't process the loss, it was too sudden. He kept expecting her to move, to get up and brush herself off. *I will not fail you.*

Nahualli had been called upon to banish evil spirits in the past. It was rare, but sometimes *things* got within the walls, called in by careless nahualli or ignorant street sorcerers. He'd read all the accounts.

"I am Bastion," said Akachi, standing tall. "I am the wall that brings peace, the wall that keeps the demons at bay. I banish you in the name of Cloud Serpent!"

Mother Death ignored him, looked to the girl standing beneath her. "And you, little shard of Smoking Mirror?"

The scarred Dirt looked at the black rectangle tattooed on her wrist and then up to the god. "Chisulo would have done the right thing, no matter the cost. To save Nuru he would have fought you with his bare hands." She turned toward Akachi. "You killed him. I am with you, Mother Death."

A needle-sharp leg, barbed like rose stems, lashed out and Akachi ducked under it. Grabbing the extended leg, he stepped in to punch the exposed underbelly. His huge fist shattered on impact. Mother Death ripped her leg free of the grip of his other hand. Those barbs, edged like obsidian, severed his fingers. Screaming, he backed away. Blood fountained from the stumps, spattered the street, ran in the gutter. His other hand hung limp, fragments of bone protruding through torn flesh.

"Mortals don't fight gods," said Mother Death.

Her front two legs stabbed at him. One punched through his left shoulder. The other pinioned his chest on the right side. Both jutted out his back.

Akachi's allies screamed and faded, devoured by the god.

Standing on her rear six legs, Mother Death lifted him. Akachi hung like a hooked worm, wriggling and writhing. Helpless.

"Mortals worship," said Mother Death. "Or they die." She tossed him aside, barbed legs tearing everything on the way out.

Akachi landed, a crumpled ruin. Torn apart, he bled out at a terrible rate. His blood joined the blood of Yejide, the woman he loved, and Nafari, his only friend, in the gutter. It flowed away toward the heart of Bastion. Flakes of ash rode the river like tiny boats.

I'm feeding the gods.

He heard sobbing. The scarred girl knelt beside the street sorcerer. Mother Death was gone. No, not gone. Something like that never truly left, never truly died.

Efra, he remembered. *The one with the scar is Efra.* Such a common nothing Dirt name. *The street sorcerer, Nuru, she's doomed.* In becoming Mother Death, she opened herself to the god. Had she been trained as a nahualli, she'd have known the dangers. The ignorant Dirt probably didn't even understand. *She sold herself.*

Smoking Mirror won. The Queen of Bastion had returned, and the only nahual who knew, lay dying.

Akachi coughed blood. He couldn't move.

Efra helped the street sorcerer to her feet. The two girls limped away, leaving behind the corpses of their friends. Neither looked back.

Is this all my fault? Had he misunderstood the visions? Where was the great war, the ranks of Hummingbirds slaughtering the filthy Dirts? Where were the Turquoise Serpents with their obsidian swords? Was that a false vision, or something still in the future?

Doesn't matter. I won't live to see it.

Smoky stone caught Akachi's eye. There, within arms' reach, lay his sacrificial dagger. Fumbling with broken fingers, he dragged it closer, lifted it to rest on his chest. He felt the weight of souls trapped within.

Efra killed Yejide with this knife.

The soul of the woman he loved was in there, trapped. Nafari, too. Only if the knife made the journey to the gods at the heart of Bastion could Yejide hope to be reborn. Out here, in the Growers' Ring, it was more likely some Dirt would steal it from Akachi's corpse, keep it for himself.

Shadow fell over Akachi. He looked up to see dozens of Growers, caked in ash and bent with age, scarred with badly healed wounds, gathered around him.

They've come to watch me die.

Did they hate him?

A Dirt stepped forward, bowed low. "Nahual, you are wounded."

Akachi coughed a bloody laugh.

"What can we do?"

Nothing. You know nothing, have no skill beyond working the soil. They couldn't patch his wounds or even slow the bleeding. Their ignorance was killing him. *We gave them that.* It was supposed to be a gift. Ignorance was freedom from worry. It seemed funny now.

I could command them to deliver the dagger—Yejide and Nafari's souls—to the nearest church. Would they obey?

It didn't matter. He couldn't let her go.

Amethyst. The Stone of Self-Destruction. He'd failed.

Clutching the stone dagger in his shattered fist, Akachi drew a bubbling breath. "Take me to my church. Lay me on the altar," he whispered.

I'll join you in the dagger, he promised Yejide. *We'll be reborn together.*

To his surprise the Growers lifted him, carried him prostrate on their shoulders.

There are still good people out here. It was easy to forget that gangs and street sorcerers and the Loa were a minority.

He saw the endless grey sky, choked with roiling clouds of smoke and ash, as they transported him through the streets. More gathered to join the impromptu parade, he heard them, their shuffling steps, bare feet on stone. No one spoke a word. More feet. All the Wheat District was here to see him off.

A thick coating of ash ate sound, swallowed the ever-present echoes of life and stone.

Far above, a falcon circled.

You're free.

He wanted to join the bird. If only he'd saved some aldatu. Perhaps he could have used his nagual training to flee this dying body.

The bird folded and fell in an uncontrolled spiralling plummet.

NURU – THE HEART OF THE LAST CITY

Obsidian daggers are brought to the heart of Bastion to be drained by the gods for two reasons: First, with each life taken, the dagger becomes more powerful. An ancient dagger is a powerful weapon indeed, capable of slicing flesh, bone, and stone. The obsidian swords of the Turquoise Serpents, Southern Hummingbird's elite, go generations without making the journey to the Gods' Ring. They cut a man in half with ease. Second, the gods don't feed off blood and worship; they feed of blood, worship, and souls

—Loa Book of the Invisibles

After collecting the carving of Mother Death, Nuru and Efra staggered away, the street sorcerer leaning on the shorter woman for support.

Is this what Smoking Mirror wanted? Had everything played out to the god's plan? Did Father Discord even *have* a plan, or did he seek nothing more than change?

Efra staggered under her weight, tears streaming down her face. "Chisulo put himself between me and that nahualli."

He knew he couldn't defeat the sorcerer and hadn't hesitated.

"He did what he believed was right," said Nuru. He always did.

Efra pawed at her tears, rough and angry. "Do you think he'd use this god? Would he use her to make things better for himself?" She hesitated and then added, "Would he use her to make things better for others, for all Growers?"

Use a god? Nuru almost laughed. *The girl never quits.* "You know the answer."

"He was good in a way I am not." Efra blinked and fresh tears ran. "We need the god."

Nuru wanted to argue but couldn't. "Where are we going?" she asked. "I killed a nahualli. There are dead Birds everywhere. Cloud Serpent will hunt us. We are dead."

"Not yet we aren't." Efra rubbed at the scar, considering their options. "Does Mother Death know everything you know?"

"No. I'm nothing to her."

"Good."

The two women limped away, leaving behind the corpses of their friends.

Nuru slid her hand into Efra's, squeezed it tight. "Tell me you didn't plan this. Tell me you didn't have some idea this would happen."

Efra squeezed her hand back. "None."

"Are you lying?"

"Yes, but only a little. I knew change was coming and I wouldn't survive it alone." She laughed, a rueful cough of pain. "I thought I could use Chisulo's natural leadership—the way folks were drawn to him—to unite the Wheat District and the Growers' Ring." She looked away, hiding the pain. "I thought we'd be together."

It was, Nuru admitted, a nice dream.

That dream was dead.

"I'll have to do it myself now," said Efra.

"No," said Nuru. "*We'll* do it."

"No one would follow me anyway."

I did.

Pain welled up within Nuru, crushed her heart in a savage fist, threatened to burst free in screams of anguish.

All my friends are dead.

Friends? The word didn't do them justice. Growers didn't have families, but Chisulo, Bomani, Happy, and Omari were hers.

She felt so alone.

"I told him he'd get himself killed doing the right thing," mumbled Efra.

Nuru pushed the pain down deep with ruthless savagery.

I'm not alone. She had Efra. She had Mother Death.

And Father Discord, whatever his reasons, was on their side.

What do I do now?

She had no idea. She wanted to run away, to hide.

But that's what Growers did.

So what don't *Growers do?*

They didn't band together. They didn't fight. They didn't take control of their lives.

The Hummingbirds with the long obsidian knives were still coming; she had no doubt. They were still going to slaughter the Growers.

With the wells filling with ash and the fields burning, there would be a war for food. All Bastion would be against the Growers. She recalled the discontent in the Crafters' Ring.

Maybe not all Bastion.

Could she unite the two rings? Could she lead the Growers?

I guess we'll find out.

She would use that discontent. She would use starvation and desperation. She would use gods and mortals alike. She would save Bastion because that's what Chisulo would do.

Chisulo. Bomani. Happy. Omari.

Dead.

Her head hurt, a throbbing behind her eyes.

Gone.

Taken.

Gods, it hurt so much.

Walking through ankle-deep ash, they retuned to the tenement to collect Isabis. The snake curled around Nuru's neck and promptly fell asleep.

Omari lay dead and Nuru went to say goodbye. She kissed him on the forehead and cried.

Efra had worried that love would make her vulnerable, that losing it would be painful. How right she'd been.

Nothing felt like this.

Chisulo.

His absence was a gaping wound carved in Nuru's soul.

Tears fell. She couldn't stop them.

She turned to find Efra crying too.

Rising, Nuru and took her in her arms. The two cried, holding each other.

"We have to go," Efra sobbed into Nuru's hair.

Nuru nodded and detached herself. For a moment they stood holding each other's hands, seeing the pain in the others' eyes and knowing it.

Finally, collecting their meagre belongings in silence, scraps of stale food, Nuru's precious carving tools and paints, they left.

The world was empty.

Exiting the tenement with Efra at her side, Nuru stopped to watch the horizon burn. She saw desperate Growers gather around ash-clogged wells. She knew the future, saw it clearly. With less food making it to the heart of Bastion, the Birds would come in force. They'd work the Growers harder than ever, desperate to feed the city.

The nahual were wrong, the gods weren't the heart of Bastion. Neither were the priests. The Growers were the heart of the Last City.

Smoking Mirror had no idea what he'd set in motion. He had no idea what he'd done when he chose Efra. Nuru couldn't imagine why he wanted Mother Death back in the city.

We're going to bring it all down.

AKACHI – HEART'S MIRROR

Worlds beyond count surround us, their realities brushing against ours, sometimes leaking through. A properly trained nahualli, with the right combination of perception-altering narcotics, can not only see through the veil separating worlds, but also summon aid from alternate realities. There are allies to be found in the smoke, in the mushroom, in the thinning of the veil. But dangerous creatures also exist beyond the veil. Evil spirits, demons, pale souls cast from the wall that were too strong to die. The wall is our protection. That veil is our shield.

—The Book of Bastion

Akachi woke on the altar in his church. His sacrificial dagger still lay upon his chest. Letting his head fall to one side, he looked out of the corner of his eye. Blood stained the runnels beneath him.

My blood.

"We all feed the gods," he whispered.

He would cut himself, let the gods have his blood and the dagger have his soul.

Soon, he promised Yejide, *we'll be together.*

Staring at the dagger, he realized he couldn't do it, couldn't bring himself to take his own life. He was a coward. Shame broke him and he cried.

Akachi summoned the last of his strength. A need to escape his failures, to flee his humiliation, drove him. An insatiable hunger built in his gut, poisoned his veins. He had no numbing erlaxatu to take away his pain, no zoriontasuna to drown him in blissful euphoria. The only narcotic left in his possession was…

Broken fingers fumbled at the pouch of jainkoei around his neck. It took several attempts before he managed to work it open. The fungus was meant to be mixed with other narcotics, not taken in its pure form. He didn't care.

One last time I want to feel the will of Cloud Serpent. There was more than enough to brain-burn a dozen priests. He ate it all and wheezed bloody laughter. *Corpses can't be brain-burnt.*

The jainkoei opened him to the will of the gods. They shone their light upon him, within him.

I failed you. Failed Yejide. Failed my father.

A snake coiled its way up the altar, slid up his legs. Akachi admired its beauty. Glowing bands of lustrous red, white, and black coloured it. The creature's eyes were green like the most perfect jade. The head rose above him, stared down.

Cloud Serpent.

His god had come. He sobbed in gratitude at this last, undeserved gift.

They died because of me. Yejide. Nafari. All of them. All my fault.

The god weaved back and forth, hypnotic.

So perfect. So beautiful.

"Mother Death poisoned you." Cloud Serpent spoke into Akachi's soul. "The stone of self-destruction ate at you. No more. You are perfect. You are cleansed." The god's words seared his spirit, burned away his pain. "The detritus of your life is gone. Your time of youth and distraction is finished. From this day forth, you serve one purpose: mine."

I'm dying.

The viper struck, sank fangs into his neck, and reared back to examine him with eyes cold and ancient.

"The Heart's Mirror is dead," said Cloud Serpent. "Assassinated. Father Death has fallen. The pantheon has no leader. The Loa have a new god, Face Painted with Bells, and she is loose within Bastion's walls. The gods war. We are riven by discord."

Smoking Mirror, the girls.

"Smoking Mirror has chosen his Heart," said Cloud Serpent. "She is chaos. She will bring about the fall of Bastion, utter ruin. Humanity will die."

Akachi struggled to form words, managed only a dry croak.

"You," said Cloud Serpent, "are *my* Heart."

"What does that mean?" Akachi managed.

"The gods dare not war directly. We act through our worshippers. Each god has chosen a Heart. You are mine."

"I don't understand."

The god's venom coursed through Akachi's blood, set his veins afire, burnt his heart to ash. The poison seared away even his ability to feel pain. It left Akachi empty, pure.

"The god whose Heart is the last standing shall rule the pantheon. Hunt the scarred girl. Cut out her heart, bleed her on the altar. Hunt the sorcerer who bears Mother Death. Throw her from the wall, once again banishing The Lady."

Pieces fell together, clicked into place like the tightest puzzle. Cloud Serpent chose him. Smoking Mirror chose Efra as his Heart, and Mother Death had no doubt chosen the street sorcerer. Each god had chosen a Heart, a representative.

They're playing with us. It's a game.

A game with world-changing results. They played to see who would rule the pantheon and humanity were but pieces on the board.

Cloud Serpent chose me.

If the Lord of the Hunt rose to rule the pantheon, Akachi would become the next Heart's Mirror. He'd be immortal. He'd have access to the Gods' Ring. Anything and everything would become possible. He could have Yejide back.

"It shall be as you command," said Akachi.

Akachi woke sprawled across the altar. Cloud Serpent was gone. The hall was empty, still. His sacrificial dagger, smoky with souls, lay upon his chest. Though the weight remained, no longer did it feel evil. It wasn't empty, the obsidian still held countless souls. Only the stain had been removed.

Or I'm so stained I can no longer feel it.

Raising his right hand, he found it whole, healed. His left remained maimed, fingers little more than stumps. His wounds, all of them, were closed. Opening his robes, he saw the scars where Mother Death impaled him.

The gods warred.

Cloud Serpent chose me.

Would his father be proud?

He realized he no longer cared. It felt like the god reached in and scooped some of Akachi out.

My god tells me what I may feel.

His father expected great things of his son. His first memories were of being told that someday, if he worked hard and was the best, he'd be High Priest of Cloud Serpent. Over the intervening years his father looked less and less proud, spoke of Akachi's position in the priesthood increasingly rarely.

But the Heart's Mirror was beyond the High Priest. No mortal but the Heart ever entered the inner-most ring of Bastion. If Akachi succeeded, if he survived to the end, Cloud Serpent would rule the pantheon. According to the *Book of Bastion*, The Lord of the Hunt hadn't held that position in over seventeen thousand years. Akachi couldn't imagine living in the Gods' Ring, being the voice for all the gods, passing down their judgement upon all humanity.

I will be so much more than you, father.

Sitting, he surveyed his church. Signs of life were littered everywhere. Items dropped by the Hummingbird Guard looked like they expected to be taken up again at any moment.

So much death. And for what?

Akachi knew the answer: Gods fed off blood and worship. The entire city was an altar, collecting blood and funnelling it to the heart. It was no mistake. Akachi saw careful thought in every gutter, in the shaped floors of every home, in the perfection of design.

The gods want Bastion to bleed and so she shall.

Cloud Serpent wanted Akachi to be the blade that shed her blood and so he would.

Casting out the sorcerer would once again banish Mother Death. For now, she remained bound to the woman's flesh. That wouldn't last forever. Eventually she'd have the strength to free herself.

What must it be like to be ridden by your god?

Akachi imagined surrendering all control and responsibility.

Examining his robes, he found them crusted with blood and ash. They stunk of sweat and death and smoke. He stuck a finger through the hole where Mother Death stabbed him.

That was real.

The massive dose of narcotics he'd been on left his memories tenuous, hastily drawn charcoal sketches, still-scenes instead of continuity.

The amethyst poisoned me against myself.

And yet because of that stone he'd been willing to ingest suicidal amounts of narcotics. Because of that stone he saw his god. Because of that stone he still lived.

The Loa failed. They made him stronger than ever.

His mangled hand caught his attention. He wriggled the stumps. *They will pay.*

They would all pay. As Cloud Serpent demanded.

The gods saved us. We owe them everything.

Jumoke, the acolyte, entered the hall. Approaching the altar, he bowed low. "Are you hungry, Pastor?" he asked as if nothing had happened.

He wasn't.

"Fetch me clean robes," said Akachi. "I hunt a god."

GLOSSARY – THE GODS OF BASTION

Cloud Serpent (Lord of the Hunt): God of the hunt. As no one leaves Bastion, all hunting happens within the city. The most common prey are escaped criminals or fleeing debtors. His priests wear robes with thick bands of red, white, and black.

Feathered Serpent (Father Wind, Lord of Storms, Bringer of Knowledge): God of wind and sandstorms. His priests wear masks that look like bone skulls eroded by sand and wind.

Her Skirt is Stars (Mother Life, Goddess of the Stars, Skirt of Snakes, Grandmother): Gave birth to moon and stars. Goddess of childbirth and women who die during it. Her nahual run the crèches where Grower children are raised. They wear the spines of snakes woven into their hair and clothes. Their vestments vary in colour, but always match the colouring of some deadly viper, depending on their particular sect.

Lord of the Root (The Healer, Lord of Wine): God of doctors, medicine, narcotics, herbs and hallucinogens.

Lord of the Vanguard: (Lord of the Nose, Nose Lord) God of merchants, commerce, and trade. Primarily worshipped in the Bankers' Ring.

Precious Feather: (The Maiden, Mother of Flowers) Goddess of pleasure, indulgence, sex, female sexual power, and protector of young mothers. Her priests are strictly female and wear robes cut to show off and accent their beauty.

Sin Eater: (Mother Sin, Mother Purity, She Who Devours the Filth, The Four Sisters, Goddess of Dirt) Goddess of filth, guilt, cleansing, sin, purification, steam baths, midwives, and adulterers. She takes confessions and purifies or punishes. Her priests are always immaculately clean. Never dirty or sweaty, they bathe many times a day. They wear robes of flawless white.

Smoking Mirror (Father Discord, The Obsidian Lord, God of storms, God of Strife, Lord of the Night Sky, Enemy of Both Sides, We Are His Slaves, He by Whom We Live, Lord of the Near and Far, Father of the Night Wind, Lord of the Tenth Day, The Flayed One, The Jaguar God): He is associated with a wide range of concepts, including the night sky, the night winds, the north, the earth, obsidian, discord, jaguars, and strife. His priests wear black.

Southern Hummingbird (Father War, The Left Hand, The Dart Hurler, Father Terror): God of war. His priests are the Hummingbird Guard.

The Lady: (Mother Death, Lady of the Dead, The Queen of Bastion, The Falcon, The Great Mother, Nephthys, Nebthet, Mother of the Universe, Kālarātri, The Black One, The Destroyer, The Lady of the House) Cast from the city after the creation of Bastion she has lived in the Bloody Desert for over twenty-five thousand years, devouring those souls thrown from the Sand Wall. She is the eldest of gods, betrayed by her husband, The Lord.

The Lord (Father Death, The Lord of the House): God of death. His priests wear long cloaks of owl feathers. Current ruler of the pantheon.

The Provider: God of fertility and water, and lightning.

GLOSSARY – NAHUALLI (SORCERERS)

Huateteo (Spirit Guides): Have the power to bring people together or tear them apart. Utilizing aspects of the pactonal art of dream walking, they can move people's souls into one of the neighbouring realities. Different realities have different rules. Some are conducive to unity and time spent in such will bind a group into a tight knit unit. Some are darker and subtly weaken the bonds of society. A powerful Huateteo can, given time and the right narcotics, alter people's personalities, plant goals and ideas.

Nagual (shape shifter): Has the power to transform either spiritually or physically into an animal form. Nagual can completely become the animal, or take on aspects or characteristics of the animal.

Otochin (Fetish Magic): Fetish magic is the creation of charms and wards. They can offer protection, imbue characteristics (strength, charisma, quickness, etc.), or be curses.

Pactonal (Dream Walking): Allows the practitioner to enter or control the dreams of others. This can be used to send messages, nightmares, or threats. A powerful nahualli can kill someone in their dreams and the victim's spirit will die, leaving the body a living shell. Since it is common knowledge that the gods speak through people's dreams, this is particularly powerful/dangerous.

Peyollotl (Totemic Magic): The sorcerer must hand carve totems of various creatures and study them while taking drugs. They imagine (and later hallucinate) the creature coming to life. The more powerful the sorcerer, the more they can control their hallucination. Truly powerful nahualli, like those in Bastion's earliest days, can cause their totems to grow to immense size and do all kinds of fantastic things like breathe fire.

Tecuhtli (Death Magic): Practised only by worshippers of The Lord (Father Death) and The Lady (Mother Death). There is great power and energy in death. The dead are ritually burned at the local temple so that an evil street sorcerer doesn't steal body parts. Curses, poisons, summoning and binding evil spirits, raising and talking to the dead are all aspects of death magic.

Tezcat (Divination): By taking the right mix of drugs (and with the right training) it's possible to see flashes of the future, the past, or even elsewhere in the present.

GLOSSARY – SORCEROUS NARCOTICS

Aldatu: A powerful hallucinogenic most commonly used by Nagual as it aids in shapeshifting. Mushroom.

Ameslari: A strong hallucinogenic. A trained user can enter the dreams of another, if that person is also asleep. Fungus grown in dark basements. Must be eaten.

Arrazoia: Improves logical thought.

Ausardia: Increases confidence and bravery.

Bihurtu: Most commonly used by Peyollotl (totemic magic). A poisonous residue scraped off the backs of a large, black frog. Bihurtu connects the sorcerer with the world of spirit animals, allowing the nahualli to channel aspects (strength, speed, armour, etc.) of various animals.

Egia: Reduces inhibitions and makes it difficult to lie.

Epelak: Cured petals from the epelak flower are used to open the third eye, found in the centre of the palm of a sorcerer's right hand.

Erlaxatu: A relaxing euphoria that numbs the user to the hurts of the world and leaves a peaceful feeling. Smoked.

Etorkizun: Milky sap from a tree. Mixed with your own blood, this is used by tezcat in divination magic.

Foku: Sharpens all senses. Edible seeds. Improves retention.

Gorgoratzen: Allows user to recall even 'forgotten' events in great detail. Any memories made while under its influence will be incredibly sharp.

Jainkoei: Opens the soul to the will of the gods.

Jakitun: Makes user physically aware of their surroundings. Increased physical aptitude, balance, proprioception.

Kognizioa: Makes the user smarter, better able to focus on problem solving.

Pizgarri: User feels sharp and alert and *very* awake. Helps with concentration.

Zoriontasuna: A euphoric. Common street drug (4th ring), mostly used as an escape from reality. A trained user can cause those around him to feel some of his high. It calms crowds, makes people mellow and happy. A leafed plant that is smoked.

GLOSSARY – LOA SORCERY

Agate: Curses and protections.

Alexandrite: Causes obsessive and compulsive behaviour, can make the subject delusional.

Amethyst: The stone of self-destruction.

Angelite: Abort unborn children and kill the sick and elderly.

Astrophyllite: The stone of torment. Drive the subject insane with nightmares.

Diamond: Create blindness, physical or spiritual, confusion, and disorientation.

Diopside, Star: The stone of truth.

Emerald: Drive subject insane with greed and selfishness.

Flint: Stone of Conflict.

Fossilized Shark Teeth: The stone of curses

Garnet: Stores many forms of energy. It can store wounds the sorcerer suffers. Those wounds can later be given to a subject. It can also steal health or strength or intelligence from a helpless subject. The sorcerer can use what the stone steals, burning through the energy. The subject doesn't recover lost energy unless the sorcerer returns it to them.

Goshenite: Stone of Unmasking.

Hematite: Mother Death's stone. Like obsidian it can store souls.

Hyraceum: Stone of Domination.

Kunzite: Stone of Distraction.

Kyanite: Knife of the Mind.

Meteorites: Increase the intensity and effects of other stones

Obsidian: Obsidian is used by tecuhtli in their death magic. This is the one kind of crystal magic not forbidden to the nahualli, though they don't think of it as such. The soul of anyone killed by obsidian will be stored inside the stone. The more souls inside the stone the more powerful it becomes. If enough souls are stored in the stone it begins to stain local reality, infecting anyone nearby. The obsidian swords of the Turquoise Serpents, Southern Hummingbird's elite, carry thousands of souls and are unbreakable. The sacrificial daggers used by the nahual are always obsidian. They are regularly returned to the Gods' Ring at the centre of Bastion to be drained of souls. Those souls are then cleansed and made ready to be reborn.

Onyx, Black: Causes nightmares, mental torment, and break relationships.

Opal: Container and radiator of negative energy.

Ruby: Clarifier or purifier of intent.

Sphene: Stone of Depression.

ACKNOWLEDGEMENTS

There are some folks to whom I owe a great debt. Without them, this would be a very different book.

Petros Triantafyllou (booknest.eu) has been my First Reader for several novels now. His advice and support throughout this and other projects has been unflagging and unfailing. He is a dude of the highest calibre, a champion of fantasy fiction. And holy shit is he a huge pain in the ass. So demanding! I am honoured to call him a friend.

Tom Smith (Grimdark Magazine) and David Walters (https://fan-fiaddict.com/) did the next round of reading. Their ongoing belief in this story has been crucial in keeping me motivated when I wanted to give up and walk away.

Teresa Frohock, author of the amazing *Los Nefilim* books (Harper Voyager), gave this a brutal critiquing. Her feedback was on point and left my beautiful story a bloody tatter. But she was right. That sex scene really was a mistake. Suggesting I rewrite this with just two POV characters was genius. *Smoke and Stone* is a much stronger story for her efforts.

Thomas Clews and Jeff Bryant did the final read. Their feedback was critical in polishing the story and convincing me that I should go ahead and publish it.

Sarah Chorn edited this little tale of narcotic-fuelled madness. She picked apart motivations, found plot holes, fixed as much of the grammar as I let her (I'm more interested in how the book reads than I am in having every comma proper grammar demands), and caught a very subtle POV error I missed when rewriting the entire &@%! book (thanks Teresa) from four to two POV characters.

Anna Smith Spark, author of the insanely awesome *Empires of Dust* trilogy, has been a good friend. If you haven't read her books, you are missing out on some of the best dark fantasy ever written. *Death! Death! Death!*

I wasn't going to hire an artist. I couldn't afford one. I was too fucking broke. Hell, I could do a "good enough" cover in GIMP for free! And then I saw Felix Ortiz's Artstation page (https://www.artstation.com/felixortiz) and thought, *FUCK!* I had to work with him. This dude is so mad-skilled it's insane.

And finally, you, the reader. Without you, there wouldn't be a fuck of a lot of point in all this insane effort. I mean, I'd probably still do it because I love telling stories, but you folks keep me going. Your emails, messages, reviews, on-line rants, and death threats make all this worthwhile.

Fuck yeah.

Up the Irons!

Mike Fletcher

ABOUT THE AUTHOR

Michael R. Fletcher was born in one of those rural towns with more dogs than people. He grew up milking goats, thinking sticks were amazing toys, and pretending that used nine-volt batteries were spaceships. He thought the rabbits in the barn were pets until one day Blackie appeared on the dinner table.

Things got a tad dark after that.

After dropping out of university in his second year of a Philosophy degree, he decided it was time to grow up and get a real job. He promptly moved to Toronto to become a rock star, which strangely involved less drugs and alcohol than his attempt at Philosophy.

After working for twenty years in the music industry as an Audio-Engineer, he decided it was time for a change and set his sights on becoming a famous author.

Once again, things got a tad dark.

Sometimes he thinks he should have become a ninja like his mum wanted.